DESIRE AND DESTINY

As they stood together in the intimate darkness, Savannah had no doubt that Skyler Reade was the man she'd been waiting for. All she had to do was keep him, or was that too flighty a dream? Their country was at war, their backgrounds making them enemies. There was so little time to be sure of him and herself.

She looked up at his strong profile, then quickly, before she had time to think, she said, "I hope I don't shock you but I want you to kiss me again."

A Southern gentleman would have recoiled in judgmental horror, but Skyler merely turned to her, his face all shadow and contour. Savannah's eyes closed as his hand brushed over the softness of her cheek. Then the heat of his mouth made her gasp as it possessed her own, moving slowly over every sweet curve until she was breathless. Her arms rose to slip over his shoulders, partly for balance and partly to hold him to her, for this moment and forever . . .

REBEL VIXEN
Dana Ransom

ZEBRA BOOKS
KENSINGTON PUBLISHING CORP.

ZEBRA BOOKS

are published by

Kensington Publishing Corp.
475 Park Avenue South
New York, NY 10016

First printing: November 1987

Printed in the United States of America

Chapter One

They were several hours from Nassau when a shout brought Savannah Russell out of her serious musings. She hurried across the thankfully steady deck in a bell of voluminous skirts to join her uncle in the group that had gathered at the rail of the *Harrier* to peer into the deep blue waters below.

"What is it, Uncle Jonah?" she asked, leaning out as far as she dared. "Debris from another ship?"

"And more, it seems," he murmured. His crew moved quickly to obey his crisp orders and returned with long boarding pikes and ropes.

Savannah watched the proceedings with interest, grateful for the distraction and the calm waters that allowed her to venture from her cabin. The February seas had been unmercifully rough and she found little comfort in the three-day journey from Charleston. All her experience on inland boats had not prepared her for the rocking misery of the ocean. When she thought ahead of the trip to England, her much-abused stomach rolled in complaint but her determination quelled it. She would learn to be a good sailor because she owed it to her father. And that ended the matter. All her family's arguments hadn't deterred her nor would her own discomfort. She always saw her debts paid.

The tangy sea breeze was sweet as perfume after the stuffy, souring confines below and the tease of the winds brought a flush back to her wan cheeks. The coattails of the storm that had tossed them about finally eased and Savannah was almost lulled by that serene face of blue cloudless sky and even bluer waters. The silky sea made the steamer's deck as motionless as a city walkway, giving her a tenuous confidence. Her sagging courage was further bolstered by the shadowy outline that grew ever larger on the horizon. She had almost given up hope of touching the beloved earth again during those long, torturous nights in the pitching cabin.

As Jonah suspected, the broken bits of planking and mast yielded more than the remnants of an unfortunate vessel lost to the storm of the prior week. The curious crew parted as the wreckage was hoisted aboard. Savannah gasped and moved forward as they stretched the limp, sodden figure of a man out beside the tangle of wood and lines.

"Is he alive?" It was barely a whisper as she knelt down beside her uncle.

Jonah put his fingertips to the side of the man's neck. The wet head lolled to one side. "'Twould seem so. This raft kept him from drowning, though I can't fathom how he's managed to hold on."

When they began to pull apart the pieces of floating rubble, he had his answer. The man's arm was crushed beneath a heavy length of mast, pinning him in a snug trap that had held his head above water in the choppy waters. It took several men to lift the massive pole from its cradle of smashed wood.

Savannah made a soft choking sound and averted her head from the sight of gaping flesh and splinters of bone. The man's forearm had been nearly crushed.

"What saved his life will most likely cost it," Jonah

6

muttered as he searched the tattered remains of clothing for some sign of identification. All compassion vanished as he touched the rapidly tarnishing brass belt buckle. He pulled it loose and stared at it fiercely. "Toss him back over, lads. I ain't going to be the one to save him."

The harsh words brought Savannah's wavering senses into sharp focus. She stood to clasp her uncle's arm in alarm. "You cannot mean such a thing," she cried, looking up into the stern visage.

"I know what I'm doing, girl. It may seem cruel but 'tis justified."

She glanced at the buckle he held in his palm but felt no such conviction. The three raised letters seemed meaningless when placed against a man's life. "I don't care, Uncle Jonah. I'll not allow it. You may be captain but this is my venture. Don't force me to remind you of it." Her words were softly spoken in deference to the pain in his eyes but firm with authority.

With a glowering stare, he turned and stalked away, leaving her to look after him in anguished sympathy. Then she spoke to the crew in a commanding tone.

"Take him down to my cabin. Gently now. Is there anyone on board who knows anything of doctoring? Fetch him. Hurry."

Forgetting her fear of the slick deck, Savannah rushed ahead to prepare the way for the carefully borne burden they laid on her turned back bunk. Keeping her gaze purposefully from the mangled wound, she arranged the linens about the now shifting figure. Uncertain of what to do beyond that point, she looked up hopefully to the man who knelt beside her.

"Are you a doctor?" she asked, but the craggy-faced man never spared her a look as he surveyed the damage with a knowledgeable frown. "What can I do? I'd like to help."

7

The doctor twisted the savaged limb, bringing a moan from the unconscious man and a hastily drawn breath from Savannah. He gave the pale girl an assessing glance, seeing her tightly clenched lips and distressed expression. "Do you plan to faint or vomit? If so, you are of no use to me," he said bluntly.

Savannah blinked and swallowed hard, forcing back the acrid taste of sickness. "No, I'll do neither. I would like to help."

Her voice was shaky but her gaze didn't waver and the doctor nodded. She would do. "Some scissors and lots of linen for bandages. Send a man for my tools."

That done, Savannah crouched at the bedside, biting her lip as the torn sleeve of navy-blue shirt was cut away. She stared hard at the slowly rising chest as the terrible wound was sponged and examined, her stomach doing a traitorous flip.

"It will have to come off, of course," he stated with casual certainty.

"What?" she gasped in dismay. "You cannot."

The doctor scowled at her challenge, then his features softened. "There's no help for it if I mean to save him. His arm's been crushed. The fragments of bone could sever an artery. He could bleed to death in minutes."

Savannah looked at the wounded man's sunburned face and her sensibilities rebelled. "And taking his arm will guarantee his survival?"

"No," he answered honestly. "But it will be easier and less painful for him."

"Perhaps physically," she said quietly. "But I cannot imagine a man wanting to wake to find himself missing a limb. Are you saying there is nothing else you can do?"

The doctor sighed. At Manassas, Fair Oaks, Gaine's Mill, and Fredericksburg no one had questioned him.

8

There hadn't been time in the makeshift surgical tents to think of the men he crippled, for only speed and drastic measure would leave them with a chance of life. He made those decisions without looking back, but the serious eyes regarding him would not be easily dismissed. "I'm saying it's the best thing for him."

The soft lips quivered then firmed once more. Her question was unforgivably blunt. "Is it that you just lack the skill for all but maiming? What choice do you think he would make if he could? Would you yourself make it if you were looking at a future with an empty sleeve?"

Unused to such bold condemnation, his frown deepened, not liking the way she pricked his conscience. Seeing him falter, she laid a hand on his arm and spoke more gently.

"I know in times of war with wounded all about you such decisions must be made, but this is not a littered battlefield. Have you the knowledge for such delicate work?"

The man's scowl grew but he said curtly, "I am a surgeon. It is not a skill one forgets."

The girl smiled at his prickly answer. "Then you'll try?"

"If he lives, he may not thank you," he warned. "It's not just setting bone, there's the pain and infection. You expect him to endure much."

"He will," she replied with a simple conviction. "You see to his arm, I'll see to his recovery."

He nodded with a reluctant smile. "If you would like a career in medicine, Miss Russell, the South could use a woman like you. I'm James Ambrose."

"Thank you, Dr. Ambrose."

The momentary lightness was gone as he turned back to his patient and selected the tools he would need. For the next two hours, he labored over the

9

shattered arm, repairing torn flesh, removing needle-like shards of bone, and piecing the rest together. The young woman at his side responded to each short command like the best of assistants, silent and efficient. She worked diligently, in spite of the queasiness that made her hands sometimes tremble and her eyes briefly close. As he snugly bound the stitched gash, he felt a too-long absent satisfaction. The feeling of futility that had haunted him on the battlefield until he fled from it was gone.

"It looks good," he pronounced, noting the absence of bleeding. He lifted the limp hand and pricked the fingers with the point of his scalpel. Each member responded with a gratifying twitch. "Now it's up to him."

"I appreciate your effort, Doctor. I'm sure he will as well."

"And I appreciate your insistence. More than you know. It's you he'll have to thank if he survives, not me." He smiled, the gesture relieving the stern lines of his face. He must have been a handsome man at one time. Then he went quickly to the task of splinting the arm to keep it immobile, while giving her instructions for his care. She asked a few pertinent questions then nodded with a capable air.

"Your niece is a remarkable woman, Jonah."

Savannah turned to see her uncle in the open door, his face still a study of displeasure. The memory of her disrespectful actions brought a flush to her face but she met his stare without apology.

"Is the dog going to live?" Jonah growled.

Ambrose arched a brow and replied coolly, "If you mean my patient, it is too soon to tell."

"Then he may oblige me yet and die. Good."

"Have you no faith in my ability?"

"You picked a poor time to decide to practice again

and an unworthy subject, James."

"She didn't think so," Ambrose concluded as if that were reason enough. With a nod to the girl, he pushed past his surly friend and returned to his shipboard duties.

Savannah sat on the edge of the bunk, posture defensive and protective as her uncle came into the small room. His angry glance fell on the unmoving figure behind her.

"Do you know what he is, Vannah?" he asked in a quiet fury.

"He's a man, Uncle Jonah, one who is helpless and injured. Beyond that, it doesn't matter what he is."

Her soft response only heightened his building rage. "Have you forgotten what he and his kind did to my brother? Your father is dead, Vannah, and the blood is on his hands. How can you forget that so easily and tend his murderers?"

Savannah's eyes clouded momentarily with the pain his words evoked, but her answer was even and strong. "I forget nothing, Uncle. I mourn my father as much as you but killing this man will not lessen that loss. If we killed every Northerner we saw, my father would still be dead. Vengeance won't bring him back to us."

"This is war, girl. He is our enemy. What compassion do we owe him?"

She took a sharp breath, eyes filling with tears that made her look painfully young and vulnerable. "I hope those who guard Darcy do not have hearts as hard as yours."

Jonah fumed and flushed uncomfortably, angry with her for drawing such an unfair comparison between her brother and the hated Yankee. But the argument was ended by her anguished plea. He sneered reluctantly, "Have your Yankee then. Tend his wounds. Restore his health so he can kill more of our friends and family. I'll have no part in it nor will my crew."

"I understand," she said faintly, feeling the lifelong bond of closeness between them fray under the strain. "And I am sorry for the way you feel."

"'Tis I who am sorry for you. You are nursing a viper, girl, and his thanks will be to strike at the hand that cared for him. Be warned."

Alone with the still figure that had torn such a rift between her and her uncle, Savannah gave a determined sigh and set to the task she had undertaken. With a wet cloth, she moistened the parched lips and bathed the caking of brine from his face. It was impossible to gauge his looks. His features were puffy and blistered from the steady searing of the sun off the mirroring waters. The stiffening of salt and sweat made even telling the color of his hair difficult. While she sponged him with the cooling cloth, she wondered if he had sisters, a sweetheart, or a wife anxious for his safety and return. The color of the cloth that made up his uniform shirt couldn't make her see him as her uncle did, as one of the nameless, faceless enemy that had taken her father. He was a man with a family and a hope for the future, just like her brother. Perhaps by saving his life, someone would do the same for Darcy in the Union prison camp in far off Maryland, and they would both see that future they deserved.

A sudden bump and the cessation of the gentle rocking coaxed Savannah from her vigil to one of the narrow windows. The steamer had docked. Nassau spread out before her in lush emerald splendor, from the clear waters to low green bluffs, a past pirate haven nestled between treacherous shoals and coral reefs. For miles, beaches of blinding white and pale pink coral sand stretched out like arms open for a warm, welcoming embrace. It was no longer a quiet, tropical port. The war had rejuvenated its glory of bygone days, making it the chief storehouse for smuggled Confederate goods. Cotton, six to eight bales deep, was stacked on the wharves, in empty lots, and even on the lawns of private homes, a testament to the boom of wealth that abounded. Confederate vessels such as *R.E. Lee, Merrimac,* and *Phantom* risked all in runs through the Federal blockade, loaded with the cotton needed in the mills of Great Britain. The Confederate government was never listed on the shipping invoices, large jobbing houses claiming ownership at a high commission. Cotton shipped from Charlestown at five cents per pound brought fifty-five in England. The profit was astronomical but so was the danger. On a single two- to three-day run, a captain could earn one thousand pounds sterling, and that lessened the fear of capture. The return profit was just as great. Ten dollars invested in quinine in Nassau brought four hundred to six hundred dollars in Charleston. The small, fast runners took cargo for the short, illegal pass through the blockade while larger, slower vessels brought stores across the ocean to this port or Bermuda and took regular remittances of cotton back.

Because of the vast amounts of monies involved, runners were often labelled mercenary privateers, serving the Confederacy by bringing in weapons and medicines but also draining its rapidly devaluating currency for luxury goods of imported liquors, coffee, spices, silks and satins, and even ice cubes. The cargo manifest was not controlled by the government but by what shipment brought the quickest, greatest return to those who took the risks.

Savannah knew her uncle was of that ilk. He loved the Confederacy but the lure of gold was more powerful. Her father hadn't trusted him to spend the monies earned, by his crop to benefit the cause. That was why he had made the ill-fated trip to Charleston, his daughter at his side. Jonah was a bit of a rascal, he often said, loyal only to his greedy pleasures and his family, in that order. Zane Russell had planned to make this trip to guard his profits, taking the money to England himself to obtain the needed supplies of quinine and chloroform and to buy clothing for those troops freezing in the North, thus bypassing the exorbitant prices on Nassau. Buying luxuries while the young men of the South died and suffered was treasonous to him. Zane Russell hadn't been able to make the voyage but Savannah vowed to see his wish fulfilled. She would guard the purse strings in his stead.

"We've docked, Vannah," Jonah called from the door. "Our ship for England leaves at nightfall. What are you going to do with him?"

"I—I don't know," she stammered in surprise. "I hadn't thought of it."

"Be thinking, girl. You wanted the responsibility. Or you could leave him to me to . . . dispose of properly."

Savannah frowned at his hopeful suggestion. "I'll see to my own arrangements, thank you" was her crisp retort.

Jonah shrugged. "Suit yourself, but this ship sails in less than two hours to catch the tide."

Savannah was pacing in a turmoil when James Ambrose came down some minutes later. His smile was sadly sympathetic.

"What am I going to do?" she asked him in despair. "If he goes back to Charleston, what will become of him?"

"He'll go to one of the military hospitals and then into one of the camps."

"What would his chances be there? Please, the truth."

"Not good, I'm afraid. There is little even the best doctor can do with so little help, little food, and in such overcrowded conditions. I would hate to see my fine work wasted."

Savannah smiled faintly. "I cannot take him with me. Do you suppose I could find someone to take him in here and care for him until I return?"

The doctor chuckled wryly. "Nassau is not exactly overflowing with the milk of Christian charity. Even if you could find someone at a fantastic fee to see to him, there would be no guarantee they wouldn't turn him out the minute you left. Northerners are a threat here."

She sighed in exasperation. "Well, he can't stay aboard. Would you help me find a decent room and move him there. I have until nightfall to think of something."

"Whatever you like," he agreed pessimistically.

Watching over the restlessly shifting man, she felt a momentary urge just to walk away and leave him to the fate her uncle said he deserved. She had made her plans, had obligations to meet. She didn't have time to be a self-appointed guardian to one who might not live regardless of her care. It was wartime. He was the enemy. No one would blame her. She touched the motionless hand and gasped slightly as the hot fingers curled reflexively about hers. She smiled in resignation. He was holding her to her word.

Chapter Two

The room Ambrose found her was small and sparsely furnished. She couldn't believe that so much money had bought such a tiny space above a grog house, when it would have netted a fine suite in Charleston. At Ambrose's instruction, the two crewmen carried in the litter bearing the still unconscious figure and shifted him onto the narrow bed. After she tipped them well, Savannah turned to the doctor with a wan smile.

"Not much, is it?" he observed, seeing her unvoiced distress. "Everything costs a ransom here. If you think to hire someone for the months you are away, I hope you have a small fortune in that little bag."

She sighed at that unhappy truth. "What else can I do? Could you stay with him while I see if I can hire someone?"

"I must be on the *Harrier* when she sails. That gives you less than an hour to find this paragon."

"Why is it I fear no such thing exists here?"

And she was right. The women she spoke to had other, more lucrative business and laughed at her proposal. The men all seemed to be transient sailors waiting for the next ship. All the local people were too caught up in their own affairs to be interested in helping anyone, even for a price. It seemed cargo was valued more highly than life.

Hot and disspirited, Savannah returned to the small room, her solemn features betraying the news. She crossed to the still figure and looked down on him in frustration. With splinted arm and sunburned, sunken cheeks, he looked so helpless. That sight tugged at her maternal instincts.

"I can't just leave him," she said more to herself than to the other man. "How much care will he need?"

"Perhaps none, perhaps more than anyone can give."

"What needs to be done?"

"Who do you have in mind for this selfless service?" He smiled as her eyes fell away. His voice was very gentle. "You don't have to, you know. You've done more than can be expected. Miss Russell, this man is a stranger to you. You owe him no further service. You've been an exemplary Samaritan. You needn't try for sainthood."

Her laugh was short. "I am hardly that. I confess this is madness on my part, but I don't take responsibility lightly."

"Do you realize what accepting this one could mean?"

"I am no stranger to hardship, sir," she stated solemnly. "I don't think anyone is after two years of war. Tell me what I need to know and I will see to it."

Ambrose smiled with admiration and respect. "I hope the reward justifies the sacrifice."

"That doesn't matter right now, does it?"

Fetched by Ambrose, Jonah entered the tiny room, face etched in angry objection. In his hand he held her worn travel bag. His resemblance to her father made her heart clutch momentarily.

"Vannah, you cannot be serious," he began slowly, as if reasoning with a willful child. "You are in my care.

18

What would your father say to you staying in a room with a man like this, all alone and unprotected?"

"Father would have understood," she stated simply.

Jonah set the bag down with a heavy sigh and shook his mane of thick black hair. "Perhaps he would have, but I surely don't. What is this man to you that you should care so greatly?"

"He needs me, Uncle. I can explain it no better than that."

Again, the futile sigh. He had heard those words before and had seen the determined set in the youthful face. Years ago, she had found a tiny foal. It had been badly mauled by some wild animal. It was weak, spindly, and oddly colored, with no sign of promise. He and Zane had urged it be put down for its own good, but Savannah had shown that stubborn Russell face. She stayed in the barn, nursing the gangly foal for three nights, and to their amazement it had recovered, growing bigger and stronger every day under her loving care. Today, Aurora was the fleetest horse in five counties, carrying Darcy to many a prize.

"So you expect me to sail off without you."

"I will be all right, Uncle Jonah. Aren't I always?"

He gave a reluctant grin. "You are too tough and capable for a female, girl."

Though true, she wasn't sure it was a compliment. She shifted the topic from herself to their original mission. "Has the cotton been sold?"

Jonah looked pleased. "Buyers were waiting at the dock, cash in hand. Zane would have been proud of the price his crop brought in."

Savannah eyed him narrowly, her father's suspicions born anew. "And will you make him proud as well by seeing to his wishes?"

"A fine question, little girl," he huffed in insult, but behind the indignant facade his resourceful mind was

19

calculating the advantages of not having his brother's righteous daughter with him. Like Zane, she didn't understand business and a man's obligation to look out for himself. Perhaps he had reason to thank the Yankee after all. Savannah was giving him that peculiar look she had, as if his mind held no secrets from her. "Never you mind, Vannah. I'll see to everything. The way Zane would have wanted it. Have you enough money to see you till I get back? Do you need anything?"

Lulled by his unexpected acceptance of the situation, his niece smiled in assurance. "I'll be fine." She crossed to him and was engulfed by his bearlike embrace. The closeness of the moment was gone when he stepped away, clearing his throat in gruff embarrassment.

"Take care of yourself, little girl. I'll be back soon."

"You too, Uncle."

She spent the evening absorbed in the routine Ambrose had given her. Sitting on the edge of the bed, she forced small amounts of liquid between the cracked lips, then cooled the burned face with a damp cloth. The time went by unnoticed, only the raucous noise from the tavern below occasionally seeping into her awareness. By the time the nagging ache in her back and temples urged her to take a short break from her vigil, faint cracks of pink appeared between the window slats. On opening them to the small balcony to emit the cooler morning breeze, she looked down on the strange tropical setting and realized for the first time how isolated she was. Jonah had gone and it would be better than six weeks before he returned. And here she was in a tiny high-priced room, caring for a man she knew nothing about except that he was an enemy. All she had was her small bag of belongings and a wad of nearly useless Confederate notes. There would be food to buy, clothing for him, and medicines. She had to see if there was a doctor somewhere near.

Ambrose had left her a vial of laudanum and that would not last but a few days. So much to do, she realized wearily. And who would stay with him while she went to see to these things? She couldn't risk leaving him alone until he was coherent. If that time ever came.

A low moan from the dim shadows of the room reclaimed her attention. She knelt down at the bedside, surprised to find bleary, reddened eyes opened and shifting aimlessly. When she touched a light hand to the rough cheek, his gaze focused with difficulty. He struggled to speak and, obligingly, she wet his lips.

"W—where am I?" It was a croaking whisper.

"Nassau. Our ship fished you out of the sea. You'd been adrift for some time. Don't try to talk now," she soothed, but he worked even harder to concentrate his blurred vision.

"Who are you?"

"Savannah. I'm going to take care of you. And your name?"

He licked the dry lips with painful slowness and mouthed with that hoarse voice, "Skyler, Skyler Reade." His eyes drifted shut and he was still for some time. When Savannah started to take her hand away, he startled her by gripping it with a sudden strength. "Don't go. Please."

She held the hot hand gently. "I won't," she promised softly. "I'll be right here. You rest now. I'll be here if you need me."

That seemed to satisfy him, for his fingers slackened and his eyes remained closed. She sat with him for a long while, until convinced he was asleep or at least resting, then eased her hand away. Skyler Reade. At least she had a name to put to him.

The sound of someone in the hall brought her quickly to the door. The mulatto girl in her garish finery turned in question when called to. She was young, too young for the cosmetics and heavy jewelry and for the profession they spoke of. Savannah discovered she too lived on the same floor, and to her relief the girl was willing to bring up a tray of food twice a day. For a fee, of course. One problem taken care of.

Savannah had time to wash and tidy her hair before the girl, Marita, knocked and brought in a tray filled with tantalizing scents. The dark eyes shifted to the man on the bed but she said nothing of her thoughts or conclusions. She took the coin and was eager to be on her way. Balancing the tray on the edge of the wicker chaise, the only other piece of seating in the room. Savannah began to feast on the fresh warm breads and fruit butters. While she ate, her gaze lingered on the figure of Skyler Reade. His clothing was in filthy shreds. Perhaps Marita could be of help there as well. Gradually the purpose of her perusal shifted from pracitcal to appreciation. Skyler Reade was a fine figure of a man. He was tall and strongly built, long of leg and wide through the chest. She imagined he would present quite a picture in formal dress. Of his face, regretfully she could tell little, but time would heal his ravaged features and broken body and she would watch the change with interest.

Savannah Russell had little use for men, least of all for the posing, proper beaux who swarmed her younger sister with pretty insincere speeches. She was never good at the coquetry that dripped honey-sweet from Hillary's pouty lips. To her, empty conversation was wasteful and annoying and a talent she never cared to cultivate. That was the reason she was still not married at twenty-one, Hillary pointed out. From childhood, she had been drawn into the dark, smoky study to listen to Zane, Jonah, and Darcy discuss crops and monies and horseflesh with a dreamy enjoyment.

22

Her father had been amused by his precocious daughter's interest and took time to explain any questions and listen in mock solemnness to her suggestions. He never mentioned that some of them proved beneficial. She was Darcy's shadow, learning to ride and shoot as well as more unacceptable accomplishments like spitting and cussing. It delighted her older brother to shock others with the inappropriate things he taught his baby sister.

When she came of age, Zane's leniency hardened and he turned her out of the room with its delicious perfumes of leather and bourbon to the frilly laces and silks of her mother's domain. Lessons in manners and graces were a painful drudgery, while Hillary, three years her junior, was an avid student. Even at fourteen Hillary was a promising beauty, and Savannah cynically deduced that many of the young men called on her just to get an introduction to her younger sister. That became obvious when Hillary attended her first party. Her bevy of admirers was four-deep, while Savannah was free to roam the edges of the men's talks of politics and agriculture.

The gentle Adelaide Russell tried to influence her wayward child, tried to instill in her the duties of a Southern woman. She was to be the keeper of the house, the tender of the sick, the always ready and accomplished hostess, the epitome of purity, beauty, nobility, courage, and charm, gentle and soothing in nature and content in her silent, subservient position. She was the fragile creature men fought over and protected, a confection of frothing fabrics and devoted smiles. And empty heads, Savannah noted unkindly. She hadn't meant to hurt or belittle her mother, who was a sweet, sacrificing woman, but she herself was too full of life, too full of ideas and opinions to become that dainty sleeve dressing for a man. She liked to talk and be heard and respected for her views, not glared at and shooed away like a naughty child intruding on an adult world. She was proud of her mind and her abilities and was eager to learn if only she could escape the barrier of her sex. But women wanted to discuss menus and childrearing, and men wanted a frilly puppet whose mouth smiled but never opened.

Jonah was the only one who treated her with any equality. He never laughed at her thoughts or indulged her begrudgingly. Darcy had been that way too, before he was caught up in the role of Southern gentleman.

Annoying as men were, Savannah was still a woman and they intrigued her. The few kisses she had received warmed her with a promise of her passionate nature. There were times she ached with loneliness and hated her sister for her effortless conquests. It wasn't that Savannah was unattractive. She had a dark, sultry allure that drew many eyes, but her forthright manner frankly frightened away her suitors who didn't know how to handle a woman who spoke her mind in public. Her gypsylike beauty made the petite, fair Hillary all the softer and more vulnerable in comparison, a comparison Savannah suffered from unfairly. Surely there must be some modern-thinking man somewhere whose masculinity would not be threatened by a free-thinking woman. At her age, it was beginning to look as though she would never find him. Hillary had received seven proposals before the war. Savannah had one from a portly planter three times her age. With so many of the South's young men cut down in the fireflash of war, it looked as though her future would be solitary. The war changed everything.

The cotton shipment had been her father's dream. He had loved his state of South Carolina and the Confederacy, willing to sacrifice all to its noble cause. And he had. He had given his life and possibly his only

24

son's. Their family was scattered and unable to draw strength from one another. A messenger had been sent to Rising Sun with the news of Zane Russell's death. Savannah hadn't returned home to relay the vague circumstances that surrounded his capture. In order to see his wishes through, she had put that heartrending word in a note to her mother. Darcy was interned up North, suffering God-knows-what at the hands of his captors, and Hillary had been stranded with her sister-in-law in the occupied port of Beaufort. And she, Savannah Russell, was voluntarily tending to one of the men who subjected them all to such misery.

She pressed her palms over her eyes, too weary to consider the oddity of the situation. When her uncle returned she would decide her course, but for now it was limited to the confines of the room. With her patient resting in fair ease, she closed her eyes and let the numbing exhaustion of the day become a soothing opiate to her senses.

A strange wailing jerked her from the dark comfort of sleep. For a moment, she was in a panic. The room was deep in shadow and it took a few seconds for her to connect her cramped position on the chaise to the mournful sounds of hurt. Had she slept the entire day away? Then she was up, ignoring the complaining aches of her body.

Setting a lamp on the floor at the side of the bed, she bent down with a concerned frown. The uneven light cast a weird play of shadows over her patient's distorted features and glittered in his unseeing eyes. Savannah shook off the paralyzing feelings of inadequacy and began to mop the fevered brow while speaking in a low, calming voice. Her efforts had no effect on his growing delirium. Fearing he would harm himself with the thrashing movements, she reached with some reluctance for the small brown bottle. Within

25

minutes, the drops had induced a heavy, unnatural sleep. Anxiously, she checked his injured arm for signs of poor color or infection. Though the area around the bandage was hot and slightly red, there were no alarming streaks or the rancid odor Ambrose had warned her of. She carefully replaced the swaddled limb on its cushioning prop of pillows and remained watchful throughout the long hours of the night.

From that point, day and night ran together with constant doses of the powerful drug needed to control the injured man. She didn't know if it was fever or pain that spurred the violent restlessness and unintelligible cries. She didn't even know if she was doing him any good, keeping a constant watch for signs of distress and administering stingy allotments of laudanum. There wasn't enough to keep him unconscious, so he wandered in a light stupor, murmuring and shifting on his bed of misery. When he was quiet Savannah fed him spoonfuls of thin broth, and when he was agitated she held his good hand and talked to him. She never remembered what she spoke of. It was unlikely that he heard her. When his eyes were open he showed no sign of acknowledgment, but she continued the soothing words in hopes of easing his fears and partly to steady her own.

Marita proved invaluable. She was never late with meals, bringing trays filled with hearty, strengthening fare and a glass of wine or an occasionally stronger brew. She wordlessly took the sweat-stained linens and supplied fresh ones. Regretfully, she refused to stay alone with the wildly rambling man even for an instant. Savannah discovered from the slight girl that the local doctor had succumbed to yellow jack and no replacement had been found. She promised to see if any of the patrons who visited her or the other girls was in that profession. Clinging to that hope, Savannah pushed

26

back the heavy hair that strayed untidily in her eyes and returned to the bedside.

On the fifth day, the laudanum ran out. She looked at the empty bottle with an anxious helplessness. Skyler's fever still raged out of control, and in spite of her careful tendering thin red lines began to creep from beneath the bandage on his arm.

"No," she moaned futilely, seeing those streaks as a defeat of all she'd tried to do. "You can't give up now. You can't."

There was no answer as the dulled eyes moved in a lazy pattern about the ceiling, lost to the effects of the opiate. She knew it would keep him subdued for less than an hour. As his pain increased, larger amounts were needed to block it out. Once he came out of this gentle lull, there would be nothing to shield him from the full brunt of his agony.

Determinedly, Savannah checked her dwindling funds. There was barely enough to keep the room and pay for food, but she knew she could do without to ease his suffering.

Running a quick comb through the tangle of unwashed hair, she pocketed the remaining notes and cast an uneasy glance at the bed. He would have to be all right. She would only be gone a short time. Surely the drug would keep him quiet that long. She checked the position of his arm countless times and sponged his sweat-dappled brow.

"I'll be right back," she told him. She expected no response. "I'm going to get you some more medicine. Just stay still."

She touched his hot cheek briefly then turned to the door, not seeing the unsteady hand he raised as if to stay her.

27

Chapter Three

The main floor of "The Pirate's Nest" was an abrupt affront to the senses. The air was stale with thick smoke and rum, and vibrant with the roar of laughter and bawdy talk. Its tables were crowded with sailors between packets, with barely enough room for the barmaids and mulatto wenches to weave between them in hopes of freeing pockets of the coin rumored to be as plentiful as dirt.

Savannah hesitated on the bottom step, alarmed by the noise and burly appearance of the patrons. She took a deep breath, nearly choking on the clouds of acrid smoke, and moved into the taproom. She didn't pause or look down at the leering faces of the men who tugged at her skirts, but walked steadily, her eyes scanning the tables for a uniform denoting some authority. She pushed her way toward a stocky man in a British captain's garb and waited for the blurry eyes to lift.

"Captain, perhaps you can help me," she began a bit breathlessly.

A toothy grin split the florid face. "A course I can, little lady," he vowed in a thickly accented voice. His beefy hand shot out to shove a companion from his chair. "'Ave a seat." When she complied, he eyed her boldly and grinned some more. "What can Captain

Rhodes be doing for you, Missy?"

"Are you one of the runners who brings in medical supplies?"

"I brings in lots a' things."

Savannah shifted away as the sweaty hand fell on her knee, and she continued in a more businesslike tone. "I'm in need of some morphine or opium. Do you have any or can you get me some?"

Captain Rhodes chuckled. "A nasty monkey you got there. Funny you don't look to be the type."

Savannah stared at him blankly, not understanding his reference. "Can you help me or not, Captain? I am in a great hurry."

"I'm sure you are," he mused. "Don't fret. The captain'll help you get square again. First share a glass with me."

"I really don't have time," she protested, but he waved her off.

"I don't barter with parched lips," he pronounced, then waved for a barmaid.

Controlling her urgency with difficulty, Savannah waited in silence until a mug was set before her. Rhodes's steady stare made her increasingly uncomfortable, so smug and certain. Whatever the name of the stuff in her mug, it was strong enough to bring tears and a fit of coughing.

Still wheezing, she demanded, "I need your answer, Captain. I have money."

"Let's see its color." When she displayed the notes, he laughed heartily. "Put away that paper. It ain't worth the ink to print it. I deal in gold. Or other things," he added with a greasy smile. His eyes began a slow assessment of her sweat-stained bodice, noting the tight stretch of fabric with appreciation.

"I have no coin," she stated in frustration.

"Don't be fretting now. I did say I'd barter, didn't I?"

He grinned at her with an ugly confidence, hand resting on her thigh. It edged upward until his meaning was clear.

Savannah went crimson with shock and fury. She was about to deal the ruddy face a hard slap when there was a quick tug on her arm. She looked up to see Marita. The girl looked terrified.

"Missy, it be your man. He in a bad way. You come quick."

Savannah rushed after her, ignoring the disgruntled shout from the captain about fickle tarts. At the top of the stairs, the sound of hoarse cries replaced the din of the barroom below.

She had underestimated the strength of the laudanum. Instead of sedating, it dulled the pain just enough to give Skyler a false sense of command. When he tried to get out of bed, he fell heavily to the floor and lay there, writing from the pain that stabbed through his arm. He fought against the hands that tried to restrain him, thoughts too fogged with fever and hurt to respond to the soothing voice. His own raspy cries made an unpleasant echo, resounding with booming thunder in his confused mind.

Savannah struggled to still the disjointed movements. Even in his weakened state, she was no match for his strength. Each slight jog of the injured limb brought more of the awful sounds. Desperated to quiet him, she sat next to him on the floor. He was too heavy for her to lift back onto the bed, so she drew him up against her, hugging him tight to restrict his thrashings. His breath raged hot and fast against her neck. For several minutes he twisted ineffectually, trying to break free, then lay limp, panting raggedly. Savannah took advantage of his laxity to turn him slightly so he rested in the curve of her arm, bolstered by the bed frame. Carefully, she lifted the splintered arm and stretched it

31

out on the mattress tick to cushion it against further abuse.

Convinced he was as comfortable as she could make him, she stroked the sweat-soaked hair and murmured quiet reassurances until his breath slowed to shallow gulps and his head lay heavy upon her shoulder. His sudden shivering despite the heat of his body prompted her to pull the thin comforter from the bed and wrap it close about the two of them. She continued to ply the dirty hair with a slow kneading movement until her own fatigue got the better of her worries and she slumbered against him.

To wake in the arms of a man was an alarming but oddly exhilarating experience. Savannah was unmoving for a long moment, eyes closed so she could savor the feeling. She had somehow ended up nestled in the warm hollow of his side, head resting on his soiled shirt front and held there by the broad spread of his fingers in the tangle of her hair. His head rested heavily atop hers, breath brushing the feathery tendrils of her hair with a faint, irregular rhythm. The shared heat of their bodies beneath the blanket created a comforting closeness, a security like that she had revelled in as a child in her mother's arms. The difference was in the subtle shift of her emotions, changing the person who held her from a helpless patient to a man capable of rousing this strange confusion in her breast. To still its unnerving flutter, she straightened, waking him with her movement.

The pale, shivery eyes regarded her with no little surprise before the pain in his arm distracted him. With a grimace, he released her to feel along the crude splint in bewilderment.

"What happened?" he muttered. "What did I do to my arm?"

"It was broken when your ship went down. Don't

32

you remember?"

He shook his head in a dazed fashion, brows lowering. "I've broken bones before. It never felt like this. Why does it hurt so?"

"Your arm was crushed beneath the mast, not merely broken. The doctor wanted to amputate but I wouldn't let him. Maybe I was wrong."

"You weren't wrong," he said adamantly. The light eyes swung back to her, the puzzled look returning. "I don't know you."

"No, you don't. I'm Savannah. I've been taking care of you. Do you think you could help me get you back on the bed? You're too heavy for me to lift."

Between them, it was a struggle to get him from the floor without a great deal of discomfort. By the time he was stretched out once more, his face was beaded with sweat and his jaw pale from the force of clenching his teeth. The lucidity was pushed away by the swamping waves of pain as he groaned and twisted in torment. There was little Savannah could do except restrain him as best she could. When his strength finally waned, she was exhausted, arms and back aching with strain. She didn't know if she could manage another hour, let alone the weeks ahead, of this draining work. Good intentions weren't enough. She needed help. She needed sleep. She needed a break from the grinding, all-consuming routine. She wanted to sit down and cry in weariness, to flee the room without looking back, but she knew she could afford neither luxury.

No features had ever looked better to her than the craggy planes of James Ambrose's face when he entered the room. She was almost weeping when she rose to greet him with hurried words of concern and apology.

"I did everything I could. He's in such terrible pain. The laudanum ran out and I couldn't get more. His arm's infected and I fear all his suffering will be

33

for naught."

"I'll be the judge of that. Let me have a look at him."

Weak with relief, Savannah surrendered her position to hover over the doctor's shoulder while he removed the dressing to examine the inflamed wound. When he prodded the swollen flesh, Skyler moaned in the depth of his delirium.

"The bone seems to be knitting but the infection is bad, very bad. I still say amputation would serve him best."

Savannah looked at the feverish face and frowned. Irrationally, all she could think of was missing the feel of both arms around her. But he was in such agony. How could she expect him to endure more of the same? Very quietly, she said, "Do whatever you think best. Anything to help him."

Ambrose gave her a long look, seeing the betraying shimmer of helplessness in her eyes, then gave a curt nod.

While he prepared his tools, Savannah knelt down beside the bed, touching the tossing head with a gentle hand. Her other hand rubbed the back of his until his fingers curled about it in a convulsive grip.

"My arm's on fire," he complained weakly. "Oh, God, it hurts so bad. I can't bear it. I can't."

"It's all right," she soothed. "The doctor will take care of it for you."

"Take care of it," he echoed, then his breath caught sharply and the pale eyes came into alarmed focus. They grew huge and round when he saw the instruments Ambrose was laying out. His stare riveted to the bone saw. "Noooo."

Savannah felt his harsh recoil and with tears bright on her cheeks continued her calming words. "The pain will be gone soon. You'll be all right. Dr. Ambrose is a fine surgeon. He'll—"

"He's going to take my arm," Skyler blurted out in horror. His chest was heaving with growing panic and his grasp crushed about her hand.

"Shh. Don't be afraid. It will be over soon."

He shook his head wildly. The frantic eyes tore away from the saw to meet hers in entreaty. "No, please. Don't let him do it. Please. I'd rather die. I beg you to stop this. You have to help me. I can stand the pain; just don't let him take my arm. Please. Please help me." His voice dwindled off as the agony brought him to a near swoon but his hand didn't lessen its desperate grip. He ground her fingers as he watched the chloroform being readied. "Please." It was a soft-spoken sob as his eyes closed in resignation.

"Doctor, wait."

Ambrose frowned at the hand that stilled his arm. His words were gruff but not unfeeling. She hadn't heard the hundreds of pleas all asking the same thing. "We've no time for sentiment here. It has to be done now while he's strong enough to recover. Waiting will only lessen his chances."

"And is there no chance he'll survive if left whole?"

Ambrose sighed. He'd heard the argument before and hadn't been able to best it. The hope and anguish in her eyes made him shrug. "He's come this far."

"Then can't we give him the chance? Please."

"Why did I know you would ask that," he said with a reluctant smile. "I'll do the best I can for him. I've brought some morphine borrowed from the last shipment, which will make him rest easier. And speaking of rest, when did you last have any?" When she couldn't answer, he lifted her to her feet. Skyler's hand fell slackly from hers. "Go and get yourself a hot bath and a change of clothes. I'll tend your Yankee."

"You won't—"

"No, I won't. My word on it. See to yourself now. Go

35

below and get a good meal. I don't want to see you back in this room before evening. Go on with you."

Persuaded by the idea of cleanliness, she gave a last long look at Skyler. He was on the edge of consciousness, not aware she was no longer beside him. Resolutely, she picked up her bag and left the confining room.

The cost of the bath was well worth the luxury. She soaked until the water's chill grew uninviting, then left the tub reluctantly, feeling revitalized. There was a mirror on the wall of the small bathing closet. She had avoided it when she entered, looking into it now in dismay. No wonder the English captain had treated her so boldly. She resembled no fine planter's daughter, with that wild tumble of hair and hollowed eyes. Methodically, she brushed out the long ebony tresses, working the snarls free to leave a mass of rippling satin that fell well past her shoulders. Her hair was her glory, thick, wavy, almost blue-black when the light gleamed against it, the hair her Creole great-grandmother had heired her father and uncle and then herself. She pulled it back from her face, arranging it in a soft roll at the base of her slender neck.

Critically, she observed her features in the dirty glass, wondering how Skyler Reade would see her. Would he be pleased or would he shy away from the intense, intelligent woman she saw there? She was no fragile beauty like her sister, but one of character and strength.

Free from the straying tendrils of hair, her face was a flawless oval, skin as pale as ivory in contrast to the framing ebony. Her mother always insisted her complexion be kept from the damaging heat of the Southern sun. When angry or set on having her way, her chin became squared with a stubborn purpose. Beneath dark, arched brows, her eyes were serious and

36

unwavering, so deep a blue they appeared almost black until lit by a mischievous sparkle. Her small, pert nose hinted at her submerged sense of humor and her petal-soft mouth at the gentleness in her nature that few ever saw. To most, she appeared too brash for a well-bred female and entirely too composed for her years. Sour, Hillary called her. A somber spinster with a waspish tongue and bullying demeanor. Savannah frowned at her reflection, wishing she could disclaim those harsh analogies. Was she indeed too prickly to invite a closer look into the softer side of her, the side that could know hurt and vulnerability and loneliness?

As she slowly dressed, she assessed her figure, finding fault because of her unfashionable stature. The belles of South Carolina were supposed to be tiny, fragile, but Savannah was neither. She was tall and amply built. She saw that as a flaw because of her sister's dainty comparison. She didn't see herself as men did, lush with full inviting bosom curving to a small waist and voluptuous hips, sensual and shaped for passion. It was her unfettered opinions that discouraged the suitors, not her lack of delicate proportion. Well, she didn't want to be a cooing, simpering plaything, she told herself defensively. But she did want to be wanted for her own merit. For herself. And more and more her fanciful thoughts were returning in unvoiced hopefulness to Skyler Reade. It didn't matter that he was a stranger, a Yankee, only that he was a man—a man dependent on her.

Refreshed, dressed in her least rumpled gown, and pleasantly full from her dinner at a neighboring cafe, Savannah couldn't find reason to stay away from where she was anxious to be. She found James Ambrose finishing the last of his meal with a flagon of wine.

"He's fine," the doctor replied to her unasked

question. "The morphine has him sleeping. I've given him some powders for the fever and have a poultice on his arm. It may or may not draw out the infection. I'll show you how to fashion one before I go."

That caught her full attention. "When is that?" There was a touch of alarm in her voice. She was unprepared to resume the full brunt of responsibility so soon.

"On tomorrow's evening tide."

"Oh," she murmured, relieved and not afraid to show it.

"It hasn't been easy, has it?" he intuited gently.

"I'm not complaining."

He smiled at that staunch answer and finished his wine.

Savannah sat down on the edge of the bed, momentarily surprised by the look of Skyler Reade. And pleased.

"I took the opportunity to clean him up some," Ambrose explained at her amazement. He chuckled at her deep blush. "I figured you being a lady might feel a bit compromised in doing so."

She shot him a glowering look that was nevertheless grateful, then returned her attention to the figure on the bed. Gone were the raggedy clothes, replaced by the cord-waisted white cotton trousers she had purchased for him but had been too modest to put on him. His chest was bare, displaying a fine down of golden hair, with only the heavy splint and bulky dressing spoiling the splendid line of his body. He'd been washed and shaved, revealing her first good look at his face. She looked long and well.

Skyler Reade had none of the classic beauty that graced her brother, Darcy. His features were bold and angular, creating a striking strength that was nonetheless pleasing. The blistering burn had mellowed to deep tan, bronzing the wide forehead, slightly prominent nose, and squared chin with warm, deceivingly healthy color. Above the brown face, his hair was a shocking contrast, pale as a silvery ash. Darker brows and thick lashes framed the pale grey eyes. His mouth was wide and heavily sensual, leaving her anxious to see his smile. Separately, none of his features were close to perfect, but together they made a compelling whole, firm and totally male. Such a powerful face could hardly befit a man who would easily be intimidated by an outspoken woman.

"He's going to sleep the night away," Ambrose told her. "I gave him a heavy dose, figuring you both could use the rest. I'm going downstairs for something stronger than this fruit juice. I've got the room across the hall for the night. You get some sleep, little lady, and don't fear to wake me should you need anything.

Savannah nodded, feeling her full weariness. Alone in the darkness of the room with only her sleeping companion, she dressed in a floor-length nightdress and settled on the chaise, trying to find a comfortable spot to spend the night. With a heavy sigh, she closed her eyes. A soft smile curved her lips as she drifted into a slumber on the stirring dream of two strong arms holding her to a golden chest while her mouth was gently plundered with a masterful desire.

Chapter Four

The days went quickly into weeks, each bringing dramatic improvement to her patient. James Ambrose had sailed after showing her how to apply the noxious-smelling hot poultice. She changed it regularly, not minding the heat that seared her fingers as she watched the dreaded streaks slowly recede. She kept up the doses of morphine and Skyler was easily managed, sleeping heavily in his drug-induced stupor. He was in a fuzzy state of consciousness only long enough to eat the hearty soups she spooned down him. She no longer found the task tiring but felt a satisfying pleasure in it. She felt needed and important, as if caring for him gave her some unspoken claim that grew stronger in her own mind as he did.

She was surprised to find those grey eyes upon her, clear and aware when she brought him his morning meal. They looked at each other for a long moment before she felt awkward, turning aside to set down the tray of sugared and creamed rice.

"Good morning," she began with a careful cheeriness. "How do you feel?"

"Hungry," he stated emphatically, eyeing the tray with some interest. Then he looked at her in the same manner. "And curious."

"About what?" she asked, efficiently lifting him on a

41

bolster of pillows.

"You mostly."

"Oh?" She looked away to stir the hot cereal so she wouldn't appear as girlishly nervous as she felt. "What do you want to know?"

"I'm sorry, but I've forgotten your name."

"Savannah."

"Oh, yes." He nodded to himself as if filing that away so he wouldn't have to ask again. He looked long into her eyes until she felt a strange shiver shake her from head to toe. "But I didn't forget your voice. The sound of it and the strength of your hand." He extended his hand with a sudden shyness, palm outstretched, for her to place hers within it. His fingers engulfed hers, drawing them to him so he could press a kiss to her knuckles. "Thank you, Savannah."

The warmth and timbre of his voice made her hand tremble in his. She drew it away, forcing a competent smile and emotionless tone. "I'm glad to see you're recovering."

"Only because of you," he concluded, gaze so intense she could feel the heat of color begin to rise in her face. "But why? If I guess your accent correctly, you're from the Carolinas. Why would you want to help me?"

"Because you needed it. Compassion doesn't see blue or grey, only a need. It didn't matter at the time that you were an enemy."

That searching stare was relentless. Savannah fidgeted with the cereal spoon to disguise her unsettled emotions. She was relieved when his attention shifted back to the swaddled arm. He watched his fingers move with a fascination.

"You said my ship went down."

"You still don't remember?"

"The storm. I remember the storm but then nothing until I heard your voice. You found no survivors?"

42

"Only you. You were caught up in some debris from the ship. It kept you from drowning."

"And you saved my life and my arm."

She flushed in humility, mumbling, "Dr. Ambrose did, actually. There was not much I could do for you myself."

"Except give me hope and something to cling to. Someday I'll repay you for that kindness."

"For now, just eat your breakfast."

Skyler continued to improve, growing stronger and restless in his confinement. He refused the morphine except for small amounts to ease him to sleep. When he was awake, his senses grew ever sharper. He never forgot her name again.

On returning from a bath at midday, Savannah was alarmed to find his bed empty. Heart hammering at a frantic pace, she rushed to the open windows. The sight of the tall, straight figure on the small balcony made her knees buckle slightly in relief and a strange stirring of another emotion much harder to identify.

"Are you all right?"

He turned at the sound of her voice, smiling broadly. The welcoming expression was dazzling, teeth flashing in the browned face and eyes glittering like silver in the brilliant sunlight. "I'm fine. I just needed to get some fresh air. I didn't mean to give you a scare. Come out and join me."

Skyler Reade was a good-sized man, soaring over her own height by an easy six inches, and built in sturdy lines. When he was abed Savannah had felt his equal, but coming to stand in his shadow she was overwhelmed by his stature. It was an unbalancing feeling that left her giddy and uncertain. And she enjoyed it.

"It feels so good here," he was saying, turning back to tilt his face toward the sun. "So warm and inviting. I can't believe it's February."

43

"Where are you from?" She leaned on the rail at his side, looking up into his face and strangely lost there.

"Pennsylvania. Philadelphia, actually. No Philadelphian would be standing outside this time of year dressed like this." His comment drew her attention to how little he wore, and her nervousness grew as her eyes appraised the sight of his broad, bare torso. "We'd be huddled in our overcoats, most likely freezing in the snow and ice. This is like paradise."

"Is that where your family is? Philadelphia?" she asked casually, trying to gain a particular bit of information without being too bold.

He nodded, eyes staring over the rooftops to the tranquil sea beyond with a look of nostalgia. "My parents have a big house there, all filled with us like a big mob. There's my older brother and his wife, their three children, my younger brother, and me. It's crowded but nice, family, you know."

No mention of a wife, she noted with a smile.

He was quiet for a time, too quiet, and she looked up in alarm. His face had gone very pale, his eyes fixed with concentration. All at once he seemed to sag and slump as if strength failed him. Savannah stepped instinctively to his side so his good arm fell heavily across her shoulders. He reeled for a moment then recovered, holding tightly to her in a shiver of weakness.

"You're trying too hard," she scolded gently, steering him back to the narrow bed where he collapsed without complaint. "You have to build up your strength slowly. Don't be so impatient."

"Tomorrow I'm going for a walk on the beach. Just see if I don't," he murmured, eyes drifting shut and awareness ebbing away.

"We'll see," she replied noncommittally, but he was already asleep.

True to his conviction, Skyler was up early the next morning, surprising Marita by taking the breakfast tray from her himself. She gave him a long, sweeping glance before grinning and scurrying down the hall.

The sound of halting movement woke Savannah from her cramped rest on the chaise. She sat up stiffly, putting a hand to her mussed hair, then blushed deeply at being found in only her nightdress. Unused to seeing him up and about, she hadn't bothered with modesty and now felt mortified and nearly naked beneath his appraising stare.

"Good morning," he called amiably, juggling the tray in one hand with some difficulty. He managed to set it down on the bed without mishap. He had taken the bulky splint off and was hugging the injured arm to his side. "I'll see if I can pour some of this coffee while you make yourself presentable. Not that I don't think you are now," he added with a quick, disarming grin.

Pouring from the heavy pot took all his concentration. Savannah took advantage of his distraction to slip one of her gowns over her head, wriggling into it awkwardly without the help of her shaping corset. Properly clothed, she came to sit on the bed with the tray between them, taking the cup he extended proudly with an answering smile.

After a silent, companionable meal. Skyler asked her help in constructing a sling. Once that was done, he announced his intention of going down to the beach. Savannah's hesitance couldn't deter him, so she walked resolutely at his side, ready to extend a helping hand should he need one. Moving slowly and carefully, he navigated the stairs and started triumphantly down to the shoreline.

The pastel sand was warm and yielding in the quiet cove, removed from the bustle of the crowded docks. A few native children were fishing beyond the point, but aside from them, they were alone. When his steps faltered Savannah was quick to aid him, and Skyler let his arm remain in a light, familiar drape about her shoulders. Of its own accord, her own arm found itself encircling his sturdy waist in a timid reinforcement.

Finding an outcropping of surf-smoothed boulders, Skyler urged her to sit beside him while he stared out over the gentle, rolling blue-green waters.

"Do you miss being on the sea?" she asked, puzzling over his wistful expression.

"Lord, no," he laughed, shooting her a quick smile. "I was a terrible sailor. I spent the first two weeks hanging over the rail. I was thinking how odd it was that I'd be the one spared."

Trying to ease the shadowed look in the pale eyes, Savannah said lightly, "That sounds like me. I couldn't keep a morsel down the whole trip here."

"Where were you sailing from?"

It was a casually asked question and she replied without thinking of who he was. "Charleston."

"And what were you doing on a runner ship?"

She looked up at him in alarm, remembering their opposite stands. "What makes you think I was?" she tried to bluff awkwardly.

"Few pleasure boats bother to slip through the Federal blockade," he chided gently.

"Lucky for you this one did."

He fell silent at her tart rejoinder, making her feel badly about the sudden distance she'd placed between them. To breach it, she explained quietly, "I was on business for my father."

"And he approved of letting you run such a risk?" Disapproval edged his tone.

"My father is dead," she told him flatly. She turned her clouding eyes back to the sea, blinking hard.

He was instantly all conciliation, picking up her

hand for a sympathetic squeeze. "I'm sorry Savannah. I didn't mean to hurt you."

"It's all right. My father was a good man and you're right, he wouldn't have approved."

He pressed her hand again and refused to surrender it. Instead, his strong fingers began a soothing massage that had the opposite effect. Instead of calming her, the gentle caress woke all sorts of disturbing prickles of sensation.

"What were you buying in your exchange for cotton? Arms for your brethren?" The condemning tone was back in his voice, intentional or not.

"I have no love for this war, Mr. Reade, nor would I willingly prolong it. I did not make it nor can I end it, but I can ease some of the suffering in its wake. My ship will supply medicines and clothing. There are enough young men injured or dying as it is."

Her curt speech brought a dull flush and words that surprised her. "I apologize to you. I've no call to antagonize you or question your motives after your kindness to me. I guess I'm sensitive because I have two brothers in the fight."

She nodded in empathy. "My brother as well but not any longer." When his hand tightened, she added, "Not dead. He was taken prisoner last September after Antietam."

"At least you know where he is."

Now it was her turn to crush his warm fingers, and he gave her a bittersweet smile. She changed the topic to a more neutral subject.

"If you're such a poor sailor, why the Navy?"

His laugh was full-bodied and tinged with irony. "To stay safe." She chuckled with him over the turn of events. "I'm one of those know-nothing politicians that clogs the gears of war. I was persuaded that blockading could earn me a distinguished rank and notice without

47

the danger. Rather cowardly, I must admit."

Seeing his awkward blush, she said firmly, "I see nothing wrong in wanting to survive."

He gave her a grateful smile. "I wish others had your outlook."

They continued to talk for some time, skirting touchy issues and speaking mostly of their families. Savannah loved listening to him. Most Northerners had a grating, twangy accent she found most unpleasant, but she was enthralled with his crisp, rapid-fire speech, his voice so full of energy and passion. She hung on his every word, eyes intent on his face and pulses racing as quickly as his delivery. Savannah had never felt so unsettled yet comfortable with any man, and she was afraid to admit her emotions were all tangled when it came to Skyler Reade.

"We'd better start back."

Savannah shook herself out of her reverie to look about, surprised to find the sun making a brilliant pool of rippling red and orange on the dark blue sea.

"Let's find some place to eat. I'm tired of dining off trays."

She was hesitant, reluctantly explaining, "That may not be wise. It wouldn't do for some to discover you are a Yankee. Your accent would betray you."

"Accent?" He looked startled. "I guess I never thought of myself as having one. Who do they think I am?"

Savannah's face flushed a deep crimson as she stammered, eyes downcast, "My husband."

He chuckled, not at all embarrassed, and said in amusement, "Then I shall be a model husband and let you do all the talking."

She laughed at his teasing, and arm in arm, they strolled back up to the crowded streets. After finding a small, secluded cafe, Skyler kept his promise, remaining silent while she ordered for them. During their meal, Savannah's eyes kept darting nervously to the growing clusters of Confederate soldiers but Skyler seemed unconcerned, devouring his food with an awkward gusto. Pouring their wine, he noted her apprehension with a touched smile.

"Don't look so guilty and no one will pay you any mind," he suggested in a hushed voice.

"Are you forgetting what danger you're in here?" she hissed back.

"And what of you, harboring the enemy?" He grinned at her sour look and stood, balancing the wine cask in the fullness of his sling so he could take her arm. "Let's enjoy this elsewhere then."

Content to let him escort her, they returned to the tiny room, so much smaller now that she was aware of his presence. She moved out onto the balcony, more comfortable in the open air darkness so the night breeze could cool the growing heat in her face and her tremors of anticipation. Hearing him approach brought that flurry of excitement to a sharpened peak until she could feel his closeness at her back.

"Your glass," he said softly.

When she turned, Savannah was startled by his nearness, having to tip back her head to see him. His eyes were dark and smoky. Before she had time to say more than his name, he was kissing her. It was a brief, impulsive gesture, more hesitant than passionate, but it left Savannah trembling in its wake.

Seeing her stunned expression and wide eyes, he said in a rush, "I'm sorry. I didn't mean for that to happen. I mean, I did but I didn't mean to offend you with my forwardness."

She drew a labored breath to expand a chest too constricted for speech. "You didn't," she assured him in an odd whisper.

He gave her a slight smile and extended her glass to break the awkwardness. But her agitation would not be quieted. As they stood together in the intimate darkness so far removed from all they knew and from the conflict that should have created a barrier between them, Savannah had no doubt that Skyler Reade was the man she'd been waiting for. She could give no reason, she just knew. His warm gaze hinted at it and his warmer kiss assured it. He was what she wanted. All she had to do was keep him, or was that too flighty a dream? Their country was at war, their backgrounds making them opponents and looming in the near future to pull them their separate ways. And if he went, would she ever find him again in the madness that ran rampant? Her uncle was due back any day and with his arrival this idyllic interlude would end. There was so little time to be sure of him and of herself.

She looked up at his strong profile in a quandary, then put her hand on his arm to claim his attention. She was thankful for the night, which hid much of her expression from him. She wanted to appear calm and in control when, in truth, she was neither of those things. Quickly, before she had too much time to think, she said, "I've been called too forward myself on more than one occasion and fear I'm about to be so again. I hope I don't shock you but I want you to kiss me again."

A Southern gentleman would have recoiled in judgmental horror, but Skyler merely set down his glass then turned to her, face all shadow and contour. Savannah's eyes slid closed as his hand brushed over the softness of her cheek, using his fingertips to lift her chin. The heat of his mouth made her gasp then sigh as it possessed her own, moving slowly, thoroughly over every sweet contour until she was breathless. Her arms rose to slip over his shoulders, fingers meshing in the moonlit hair partly for balance and partly to hold him to her. She thought no pleasure could be as intense and thrilling as the searching part of her lips by the fleeting touch of his tongue.

Eager for more of this discovery, Savannah leaned against him, the sudden shift putting him off balance. Instinctively, he reached out both arms to hold her. His sharp cry of surprise and hurt shattered the mood as he clutched his arm with a pain-filled grimace. Savannah helped steady him. Her face was pale with upset.

"Oh, I've hurt you. Forgive me," she pleaded as he struggled to keep from succumbing to the swirling nausea.

"No, I hurt myself and, I fear, my chances," he managed with a wan smile. "This arm is blasted inconvenient."

Providing a steadying shoulder, Savannah helped him back to bed. He sat heavily, pulling her down beside him.

"I shouldn't have let you do so much today," she continued to berate herself.

"I only regret not being able to do more." He said it teasingly but his eyes were serious. It took him a moment to straighten, then his fingertips grazed her cheek. "Is there someone at home for you, Savannah?"

Her surprise made her blank for a second, then she answered, "No. And you? Have you someone waiting?"

"No one special," he replied quietly. "I've a feeling that you'll be special though. I'd like to call on you if you'd let me."

Savannah sat very still, heart beating madly as she tried to hold onto her sensibilities. "That's not very realistic. You're forgetting the war."

"Another inconvenience," he dismissed mildly. "Do you think I'd let a war stop me?"

"I hope not." She said it softly but with a strength of passion as her eyes rose to his in bold answer.

"I think it would be a foolish mistake to let you go and slip away from me as easily as you do our blockade ships. Be warned, I won't let that happen. I should know your surname though."

"Russell."

"Savannah Russell, I mean to court you and I mean to have you. You'll have to settle for that promise because I feel too awful to give you more than words. I'd better lie down before I faint."

Still left atremble by his vow, Savannah eased him back, concerned by the pinch of discomfort about his mouth and eyes. "Do you want something for the pain?"

"No. I want my head clear. It's not that bad," he assured her with a forced smile to tell her he was lying nobly.

"Sleep well, Skyler," she said softly, touching a fingertip to his moist lips before moving quickly away.

In the darkness, she shed her heavy gown that had been so stifling throughout the day. The night air was cool and silken upon the skin left bare by her thin chemise. Languorously, she unpinned her hair and shook it out so the ebony waves tumbled about her shoulders in a ripple of weighty satin. After brushing it well, she tied the heavy mass back in a single fall to keep her neck bare to the cool of the evening. She settled on the unyielding chaise, curling into an awkward knot so it would accommodate her long, slender legs. She stayed in that cramped position, tired but too elated to sleep. After twisting this way and that, a softly spoken offer stilled her.

"You can't be comfortable on that thing. I've plenty of room here if you don't mind the sharing."

She was silent for a long beat, tempted but held

by uncertainty.

There was the sound of his hand patting the inviting space. "Come on, Savannah. It's not as though we're strangers, is it?"

"No." With that small word, her decision was made. Ignoring the modest cries of her proper conscience, she crossed the room on silent bare feet, a flitting shadow in the broken light from the slatted windows. Her weight created hardly a dip as she lay back in the small spot left her. Though the space was far from ample, it was heaven to stretch her toes out full length, and then there was Skyler. Just his closeness was reward enough.

"Have you enough room?" he asked, shifting slightly to make a beckoning hollow next to him. "There. Now that's better." His good arm slipped about her shoulders, drawing her against him until they fit snugly and perfectly together. A small, timid hand moved to rest atop the slowly rising chest with its mat of fair hair.

"Much better," she murmured drowsily. She had wanted to stay awake to savor the feel of him beside her, to replay all the words he'd spoken, but safe and warm in his strong embrace, her wistful thoughts became sweet dreams.

Chapter Five

The pounding began somewhere in her subconscious, then focused to become an impatient hammering on her door.

"Vannah, are you there, girl?"

With a gasp, Savannah sat up, leaving the warm burrow her cheek had found at the base of Skyler's throat with a guilty flush. What had seemed so innocent and right in the intimate darkness of the room they shared alone would become an unforgivably wanton act upon discovery.

"Who is it?" Skyler asked her quietly, light eyes flickering between annoyance and alarm.

"My uncle," she replied in agitation. "He can't find me like this."

Frowning to himself, Skyler watched her hurry about the room, frantically dressing and twisting her dangling hair into its conservative netting. Her upset seemed in direct denial of their closeness, and even before meeting him, Skyler didn't like this uncle who could push her into such a panic.

"What took you so long, girl? I've been standing here forever," Jonah grumbled as he cast a suspicious glance at her flushed features. His no-nonsense niece never looked flustered. Then his cold, dark eyes moved behind her to the half-dressed man struggling to sit up,

55

favoring his left arm. "See you kept him alive after all. He'll be good and healthy for the stockade in Charleston. Or better yet, you can leave him here. I understand the lads would love to get their hands on a Yankee blockader."

"Uncle Jonah, please," she beseeched, giving Skyler an apologetic look.

"Let's get some breakfast, girl. We have things to discuss." With that, he began to walk away down the hall.

Seeing her turmoil, Skyler urged, "Go on. I'll be fine."

"I'm sorry," she stammered and hurried after the rigid back of Jonah Russell.

While they waited for their meal in a crowded dockside cafe, Jonah leveled that disapproving glower, only to have it parried with an unblinking stare of cool innocence.

"He seems fit enough," Jonah commented wryly. "Awfully close quarters to be sharing with a man so obviously recovered."

"Oh, please," she snapped irritably to hide her blush. "The man nearly died. I don't think he's a great threat to my honor. Now tell me how your journey fared."

Jonah harrumphed at her skillful evasion but warmed to the subject. "You wouldn't believe how much we saved by avoiding these thieving middlemen. The Brits were very obliging. I've everything stored until our ship gets in tonight. I even got you ladies some pretties."

"You didn't have to," she protested, but Jonah laughed.

"Hillary won't like you treating her box of bonbons so lightly."

"I'm sure she would think of her comfort above any one else's," she said unkindly, then looked chagrined.

56

"But then she is yet a child and I shouldn't judge her weakness so unfairly."

"And what of your weakness for the Yank? How would you have us judge you?" he asked shrewdly.

Savannah frowned and remarked tartly, "Skyler is my affair and I don't care what anyone else thinks."

"Skyler, eh?" he observed with a sad sigh. "Vannah, he's wrong for you. It's wrong for you to care about him. I know your weakness for helpless creatures but don't be confusing him. He's no hurt little boy that needs your tending. He's a grown man. He's dangerous and an enemy to all of us."

"I can't help how I feel and I care very much."

She was as startled by the admission as her uncle but backed it with a determined jut of her chin, while Jonah grew pale then red trying to control his outrage. His words were stilted.

"Girl, you don't even know the man. With all the good, self-respecting stock in your own state, you pick the likes of him to pin your heart to? For God's sake, Savannah, for your dead father's sake, think of what you are doing."

"Skyler Reade is more of a man than any of your porch-lounging aristocrats. The color of his uniform doesn't change the man," she argued hotly.

"And just what are you going to do with this fine man of yours? Take him home to meet your family? Do you think your mother or Darcy's wife will welcome him with open arms? And what of him? Do you honestly believe he'd proudly take you home with him, showing off his little Southern gal on his arm? Not likely. He's a man and there's only one thing he wants from you. Now don't go giving me that huffy look. Like it or not, we're at war with him and his kind, and I for one won't allow you to cozy up to him when he could be killing your loved ones tomorrow in the name of his

57

precious Union. Send him to prison where he's sure to do no more harm."

"No," she shouted, bringing curious stares from all about them. Scowling until heads turned away, she continued in a low, purposeful tone. "You've no say in this, Uncle Jonah. I'll listen to you because I love you but my decisions are my own. I am twenty-one and of legal age to do as I please. You are not my father or my brother. Skyler Reade is my responsibility to do with as I please and I'll deal with him in my own way."

Jonah's jaw clamped shut, conceding her point, but the victory was bitter. With the world at odds, she needed the closeness of her family more than ever. Skyler would be a wedge to that closeness because of what he was and what he stood for. Looking at her uncle's sullen expression, she wondered which was more important.

She was still quiet and reflective when she returned to the small room. It no longer felt like a secluded hideaway where romance could flourish. That myth was spoiled by the intrusion of reality. She went to join Skyler on the balcony. He didn't turn to greet her but continued to stare out over the rooftops.

"Our ship sails this evening," she began softly. He nodded but said nothing. "You'll be going with us."

She felt more than saw his body tense. "I see," he remarked noncommittally. "To Charleston?"

"Yes."

He grew more distant, mouth taking a downward curve and eyes troubled. "What's it like there."

Puzzled by his hushed tone, she asked, "In Charleston? Why?"

"If I'm to be there for the duration of the war, I'd as soon know what to expect." He took a deep, steadying breath, then turned to look at her. The grey eyes were clouded with many things but none of them condemnation.

Savannah understood then and put a gentle hand on his arm. "Skyler, we're not taking you into Charleston."

"But you said—"

"Our ship sails there but you aren't going all the way. We'll put you ashore outside of the harbor. It won't be easy, but you should be able to return to your troops." Mistaking the odd look in his eyes, she blurted hastily, "It's the best I could do. Really. We're carrying contraband. You can't expect us to escort you to one of your ships. I wish I could make it easier for you but—"

His sudden hard embrace drove the rest of her apology from her as she was crushed to his chest. His shaky laugh rushed past her ear.

"Oh, Savannah, I've no complaints. When you left with your uncle I was going to run and take my chances, but instinct told me to trust you. I'm just relieved to know I made the right choice."

He held her for a long moment, cheek pressed to her hair, then asked very gently, "Would you come with me, Savannah?"

She leaned back in the curve of his arm, expression regretful. "I can't. Not now. Not with things the way they are."

"But you're not saying no forever," he prompted.

"I want very much to see you again, Skyler Reade," she told him with a simple sincerity. "Don't disappoint me."

"I won't."

He bent down, lips parting softly to capture hers, when a brusk knock brought them apart.

Repressing a curse, Savannah strode to the door, but her anger at the interruption was tempered when she saw James Ambrose.

"'Morning, Miss Savannah. I understand we're going to be sailing together. I offered to share my quarters with this unpopular fellow and thought I'd stop and see if he needed anything."

"Some clothes would be nice," Skyler suggested, extending his hand in greeting. "Anything but grey would do fine."

Ambrose grinned as he shook his hand, then took hold of his other wrist and slowly drew out his injured arm. When he turned it slightly, Skyler's breath sucked in noisily.

"Still hurt you?"

"Like a bi—bear," he concluded, eyes flashing to Savannah in deference. She rewarded him with a teasing smile. "But better the discomfort to remind me I still have an arm. I thank you for that."

"The little lady's the one you should thank, but then I have a feeling you already have." His glance went between them in smug amusement. "A good gambler, that gal."

Skyler nodded, eyes warming as they touched hers.

"Well, I've come to see this dangerous Yank to his quarters. Jonah will be up for you in a bit as soon as he sees to some provisions."

"Now?" Savannah protested a bit too strongly.

"I'm his keeper until we put off. Get your things, Yank."

"I don't think I have any. Lead the way."

Savannah reached out a tentative hand as if to stop his departure, but he flashed her that brilliant grin and was gone.

The *Harrier* set sail on the evening tide, on a calm sea awash with moonlight. As she paced her cabin, the same one she'd confined herself to on the voyage over, her thoughts were too full and sundry to consider any ill effects of the rocking floor. She missed Skyler with the same deep ache she'd known when she heard of Darcy's capture. Knowing he was near didn't lessen his absence. She wasn't sure but she suspected Jonah ordered them kept apart, for she hadn't seen a glimpse of him on her frequent tours of the deck. When she cornered Ambrose, he explained uncomfortably that her uncle had ordered him confined to his room but assured her that he was well. Assurances did little to ease her restlessness, knowing their destination and parting was a day away. She continued to mope and pine in a most uncharacteristic way until a hurried knock sounded on her door late that night.

"Miss Savannah, it's Ambrose."

His agitated voice chilled her as she peeked her head out. "What is it?"

"It's Reade. He's gone. Jonah'll have my head if he finds I've let him give me the slip. Is—is he—" He cleared his throat in awkward embarrassment.

Concealing her surprise, she gave a slight smile and bluffed, "He's with me, James, so don't fret. Please don't tell Jonah."

He shuffled his feet uncomfortably and muttered, "Just see he finds his way back all right."

"I will," she promised before shutting the door. She leaned against it in a panic. Skyler was wandering somewhere about the Confederate vessel. She didn't even try to guess her uncle's reaction if he was caught. Suspicion, sharp and nagging, began to surface. Snatching up her robe, Savannah tied it about her and lifted her lantern high as she hurried along the dim corridors. Hating herself for it, she reasoned the best place to look for a Yankee was in the hold with the smuggled cargo.

As she rushed by a dark stairwell, a hand caught her arm, spinning her about and up flush against an unyielding chest. Before she could express her alarm, a silencing finger touched her lips. She let her breath out in a gust of relief.

"Skyler, where have you been?" she began in a shaky accusation. He was undaunted by her suspect gaze, grinning down at her.

"Looking for you."

His sudden kiss stilled any questions she had, and with a sigh her arms encircled him trustingly. His mouth was eager and hurried, stealing away her senses with that shock of urgent passion. She clung to him weakly in a world careening wildly without balance. If he hadn't released her, she feared she would have swooned in heady breathlessness.

"I missed you," he was crooning as his lips brushed hotly over her flushed face then down the slender column of her neck, pressing to the frantic pulse that fluttered there.

"Skyler, please," she moaned faintly, the fear of discovery nudging aside her delight. "Not here."

But he wasn't discouraged. He continued to nibble the tender feast of her throat until she twisted away, panting unevenly.

"Will there ever be a right time and place if we don't make them?" he argued, holding her close so the fullness of her bosom was mashed against his shirt-front. "I want you, Savannah. I want you more than any woman I've ever known. We've no time for a proper courtship. After tomorrow, I've no guarantee of seeing you again. I don't want to rush you but I need to know how you feel. Savannah, do you care for me?"

It was all going so fast. Her mind was in a whirl. Never had she experienced such a painful confusion of emotion. Her famously cool head was afire with feelings she had oft times scorned as those for insipid daydreamers. Giving her heart full rein, she breathed, "Yes, I do. Very much."

"Then I'll find you. No matter where you are, I'll come for you. My enlistment is up in September, then there'll be no uniform to come between us. I want to be with you, to spend time with you away from all this madness. I've never met a woman like you, with your courage and determination. I know we're really strangers to one another, but then we're not. There's a bond between us that I don't understand. I've never felt closer to anyone before. Wait for me, Savannah."

"I will, Skyler, for as long as I have to."

Their lips met to seal the vow, and in the darkness of the stairwell, Savannah felt herself lose her grip on all sensibilities. Pressed against him in just a thin gown and robe, there was no disguising his desire and she was a bit frightened by the bold feel of his man's body. Hillary had often joked about leaving a line of bulging trouser fronts, but Savannah had no such experience. Just the knowledge that she had that effect on him made her more aware of herself as a woman, more aware of those strange shivery feelings he was arousing in her, feelings of yearning and need, curiosity and excitement. When he stepped away, she knew she couldn't let him go without pursuing those urgent emotions a bit further.

"Skyler, come to my cabin with me. Stay with me. We've so little time," she pleaded anxiously.

He gave a shaky little laugh and a strained smile. "Oh, Savannah, there is nothing I'd like more, but you were right, this isn't the place. I'm dying to take you in my arms, in two good arms and love you, but not here like this. Be patient. We'll have the time. I'd better go before I make a liar of myself. Good night."

His lips brushed her forehead and then he was

hurrying away, leaving her with the powerful stirrings of passion unmet and untried. Those feelings were still uppermost in her mind when the steamer came to a stop outside the line of Union vessels.

Iron-hulled sloops of war and shallow draft gunboats patrolled the Gulf Stream courses and Confederate rivers since the fall of Fort Sumter. Lincoln had ordered the blockade of the Southern coast from Virginia to Texas, starting the dangerous trade of running that line. The *Harrier* was painted a lead grey to blend with the haze of dusk or dawn, when discovery was at its highest risk. It was a matching silvery silhouette against the dune-lined shore, where it waited in a small inlet for darkness and the tide, enabling it to slip out and cross the barrier of gunboats by hugging the shore. It was a dangerous few miles, in which no lights or smoking were permitted. Even the engine room hatches were covered with heavy tarpaulins, at the risk of suffocating those below, so no telltale spark would give them away. The runner ships were unarmed, and if spotted, their only recourse was to run intentionally aground in hopes of beaching some of their cargo before capture. Once through the Union gauntlet, they would head for the West Point Mill wharves and depots at the end of Tradd Street. The constant shelling had already closed the Cooper River wharves. For now, they could do nothing but wait until the right time to make their desperate run.

As they continued their tense watch, a small boat was lowered and rowed toward the deserted beach. None of the three aboard spoke as they skimmed the orange-tinged waters of sunset until the belly of the skiff rubbed bottom.

The sailor frowned as the Yankee handed out the lovely niece of his captain. He said nothing. His orders

64

were to see the Yank ashore and the lady back to the ship.

Savannah lifted her heavy skirts to keep them from dragging in the deep sucking sand. She accepted Skyler's arm gratefully as they climbed a small dune to find privacy in its shadow among the tall grasses and scrub palms.

"How long do we have?" he asked quietly, turning to face her. Her eyes were as deep as the distant heavens and his as cool as silvery waters.

"Not long enough," she answered in soft regret. "Oh, Skyler."

Her arms went impulsively about his neck, her suddenly damp face hiding in the hollow of his throat. Feeling her tremble, he held her tightly.

"It won't be forever. Knowing that will make the time go faster," he soothed, not immune to her panic at the thought of parting and the uncertainty of all else.

"I don't want to wait. I want you now in this time we have together. I may never see you again," she cried in anguish.

"Of course you will."

"Can you promise me that? Can you guarantee it?"

He looked into the wide, searching eyes and answered honestly the only way he could. "No."

"Then don't ask me to wait when there may be no other chance." Her fingertips traced the strong line of his cheek and jaw, trembling slightly when they brushed his wide mouth. "Make me yours, Skyler. Love me and leave me with that knowledge."

His expression was hesitant as he caught her hand and pressed hot kisses to it. "Do you know what you're asking? You can't mean to give yourself to me knowing you might never see me again. You want to save that for the man who shares your life with you." His words were gentle with care for her, but she didn't want his consideration.

"Don't tell me what I want or need," she growled. "I know my own mind." To affirm that, her hand locked behind his head, pulling it down abruptly to meet her determined kiss. His reluctance was quickly overcome, and together they sank down on the dirty slope of sand, mouths eagerly exploring and desires beginning to flare.

Savannah lay back, eyes closed and heart racing as his lips burnt down her throat to the soft curve of her bosom. The bodice of her gown was too tight, crushing the swell of anticipation that rose within her. Then it loosened and she took a grateful breath, catching it sharply in delighted surprise when his hand eased over her slightly clad breast. It followed the contour of its fullness with a maddening deliberation, cupping it lovingly in his palm while his mouth scorched over the tight, aching peak burning through the thin fabric to incite sensations that made her moan in wondering rapture.

When his mouth returned to hers, he found her lips parted in invitation, accepting the lingering quest of his tongue while molded to his in willing abandon. Her fingers twisted and twined in his hair, kneading it in quick, convulsive clutches. So lost was she to that deep, soulful kiss that she didn't feel him push up her voluminous skirts and petticoats until his hand lay warm and possessive on her thigh. That unexpected touch awoke a new realm of tingling feeling, fluttering in her belly nervously and spreading slow and honey-sweet through her loins. She wouldn't have dreamed of stopping him then, the momentum of passion moving too rapidly. When he sat up, she said his name in bewilderment.

"Stay right here. Don't move," he crooned, voice low

and rough with emotion. "I'll be right back."

"Skyler?"

"I want to have a word with your man. We can't have him looking for you, now can we?"

She smiled languidly and nodded, pulses slowing to a hard, hammering tempo of insistence. In his absence, she stared idly at the darkening sky above, eyes following the soaring flight of a single gull. Her emotions were like that bird, aloft and free, floating, diving, cartwheeling unfettered by the earth below. She had no doubts about the seriousness of what she was doing. In her heart, she knew the rightness of it. Skyler was the man she wanted to spend the rest of her life with, and if he didn't return, she knew there would be no other. Whatever they shared on this lonely beach might have to make the memories of a lifetime and she wanted them to be spectacular. Then she could face even an empty future. If she were to be cheated of sharing a life with him, at least she would have this moment of intimate exchange. She would trade innocence and ignorance for a priceless knowledge, knowing he had changed her and shown her the way.

His kiss was deep and bruising as he came down to her in a sudden hurriedness, slightly out of breath and strangely intense. His mouth moved over her face in a searching urgency and even his softly spoken words had a tense immediacy to them.

"I love you, Savannah. You cannot know how deeply you've touched my life. Please believe how much I care for you. If this is all the time we have, let me make it special for you. I want you to remember me, to remember that I loved you so."

She had no time to reply, for her lips were claimed and her senses set awhirl. He was no longer moving at a slow, careful pace but plunged her headlong into the swirl of consuming, excited pleasure. Continuing the

67

deep, probing kiss, his hand slid up the silk of her bared leg, pausing briefly in a tangle of lacy undergarments, then touching her, stroking her boldly and purposefully until her mind and blood seemed afire. It was like madness, the sudden pulsing rush of feeling, frightening in its strange, awesome power. Her senses were flooded, but the drowning was so wonderful she almost wept his name against the now-tender mouth.

At first she thought the sound a part of the thundering within her, that whining sizzle flaring to a massive boom. Her eyes snapped open, meeting the grey eyes briefly before she rolled over in a jumble of twisted skirts to scramble up the dune. From its crest she could see the bright trail of the rocket from its launch on the beach below where the sailor lay sprawled insensibly to its showy starburst above the *Harrier* where it lay vulnerable in the inlet. In the distance but perilously close, a dense column of answering black smoke rose from one of the fast, oceangoing Yankee cruisers, signalling its sister ships.

"No," came a low, wailing moan from Savannah as she saw the trap close about her uncle, a trap she helped set by trusting the man she had almost let be her lover.

"Savannah."

She turned fiercely to face him, eyes bright with tears of anger and hurt and betrayal. "You." She couldn't bring herself to say more.

"Savannah, I love you. I couldn't let you be taken. I know you can't forgive me but please understand. It was my duty," he said in a rush, trying to get his explanation out before the rage he saw building in her face came to a head. "Savannah, I had no other choice. The ship was carrying—"

Her slap silenced him, stinging with the bitterness of her hurt. The return carried the force of her hate, splitting his lip and rocking him off balance. When her fist cuffed him, he misstepped and tumbled backward down the slope, head over heals until he spilled out at the bottom on his knees, hugging his arm to him in an oblivious fog of agony. He looked up blearily, seeing her at the top of the dune, sandy hair swirling about her shoulders like a black cloud. He tried to say her name but that blackness spread, dropping him facedown into unconsciousness.

Chapter Six

Lieutenant Commander Skyler Reade sat listlessly at his makeshift desk, a scattering of letters and reports spread out before him, a blur before his tired eyes. His temples ached dully from the shared spirits the night before, adding to his general ill-humor. One of the letters lay unopened. He was in no mood for Rhea Sherwood's prattle about Washington. Another was smudged from constant rereading. It was from his mother, filled with news, or the lack of it, of his family. Palmer had received another field commission. His father was probably strutting about in a swell of pride. There was no mention of Brent, off in the wilds of Virginia with the unabashed Joe Hooker who, despite his reputation as a loud debaucher, had succeeded in boosting the army's sagging morale after Burnside's disastrous "Mud March" the year before.

Since his return, much had been made of his part in the capture of the Rebel prize. He had accepted his twenty percent of the reward dourly, his reluctance raising many questions, as had his sketchy report of the incident. Rumors of a Southern woman being involved fueled speculation, but a cutting glance from the severe grey eyes discouraged the curious. His injury and notoriety granted him a desk position, for which he was thankful, but little else pleased him these days.

71

Always well liked by his command for his leniency and tireless good humor, his men were at a loss with the sharp-tongued, overly critical despot who preferred the stifling interior of his tent to a cool drink with his troops. Much could be excused because of the pain in his arm, but others hinted privately that the agony lay closer to his heart.

The arrival of his childhood friend, Captain Anthony D'Angelo, had raised hopes of cheering their commander's mood. After two nights of almost-silent drinking together, even the unflappable Tony D'Angelo wondered what had become of his amiable companion.

Skyler frowned when he heard voices outside his tentflaps, his scowl deepening at their words.

"Is he inside?"

"Go in at your own risk."

"Still cutting his teeth on everything in sight?"

"Be careful lest it be your butt."

The flap lifted and his aide appeared with a flawless military stance. "Good morning, sir. I hope I'm not intruding."

Eyes red in the unshaven face and squinting against the backlight of the sun, he growled, "Now that you have, what is it, Cochoran?"

The lanky Michigander turned to close the tentflap with a conspiratorial air, fueling Skyler's annoyed curiosity.

"It's about that matter you asked me to check into."

The change in Skyler Reade was instantaneous and startling. The dulling apathy vanished from his expression, the grey eyes growing bright and keen as he leaned forward, palms pressed to the plank of scarred wood that served him as a desk top.

"You found her?"

"Yes, sir," he replied, shifting awkwardly at the

emotion in the other's voice. "Right here in Beaufort."

"Sit down, Cochoran. Help yourself to a drink."

"Thank you, sir."

Skyler used the delay to gather his shaken control and get a tight rein on his features. Inside, his wits were scattered by the sudden race of hope and excitement. She was here. It was almost too much to ask and he felt like shouting his elation. Instead he said, with a forced calm, "Tell me what you found out."

Warmed by the liquor and his superior's sudden shift of temperament, Cochoran began to recite, "She's at her family's plantation on one of the islands. Came across her by accident while going over some reports. Seems she's suspected of harboring Rebs."

Skyler gave a slow, spreading smile. "I'll see to that," he murmured distractedly, eyes vague and distant.

Some time later, a low chuckle interrupted his musings.

"What have we here? She must be some lady."

Skyler paused in his shaving to glower at Tony D'Angelo in his mirror. When the dark-complected man continued to smirk, he gave way and grinned broadly.

"I'm going to marry her, Tony," he announced matter-of-factly.

The captain's jaw dropped perceptibly. "What? Sky, are you serious?"

"Oh, yes." He towelled the remaining lather from his cheeks and regarded the results critically.

"But I thought you and Rhea—"

"That was her thinking, not mine. I never gave her any promises."

The curly black head shook in amazement. "Who is this lucky woman?"

"Savannah Russell. She saved my life."

Tony snorted. "I had a fat boy from Vermont save

73

mine, but I didn't want to marry him. Sky, is this a Southern girl you're taken with?"

"I love her. I don't care what she is."

"Lord, I need a drink."

Over hefty glasses of bourbon, Tony pried the story from his friend, of Savannah's care and diligence in saving his arm, and her reaction to his betrayal.

"And she's agreed to marry you?"

Skyler flushed, looking a bit sheepish. "Not yet. I haven't exactly asked her."

"Sky, you're a dreamer. She most likely hates you for what you did. I doubt she cares if you love her."

"But she loves me too. I know she does. And she hates me as well. It'll take time but we'll sort it out. If she doesn't shoot me off her porch, I'll take that as a yes."

Tony shook his head again, smiling wryly at his friend's glassy-eyed expression. Skyler Reade was a man of few commitments, but when he made one, it was total and all-consuming. He grinned wider, wishing he could see the smug Rhea Sherwood when she heard her safely snagged catch had slipped the hook.

Beaufort, South Carolina was a quiet, lushly beautiful setting, unspoiled by the scarring of commercial business. Its Sea Islands were dotted with sprawling cotton plantations. In the summer months it was deserted by its white inhabitants, left to overseers because of the heat, but in the spring it was a paradise of balmy breezes. Miles of channels wove between the network of low fertile islands. Some were wide as a great river and others narrow enough to jump from bank to bank. In his rush, Skyler overlooked much of the exotic splendor. He didn't notice the expansive

74

cotton fields amid the graceful swamp palmetto and clumps of soaring pine. His eyes were filled with the white planter's mansion with its surrounding Negro village. The home of Savannah Russell.

Beaufort had fallen to the Federals in December of 1861 and was held in a state of martial law. Most of the planter families had fled and those remaining had their movements carefully monitored. Many of the fine white houses lay in ruin at the hand of Union renegades or restless slaves, but the Russell home seemed to suffer no ill effect. It was an impressive pre-Revolutionary War structure with three tiers of verandas. Six massive pillars rose to the top of the second floor. It was decorated with long windows, dentilated eaves, and a spreading attic fanlight. The blinding green lawn was surrounded by groves of oak, cedar, and magnolia. When his prancing stallion emerged from the trees, a small cluster of servants gathered on the main porch and yard, wide, fearful eyes on the blue of his uniform. They scattered when he reined in, one old man remaining to take his horse while he dismounted. His eyes rose to the straight, proud figure on the steps.

"I told you I'd find you. Hello, Savannah."

When she heard a Union officer was approaching, Savannah had rushed out, clutching a heavy pistol for the protection of her home. One Yankee was as dangerous as a dozen, but she would have preferred a dozen bent on mischief to Skyler Reade. Seeing him at the foot of her stairs rattled Savannah badly with an influx of fury and desire, the latter making her all the more angry because of her weakness. Voice deadly calm, she said, "You are the last person on earth I wish to see here. What are you doing here?"

With a matching cool, Skyler drew off his gauntlets, folding them meticulously. "Business, I'm sorry to say. As Lieutenant Commander of our fortifications here in

Beaufort, it's my duty to follow up on reports of certain activities."

"Your duty. Yes, of course," she sneered, pain heavy behind her sarcasm. "You mustn't let anything stand in the way of that."

"I'm an officer in the United States Navy and at the moment you are one of the conquered populace, so you would do well not to antagonize me."

He knew it would make her angry, her eyes growing dark, narrow, and dangerous. "Or what? Would you place me in irons, Lieutenant?"

He pursed his lips as if the idea was not unappealing, then smiled easily. "It would serve no purpose to bruise such tender flesh but don't tempt me too far. I've come to check a rumor that fugitives are being harbored here on your lands. I would prefer your cooperation, but with or without it, I plan to look around."

He could see her features tighten but her reply was admirably indifferent.

"Search away, Lieutenant. I will walk with you to make sure no one mistakes you for vermin and puts an end to you."

"Such concern, Savannah. I am touched," he teased.

His wide grin flustered her briefly before her lips firmed. "No such thing, sir. I would prevent more of your kind from swarming my property."

"Of course," he remarked, lips twisting with mirth. How good she looked. How good he felt just looking. He noticed a new toughness to the set of her features that would deny any softening, as if her naivety had born a hard cynicism. He didn't have to look far to know the reason for that change. The dark blue eyes that had been so adoring cut through him fiercely. "Shall we start in the outbuildings?"

"Lead on."

Following in his wake, Savannah struggled to

control her anxiousness and also the traitorous stirrings of another source. She had forgotten how tall and commanding he was, but little else escaped her tortured thoughts. His presence, his nearness, brought it all back with stunning clarity, the attraction and desire running too deep to be denied. That made her hatred all the sharper. She had hoped, even prayed, never to see him again after she had used the small boat to flee the inlet in a maze of tiny channels until she was able to work her way back to Beaufort. Looking on him now was a bittersweet pleasure, the way he fired her blood with such strong emotions, hating him, wanting him, and hating herself for the wanting. That he showed no sign of being affected by her was an added insult as he strode through the series of sheds and barns, never sparing her a glance.

When he marched into the main stables, Savannah lagged back, uncertainty clutching her chest as tightly as her hand did the primed pistol. She looked at the broad blue back steadily, willing her nerves to bear whatever was necessary.

Skyler poked about the tack room and stalls while Savannah fingered the gun nervously, trying to keep her eyes from the loft above them. If he was aware of her distress, he gave no sign.

"What an odd-looking creature," he remarked, pausing at one of the stalls.

Defensively, Savannah pushed past him to stroke the yellow nose that stretched out toward her in greeting. She rubbed the velvety muzzle lovingly.

"Aurora can best anything on four legs. None of your lanky Union cart horses could come even close," she countered tartly.

He peered over the half gate to mutter, "Looks a bit shallow in the chest for such a claim, but if you were a man, I'd put a fair wager mine could outdistance this one."

"Oh? If I were a man? Are your principles above betting with a woman or wouldn't your pride allow you to take a beating at the hands of one?"

"Depends on the stakes." He grinned and patted the dun-colored neck. "But we can talk of that another time."

To her horror, he crossed to the sturdy ladder and began to climb. She drew the pistol out, leveling it on him, but it shook so badly she had to brace it with both hands. Oh, Skyler, please stop, she moaned to herself. Her finger tensed on the trigger when he reached the blocks of hay and looked around. A sob in her throat, she lowered the gun, realizing she could no longer fool herself into thinking she would actually use it.

After a pause, Skyler backed down the ladder and turned to her, dusting off his hands. "Well, I'm satisfied. I won't abuse you further by intruding in your house."

"Thank you," she mumbled in a small, tight voice. Her face was very pale and her eyes downcast without the earlier boldness.

"I'll escort you back up to the house," he insisted, cupping her elbow in his palm and steering her around. She was too unnerved to object and walked docilely beside him. He didn't speak again until they had reached the sprawling veranda. "If you didn't plan to shoot, you should have given the gun to the woman watching us through the window. From the looks of her, she wouldn't mind pulling the trigger."

Savannah followed his glance, then gave him an uncertain look of sullen humiliation that he should know of her failure. But his gaze didn't chide her for her weakness.

"I saw nothing to report and I trust when I send out a follow-up patrol this afternoon, they'll find nothing

78

either." His forefinger touched beneath her chin. "If they did, you could find yourself in irons after all, and I wouldn't like that. Dangerous risks have dangerous consequences."

Her head jerked back, eyes all hot with fury once more. "You taught me that well, didn't you? If you are finished here, I suggest you go. Now."

"Well I declare, Savannah Russell, the first real man we've seen in ages and you go shooing him off. Shame on you."

Savannah scowled up at her sister, then glanced at Skyler to gauge his reaction. Being a man, it was no different than the others. Hillary Russell was a heavenly creation, petite, pert, and well aware of her effect on the opposite sex. She dimpled prettily as Skyler's eyes swept over her in honest appreciation.

"Aren't you going to present me, Vannah?" she prompted with a coy flutter of lashes.

"Lieutenant Commander Reade, my sister, Hillary."

The grey eyes flashed between the two women in unabashed surprised, just as Savannah knew they would. No two more unlikely sisters could be imagined. She felt a sharp, unwelcomed stab of jealousy, knowing how she would fare, but then she had no claim or interest in Skyler Reade, nor wanted one.

Hillary was a confection of dainty laces and pink tulle. Savannah realized wryly that she must have just changed, having seen a male visitor ride up. Hillary wouldn't care if a man had horns and cloven feet as long as he paid her due court. She knew she deserved it, having been told so since the cradle. She was a true beauty, with a pale, heart-shaped face, huge baby-blue eyes, and bowlike mouth beneath a spun halo of golden hair. Her every move was carefully studied to signal "Help me, I'm vulnerable" to the protective male instinct. Her drawl was sweet as syrup and her giggle a musical tinkling, all meant to soothe the ear, and her simple conversation to bolster the pride of a man.

All her best devices were in play as she minced down the steps, hand extended. "How nice to meet you, Lieutenant Reade. Whatever brings you way out here?"

Her tiny hand disappeared in Skyler's grip as he bent cordially over it. "Some business and to see Savannah."

The limpid eyes snapped to her sister in surprise, then she was all cooing sweetness. "Why, if you are a friend of Vannah's, I must insist you come inside for some cool refreshment." She had twined herself about his arm, eyes rising in hopeful supplication.

"He can't stay," Savannah snapped brittlely.

Skyler glanced at her, reading the irritation in her deep eyes. Then he smiled and disengaged himself. "I really can't," he told the pouting young woman. "I must get back. Perhaps another time."

As he swung up on the back of his showy chestnut stallion Savannah saw him as Hillary did, and the effect he had frightened her. He looked handsome and powerful in his double-breasted Federal uniform jacket of navy fine flannel. The white drill trousers accentuated the long, strong line of his legs. He looked fit, all tanned and well-groomed, the fair hair swept aside with careless fingers and white teeth flashing in that broad, captivating smile. He was all virile, desirable male, too much so, Savannah groaned in misery, but her stony expression never altered as he tipped his head to her and reined about. Her relief at his absence was short-lived, for Hillary turned on her in a fury.

"What did you chase him off for?" she demanded, stamping a slippered foot. "You'd think we had attractive men growing in the fields the way you pick and choose. You may not care if you die a spinster, but I'm not going to."

"Skyler Reade is not going to save you from the disgrace of virginity, so I want to hear no more about him, do you hear?"

Even used to her sister's sharp tongue, Hillary gawked at her in shock, then fumed indignantly, "Well, at least I don't wear it like a badge of martyrdom. I swear, Vannah, I think it would please you to no end to go to the grave without ever knowing the pleasure of a man."

Savannah flushed darkly, hurt by how true those words could well be. "I am a little more discriminating than you, is all. I don't jump after anything in trousers."

"Even trousers cut as nicely as Lieutenant Reade's?" she taunted, then giggled when her sister went alarmingly pale. "Just how good of friends are you and Mr. Reade?"

"Skyler is none of your business. Stay away from him. He is responsible for Uncle Jonah's ship being taken. He is no friend of mine nor of this family."

Hillary smirked saucily. "So you say." She flounced up the stairs in a puff of petticoats, undaunted by her sister's fierce glare.

Slowly, Savannah followed into the house, thoughts too full of Skyler Reade to worry over the cunning look in the blue eyes. Skyler was here. How would she ever bear it?

"Is that Yankee gone?"

Savannah looked up at the speaker of the angry tone. Caroline had reason to be so bitter, she supposed, more reason than she herself did. When Darcy left West Point, he'd rushed home to wed her, leaving with Wade Hampton's cavalry unit the next morning. She had only seen him once since then, on a two-day leave that had her now heavy with his child. She hated the North for keeping her husband from her and hated Northerners for perpetuating a war Darcy had promised would only last six months.

"Yes, and hopefully he won't be back."

Caroline nodded grimly to that sentiment, then walked awkwardly back to the kitchen to check on the boiling potatoes. She had taken over the cooking, since most of the house servants had disappeared as had the majority of the field hands, enticed by the lure of freedom in the North. While the land lay fallow and the livestock fell prey to vagabonds and prowling Yankees, they dined on what they grew in the small garden. It seemed like months since they had had fresh meat.

"Potatoes and corn cakes again?" Hillary groaned as she flopped down at the table. Her frilly dress had been replaced by a simple calico. "I declare, I am going to simply perish if I don't get something decent to eat. I am sick to death of this horrible stuff."

Seeing Caroline's eyes cloud in hurt, Savannah said sharply, "Be glad you have anything and a roof to eat it under."

"I just hope Darcy has as much on his plate," Caroline said quietly to herself. Her shoulders rose and fell heavily.

"Doesn't anyone care that I'm unhappy?" Hillary wailed pettishly.

"At least you don't have to depend on strangers for your meals." With that soft cry, the pregnant woman pushed away from the table and fled to the kitchen, weeping into her hands.

"Now what did I say?"

Savannah glared at the vapid face, anger at the day's events coming to a boil. "If you would ever think of anyone but yourself before opening your mouth, you would know."

"You are so mean," the girl accused with teary eyes. "I hate you."

Alone at the table, Savannah slumped wearily, covering her eyes with her hand. She was near tears herself but she forced them back. Slowly, she began to gather up the uneaten food they couldn't afford to waste. The strain between the three of them was growing daily and it was up to her to keep the peace. She couldn't blame Hillary for her tantrums. She had been taught to gain her own way with pouts and tears. She could only sympathize with Caroline's melancholy, for she shared it too. And now there was the matter of Skyler to add as well.

She longed for her home, wanting to flee from the ever-present blue coats to the safety of Rising Sun. She wanted to see her mother, to pour out her troubles to the gentle soul who would have the right answer. Savannah wanted to hand the problems of day-to-day survival to someone more capable. She was tired of dealing out the often harsh discipline needed so they could continue to eke out an existence. She was tired of maintaining a brave front and coming up with answers to impossible situations. But she was trapped in Beaufort. Passes were needed for Southerners to travel the main roads, and Hillary refused to be conveyed in less than comfortable style. Besides, Caroline's time was too near for such a strenuous trip. For now, there was nothing to do but make the best of their circumstances and hope for things to get better. Or at least to get no worse.

Skyler. He was the one burden she could not carry gracefully. Seeing him hurt. Talking to him was agony. Bearing his touch was torture, watching him ride away was misery. She was not the same woman who stood on a sandy dune believing with an innocent heart. In that single moment, she had shed that naivety like blinding scales and life had shown her its bitterness. She hated Skyler Reade for using her, for showing her love then turning it into the vilest of things. She had stepped out of character, becoming a flighty, mooning female eager to trust his words and lost to his initiating caress. How foolish she had been but no more. She kept forcing the image of that damning rocket trail to reappear, the symbol of his betrayal, but other pictures kept intruding, images that set her heart afire. They were of clear grey eyes smoky with passion, wide mouth parting to taste hers, the golden chest so warm and firm beneath her cheek, the strong profile against the sunset sky in Nassau. And there was the look in his face when his treachery was discovered.

She had to find a way to escape before her defenses weakened to the softening emotions he stirred in her breast. She couldn't afford to weaken any more. Not for Skyler Reade. Not ever.

Chapter Seven

Skyler looked up gratefully from the shuffle of papers that failed to hold his attention to distraction in the form of his aide. Cochoran hastily composed his smirking features and stepped in smartly.

"A message for you, sir."

When he took the envelope, a waft of perfume made his expectations take a hopeful leap. "That will be all," he said cripsly to the lingering man.

Clumsily, he tore open the flap and frowned in a moment of disappointment. Then he smiled. An invitation to dinner from Hillary Russell. The little minx, he thought, tapping the scented paper on his desk top. No matter who it was from, it was an open door to the Russell's and that was all that mattered.

For a foolish second he had been hoping the note was from Savannah, thanking him for sparing the three Confederates he had found hiding in her barn. He sighed when he thought of those ragged, bloodied children with their terrified eyes. Let them go home to their mamas where they should be, not fighting in a man's war or locked away because of it. Letting them slip through was a failure of duty, but he wasn't a professional soldier nor did he want to be. He saw faces behind the uniforms and he couldn't hate them indiscriminately. Some of his men spat in contempt on everything Southern, and that kind of blindness frightened him when he thought of Savannah and her vulnerable position.

He leaned back in his creaking chair and smiled, remembering the bold blue eyes daring him to find anything when she knew what was at stake. How like her to be so brave and careless of her own safety. He hoped his visit scared some sense into her. Perhaps she would think twice before taking such risks again or at least be more careful. His desk was full of cases of brutal treatment of discovered traitors and he swore he would not see her name affixed to one of them.

Then he thought of the pistol she carried. She didn't shoot him. She couldn't. Whether she was incapable of taking a life or just his own he didn't know, but he wished fervently it wasn't the former if she were threatened. His own men weren't his only cause for worry. Since the Federal occupation, there were increasing numbers of slaves revolting against former masters and attacks by large numbers of vagrant blacks who had run off and found making their way North too difficult. The whole area was a powder keg and he didn't want Savannah to be caught up in the ensuing percussion. There was nothing he wouldn't do for Savannah Russell. She was his constant preoccupation. Seeing her on the porch, it had taken all his will not to rush up and sweep her into his arms. But her cold glare had convinced him to be cautious. He wasn't discouraged. She hadn't shot him, had she? And now he had an invitation to her table. It would only be a matter of time before that invitation extended further. He had tasted her passion in the heated kisses and it was more than the desire of the moment, just as his had been.

A night did not pass when he didn't imagine what it

would have been like to follow her to her cabin on the *Harrier*. Just as often he weighed the consequence of his choice on the beach. He could have taken her then but he couldn't force himself to take advantage of her vulnerability, not full knowing what would happen when the fuse he lit ignited on the rocket. He couldn't use her that way no matter how desperate his own need. His feelings were too strong to be satisfied by fleeting intimacy. He wanted to possess Savannah Russell. That realization had stunned him at first but now he relished the idea with a warming certainty. Now, he only had to convince the lady he was right.

As the heat of the day mellowed into a balmy evening, Savannah was drawn to the rear of the house by smells so enticing she thought it must be some rapturous dream. But the sight of the roasting ham was no illusion. When she gave a questioning look to Caroline, she shrugged and said, "Ask your sister."

She found Hillary in her frilly room in the middle of an elaborate toilet. A rainbow of silks and satins was spread across her bed in typical indecision as the young woman struggled with the ties of her corset to whittle her tiny waist to near nonexistence.

"Give me a hand, Vannah, and don't spare me."

Taking the laces while her sister held to the back of a chair, Savannah asked, "Where did you come up with a ham?"

"You can't expect us to serve a guest potatoes and yams" was the evasive reply.

"What guest?"

"Why Lieutenant Reade, of course."

Savannah gave a jerk that made Hillary gasp and wheeze as the corset became a sudden torture device.

"What is he coming here for?"

"Vannah. Vannah, please. I can't breathe. I invited him."

The stays pulled tighter until the young woman was nearly faint. "And he sent over the bountiful charity feast, I suppose."

"Yes. Vannah, please."

Hillary staggered and sagged to the floor, holding her aching ribs and sucking air while her sister paced. She had never seen Savannah in such a fury and was cowed by it.

"How could you do such a foolish thing?" Savannah raged. "How could you ask that . . . Yankee into our home. Have you no thought for your father in his grave or Darcy and Uncle Jonah imprisoned in some Union hellhole or poor Caroline worrying away to nothing? How could you think only of your own selfish pleasures at such an expense?" Unconsciously, she had echoed much of her uncle's speech to her but was too upset to recognize it.

The sound of pitiful weeping stilled her tirade. Looking down at the crumpled figure in its pool of petticoats, her anger lessened to an impatient exasperation. "Oh, for heaven's sake, Hilly, stop that noise before your face swells up like a beet." The unflattering comparison had the desired effect, for she sniffed loudly and straightened.

"I just wanted to have a nice evening with a decent meal for all of us," she whined, eyes reddened and aggrieved. "What's so wrong in that?"

Savannah sighed heavily and shook her head. "Nothing, I suppose. Let's just get this evening over with."

But dinner was worse than she could have imagined. When she found out who they were entertaining, Caroline retreated to her room, refusing to sit at the table with a Yankee. It was all Savannah could do to persuade her to eat from the tray she brought up. The dark eyes looked at the juicy slabs of ham as if they were contaminated by the blood of her husband.

Skyler arrived promptly, handsomely attired in dress uniform and bearing a bottle of champagne. Seated on the far end of the table from him, Savannah watched him exchange a playful banter with her sister. Stubbornly, she had refused to don her finest gown. She chose instead a somber, unadorned cotton, appearing the crow next to Hillary's fluffy canary. It suited her mood, she told herself dourly, and besides, Skyler hadn't come to look at her. That much was obvious. She saw her role as chaperone and met any attempts to draw her into conversation with a frigid word or even icier glance. Hillary seemed oblivious to the tension. She was flushed and animated, as if Skyler Reade was some highly eligible beau and not an enemy and betrayer of her family. Her small hand found every excuse to touch the blue sleeve and her eyes kept up a lively, teasing dance with those of admiring grey.

The food was delicious, a true feast after so long a depravation. The champagne flowed freely into all glasses. Savannah depended on it to steady her frayed emotions. As much as she longed to flee the table, the thought of the two of them alone held her in her discomfort, brooding in her misery. With no servant to wave the carved punkah above the table to stir a breeze and fan away flies, the room was oppressively hot and her head buzzed with the drone of insects and heady effects of the drink. When Hillary coyly suggested an evening walk, it awoke a fierce rebellion in Savannah but she had no right to speak. As they strolled off arm in arm on their romantic turn about the fragrant garden, she began to clear the table with mechanical efficiency.

She had just finished the dishes when Hillary waltzed in, all starry-eyed and pretty smiles. Her expression sobered when she saw the other's seriousness. Savannah didn't look at her again, stacking the dishes away with a vigor that rattled the delicate porcelain. Hillary lingered, fidgeting with the sash of her gown.

"Skyler is coming by tomorrow afternoon to take me for a buggy ride." She held her breath as Savannah's back stiffened. When there was no comment, she hurried on with her rehearsed speech. "He can be of use to us, Vannah. He's promised to see a parcel to Darcy and he can get things for us like flour and real coffee and—Oh, Vannah, please don't hate me."

The strong shoulders slumped, echoing the weariness in her voice. "You know I don't, Hillary. You just do what you have to. I cannot be your judge. Go to bed now."

"Good night, Vannah."

Savannah didn't move until she heard the rustle of skirts as her sister hurried up the stairs, eager to get away. Then she sat down on a stool in the dark shadows of the kitchen and wept into her hands. She had no specific reason other than the tearing heartbreak for all things hoped for and lost. After ten minutes, she dried her eyes and went slowly up to her room.

Hillary had forgotten all the uses for a Yankee suitor as she sat next to Skyler Reade. The day was pleasant and so was the company, and she was determined to enjoy it to the fullest. It had been so long since she had been on an outing and even longer with so handsome an escort. Coquettishly, she slipped her arm through his and leaned against him, the soft swell of her breast pushing upward to make a daring display above the lacy neckline of her gown.

Skyler wasn't naive enough to miss the careful artifice of her action but was too much a man not to ogle the fair sight in appreciation. He snapped the reins down on the back of the horse, causing the buggy to jerk forward. Hillary was jostled back against the seat and clung to the side in alarm as he smiled to himself.

They had a guest for dinner again that night, but he and Hillary were the sole occupants of the spacious dining room. Though she tried to be a charming hostess, Skyler seemed distracted, often not hearing her witty repartees until she repeated them more than once. When she had him alone in the cool darkness of the veranda, she studied him in bewilderment. She had gone through her best repertoire to entice him, fluttering her lashes and dropping dainty hints, but still he remained politely aloof. She didn't understand it. Just moistening her pouty lips was enough to send her previous beaus into a nervous frenzy. In a last resort to gain his full attention, her gloved hand rose to turn his face toward her. She stretched up to press a kiss on his mouth. After a moment she came off her toes in puzzlement for his response had been so vague it was insulting to her femininity.

"Lieutenant Reade, don't you like me at all?" she demanded petulantly.

"I like you very much, Hillary," he replied easily.

She pouted prettily, tapping her foot in aggravation. "Why did you come out here if not to court me?"

"You invited me."

She scowled at his answer. "My dear old grandaddy used to like my kisses better than you seem to."

He laughed softly but not unkindly. "I'm sorry, Hillary. I'm not being fair to you. I should have told you I was taken."

She digested this and peeped up at him through the sweep of her lashes. "The North is a long ways away, Lieutenant."

"She's much, much closer than that," he confessed, eyes going to the silent house in a wistful longing.

Hillary opened and shut her mouth several times like a gasping fish, then blurted incredulously, "Savannah?" At his nod, she cried, "But she hates you."

He shrugged and said indifferently, "Perhaps she thinks so."

"So you've been using me. I ought to be furious with you." The dimples creased her cheeks with amusement. "But I'm not. Good night, Lieutenant Reade. I hope to see you again soon."

As he watched the petite figure head back into the house, he was aware of another presence and glanced to her briefly.

"She's a saucy little thing, isn't she?"

Whap!

The force of her hand snapped his head back.

"I won't stand for it, Skyler. I won't have you sweet-talking my baby sister. She's just a child and I'm not going to let you hurt her. Find yourself another saucy piece of skirt to amuse yourself with. I won't let you break her heart."

Skyler stood silent throughout the ranting torrent of words, hand rubbing his jaw and eyes thoughtful. When she was through, he said softly, "I'm not interested in wooing Hillary."

"Then why—"

"I came to see you. I used Hillary as an excuse because I knew you would never ask me."

Savannah's eyes grew round and disbelieving. "Me? You came to see me? Why on earth would you do that?"

"You know why," he answered simply.

Before she could object, his hand cupped the back of

her glossy head, stilling it as he dipped down to catch her frowning lips in a long, thorough kiss. His other arm pinned her to his chest so tightly she couldn't struggle as her feet cleared the ground. She hung there rigidly as his mouth lingered over hers, taking his time and enjoying even the taste of her resistance. When he settled her back, he sidestepped quickly to avoid her palm.

"How dare you!" she sputtered in shocked outrage, scrubbing the back of her hand over her abused lips. "How dare you think I would welcome that or you, that I would let you—"

"I love you, Savannah."

"No," she shrieked at him, pressing her hands over her ears and eyes screwing up as if in pain. "Don't say that to me. I don't want to hear it from you. You've no right after what you've done."

He reached out to try and bridge the gap between them, but she stumbled back, panting and seething, the deep blue eyes black and shiny in rage.

"You saved my life, Savannah, and I saved you. What have I done that's so wrong?"

"What?" she spat. "I'll tell you what. You put my uncle in prison because you convinced me to trust you. You and your kind have torn my family apart. You put my brother in chains and murdered my father. I don't even know where he's buried. You intrude in my life, trying to buy favor with the very things you deprive us of, and yet you expect me to welcome your presence and your kisses. I hate you. I loathe the sight of you. The idea of your affection sickens me. I want you off my property. I want you out of my life. I never, ever want to see you again."

He said nothing for a long second, then gave a slight smile. "All right, I'll do as you wish." He continued before the relief could overwhelm her. "But you have to earn it."

"How? What game are you playing this time?" she demanded suspiciously.

"One you suggested. A friendly wager on your odd little yellow horse against mine. You win and you'll never see me again."

"And if I lose?"

"Nothing so terrible," he assured her with a grin that said it was. "You on my arm at a regimental ball."

"You must be mad," she gaped. But when he only smiled, she looked at him narrowly. True, he was a man, but she, next to Darcy, was the best rider in their county and many beyond. She'd grown up in the saddle. She had much to gain and replied coolly, "All right, Lieutenant Reade. I accept you wager and expect you to hold to the outcome."

"As I will you," he countered. "Good night, Savannah. I'll see you tomorrow."

He gave her a smart salute and went to untie his horse. His teeth flashed white in the darkness and Savannah had the uncomfortable feeling she had already lost too much.

Aurora was in high spirits as Savannah rode into the yard the next afternoon. The filly's exuberance was contagious and she soon forgot her doubts of the night before. She managed a confident nod in Skyler's direction before cantering down the drive with his powerful stallion on her heels. When she reached a small copse of trees, she pulled up and sketched out the course she had taken many times in the past to victory.

"If you are ready, I'll wait for you back here." With that, she slapped her palm down on her mare's flank and set her off at a gallop.

Grinning, Skyler applied his boot heel and was after her.

Savannah couldn't blame Aurora. The filly gave her all as she always did but she was no match for the leggy chestnut who finished a full length ahead of her. Begrudgingly, Savannah had to admit much of the victory was due to Skyler's excellent handling of the reins. He was a superb horseman, even rivalling Darcy. She dismounted stiffly and turned to face her opponent stoically.

"Congratulations, Lieutenant. You sit a fine saddle."

"So do you. I should have told you I purchased Beauty in Virginia, where they brag of having the world's best horseflesh. The Beauty of course being for your Jeb Stuart."

"I should have known it would take a Southern horse to best me," she said sourly.

Skyler gave a short laugh, then grew serious. "As to the wager?"

"What time shall I be ready?"

He smiled at the gruff question and replied, "At seven."

"I'll be ready. I keep my word no matter how unpleasant.

"You are an admirable woman" was his amused comment.

"You are a charitable winner, sir. Do you lose with as much grace?" she grumbled, tugging her gloves back on.

"I don't know," he said casually. "I've never lost anything I really wanted. You might remember that."

"I will consider it a threat."

She turned away from him to remount. Halfway up, he moved to assist her, but the feel of his large hands on her waist gave her a violent start. She swung back at him, at the same time losing her balance. The unfamiliar movement startled her horse, and as she fell back, it bolted off toward home, leaving Savannah in the awkward position of having Skyler catch her in a strong embrace. His arms stayed about her a moment too long and she flailed at him with her elbows until she was released.

"Now look what you've done," she accused, looking down the lane her horse had taken with a huff of annoyance.

"I was merely being a gentleman," he said in his own defense. "Let me be so again and offer you a ride back. Or does your pride insist you walk?"

She bristled at his mocking tone, but the thought of a five-mile hike in the fashionable but hardly practical half boots tempered her tongue. "I have no choice," she snapped brittlely.

"What a graceful acceptance."

He swung up into the saddle with an easy grace and held down a hand to her. Scowling, she took it and settled behind him, vowing not to make contact with his hated person. To complicate matters, he nudged his horse into a trot, the jouncing gait forcing her to cling to his lean waist in self-preservation.

"This isn't the way," she complained.

"I've somewhere to take you first, so hold on and enjoy the ride," he called back, then urged a rolling canter. He smiled at the feel of her pressed reluctantly to his back.

After fifteen minutes had passed, Skyler reined up in a small clearing and swung his leg over the pommel to jump down. Savannah slid into his sturdy embrace but he didn't antagonize her by trying to prolong it. She puzzled over the solemnness of his expression.

"Where are we?" she asked, glancing about the stretch of unevenly spaded earth.

"Savannah," he began softly, taking up her slack hand, "I asked some questions and found this spot."

"What is it?" she asked in growing dread.

"Your father is buried here."

She took a shaky breath, eyes clouding with disbelief and grief.

Clutching her hand tightly, he went on. "I'm sorry I couldn't find out exactly where, but his body is somewhere in this field. Political prisoners are buried here."

When her glazed eyes turned to scan the many mounds of unmarked dirt, he released her hand and stepped away in awkward sympathy.

After standing with bowed head in a rigid silence for several minutes, her voice came low and steady.

"How did he die?"

"He was being interrogated to find out the departure date of his shipment. The men got a bit rough with him." His words deepened in embarrassed guilt. "He broke away and leapt through a window and fell a story to the street below. He broke his neck. It happened instantly." He waited quietly for some response from her, either anger or tears, but her calm surprised him.

"I'd like to go now."

He nodded wordlessly and helped her into the saddle. As they rode in silence, he felt her head lean against his shoulder. The dampness of her tears soaked through his shirt, but when they arrived at her home, her eyes were dry and emotionless.

"I'll be ready at seven," she said flatly and disappeared into the house.

Chapter Eight

Skyler was greeted at the door by a small woman huge with child. Her dark eyes were bright with hatred. That harsh emotion looked so out of place on her delicate features he was taken aback.

"Savannah will be down in a minute," she clipped out with none of the expected Southern hospitality. "You wait out here."

"Yes, ma'am," he began formally, but the door closed between them like a slap.

He stood awkwardly on the dark veranda, looking about the deserted yard with an odd feeling of uneasiness. It made his neck prickle defensively, as if unseen eyes were measuring a spot on his back. That apprehension was forgotten, as was all else, when the door opened again.

"Good evening, Lieutenant. I trust you haven't been waiting long."

It took him a moment to shake off his stupefaction and mumble an apt reply. The sight of Savannah Russell had quite undone his senses. She was as deep and mysterious as the evening sky. Her formal gown was a fashionable combination of satin and lace. The black lace overskirt rose in scallops to join at a tiny pointed waist. Beneath it was a shimmer of dusky rose. The off-the-shoulder styling left a great deal of pearlescent skin bare above the neckline flounce, with its narrow strips of black lace to match the sweeping ruffle at the hem. Gloved hands clutched a folded fan and heavily beaded bag with a tension that betrayed her nervousness. The heavy waves of raven-black hair were drawn softly back from a center part to form a chignon left unadorned in a simple jet-studded net. The stones were repeated in her weighty necklace, ear fobs, and bracelets. The overall impression was far from flirty or frothy. She was a stunning woman of uncommon bearing. Some would have unkindly called it overbearing, but for all the cool dignity, Skyler sensed a submerged softness that was both sensual and vulnerable. The combination had him quite unraveled. He took her extended hand, hoping his wasn't too unsteady or damp, and assisted her into the sling-shaped barouche he had hired for the night.

With the top folded down on the warm evening, they sat silently side by side as the carriage whirred along the roads. Skyler was no longer certain. He could deal with her emotions but not this strange lack of them. She was here with him, close, accessible, smelling deliciously, satin brushing against his leg. The nearness had him clammy with agitation and anticipation. Her seemingly easy acquiescence had him off balance. He wasn't fooled by her honorable intention to see their bet through. Was it then because she wanted to spend time with him? Her distant manner and rigid posture said not, but his memory of her on a sandy dune said otherwise. She was remarkably calm for one about to engage the enemy on a grand scale but then, he mused proudly, little unnerved Savannah Russell. No matter what her reasons, she was his for the evening, and it wasn't a pleasure he was going to spoil with lengthy suppositions.

When the carriage turned in at one of the stately

mansions, Savannah asked, "Is this where we're going?"

"It was commandeered for a temporary headquarters. Beautiful, isn't it?"

"Very. I used to play here as a child."

He glanced at her sharply but her features were still composed, betraying no sense of the bitterness her words held. Quite coolly, she had made him feel very much the interloper. Not knowing how to respond, he fell silent as a groomsman took the reins, leaving him free to help Savannah down. When their eyes met, there was no disguising the anger in the deep blue depths, anger at the situation and at him for placing her in it. Contrarily, she placed a gloved hand lightly on his sleeve and waited to follow him inside.

The rooms of the deserted home were filled with blue dress uniforms, army and navy mingling amid the free flow of champagne. Musicians played from some hidden alcove while a troop of servants bustled efficiently between the brass and oak leaves, bearing silver trays laden with delicacies. The uniformed men outnumbered the few women nearly eight to one. Most of the ladies in attendance were the wives or daughters of the officers. Skyler's arrival with a tall, unfamiliar beauty on his arm caused an immediate stir, which became a mixture of speculation and disgruntled complaint when the soft lull of her voice was heard. Some saw her as a lovely woman but others as an enemy who had no business intruding in their affairs.

Savannah felt the hostile undertone in the room, especially from the women, who glared at her as if she were the sole reason their husbands and sons were gone from them. She bore up under their accusing eyes with a proud tilt of her head but her grasp was firm on Skyler's arm.

"You made a mistake in bringing me here, Lieutenant," she murmured in a low voice.

"Really? Why do you say that?"

Could he be so deaf to the malcontent whispering? "These people would like to hang me and you alongside me."

His laugh was easy and unconcerned. "Nonsense. They're just jealous because I have the most beautiful woman here." His warm fingers traced along her back at the top of her neckline, evoking a shiver as she jerked away, lips narrowing in warning.

"I do not think that is the reason."

"Here, have some champagne and act as though you enjoy the company."

She took the glass from him with a sour look. That scowl deepened when he grinned in amusement. He took too much enjoyment from her discomfort.

"Wonderful bouquet, this stuff," remarked an officer next to them. He raised the glass to Skyler. "We owe a toast of thanks to the Confederates for bringing it in for us. I hear you profited handsomely from the bounty on that steamer last month, Reade. Perhaps this affair is catered by your handiwork."

Feeling Savannah stiffen at his side, Skyler repressed a curse as he brushed off the remark casually and moved away with feigned ease. He knew the statement would not go unchallenged. He could sense the rage boiling in the woman beside him.

"So your treachery won you a nice reward," Savannah said icily. "And I thought you were only motivated by duty. Silly me."

"Savannah, I want to tell you something about your uncle," he began.

"I don't want to hear more lies from you. Excuse me while I freshen up a bit. I feel quite warm."

She pulled away from him and hurried through the crowd with a regal poise. One of the large bedrooms had been set up for the ladies to retire in and was thankfully empty. She bathed her face in shaking hands and regarded her reflection. The flush of upset was becoming to her features, giving them a sultry warmth that would doubtlessly draw many an appreciative eye. But she didn't want to be ogled by the hated Yankees, especially by one in particular. Had he brought her here just to humiliate her? Well, she was made of stronger stuff than that. She would see this odious debt paid, then heaven help him if he ever came to her door again.

Angry and smarting with indignation, Savannah retreated to a recessed window seat where she could sit in darkness and look out over the familiar lawn. She toyed with the idea of remaining in the sanctity of the ladies' room until the hour grew late but dismissed it as too cowardly. Her bruised pride refused to let her return to the smug Lieutenant Reade until she had some plan of retribution, some means of dealing him the same embarrassment he had given her.

While she sat plotting, her thoughts were disrupted by two Northern women. They were gossiping busily in their twangy, unpleasant voices, too involved in their conversation to notice Savannah in her secluded seat.

"What a lovely house," one of them was saying.

"Built by the broken backs of their slaves, no doubt," said the other as she regarded her pitted face in the glass and began to heavily powder the pockmarks.

"Can you imagine living like this, never having to lift a finger for yourself, having all those Negroes waiting to please your every whim."

"Those Southern women are raised to be pampered whores. All they're good for is sweet-talking their men into bed, but then I hear Southern men are more interested in their nigger wenches and producing more coffee-colored slaves."

103

"Abbey," her chubby companion cried in titillated shock. "Surely you can't mean—"

"I do. Jasper told me all the sordid details. Since they can't bring any more coloreds over, they breed their own in those little shacks out back. No wonder the women are so eager for our men, with their own so busy producing a bumper crop. Jasper told me they throw themselves at his officers like the cheapest sort of hussies. He said they brag about how many they've bedded. Of course, my Jasper would never seek out such obvious charms."

"I don't understand how they can hold themselves so cheap," her friend exclaimed in moral indignation.

Abbey chuckled slyly. "Some of them aren't so cheap, I've been told. I wonder how much that doxy on Lieutenant Reade's arm is getting for the evening. Imagine her strutting around with those regal airs when everyone here knows what she is. Such a fine-looking man, too. I can't see why he'd have to resort to a harlot when he could have a decent woman."

A sudden clatter brought their attention to the window. They stood in wide-eyed dismay as a graceful figure bent to retrieve her evening bag. There was no doubt about who she was. She straightened with a sunny smile.

"Excuse me, ladies," she purred, voice dripping with a heavy accent. "I didn't mean to interrupt y'all but I really must get back to Lieutenant Reade before he thinks he's not getting what he paid for. It was so nice of him to sport with me while my menfolk are out propagating the nigras, so I don't want to keep him waiting."

She swept past them while they gawked in ill-concealed horror. Once in the hall, Savannah swayed and leaned against the muraled wall for support. Her head swam with a fever of shock and outrage. His whore. They all thought she was Skyler's whore. Tears of hurt burned hot behind her eyes but she blinked them away. Why should this misuse of her come as any greater surprise than the others? He had broken her heart without compunction, so why should she expect him to spare her feelings?

She drew herself up with a fierce dignity and smoothed the bell of her skirt. If it was a whore they thought her, that's what they would get.

Skyler started in surprise when cool fingers rubbed over his in a light caress. More surprising was the sweet smile on the beautiful face that tilted up toward his.

"I hope I haven't been gone too long," she cooed, eyes melting and soft behind a flutter of lashes. "How unkind of me to desert you. Did you miss me terribly?"

The sudden press of her breasts against his arm halted his immediate reply, then he managed to say somewhat hoarsely, "Yes, terribly, but I don't plan on letting you leave me again."

"All night, I hope."

Skyler looked at her sharply but she was all inviting smiles. As the evening progressed, her overtures became more blatant. Her hand stroked his shirtfront as he spoke to fellow officers, the warmth of her body pressed close to brush his arm and hip like an eager cat when he tried to follow a conversation. Though far from unaffected by her calculated seduction, he was wary of its reasons. The coy, teasing nature wouldn't surprise him from Hillary, but from Savannah it was so artificial it had him suspicious. He found her bold, fiery manners more appealing than the coy pretense. Knowing of her almost innocent reserve, he couldn't fail to wonder at the sloe-eyed siren who cuddled up to him with all the discretion of a paid escort. If she wanted to subtly coax his favor, he had no objection, but she went beyond that, seeming determined to make a conquest of every man in attendance. And few of them had any objection, either, eager to please the soft-spoken Southern woman who enticed them with such a sensual simmer. She danced every dance, flirting in deadly earnest with each partner, especially with two older officers whose wives looked on with apoplectic pastiness. After each spin around the crowded floor, she returned to his side, attentive to the point of embarrassing. But still he couldn't bring himself to end it. He was too hungry for her agreeability. He excused her bad manners as signs of her nervousness and the great quantity of champagne she had consumed. And she was so provocatively beautiful.

"So this is your lady," Anthony D'Angelo said with a grin, observing the way the pretty woman molded herself to his friend's side. The dusky eyes turned to him with a curious sharpness, then her smile warmed them.

"So Skyler's told you about me. Nothing compromising, I trust." She laughed gaily and rapped her escort's knuckles with her fan. It was a stinging blow.

"Not nearly enough," Tony assured her gallantly. He lifted her hand for a brief kiss. "He didn't tell me how beautiful you were, probably in his own defense."

They talked for a while and Tony grew more and more puzzled. Savannah Russell was lovely enough, but shallow women didn't usually hold his friend's interest and he was clearly infatuated with this one. She seemed the type one would take to bed not to the altar, and that image didn't hold with the one Skyler had painted for him. He had expected some larger-than-life heroic saint. The woman on Skyler's arm was much closer to the earth. If his interest had been solely in the lush figure so tantalizingly displayed in the fetching gown, he could understand it, but this was the woman

106

he said he wanted to marry. A man just didn't marry a woman anyone could have.

Skyler could see his friend's bewilderment and couldn't blame him for it. The woman he was seeing was not the one he had described. He would let Savannah play her game for the duration of the evening, then he would have the truth of it.

He had his opportunity sooner than he expected. Savannah coaxed his head down to whisper softly in his ear. The impact had an immediate effect on his body.

"Skyler," she murmured breathily, "can we go now. I want to be alone with you."

Shock waves of longing swept through him in an unsettling wash, weakening the logic that told him not to believe what he was hearing. He wanted to believe it, wanted her to convince him. When she tugged on his hand, he followed in a daze. While they waited for their carriage in the shadow of the great house, the touch of her soft lips on his scrambled his thoughts and the teasing flicker of her tongue nearly cost all his control. Determinedly, he straightened and searched her face in confusion for some clue to her feelings, but the deep eyes were secretive, holding that knowledge from him.

"Savannah," he began dryly, but her fingertips pressed to his mouth.

"Shh. Not now," she insisted in that same husky voice that sent his nerves trembling. "No talk tonight."

Once in the carriage, Savannah snuggled close into his side, one hand resting familiarly on his thigh and the other rubbing the small of his back beneath his coat. Her head found a comfortable rest on his shoulder and she smiled smugly to herself. She would have more respect for Hillary in the future. Playing with a man's lust was a skillful game whose benefits were obvious to her now. Her half-veiled suggestions had Skyler panting with expectation. Well, let him simmer in that fervor of anticipation a while longer until it reached fever pitch at her front door. Then when he expected her to comply to his well-stoked passions, she would cut him to the quick, scorning him and laughing in his face. That humiliation in tandem with her embarrassing behavior before all his friends should keep him from haunting her door and teach him that she wouldn't be toyed with. Whore, indeed. How could he think she would so easily forget and forgive? As long as the memory of that rocket burned in her thoughts, her hatred would flare just as brightly.

The ride was a long one and the effects of the champagne seditiously lulled her abused feelings. Skyler was warm and solid beside her. The circle of his arm created an aura of well-being. Unconsciously, her hand massaged the hard muscle of his thigh, sliding naively upward until his clamped over it to halt the dangerous progression. She noticed the sudden irregular movement of his chest and the tension of his body, and realized with a pleased satisfaction how much he wanted her. That notion of power over him was as intoxicating as the bubbling wine. Thinking of her vengeance, she closed her eyes.

"We're here." His voice sounded odd.

Savannah straightened in surprise to see the soaring pillars of her home before her. She let Skyler lift her down and sagged briefly in his arms before she could get her legs to support her. Her mind whirled in a giddy fog in which he was her only point of reference.

"I'd better take you in. You look a little shaky."

"I'm fine," she slurred, stumbling along at his side with uncoordinated steps. How tall and sturdy he was in her tipping world. She clung to him gratefully as they

108

navigated the steps and he turned to her as they stepped into the dark hall.

"Are you going to be all right, Savannah? Shall I call someone?" he asked gently as she reeled against him.

"So you can make a joke of me in front of more people?" The sneer in her voice made him blink. "Wasn't it enough to show me off as your newest whore, the Southern slut you're whiling away a few idle hours with? Did I act the part well enough for you and your friends? Were you expecting more of the same when we got here? Something like this perhaps?"

She moved up against him. Her arm snaked about his neck, jerking him down so she could catch his mouth. She bruised his lips with her anger and hurt. The dark blue eyes were shimmering with tears when he pulled her away.

"Savannah. Savannah listen to me. Stop this foolishness."

"No. I don't want to listen to you. I hate you. I hate you."

"No, no, no," he soothed, drawing her into a close embrace. He held her tightly in spite of her struggles. "You have to hear me out. I didn't take you tonight to embarrass or hurt you. Oh, Savannah, I just wanted to be with you, not Hillary, not some easy bit of skirt I could bed at the end of the night. I didn't expect a conquest when I brought you here. I'd be lying if I said it wasn't what I wanted, but not like this, not against your will. I should never have made you go with me tonight but it was the only way I could be near you. I didn't know what else to do. I love you, Savannah. I can't give you up. I can't."

She had gone limp in his arms, the fight drained from her. When he lifted her chin to tilt her face up, her cheeks glistened with the dampness that clung jewellike to her dark lashes. When he kissed her lightly, she offered no resistance. Her soft lips parted slightly. That sweet submission made it impossible for him to release her. The nagging logic that warned him to go slow, to give her time, to wait until she returned some feeling for him, was lost in that heated flood of desire. And when her hands timidly touched his back and glided up to cling to his shoulders, he forgot he had planned to leave her this night.

Leaving the open hall, he steered her into one of the side parlors. Savannah was no longer hesitant when they came together in the concealing darkness. Her arms stole about his neck, all her emotions rushing back to a sandy beach and the arms of the man she'd been waiting for all her life. What passed between that perfect moment and this was forgotten in the rekindling of passion, so hot and intense with need and want. There was only Skyler, and she loved him completely with no reservation. She met his kiss with all the urgency that bubbled and boiled through her, eager to know once again that surge of ecstasy he had shown her and what more she knew awaited her beyond that.

His mouth broke away from hers to move along the smooth satin of her sloping shoulder. In a thrill of expectation, her eyes slid closed as fingers clenched in the silvery hair. A low moan was torn from her as those warm kisses scattered over the swell of her heaving breasts. Impatiently, she worked down the fastenings at the back of her gown, his hands taking over when she could reach no farther. The heavy yards of lace and satin sighed to the floor followed by the circle of her hoops and stiffly boned corset. Clad in only her wispy undergarments, she leaned back into his arms, seeking out the consuming kisses.

She was so warm, so pliable in his embrace he could

hardly believe just moments ago she had professed her hatred. There was no question of her willingness. Her kisses returned in kind and her hands pushed off his coat and began fumbling with his shirtbuttons. In the scanty clothing, she was supple and slender beneath his roving hands, so inviting, so perfect. The gentle curve of her back and rounded hip fit the spread of his palms as if made for him.

"Skyler," she whispered huskily against the fierce throb of his throat. "Skyler, take me upstairs."

She was surprisingly light without the cumbersome attire. He paused at the foot of the stairs to kick off his boots so he could ascend the uncarpeted steps silently. Her room was shadowed and cool, a pleasant contrast to the heat they were creating between them. When he laid her upon the coverlet, her arms tugged him down with her. For a moment they shared a deep, searching kiss until, with a sound of contentment, she turned her face away.

"So dizzy," she mumbled. "The room won't stop spinning."

Reluctantly, Skyler leaned up on his elbow and looked down at her. His mouth still pulsed warmly from her kiss, the taste of surrender and champagne a heady combination. The powerful force of his desire insisted he take her. Did it really matter that she had had too much to drink? She had invited him up. She had encouraged him with the availability of her sensuous body. Lust born of lonely dreams and expectation urged him on, arguing that once he had her, the bond between them would be even harder to deny. But what if she woke in the morning, feelings unchanged? How much more would she detest him knowing they'd been lovers while her mind was numbed by drink?

111

"Skyler?" she called groggily, reaching up for him. He allowed her to draw his head down, savoring the way her lips moved so sweetly on his, asking, needing, wanting what he longed to give. It was her words, so oddly out of time and place, that halted the demands of his passion.

"Skyler, we've not much time. Love me now so I'll know you'll come back for me."

Kissing her tenderly, he murmured, "You know I will, Savannah. I can't stay away." His smile was bittersweet. In her confusion, she had made him the man she'd cared for, not the man who betrayed her, the one he was to her now. If he went any further, that betrayal would become insurmountable. "I love you but I have to go now."

"Go?" Her eyes flickered briefly then struggled to focus. "Don't go." Her hands slid up and down his shirtsleeves. "Please stay with me."

"Another time, I promise. If you let me love you tonight and deny me tomorrow, you would be hurting me most cruelly. When I make love to you, I want you to belong to me and I want you to know it. It has to be right. It has to be special. It has to be forever. If it can't be those things, then it's better if I let you go untouched, for once I take what you offer, I won't be able to walk away. Let me go, Savannah,"

"Kiss me first," she bartered languidly. Her lips moistened then parted to cushion his. What a wonderful mouth he had, so warm and giving. Her fingertips rubbed over the angular planes of his face, the strength of his features making her feel delightfully weaker. "I love you, Skyler," she whispered into his kiss. "I love you so much."

Eyes tightly closed, he rested his forehead against hers with a heavy sigh of longing. "Oh, Savannah, please say that to me tomorrow."

She only muttered sleepily. Her hand fell slackly to the mattress.

He kissed her forehead lightly and sat up. The image of her stretched upon the bed, features relaxed and lovely in sleep, her enticing figure so briefly clad, would burn within him with aching clarity for a long time to come.

"Good night, Savannah," he said softly.

Chapter Nine

Savannah's first conscious action was to pull the covers over her head to block out the sun. The next was to give a heartfelt moan of misery. Her temples beat unmercifully and her mouth was as dry as an old wool blanket. She lay still so the ache in her head would stay a throb instead of a pounding, trying not to think lest that bring on more of the hurt. What on earth was wrong with her? In trying to moisten her lips, she tasted stale champagne and she remembered.

Skyler. She sat up with a gasp, ignoring the harsh echo it made. Her dismay grew when she found herself in her dainty underthings. Vaguely, she recalled the sound of boots falling at the foot of the stairs. Skyler had carried her up to bed. She pressed her hands to the clammering temples and tried to bring the scattered bits of memory back into focus. She had kissed him. Not just kissed him but begged him to make love to her. His mouth, his hands, his body, the feel of them rushed back to her in painful detail, the searching kisses, the tenderness of his touch, the hard, unyielding strength of him. Even now, she was aware of stirrings she couldn't control.

Cursing her weakness for him and the alarming gaps in her memory, she stood tipsily and washed in a basin of cool water. It did much to refresh her spirits and her mind. Foremost upon it was a serious question she feared to form. Had she let Skyler make love to her? she wondered in naive anguish. Had they come together in her bed, under her father's roof, an affront to all they had suffered? Could she have been that disloyal? Had she lost sight of the game of vengeance she sought to play, turning it on herself in bitter irony?

Moving slowly in deference to her splitting head, she slipped on a robe and eased her way downstairs. Thankfully, it would be hours before anyone else rose. The scene in the parlor was even more damning than her patchy recall. Her clothing lay in an abandoned scatter on the floor. On the arm of the settee, Skyler's coat was a blue blaze of betrayal. She lifted the garment gingerly. The clean masculine scent that lingered on it assailed her like an unexpected blow as she clutched it tightly, hands shaking in a confusion of want and anger. Fiercely, she flung it from her, hating its color and the man who wore it.

It was later that morning when Skyler rode up to the house. He could wait no longer to discover Savannah's mood toward him. His nervous apprehension was well hidden by a bland expression and a cooler reason that warned him not to have too much hope. Savannah Russell was a strong-willed woman and the thought that she had suddenly succumbed to his charm was unlikely. Chide himself as he would, a part of him wished the woman he loved would come to him with a matching affection to tell him again the words she spoke in the soothing arms of champagne.

His brief knock was answered by Caroline Russell. The dark eyes chilled with immediate hostility. At his request to see Savannah, her reply was equally frosty.

"Savannah is indisposed this morning and doesn't wish visitors."

Disappointment weighted his features unknowingly,

then he asked, "I've really come by because I left my coat. Do you know where it is?"

Caroline nodded crisply. There was no invitation for him to enter. She returned with the coat and extended it as if contact offended her.

"Thank you, ma'am. Good day."

As he started about, her quick words held him.

"Lieutenant Reade, wait." She looked at him anxiously, never quite meeting his eyes as if in some great indecision. "Hillary told me you could see a package through to my husband. Are you still willing to?" She looked up at him then, humility and desperation not overwhelming the intense dislike in her gaze. Bending her pride to so loathsome an enemy was a distasteful chore.

"Yes, of course, Mrs. Russell. Do you know where he is?"

"I have it right here. Just a moment." She came back with a hastily wrapped parcel. "He's at Point Lookout in Maryland. I've gathered some warm things and some of his books." She broke off, averting her eyes so he couldn't see the pain that was so heavy in her tone.

Very carefully, Skyler took the bundle from her. "I'll see he gets it, ma'am. Don't fret."

Her eyes snapped up, shiny but hard. "Don't tell me that. I'll stop fretting when he's home safe where he belongs."

"Yes, ma'am," he said gently, awkward in the face of her wrathful indignation. Unable to give her any other assurances or comforting words, he merely nodded and strode back to his horse. After tucking the package safely behind his saddle, he was about to mount when a low voice called to him.

"Lieutenant?"

His fair head jerked up, the grey eyes wide with a sudden flash of irrational expectation. Even his heart seemed to stop for a second, then resumed with a hurried beat. Savannah stood at the rail of the second-story veranda dressed in a plain morning gown, black hair loose about her shoulders in a glossy cloud. Her expression betrayed nothing.

"Please come up. I wish to speak to you. There's a stairway on the right."

He quickly retethered his horse and bounded up the steps. When he got close enough to meet her eyes, their emotionless distance nearly shattered all hope.

Savannah said nothing for a time, letting him hesitate in uncertainty. The eager softness in the silvery eyes hinted at what he wanted to hear from her. His whole attitude gave her an uncomfortable dread as to the answer to her unasked question. Finally, he spoke first, relieving her of the difficulty.

"Savannah, I'd like to apologize to you. It was thoughtless of me to make you go to that party last night. I should have realized you would have a problem with the people and the politics."

"On the contrary. I had no problem with either." Only with you, her heart mourned. Very stiffly, she continued. "I would apologize as well. I had too much to drink and acted badly. You must have been quite embarrassed." She didn't sound unhappy about that.

It was his turn to object. "You didn't. I enjoyed your company."

How much? To what extent did you enjoy it, she wanted to shout at him. Why did he have to make it so difficult? How could she ask him?

"I'm not accustomed to strong drink and fear I acted foolish. It was kind of you to see me . . . home." She had almost said to bed, she realized, flushing darkly.

"Is there something you wished to ask me, Savannah?" His tone was smooth. Was he mocking her?

Back rigid and teeth gritted in misery, she ground

118

out, "Yes. Skyler, last night when you brought me here and put me to bed did you—did we—?"

"Are you asking if I bedded you?" he supplied calmly.

Oh, damn you, she thought murderously. "Yes. Did you?" She turned her back on him, unable to bear the cool grey eyes upon her. She jumped slightly at the touch of his hands on her shoulders. His words were low and silky with promise.

"When I make love to you, Savannah, you will remember it."

Her shoulders slumped in brief thankfulness, then squared at the confident insinuation of his statement. She pulled away and faced him indignantly, the chill of that assumption making her more defensive. "You speak as though that might happen. I assure you, Lieutenant, it will not. Not ever."

He regarded her with a half smile. "How can you say that after last night and all you said to me? You told me you loved me, Savannah."

Her face went white with shock and disbelief. "You lie," she said hoarsely.

"Do I? Can you deny this?"

He caught her to his chest, one arm curled about her waist while his hand held her rebellious head still. His mouth moved slowly, devastatingly over hers, until she was panting in rage and confusion. He let the kiss deepen. Her lips slackened with a forlorn moan of protest. Her hands came up to rest on his broad shoulders, kneading them briefly. Then she was shoving him away.

"You see," he explained reasonably. "It's only a matter of time the way we feel for each other."

"We feel?" she cried frantically. Her hand dashed across her damp lips as if she could wipe away the delicious tingle that lingered there. "You are fooling yourself, Lieutenant. It will never happen. I will never come willingly into your arms."

"I don't believe you. You don't believe it either. That's why your eyes are so afraid. Don't be afraid of your feelings for me."

"You're confused, sir," she insisted, voice growing stronger and force of will returning to brace her wavering emotions. "I don't love you. All the kisses in the world won't change hate to love. When I look at you, I see my uncle betrayed by his love for me. You used me and I'll not forgive that. No amount of sweet kisses can change what you did. I will always hold you responsible and I will curse you every day of my life."

Her words were so sure and strong, he paused in his certainty. "But there is more, isn't there? You cared for me once. I think you still do."

"Just because you want it to be so, you can't make my feelings different. Yes, I'll admit I could have loved you. Oh, Skyler, I wanted to love you but you ruined it, you soured it with your treachery and the taste of it will always be bitter. We can't go back and I cannot overlook the past to go on. You hurt me and broke my trust and I could never, ever feel safe with you. I'm sorry that's not what you wanted to hear but you must believe me. I cannot love you."

"I believe you," he said quietly. There was so much unhappiness in his eyes she almost wished she could call back the words but she didn't. Skyler Reade was too dangerous to her vulnerable heart. Then he smiled, the confidence returning. "I believe that's the way you feel now but I don't believe in forever. I will make you care for me."

She stomped her foot in frustration, fist striking his chest for added effect. "No. No, you won't because I won't let you. I will not let you get close to me."

"Are you that afraid of the truth?"

She whirled away, shaking her head in agitation. "Don't make me hurt you, Skyler. I don't want to hurt you. I just want you out of my life before you harm my loved ones any further."

"Savannah, I'm no monster. I didn't keep a ship full of clothing and medical supplies from reaching your troops. I wouldn't have done that, duty be dammed. Your uncle was carrying weapons and liquors. That I couldn't overlook. I couldn't."

Her slap was hard and angry. "Liar. You liar."

"I'm not. I'm not lying. The hold of that ship was full of guns and champagne. Didn't you think to check for yourself? Look at me. I'm telling you the truth."

She did look. The imprint of her hand stood out in bold relief. The grey eyes were desperate with sincerity. She hadn't looked into the hold because she had been blinded by him, but now she believed him. She knew her uncle.

"It doesn't matter, Skyler. It's too late. It's too late for us just like it's too late for our country. The wounds are too deep to heal. When they fester that badly they must be cleanly cut."

"No. That's not true." He put his hand on his left elbow. "You fought as hard as I did to heal an impossible wound once before. We can do it again. Time helps heal things."

"Not for me." She said it with a flat finality, that very determination he so admired in her a barrier he couldn't surmount. At least for now. Savannah sighed wearily and looked at him long and sadly. When she spoke, her words were not unkind. That charitable gentleness made them cut all the deeper. "If you love me, Skyler, and I believe you do, go now and give me some peace. I can't give you what you want. It's too painful seeing you and thinking of what could have been and can never be. Please leave and don't come

121

back. If you do, there will only be more unpleasantness. It's hard enough as it is without having to deal with you too. Please, Skyler. Please go."

His hand reached out to stroke along her cheek in a wistful gesture that touched her in spite of her brave claims, and his softly spoken words touched her even more. "I've never wanted anything so much in my life. Do you really want me to walk out of yours?" At her stiff nod, his hand fell away. "All right, Savannah, but be warned. As I said, I don't believe in forever. If you change your mind or need me, for anything, I'll be here for you."

"I won't."

He pursed his lips regretfully. "You're an independent woman and a thickheaded one, but I love you and I always will. Don't forget that. At least let me offer you some protection. I could arrange for a regular patrol to swing by and check on things."

Her smile had a bitter twist. "No, thank you, Lieutenant. I have more to fear from your men. Just leave us alone. We'll be fine."

"How many of you are there? Are there any men who could put up a defense?"

"We don't need any men to see to our safety," she vowed staunchly.

He laughed at that. "You, a pregnant woman, and a little girl? A truly fearsome defense."

"Don't laugh at me. I don't give up what's mine easily."

"Nor do I." He tapped her under the chin with a grin, then added somberly, "Forget your pride and send for me if there's any danger."

"Good-bye, Lieutenant," she said firmly.

"For now, Savannah."

When he started away, she called after him, "Skyler, will you still see the package to Darcy?"

He looked surprised at her doubt. "Of course. That has nothing to do with us. That's just plain decency." He snapped her a jaunty salute and continued down the steps.

Savannah could forget neither the man nor the peril of their situation. Every day one or two or even three of their slaves disappeared, some bearing off irreplaceable stores. When Hillary had surprised one of their field hands, weighed down with sacks of cornmeal, he had threatened her with a pitchfork. After that, Savannah began carrying her father's pistol in her skirt and insisted no one go outside at night or even during the day alone. The idea of being virtually a prisoner in their own home created a tension between them. Hillary moped about in a disagreeable temper but never challenged her sister's orders. Caroline was weepy and depressed in her discomfort as the babe shifted lower and constantly bemoaned Darcy's absence. Guiltily, Savannah tried to avoid them both, her own thoughts grave with concern over their predicament. The reoccurring solution was one she would not hear of. She would not go to Skyler Reade for assistance and open the door to give him a means to intrude in her life.

Despite her convictions, her wayward thoughts often strayed down the drive, as if expecting to see the tall, fair-haired Yankee who lingered in her heart. But as he promised, Skyler stayed away and his absence tormented her as painfully as his presence. Even when she escaped the daily drudgery to dream of Rising Sun, he was there, blue coat replaced by Confederate grey. He was the master of Rising Sun and she was at his side, loving him with all her heart. And when those happy dreams carried her to a shared bed, she would

123

awake clammy with anticipation to the crushing disappointment of reality.

She was having that dream again when shaken from it roughly. Hillary's pale face was bent close, illuminated by a sheltered candle.

"Hilly, what is it?" she asked groggily.

In a high, thin voice her sister shrilled, "Vannah, there are some men out in the stables. They're taking the horses. They're Yankees. What are we going to do?"

Sheer outrage brought Savannah from the bed to the window to peep out cautiously. In the darkness below, she could see shadowy shapes moving about the yard. From the barn, there was the sound of horses' nickering. Aurora was among them. Her fist beat against the sill in impotent anger, then she turned to her terrified sister.

"We do nothing," she said tightly.

"But Vannah—"

"Let them take what they want. Just pray they're satisfied with what they find outside." With a forced calm, she tied her robe about her and checked the heavy pistol. "Where's Caroline?"

"She went downstairs to make sure the doors were locked." Her teeth were chattering so hard the words were nearly unintelligible.

As if locks would keep them out, Savannah thought bitterly. Her fear was edged aside by a cold indignation that dirty boots would track on the floors her mother was so proud of, that twangy voices would fill the same air that had known music and laughter, that precious belongings would be misused by unappreciative hands. Then she looked at the trembling girl at her side, seeing her fragile beauty and defenselessness. Her anger became a fierce determination.

"Hillary, lock yourself in your room and don't come out no matter what you hear. Do you understand?"

124

The sharpness of her voice made the blond head jerk up and down like a pretty puppet, but it took a push to get her moving.

From below, there was the sound of breaking glass and a scream from Caroline that sent Savannah racing to the stairs in a panic. They were in the house.

Miles away, Skyler was out walking. He often did that in the evening when sleep was hours away. The cool night air and exercise eased his moodiness. He was trying very hard to push his life forward when the most important part of it remained unbudgingly in the past. The road to the Russells' was wide and inviting. He walked because he feared if he rode, he would be down that avenue without a thought to promise or consequence. His heart refused to let his mind consider that road might be closed to him now. Savannah Russell would be a part of his future if he had to drag her into it kicking and fighting all the way. The only drawback to that plan was an annoying sentimental streak that wanted her to come willingly. He hadn't heard from her nor did he expect to, and he hadn't found a good enough reason to go to her. Desire and loneliness weren't reason enough, and he knew the harder he pushed the deeper her stubborn heels would dig. Compared to Savannah, everything else seemed so temporary and unimportant. That included his military position, his semi-ambitious political hopes, and even the war. He could visualize the end of all those things but not the end of his future with Savannah Russell.

His aimless stroll took him along the line of horses. He paused to rub the velvety nose that pushed out at him. Beauty blew warmly into his hand and nudged the front of his coat in search of the sugar lump that teased its nostrils. Patting the arched neck, he smiled as it disappeared from his palm. He started back toward the sweltering enclosure of his tent when the approach of riders brought him up curiously. A half-dozen men he recognized only slightly reined in, talking among themselves in obvious drunken revelry. The sight of a superior officer quieted them only slightly.

"Evening, sir," one of them called then belched into his hand. That brought a round of loud laughter.

Skyler returned the sloppy salutes with an ill-concealed grin, then all traces of humor were gone. He pushed between the startled horses to snatch the reins of an oddly colored mare. After looking at it more closely, he gave a snarl of rage and gripped its rider by the coat. With a hard jerk, he pulled him out of the saddle. The man fell awkwardly with a cry of surprise. He swallowed the sound when the barrel of Skyler's revolver clanked against his teeth.

"Where did you get this horse?" he demanded. "You lie to me and you'll have a draft running clean through you."

"We were just having some fun, sir," the man whimpered, seeing the shortness of his future in the cold, silvery eyes. "We didn't mean no harm to anybody. We just got carried away is all."

"They'll carry you and your friends away on stretchers if anything has happened to those ladies. Get up."

With Skyler's knee off his chest, the wide-eyed man scrambled up, exchanging alarmed looks with the others. A short call brought a sentry.

"Put these men under guard and confiscate everything they're carrying. I want to see them first thing in the morning." The steely stare turned back to the silent men. "If those women are hurt, you'd be safer to desert than to be here when I get back."

126

Pausing long enough to throw a saddle on his horse, he grabbed the reins of Savannah's mare and kicked his stallion into a full gallop.

As he bent low over the stinging mane, his thoughts raced ahead in fear of what he would find. Memories of the grim atrocities on his desk urged him to use his heels mercilessly. He cursed the criminals the war honorably called soldiers, and himself for giving in so easily to Savannah's stubborn insistence.

A smudge like a black cloud hung heavy on the evening sky. Over the treetops rose a haze of flickering orange and crimson that preceded the acrid smell of smoke. Uttering another oath, Skyler flailed out with his reins as well.

Chapter Ten

"Get out of my house."

The low, fierce words made the three men freeze in the hallway. Their eyes lifted in surprise to the woman on the stairs. She was tall and wildly beautiful, black hair tumbling about the lightweight wrapper she wore. There was nothing soft and feminine in her cold stare or in the heavy pistol she wielded steadily in both hands.

"I won't tell you again. Get out of this house or I'll blow you through that door." To emphasize her words, she cocked the hammer, having to use both thumbs to do so. She was thankful for the flowing silk that hid the shaking of her knees. A low moan sounded from where Caroline had collapsed to the floor and it was difficult to keep her eyes from stealing a glance at her. Her only hope was bracing a brave-enough front to intimidate those below into leaving peacefully. All she could do was boldly bluff and hope they weren't determined to see their mischief through.

"I'm warning you. This house is under the protection of Lieutenant Commander Reade and he'll not take kindly to your intrusion."

"How do you know he didn't send us with his best wishes?" one of them chuckled.

"Vannah?"

The frightened voice from above drew her attention only for a second but it was long enough. The rush of movement brought the gun up and she fired reflexively. The recoil was massive, knocking her back on the steps. She gave an angry cry as the gun was wrenched roughly from her grasp and hurtful hands jerked her down the rest of the stairs.

"You come on down too, Missy. We ain't gonna hurt any of you. You just stay quiet and don't get in our way."

Hillary crept down and hurried to Caroline, who was recovering from a faint. The man holding Savannah gave her a push, sending her stumbling toward them. She crouched down and placed a comforting hand on the moaning woman's shoulder while her eyes blazed up at the intruders.

"Take what you want, just leave us alone," she bit out, unable to humble herself or her tone in spite of her fear.

"We intend to, ma'am," one of them said with a grin.

The next minutes could have filled a lifetime as they huddled together in the darkened hall while their home was raped by strangers. Hillary whimpered helplessly as she clung to Savannah's skirts, but she was more concerned with Caroline. The fright had caused her to fall heavily and now she was writhing with discomfort.

"Savannah," she whispered hoarsely. "It's the baby. The baby's coming. What am I going to do?"

She stroked the beaded brow gently and answered in her calmest voice, "You're going to relax and take deep breaths, and as soon as these animals are gone, we're going to deliver a healthy child for my brother."

"Darcy. I want Darcy. I need him. Get him for me, Savannah. Promise me you'll get him."

"I will. You just rest now. I'll get Darcy for you," she soothed absently. "I'll see to everything."

130

By the time Skyler rode into the yard, the out-buildings were ablaze, the stable already a smoldering ruin. Thankfully, there was no wind or the house would have been consumed as well. As he drew up, a lone figure rose from the shadows on the veranda. Heart in his throat, he slid off his horse and bounded up the steps in two long strides. The sight of her stopped him. Her eyes were dull and empty. The front of her robe was splotched with a drying crimson. That they had raped her was his first thought, freezing his insides with horror and rage.

"Savannah?" Her stare rose blankly. "Are you hurt? Is everyone all right?"

She blinked several times then rubbed her hand over her eyes in a weary gesture. "We're fine. I delivered Caroline's baby."

A lusty wail from above reinforced her claim, and with a soft cry, Skyler took her in his arms. She neither resisted nor responded to that crushing embrace but merely leaned upon his chest in exhausted relief. His heart was hammering frantically beneath her cheek and his voice was rough and unsteady.

"When I saw them ride in with your horse, I thought—I thought I'd lost you. Oh sweet Christ, Savannah, I was so afraid they'd hurt you. Are you sure you're all right?" At her faint nod, he simply held her, trembling as the tension of the long ride left him. His quick, gulping breaths ruffled the loose tumble of her hair.

Too numb to think beyond her gratitude for his solid strength, Savannah couldn't control the shivers of shock and outrage that ran through her. His arms tightened until they were almost forged into one being. She could find no objection to the comfort she took in his closeness. Slowly, in the midst of that spreading security, an ugly insinuation returned to plague her.

131

"Skyler," she asked quietly. "Were those your men? Were they acting on orders?"

He released her so abruptly she staggered. "My orders, you mean?" he demanded incredulously. "Are you asking if I sent them to hurt and terrify you? Do you think I would do that?"

She turned away from his shattered expression with a shake of her head. "No," she told him. "No, I know you wouldn't. I'm just so tired I don't know what to think." She sagged against one of the majestic pillars, eyes closing in helpless pain.

"Let me take you inside," he offered, putting a supportive hand on her shoulder.

"No," she cried, shying away from him. "I don't want you in there." The unfair hurt those sharp words brought to his eyes made her rephrase quickly. "I just don't want to go in right now."

In truth, she knew she couldn't look at what they had done inside without breaking down completely, and she wanted to retain a bit of dignity in front of the tall, blond Yankee.

"Is there anything I can do for you?" he asked lamely, feeling uncomfortable and unneeded.

"No, thank you," she began proudly, only to have him grip her shoulders tightly.

"Stop it, Savannah. Don't pretend with me. I know they scared you. I know how upset and angry you are that your home was violated."

Her hands slipped over his and pulled them off so she could pace as the remembered horror rose again. "How could you know? How could you even imagine the helplessness of watching everything you cherish being desecrated? I couldn't stop them. All I could do was stand by and pray they wouldn't touch me. I've never been so terrified and so alone in my life. Hillary and Caroline are counting on me to make everything right.

Hillary expects me to turn this nightmare into a safe, secure home again. Caroline expects me to bring Darcy back to her. I wish he were here. I wish he were here so I wouldn't have to manage all alone any more. I'm so tired of everyone counting on me to fix things, to find food, to protect our home. I can't do it. But how can I tell them I'm just as weak and frightened as they are? I'm just so tired."

He wanted to touch her, to hold her, to share his strength, but the dignity in her quiet weeping wouldn't allow it. She wasn't speaking to him or asking him to carry her burdens. She was asking for a solution that would lift the weight before it crushed her.

"I want to go home. I want to leave this place. I don't want to live in fear of blue uniforms snatching away everything that's mine. I want my brother home so he can see his son. If Darcy were here, everything would be so different. He would know what to do and I wouldn't be so afraid."

"And if I could arrange that for you?"

She turned at the quiet words, cocking her head as if her hearing had failed her. His features were all shadowy angles and his eyes a pale glimmer of silver. "What did you say?"

"What if I got your brother released and arranged passes for all of you to leave Beaufort?"

"You could do all that?" she asked with a hopeful skepticism.

"I could."

"But would you?"

"If you asked me."

"And?" She waited, knowing there was more, sensing it in the sudden tension of his stance and deepening of his voice. His very intensity alarmed her as to the seriousness of the condition he would name but she wasn't prepared for the incredible magnitude of

133

his proposition.

"Marry me, Savannah."

She gave a nervous laugh. "Skyler, I am in no mood for silliness."

"But I am very serious. I want you for my wife. In exchange, I'll arrange your brother's release and see you safely to your family's home. That is the cost of my help. If you have a better offer, I'll understand."

Savannah stared at him. She wanted to laugh. She wanted to strike him. She wanted to cry. But mostly, she wanted time to think. Her head was swirling with the events of the evening and too weary to fully comprehend what he asked.

"Why?" she asked faintly. "Why do you ask that? You can't want a wife who holds no affection for you. You are the last man in this crazy world I want to share a life with."

"It's always been my intention to marry you. I had wanted to wait until you realized you cared for me, but the danger of your situation doesn't give us that kind of time. I won't let any harm come to you even if it means offending your stubborn pride. If the only way I can keep you safe is to force you into a marriage you don't want, so be it. It's what I want, and in time, I think you'll find it's what you wanted too."

"But I don't want to marry you," she wailed impatiently. "Can't you help me without chaining me to a future I loathe?"

"No. I'm sorry. If I'm to have any control over your impulsiveness, it has to be this way. I want you safely tied to me so I don't have to worry about losing you. Agree to it, Savannah. You know it's your only chance. What other choice do you have?"

She looked out over the flaming buildings, the flicker reflecting in the wetness of her eyes. The sense of helpless panic was nearly overwhelming.

Very gentle fingertips brushed a straying curl from her cheek, then stroked through the tangled mass. "Think on it, Savannah. I'll be by for your decision in the morning. Unless you'd like me to stay." It was a thoughtful offer meant to give her peace of mind, but she shook her head vehemently.

"Please go."

He hesitated, not wanting to leave her in such a fragile state, but he realized his presence only added to her distress. He wanted to hold her, if only briefly, and tell her how much he cared, but she wouldn't welcome that from him either. Reluctantly, he backed away, feeling a strong stirring of pride and devotion as he gave a last look at her poised, self-contained figure. What an admirable woman she was, and the sooner she wore his ring, the better he would feel about leaving her alone. He secured the reins of her horse to the front rail, then swung up on his own mount. He had much to do in the few hours before daybreak and his return for her answer.

Hearing him ride away, Savannah exhaled wearily. She wouldn't think any more on his proposition tonight. Her emotions were too wired and her fear too close to the surface to choose rationally. At the moment, his offer was both insult and rescue, and she didn't trust her weakened state to decide. He was right about one thing—the danger they were still in. She only had to enter the house to support that. Tears began to well once more as she looked about the intentional destruction. Furniture had been overturned, upholstery ripped savagely to expose its stuffing. Paintings were viciously slashed and the rugs torn from the floors, all in search of hidden valuables. What few they had had were sold long ago for food and information about Darcy, but they wouldn't have believed her had she told them.

Slowly, she began to right and straighten things, wanting to spare Hillary and Caroline the upset of seeing the malicious damage. As she swept up shards of glass and porcelain, she realized sadly that she could never feel safe here and call it her home. They had torn that security from her. She wouldn't rest easy until she was once again at Rising Sun. That was the important thing, wasn't it, getting away from the atmosphere of hate and threat, getting Darcy back to head the family? Did the means matter more than the safety of her family? It wasn't as though she had to stay married to him. An unconsummated marriage to a Northerner could be easily dissolved.

Too tired to think or rebuild, Savannah climbed the stairs to her room. Emotionlessly, she turned the mattress so the slashes in the tick wouldn't show. Most disturbing of all was her dream that night of going joyously to Skyler Reade's marriage bed.

The purification of morning light pushed away the darker shadows of memory and Savannah rose with renewed energy. She checked on the others, finding them still sleeping soundly, then checked in on the sleeping infant with a bittersweet glance. How sad that Darcy would miss seeing the tiny curled bundle. Even braced for it, seeing the ruinous wake of the first floor was a rude shock, but she plunged headlong into the task in the kitchen, where the damange seemed the worst. As she scooped and swept and mopped it was as though she were working in someone else's house. There was no longer the sense of private hominess in the rooms or the pride of ownership.

She had just finished stacking the small amount of unbroken dishes when she heard a single rider approach. Her hands went instantly to the turban that covered her hair, then fell to her sides. Her head gave an arrogant tilt. Who did she have to impress?

Skyler was tying his horse when she appeared on the steps. His gaze lingered over her warmly, noting the rolled-up sleeves, the perspiration and flour blotches on the snug bodice, and the red petticoat that showed where her overskirt was looped up to tuck into her waistband to protect it. How capable and domestic she looked, and how eager he was to have her in his own home. There was no sign of the frightened, uncertain woman in her composed features. For a moment, he feared he might have lost her.

"You know why I've come, Savannah," he began, eyes intent on hers. "Have you an answer for me?"

"What you ask of me is impossible. You ask me to betray my family, my state, and my own conscience, and I hate you for that, but yes, I will marry you."

He flashed a quick, tremulous grin and started up the steps to take her in his arms. A hand on his chest halted him.

"No," she said adamantly. "Don't touch me. You've no right. You haven't bought me yet. I want proof of Darcy's release first and free passage out of Beaufort."

He smiled, taking no offense. "I don't trust you either, little Rebel. When I've the papers on your brother, we will wed. Then you get the passes."

She gave him a vinegary look but nodded. "Fair enough. One thing I insist on though. I want to tell my family. I don't want them to hear of it from you."

"Fair enough," he agreed somberly. "It should take a few days to arrange. Can you be ready by then?"

"What do I have to ready?" her reply was tart and angry. "It's not as though I am marrying a beau of my choice in a grand church with family and well-wishers in attendance. I'm sneaking off to wed an enemy I despise to get out of a dangerous corner. It is blackmail, not true love that drags me to the altar."

"No one is forcing you," he pointed out calmly. That observation only increased her temper.

"Just like there is no one forcing me to buy coffee at twenty dollars for four pounds or ten pounds of bacon at ten dollars instead of one dollar and twenty-five cents. You have to pay the price if you want it. You are profiting nicely from the price of war. You prey on three vulnerable women who are alone and in danger. Just what does that make you?"

He met the fire of her accusation with eyes of polished steel. "No better or worse than men who would bleed your treasury and let good men die to supply luxury and liquor to those who can afford it." He caught her hand before it reached its mark and held it tightly. "I did not make the moral rules of this or any war, but I am not above taking advantage of them. If that makes me all the more loathsome in your eyes, I will deal with that later."

"And how will you deal with a wife who hates the sight of you?" she challenged hotly, wresting her hand free.

"For the time being, I love you enough for both of us. I don't mind your hate. I can live with that. What I can't live with is the worry for your safety and the fear that I will lose you. I need you, Savannah, and I'll take you any way I can get you."

"Then it will have to be by force," she vowed darkly.

His eyes were as cool and chilling as ice, with an edge as sharp as glass. "No," he said in a low, firm voice. "You will be my wife in every way. You may hate me as you will but you will submit to me. There will be no battleground in our bedroom. I don't insist you love me but I do plan to love you and love you well. If you can't agree to that, then say so now. I'm taking you for a wife and I expect you to fulfill the duties of one. Are we in

138

agreement, Savannah?"

She shivered uncontrollably, his audacity enraging her and his demands giving her an unwelcome tremor of anticipation. Her reply was as frigid as his stare. "I will hold to my end of the bargain, Lieutenant."

He reached out to lightly brush a smudge of flour from her cheek and told her with quiet emotion, "If I thought you truly hated me and the idea of this marriage, I would put a stop to it. I don't want you miserable. I know I can make you happy if you'd let me. It only has to be as bad as you want to make it."

"You expect me to love thy enemy, Lieutenant?"

The corners of his mouth twitched at the acid remark. "That's up to you."

When he presented her with the signed orders authorizing the exchange of Captain Darcy Russell two days later, she fell silent, staring at the papers as if they contained her death warrant as well.

"We have a wedding to go to, Savannah," he said softly. He'd spent two days drawing on every connection and political favor he was owed. It was difficult arranging the release of a Confederate officer. The Federals weren't hurting from the lack of manpower and accommodations the way the South was. It had been difficult but not impossible to gain what he needed, in effect his marriage license.

Her words were unexpected. "I'd like to change first."

"Of course. Take all the time you need."

Skyler waited somewhat anxiously on the steps, superstitiously fearing something would go wrong. When she appeared with unfashionable promptness, he stood, hat in hand and emotions tightening in his throat.

As much as she disliked the choice of groom, Savannah was determined to be a beautiful bride. Even while cursing the circumstance, she had spent a great deal of time selecting her wardrobe for that moment she had dreamed would be so special. She had no time to effect a wedding gown but had chosen one of simple, delicate charm. Layers of ivory lace draped gracefully over bell-shaped hoops in a series of overlapping flounces at the hem and wide bertha. Instead of fussy festoons and ribbons, the gown's only decoration was a series of ivory satin rosettes set about the neckline where undersilk meshed with sheer Chantilly that rose modestly to her throat. Small pearl clusters adorned her ears and were set among the rosettes and wisps of lace in combs that held the heavy mass of her hair. The effect was one of feminine sophistication and a fragile purity with no trace of girlishness.

"I'm ready, Lieutenant," she proclaimed in a low, throaty voice.

He took the lace-covered fingers up to his lips. His smoky eyes claimed hers with a possessive intensity. "Today you make me the happiest of men," he vowed, tone rumbling with the strength of sincerity.

"I make no promise that you will remain so," she countered smoothly, provoking his wide grin.

"That will be up to me, and I plan to work at it diligently. Shall we go?"

He handed her up into the carriage and slid in beside her. He cast a puzzled glance toward the house. "Your sisters didn't want to see you marry?"

"They didn't consider it an occasion for celebration" was her crisp reply. The rest of the ride she graced him with a dignified profile and a stony silence.

The ceremony was held in the tent that served as a chapel. Of the witnesses, Savannah knew only Tony D'Angelo. Some of the others she had seen at the party and wondered shamefully if they all remembered her for her performance. All were in spotless dress uniforms, with a somber air more befitting a burial than the sharing of nuptials. Only the groom seemed really pleased with the proceedings as he repeated his vows fervently. In contrast, Savannah's voice was a hoarse whisper, her eyes downcast until the moment she was turned for the kiss to seal the exchange. When the large hand warmed by its circle of gold cupped her cheek, she looked startled, as if suddenly aware of the reality of it all.

"I love you, Mrs. Reade," Skyler whispered softly before he bent to kiss her. Not deterred by her sharp recoil, his mouth moved firmly over hers with the demanding authority of ownership. He laid claim with that bold, searing twist of his lips, dominating her will until she lay in a near swoon upon his blue-clad chest. When released, her eyes stayed closed for a moment, then opened to look into his almost fearfully. The adoration that warmed the pale grey eyes gave her a guilty twinge, for she had no intention of living the words she spoke so monotonously and obviously he was eager to begin.

Her discomfort was spared when an aide tugged on Skyler's sleeve and murmured something low to displease her new husband. Frowning, he turned to her.

"This is poor timing but I have to leave you for a while. I should be done before evening, then we can get on . . . with other things."

The darkening of his dusky eyes made her flush and look away.

"You can wait for me here."

Her gaze snapped up in alarm. "No. I mean, I'd feel more comfortable going home if you'd let me take the carriage." She glanced uneasily about the company so he would understand her reluctance.

"Yes, of course you can. I'll have a driver—"

"No." Again the curt objection covered by a shy, pleading look. "I can manage myself."

In the mood to deny her little, he smiled and brushed her cheek with his fingertips. "All right. I'll come straight there when my business is finished. If I'm delayed, wait up for me." His voice lowered huskily. "I'll be a good husband to you, Savannah."

She had no comment and fidgeted uncomfortably before blurting out, "Skyler, I've seen to my part of the bargain. Will you see to the rest of yours?"

"Say no more."

He drew the authorized passes from his coat and pressed them into her hand.

"Thank you," she said quietly.

"I'll see you tonight."

"Good-bye, Skyler."

When he bent to kiss her, she rose on tiptoe to meet him, arms encircling his neck in a warm if not passionate embrace. The sweetness of her response made him calculate the risk of abandoning orders to see her to the nearest cot. But she stood away from him, deep blue eyes serious as she touched his mouth gently.

"I wish I could be the wife you expected."

"You're the one I wanted and I'm happy with my choice."

Again she was silent, looking long before turning to hurry to the carriage.

The day wore on tediously while Skyler chafed at being kept away from his bride. When finally released from his duties, he sent his stallion racing across the fields at a mad gallop to match the fierce tempo of his heart. It was nearly twilight when he reined up in the yard. The house lay strangely silent. He knocked, then pushed the door open.

"Savannah?"

There was no answer and he realized in dismay that there wouldn't be one. The house was empty. He checked upstairs mechanically, knowing even before he saw the open closets that the ladies of the house were gone. With the passes he supplied them.

Smiling wryly at Savannah's cleverness, he descended the stairs slowly, noting for the first time the desecrating ruin all about him. No wonder she hated him for being one of the same who had invaded her home. He had invaded her life, forcing his emotions upon her. Why was he surprised that she would bolt given a way to safety? But he wouldn't be tied to Beaufort much longer and the South couldn't hide his wife from him.

He shut the door carefully and gave the house one last look before riding back to his solitary tent.

There was no answer and he walked to the steps that
there would be one. The house was empty. The
phone . . . was it . . . there . . . the . . . Roy . . . seven . . .
before the crouch . . . . . . the . . . . . . of the house was
gone. But the same as ever . . . from . . . . . .

. . . . . . with a . . . . . . I suppose . . . he . . . . . .
he stared down . . . . . . at . . . . . . and . . . . . . he
. . . . . . and . . . . NO . . . .
put her one . . . of the many . . . and lowered his
body. He . . . . the forced . . . without
upon her. Why him he . . . . . . that the would that
never a new to know why he . . . didn't he . . . .
Realizing what lesser had the South captor. Now we
will grip him.

He shut the door tonight and gave the house this
last look before riding back to his suburb from . . . . .

Chapter Eleven

Savannah sat rigidly at the reins while the Yankee examined her passes. He seemed to take his time, his eyes wandering covertly to Hillary then back to the papers.

"Is everything in order?" she inquired sweetly. This was their last roadblock before freedom. In her mind, she envisioned Skyler in pursuit.

"Looks fine. A shame to be losing such nice-looking females. Have a safe trip now." He flashed them a broad smile and returned the papers.

"Why thank you, sir," Savannah cooed, then slapped the reins.

They moved through the sentry post like casual travelers, showing no sign of the frantic preparations for the unexpected trip. When Savannah announced on her return that they were leaving in an hour, the house was thrown into chaos. In spite of Hillary's wailing at leaving some of her finest dresses and Caroline's protests over her frailty, they were bundled into the carriage within the set time, sullen but glad to leave. Only Hillary's maid, Sally, and the baby Jeffery's wet nurse, Minnie, accompanied them. The rest of the servants had disappeared as soon as the rumor spread that they were fleeing the Yankee stronghold.

Despite Savannah's rigid stand on what belongings

145

could be taken, the carriage was uncomfortably crowded. She and Hillary sat in front, wedged between bandboxes and small trunks. Caroline and the baby occupied the back seat, with the nurse seated on the floorboards. Sally followed round-eyed in terror on the back of Aurora, who was securely tethered to the rear of the carriage. All the foodstuffs they could find were strapped behind the saddle. Ignoring the moanings from all quarters, Savannah started down the road. They were going home.

She drove straight through the last sentry post heading South, then looped sharply up toward Columbia. That was to confuse anyone who might be following. She said nothing of how she had obtained their freedom nor did she mention Darcy's possible release. She wasn't certain that on finding her gone, Skyler wouldn't put a stop to his exchange. She could only hope he would do the "decent" thing. She had taken off his ring the moment she had left the Union camp, intending to throw it away on the roadside, but holding the small circle of gold and commitment in her hand, she felt a strange reluctance to discard it so callously. It traveled with her now, nestled between her breasts on a thin gold chain. She made no attempt to justify the sudden sentimentality or her odd sadness on leaving Beaufort, leaving part of her life and her hopes behind.

They made good time even with the uncooperative passengers. She drove them straight through the first night and the next day. Though the weariest by far, Savannah had no complaints about the rough, hot ride. She forced what she had left behind her and concentrated all her energy on what lay ahead. Next to her, little Jeffery proved the best traveler, either sleeping contentedly or gurgling in easy amusement. Caroline didn't fare as well, even pampered on the well-padded bed of quilts and shaded by the fringed top. She was constantly whining of her discomfort, begging her heartless sister-in-law to consider her in frequent stops. Savannah told her curtly they would stop only when necessary and Caroline clammed up tight in aggrieved sulking.

Hillary grew more quiet as the miles between them and Beaufort widened. She was mixed about going home. She would be glad for the safety there but not for the isolation. There were no men at Rising Sun. She thought wistfully of the Yankee soldiers who had flirted with her when they purchased supplies and of the manly form of Skyler Reade. She glanced at her sister, wondering if her Yankee suitor had played a part in their escape. Perhaps she would ask when the look of determination left Savannah's face.

It was a long journey under the best of circumstances, and slowed by the delicacy of the carriage's occupants, it seemed endless before the countryside grew familiar and spirits took an upward lift. Even Caroline ceased her moaning and sat straight in her seat, eyes anxiously on the way ahead.

Rising Sun stood facing the East, sturdy and welcoming like a patriarch with open arms. The red brick and white trim were warmed by the morning sun that shimmered in the elliptical fanlight above the door. It was a stately, graceful structure with a four-columned Grecian entrance and outbuildings ornamented with the same soaring arches and tapering pillars of native cypress. They had played on the recessed porches and terraced gardens as children. Even the pale blond woman who stood on the steps watching their approach seemed little changed since those happy years.

Adelaide Russell was an older, more refined version of Hillary. She was the epitome of the Southern woman, delicate exterior masking an inner strength that all depended on. Seeing her, Savannah felt tears of weary relief prick behind her eyes. She was home. Her mother would hold her and make everything all right. She no longer had to be the stablizing stronghold of the family.

It was a weepy reunion, with much hugging and fussing over the new baby. As one of the house servants brought out a tray of cool lemonade, the women of the Russell family sat together, squeezing hands and wiping damp eyes. Rising Sun seemed untouched by the ravages of war in all but two important exceptions, the lack of masculine voices.

Savannah leaned back in the wicker chair with a satisfied smile. Her mother looked well and everything was in order about her as always. It was hard to believe her father was gone until Adelaide regarded them with a sunny smile.

"Wait until your father gets back from Charleston and finds you all here. He'll be so pleased."

Savannah felt a cold twist of fear in her heart as she looked at the serene features so blank of any knowledge. Hillary started to speak but she waved off her words quickly.

"Mama, didn't Tobias get back with a message for you?" she prompted softly.

"Oh, yes, but I can't for the life of me remember what it was about. Something about your father being delayed." The vague look intensified on the lovely face.

"But, Mama," Hillary blurted in teary upset, "Papa's—"

"Still delayed," Savannah interrupted smoothly with a warning glance at her sister.

"How like him," Adelaide mused with an absent smile of fondness. "He isn't one for timeliness. Well, I must see about dinner while you girls get settled. It's so good to have you home."

While the others saw to their unpacking, Savannah hurried down to the slave cabins to seek out Tobias. The elderly black man stood awkwardly before her questions. When asked if he had brought word of his master's death home, he replied, "I done tole Missus Adelaide jus' like I was supposed to."

"And what did she say?"

"She didn't say nothing. She jus' looked at me all queer like and went back in the house. She been pretending to herself that the Massa be coming home jus' like she never been tole any different."

"Whose been running things here?" she went on, ignoring the heavy ache in her chest.

"Missa Tyree, ma'am. He been seeing to us folk." The liquid eyes shifted with unsaid sentiments. Ben Tyree was hated and feared on Rising Sun. It was a feeling Savannah shared.

"Where is Mr. Tyree?"

"He done took up in your papa's office." This time there was no concealing the contempt in his voice.

Ben Tyree had been the overseer at Rising Sun for nine years. He took his position seriously and insisted all others did as well. He wasn't a big man but was as broad through the chest as a man twice his height, his forearms nearly as bulky with muscle as his thighs. Atop a stocky neck, his head was oversized and crowned by a slight fringe of brittle grey hair greased and combed across the shining pate to simulate thicker growth. He had no schooling and was offensive and coarse in manner. His presence so terrified the house girls that Savannah insisted he not be allowed past the porch. She was rarely intimidated by a man, but Ben Tyree made her flesh creep when his tiny blue eyes feasted on her.

That rude, insulting gaze met her as she pushed open

149

the door to her father's office. It was a small building between the house and the cabins.

"Why, Missy Savannah, I didn't know you was back," he drawled. He didn't bother to stand, leaning back in her father's fine leather chair with hands clasped behind his head. The armpits of his faded shirt were ringed with the sweat of several days.

"I understand you've been seeing to things," she began brusquely, unwilling to exchange pleasantries with the man.

"I sorta' did seeings how nobody else was able." He smirked to himself as the beady eyes strayed to the bodice of her gown."

"I am quite capable. I'd like to see the books."

He blinked, then laughed heartily. "Would you now?" he chuckled in amusement.

Her hand flung out to sweep his feet from the littered desk. His heels hit the floor with a jarring clunk.

"I'd like to see them now and that is not a request. I'll be using this room in the future, so you can take your things back to your cabin. I'll be back after supper and I expect everything ready to be inspected."

She turned on her heel, hearing him mutter about "ungrateful" and "uppity" females before she let the door bang shut.

Savannah spent the entire evening hunched over the books in the uneven flicker of lamplight. Immersing herself in Rising Sun made the problems of Adelaide and Skyler lessen. The ledgers were a disaster. What Tyree managed to record in his nearly illegible pen noted either gross overspending or unnecessary purchases. It was like working a Chinese puzzle box where none of the pieces would mesh into a balanced whole. When she had finished near dawn, what she managed to decipher was a frightening tale of incompetent stewardship of the plantation's funds. The glaring

150

figures showed a deep hole of debt into which Rising Sun was sinking. By the time the sun streamed through the windows of the office, she had outlined a plan to see their crops in and stores in their larder. Thus satisfied, she sought out her room for the first time and was able to sleep through the deep, disturbing dream about Skyler standing at the foot of the stairs.

Savannah's plan crumbled through no fault of her careful planning. The crushing blow fell as she sat across the desk from Philip Aiken, her father's banker in Columbia. She simply stared at him in numb disbelief, all of her jewels spread before them on the blotter winking with deceiving worth.

"That's all?" she blurted. "For all of them? But the rubies alone are priced at—"

"Were, Miss Russell," he amended gently. "Forgive me for saying so but the South is smothered with such treasures. There is no market for them. I cannot guarantee a tenth of their worth, if that. If there is sentiment attached to these pieces, I suggest you keep them for all the good they'll do you."

"Sentiment will not feed my family," she said stiffly. "Sell them for the best price you can get. What about another mortgage on Rising Sun?" She said that with less enthusiasm, pain darkening the deep blue eyes.

"Savannah, the best I can do is offer to buy it from you. There is no money to invest in such properties. I wish I could help you."

"And if I sold, what would it bring me?" she asked faintly, studying her tightly clasped hands.

The price he mentioned tentatively was absurd. It was less than five cents on the dollar. It was an insult. It was blatant thievery. She would have said as much had he not been her father's trusted counsel.

"Selling, of course, is out of the question," she said with a tilt of her chin. "Take care of the jewelry for me,

151

and beyond that, we'll just have to have faith."

"Faith won't feed you either," he pointed out kindly. "My advice is to sell now while you can get anything at all. You have no men to manage things. You won't be able to hold out for the remainder of the year."

Savannah stood tall and proud. "Yes, we will. We'll make it just fine. See if we don't."

"I hope you do. I really hope you do."

The next weeks were made of long, exhausting hours. Savannah worked efficiently to utilize the small sum her jewelry brought to plant a quarter of their normal cotton crop. She reigned hard over all those at Rising Sun, including her bewildered family who thought her tyrannical and stingy. She watched every morsel of food that went into the pot, giving the cook strict orders on what and how much to prepare at every meal. The pantry was supervised so closely that even a handful of grain would be missed. She was constantly checking on the progress of the crops, much to Ben Tyree's annoyance. As a woman, he had great interest in Savannah Russell, but as a boss, he found her official bearing offensive and insulting. The only way they could coexist was by laying firm rules. He would agree to her demands as long as she left the handling of the workers strictly to him. She balked at that, knowing he had a heavy hand, but consented reluctantly. A good overseer was too hard to come by, especially one who could keep the men in the fields instead of on the Freedom Road North.

Savannah found the frustration of running the plantation far easier than coping with family life in the great brick house. It broke her heart to see her mother in her blissful dream, serenely awaiting the return of her husband. She took only a vague interest in all else. She was perfectly content to let her daughter take care of everything. Savannah decided to let her stay in her fantasy world at least until Darcy returned. If he returned.

Hillary regressed to a pouting, spiteful child, bemoaning her boredom and deprivation at every meeting. She cried for her lost pleasures of fancy new clothes, entertainment, and pampered luxury as if she were being cruelly punished. When Savannah discovered she had made a secret trip to Columbia to purchase a new frilly bonnet for the staggering price of two hundred fifty dollars, she nearly snatched her sister bald in her fury. Hillary accused her of becoming a penny-pinching miser who enjoyed making her miserable and fled to her room in a flood of tears. That deluge lasted two days, then extended for a week when she found the precious bonnet had been returned and the money used to purchase feed for the livestock.

When she wasn't doting on Jeffery, Caroline had become a staunch supporter of the South. Together with the neighboring wives, she sat for tireless hours knitting socks and mufflers for the Confederate troops. She worked with a single-minded purpose, much in the same way Savannah did, to ease the torment of thought and loneliness.

They were sitting on the front porch one lazy June evening, Caroline at her knitting, Jeffery cooing in his basket at her feet, and Savannah busy with her ledgers over her knees, when a rickety wagon pulled up at the steps. They looked curiously at the unfamiliar driver then at the gaunt man who climbed awkwardly down from the buckboard.

Knitting fell in a forgotten tangle as Caroline surged up. "Darcy!"

It was hard to associate the dirty, ragged scarecrow with the dapper Darcy Russell who had ridden off nearly two years earlier with plumed hat and tasseled saber to join Wade Hampton's South Carolina legion.

153

This slumped, tired man showed no such optimism. He looked beaten and defeated. He embraced his wife for a long, timeless minute, then reached into the wagon to draw out a crude crutch. When he walked toward the house, his limp was painful and obvious.

Savannah welcomed his hug, ignoring the stench and grime that clung to him. Her brother was home.

After a large, wasteful meal, the family, nearly complete, sat in the parlor sipping claret. Darcy had washed and put on fresh clothing, but the pallor stayed with him and his clothes hung in reminder of what he'd been through. He told them sketchily of his injury at Antietam, when he took a minnie ball in the calf. To save his leg, the surgeon trimmed away the splintered ends and pieced it together. The leg had mended but was almost three inches shorter than the other. He would never walk without the limp or the crutch. He refused to discuss Lookout Point, saying it was no fit topic for women. He retired early, pleading exhaustion, taking his wife and the rest of the liquor with him.

If Savannah had hoped Darcy would be eager to take control of Rising Sun and its problems, she soon realized her disappointment. He lay in bed often until afternoon, then if he bothered to dress at all, he hobbled to the front steps to stare out over the green lawn, tumbler of homemade mash in one listless hand. When she tried to approach him and coax his interest, she was met with a surly rebuff. Caroline coddled and protected him, defending his apathy by saying he needed time to recover. Savannah thought just the opposite, fearing he dwelled too much on what he'd suffered. She felt he needed to focus on problems other than his own, but they wouldn't listen. She gave up trying to seek his help and returned to shouldering the burden alone, trying not to view him begrudgingly as another mouth to feed.

154

The summer continued hot and searing. The crops flourished and their larder grew smaller. Savannah's weariness was a constant state. She often fell asleep with an open ledger as a pillow. Her absence from the house was seen as a blessing by the others who bore the brunt of her short, biting temper. Her forced dealings with Ben Tyree did little to ease her disposition. With Darcy's return and failure to assume his place, he grew more bold in his dealings and more often Savannah caught him eyeing her in a speculative way. He was constantly lurking about her office on some excuse to speak with her, his sweaty body standing too close and his look too undressing. She kept reminding herself that they needed him if Rising Sun was to weather the storm of war. Once things were restored, she would have no qualms about showing him the road. It was too close to harvest to cause trouble now. She knew it and so did he. Both knew she couldn't handle it alone.

Savannah took to her bed early in an unaccustomed bout of depression. She couldn't bear to see the once-loved faces of her family scowl at her over their paltry portions at the table as if she were at fault for their hunger. She lay in the sweltering darkness trying to block out the hopelessness of her struggle when a commotion below intruded on her melancholy. She could hear Darcy's voice raised hot and angry, and another man's, not Tyree's, too low to understand. Frowning, she went to the head of the stairs. Darcy was in the alcove below, pistol lifted. She heard her own voice cry out shrilly.

"For God's sake, Darcy. Don't shoot him. He's my husband."

Chapter Twelve

The silence was thunderous as Darcy stared up at her. Then his face congealed with rage.

"You married this—this Yankee?" he roared. "I don't believe what I'm hearing. How could you do such a thing?"

The contempt and outright disgust in his voice touched off her pent-up frustration and anger. That he would dare judge her sparked the volatile temper she could no longer keep in check.

"Yes, I married him and I'm not ashamed of it. Someone had to take care of our family and free you from imprisonment. How do you think your exchange was managed? I saw to it the only way I could. I've had to see to all of it. Since no one has been eager to lift that yoke from me, none of you has the right to question how I sought to do it."

"You sold yourself to him like some common—"

A silencing hand gripped his lapel, jerking him up sharply. The low voice rumbled in warning. "Be careful of your words. You've no cause for them. Your sister is a decent, honorable woman and I'll hear no different from anyone."

Abruptly released, Darcy stumbled, reeling on his crutch for balance. His blue eyes were dark with hatred, but it was his sister's pitying call that forced him

157

to limp from the room with broken spirit.

"Darcy? Darcy, please listen," Savannah cried after the hobbling figure, but he wouldn't acknowledge her. Slowly her eyes turned to the man at the foot of the stairs. The likeness to her dream made her heart skip with an irregular flutter.

Skyler Reade stood bold and handsome, the cool silvery eyes assessing her with a growing warmth. Instead of the hated blue uniform, he wore civilian clothes. They were well tailored for his tall, broad, and tapered physique. Even the circumstances couldn't keep the sight of his strong, angular features from stirring her emotions with unsettling results. His low, rapidly spoken words only added to her apprehension.

"I would have thought you'd rather he shot me than to see me again."

"I still might ask him to," she countered tersely. Why couldn't she control the feverish rush of her blood? "What are you doing here?"

A slow, silky smile spread wide across the rugged face. "Can't you guess? I've come for the wedding night you promised me."

Savannah was motionless as he started slowly up the steps. The intense grey eyes held her mesmerized. By the time he stopped on the stair below her, she'd forgotten to breathe.

"I'm a patient man," he continued quietly, "but six months is not a reasonable time for a bride to play the modest virgin. The time for patience is over. Which room is ours."

Ours. Her breast tightened in panic. "You—you can't stay here," she stammered nervously. Her mouth was as dry as her palms were wet.

"Summon the entire Confederate army if you like. Nothing is going to keep me from this night with you. If you prefer the stairs to the privacy of your room, after six months of thinking of you, it makes little difference to me."

With a gulping breath, Savannah retreated up the top few steps, then hurried to her room. It crossed her mind to latch the door, but logic told her that Skyler Reade wouldn't be kept from what he'd come for and he'd come for her.

The soft click of the door behind her echoed like the snap of a trap, closing her into a situation she never thought she'd have to face. After her desertion in Beaufort and the time in between, she never dreamed he'd come after her. Yet here he was, demanding payment. Her anxiety made her voice brittle.

"My feelings for you haven't changed."

"Nor have mine for you," he vowed huskily. He moved up behind her so she could sense but not feel his presence. It engulfed her with a dizzying heat and power. "I want you, Savannah."

"So much you'd take me against my will in my own home?" she asked stiffly.

"By your own word you said that wouldn't be necessary," he reminded her smoothly. When his hands rested on her tense shoulders, he felt her tremble. "Are you afraid of me? You needn't be."

She couldn't find her voice to deny it bravely. She could only stand mute while his large hands stroked down her arms, then began to work up the fastenings of her gown. With a slight encouragement, it fell to the floor. His mouth was hot as it teased along the line of her shoulder, providing a disturbing distraction as he efficiently removed the petticoats, cage of hoops, and protective corset. He heard her hoarse gasp as his hands slid up to cup the full heaviness of her breasts. The rapid panic of her heart was apparent beneath the thin, gauzy covering. Her timid fright moved him with a warm swell of emotion, instilling feelings of

159

protectiveness and caring for this precious woman he loved so completely.

Wanting to ease her apprehension, he nuzzled her ear and whispered softly, "Don't be afraid, Savannah. I know you've no experience in these things and will see you've no cause for fear. I want this to be a special time between the two of us, one you will remember always. You've no idea how a man feels to know he's the only one to share himself with the woman he loves. It makes what we have all the more wonderful, all the more binding and perfect."

Savannah closed her eyes and swallowed the hard knot of her terror. That he would sound so pleased and proud to have unfairly won her virginity awoke a fierce sense of denial. How dare he make his conquest seem a romantic moment and her surrender one of willingness instead of forced payment. Her indignation would not allow him that blissful self-deception. She could not give him that kind of satisfaction as a reward for his betrayal.

She turned to him with a haughty tip of her head. Her deep eyes were as cold and hard as the edge of her voice. "You assume wrong, Lieutenant. I am no untouched maid you can woo with pretty sentiments. This road is not unfamiliar to me. You will not have the honor of being my first lover."

He looked blank and stunned with disbelief. "But on the beach—"

"That was a long time ago and I was naive in many matters. It seems you are the one who is being naive now. Do you think I would shame myself by allowing the likes of you to compromise my virtue if it had not already been breached? You are not the first to demand such degrading payment in barter for goods I had to have. My brother's words were not far from the truth. See your price met but don't expect it to be special

160

to me."

The grey eyes darkened in anger and a deeper hurt as he blurted, "You were unfaithful to the vows we took?"

Her laugh was a cutting edge of glass. "Unfaithful?" she sneered. "I feel no obligation to you or to the sham of our marriage. You must be mad to think I would. I don't care about you. You knew that when you pushed me into this farce. Nothing binds us together but a mockery. Release me from it now. You cannot choose to be wed to a woman who holds you in contempt and cuckolds you in your absence."

His lips had narrowed into a long, thin line and she could feel the mounting anger seethe from him. When she took a step back in alarm, he seized her up tightly by the forearms until she could feel his breath, harsh and fast, upon her face.

"You are the only woman I would be wed to, Savannah. I may not be your first lover, but by God, I will be your last. Since you confess such an extensive knowledge, I see no need to court you gently. It's time this marriage was consummated."

She gave a shriek of outrage when he scooped her up and deposited her unceremoniously on the bed. She scrambled to draw the covers around her and glared at him murderously. He only smiled and began to remove his clothes.

The room was lit with one small candle but it was enough to display the dangerous strength of his body to her ever-widening eyes. It basked the broad chest in golden light and shone whitely against the curving scar on his arm. And when his trousers dropped to the floor, the boldness of his manhood appeared in stark definition. She could only stare in shocked amazement, fingers clutching the coverlet defensively. She wasn't totally ignorant of the facts of mating but seeing his proportions made her doubt the possibility of it. He

161

certainly couldn't intend to—

"If you are making comparisons to your other lovers, I trust I don't disappoint you," he mocked wryly as he gave his drawers a freeing kick.

Her eyes flashed in an embarrassed alarm, then narrowed fiercely.

"If you're interested in comparisons, let's see how you fare next to my others." With that, he ripped the concealing covers from her.

Savannah snarled in rage and tried to roll away, but he anticipated her. The crush of his weight atop her momentarily ended her fight. When he began to tug at the laces of her delicate chemise, her energy returned in desperation.

After receiving two hard cuffs to the head, Skyler caught the vicious fists and held them harmless in one hand while he continued to disrobe her. Her lithesome body bucked and twisted in an attempt to topple him, but when she saw the unwanted result of her struggles, she lay rigid and panting.

The parted chemise revealed soft creamy skin flushed invitingly by exertion. She felt warm and firm and pliable beneath his questing hand. When he began to tease the dark tip of her breast into a hard peak, she cursed him.

"Stop your pawing and get on with it," she raged through clenched teeth. In truth, she didn't know how long her courage would last and she couldn't bear to beg any gentleness from him. And there was also the alarming feel of his hot, bare skin on hers that was strangely exhilarating.

"If you are that eager, I suppose we have plenty of time to get acquainted later. At this point, I don't need much encouragement."

Her linen pantaloons were tossed to the floor and for the first time she felt the press of him between her thighs. Her resolve failed in a sudden rush of panic, but before she could plead with him, there was a splintering pain as his possession of her was complete. Biting back her cry of surprise and hurt, Savannah squeezed her eyes shut. Her hands clenched until small crescents of crimson dotted her palms. The sense of unfamiliar invasion persisted, becoming an unbearable stretching and tearing as he moved above her. Tears stained her cheeks as the burning friction intensified to a thankfully quick conclusion. His passion had been too long in check to be subdued for long.

She let her breath out in a soft sob as he lay heavily upon her. He murmured something low and unintelligible against her hair before rolling to one side. Even when he was gone from her, the hurtful ache remained. While she let her silent tears fall, his breathing slowed and deepened in an exhausted sleep.

Skyler stirred some time later, pleasantly drowsy and body languidly satisfied. Without opening his eyes, he stretched out his hand to search the cool but empty sheets beside him.

"Savannah?" he called softly. When there was no reply, he slit his eyes to glance about the room.

She was standing at one of the windows, gazing into the night. A light robe did little to hide the curves of the supple body beneath it. She made no sign of having heard him.

"Savannah, what is it?"

The sound of his voice incited a mighty trembling. She hugged her arms about herself, trying to contain it, but the tremors only worsened until helpless sobs were shaken loose.

Puzzled, Skyler started from the bed when the sight of dark spotty stains on the sheet made him hesitate. In stunned awareness, his eyes rose slowly to the shivering figure at the window. Groaning inwardly, he went to

163

her still naked and drew her back against his chest. She stiffened at the contact but he wouldn't relent.

"Why did you lie to me, Savannah?" he questioned softly. But he knew. She had wanted to wound him and she had, but her punishment had been all too severe. "It should never have been like that. If I'd known I was your first, I would have taken such care with you."

"Just leave me alone. Please," she whispered faintly. "You've gotten what you wanted, so please go."

Contrarily, he turned her to face him, taking the dark glossy head between his hands. "You don't understand, do you?" He noticed for the first time the circle of gold that lay between her quivering breasts. She had kept his ring. He lifted it reverently and slipped it from the chain. "Savannah, I married you not because I wanted to sleep with you but because I wanted you for a wife. I wanted you. I do want you. I told you we'd be together when the time was right. This is that time."

The ring felt cold as he pushed it onto her finger but warmed quickly beneath the press of his hand. This sudden claim of permanence was more upsetting to her than the thought of enduring him for the night.

"But it's not right," she wept miserably. "It will never be right for us. Skyler, please let me go."

"It's too late. I can't. I won't. You're mine, Savannah, and I promise someday you won't mind that so very much."

She started to shake her head in denial but he stilled it with fingers gliding deeply into her hair. His head dipped down, mouth finding hers even as she sought to evade him. His kiss was tender and persuasive, growing more confident at her slight response. He lifted her easily and lay down on the bed with her. Feeling his weight, she started to struggle fearfully but he overcame her complaint by deepening his kiss and supporting himself on his elbows so she wouldn't feel so threatened. She lay still and submissive until the gentle probing of his tongue made her turn away with a moan of objection.

"Don't, Skyler. Please. I don't want this."

"Yes, you do," he argued huskily. "Remember how it was on the beach? Let it be like that again."

"It can't be."

"Yes. Yes, it can. Stop fighting yourself and let me make you remember."

She surrendered reluctantly to his searing kisses, tasting the intoxicating desire of them as they scattered over her lips, face, and throat. Slowly, he parted her robe. His hand rested large and warm on her rapidly moving rib cage, remaining there until she grew used to it letting it slide up gradually to be filled with a soft, rounded breast. Again, he let it stay there while he kissed her lips. Her breath caught as his thumb rubbed over the delicate peak but soon resumed, light and fast and shivery. And when his mouth moved down to tease that tightening crest with gentle nibbles and swirls of his tongue, she gave up all pretense of not enjoying what he was doing to her. She let the denying tension flow from her with a shaky sound of wonderment. Unsteady hands rose to lay atop the fair, silvery hair, plying it mindlessly as sensations began to build in giddy spirals. She closed her eyes to let them carry her aloft, like that soaring sea gull, to a place she'd visited only once before. And she wanted him to take her higher.

When he returned to seek her lips, the sudden urgency of her reaction surprised him. And delighted him. Once the cold, angry barriers dropped between them, she was warm and sensuous in his arms, her sweet, avid little mouth tasting and exploring his with unashamed passion and curiosity. Her hands stroked

165

over the sleek satin of his shoulders and back, thrilling him with their shy, eager inexperience. She clutched him close while the firm, tempting tips of her breasts pressed up to his chest in undefined longing. That supple encouragement stiffened in rejection as his touch strayed down to the tops of her tightly clenched thighs.

"Don't," she whispered tremulously against the thundering pulse of his throat. "Don't do that to me again. You hurt me so."

He lifted up slightly so he could see her face, so pale and frightened. The eyes were deep midnight pools of pleading, beseeching some kindness from him. Tenderness for her surged up warm and encompassing, and he feared he would burst from loving her. He made his words as soft and gentle as his caress had been.

"I won't hurt you, Savannah. It's a part of loving I want to share with you and perhaps someday you'll want to share with me too. I'll make you ready for me this time so there'll be no hurt. I promise. I would never knowingly hurt you."

She looked long into the clear, crystal eyes, doubt registering in her own. Certain she would refuse him and unwilling to frighten her more, Skyler began to turn away. Her slender fingers brushed his cheeks, drawing him back down. Her kiss was desperate but determined, and he smiled against the press of her lips.

The heat of that kiss fanned the fires of passion. He let them burn hot and consuming for a long moment before attempting any advancement. This time, her thighs parted at his touch. Her lips trembled beneath his for a brief instant, then were still in slack amazement as he soothed her raw, bruised flesh with a gentle magic. The trembling returned but not from fear. Her insides felt hot and fluid, tingling, aching with a need so strong and sure she sobbed his name in awed and urgent longing. When he came to her that second time, there was an instant of pressure giving way to a spreading sense of fullness. And it felt so very right, so completing.

Mistaking the reason for her sudden tears, he asked worriedly, "Am I hurting you?"

Her eyes opened, all misty and dazed as a small dreamy smile played upon her lips. "No," she breathed against his mouth. Her plunging kiss conveyed that further, shocking his senses with the fiery probe of her tongue until the hard swell of desire began to pound in his temples.

He had wanted to be slow and gentle with her but her insistent fervor made that all but impossible. With the urging of her hips, his thrusts grew deep and powerful, sensations of hot and cold searing his mind with lust and love and a desperate need for her to share these shattering experiences. Her response spurred him on, prompting him with soft moans of pleasure and the enticing motion of her body.

It came upon her so unexpectedly she cried out, body arching with tension then falling limp and gloriously spent. Never had she felt such a concentration and binding of sensation before it had broken free in a scattering of heat and light and ecstatic shiverings. She was vaguely aware of Skyler's weight, heavy and still upon her, and of the scorching gasps of breath against her neck. Tentatively, she touched him, stroking the slick heat of his back up to the silken spun moonlight of his hair.

She turned her head, surprised to find his eyes open and intent on her. She let her fingertips run down the sharp line of his jaw, then over the prominent cheekbones. He turned slightly to kiss her palm but his eyes never wavered. Feeling suddenly awkward with him, she ducked her head into his shoulder. Smiling, he

167

rolled onto his side, pulling her close to him so their hearts beat as one.

Held so securely in his arms, Savannah closed her eyes to savor the heavy luxury of peace and contentment that settled upon her. She had been so long on edge, pushing herself to the limit of exhaustion day after day, that simple relaxation was a pampered dream and the languorous satisfaction he gave her like a blissful, calming drug. It felt so marvelous to surrender those nagging fears and worries even due to such an improbable source. Just to be held and loved unconditionally, undemandingly, was a tonic to her soul, and if nothing else, she could thank Skyler Reade for giving her a moment of self-indulgence. Her body ached and throbbed with delicious laziness. The sound she made when nuzzling his warm throat was a vibrating purr.

"Happy?" he asked quietly, brushing back the heavy wave of her hair.

"Umm," she murmured. "Very."

"I love you, Savannah. The only thing that could make this more perfect would be for you to tell me the same."

"Skyler, please," she whispered uncomfortably. "Don't spoil it."

He sighed into the tumbled curls. "All right," he agreed. He tipped her face up and kissed her. The gesture was so sweet with tenderness and so achingly personal that she drew away in confusion, hiding her face in the stronghold of his chest. His hand moved slowly atop her head, slipping through the glossy hair with long, lingering movements.

"Have you had many lovers, Skyler?" she asked with surprising directness. Startled, his hand stopped in midair then continued.

"No," he answered honestly. "Quite few actually. It's

168

not a frivolous matter to me and never has been. I have to care to want to give of myself."

She was silent for a moment, wondering why it was so important to know of those he'd been with before her. "And did you ever want to marry any of them?"

"No."

"And how do I compare?"

The testiness of that question made him chuckle. "It would be unfair to the others to rank them alongside you. I love you, Savannah. There is no comparison. I was just being disagreeable before."

"Why me? Why would you want me?" she asked in bewildered frustration.

"You—you make everything else so unimportant." He sighed in exasperation, struggling to find a way to explain how she had conquered him so completely. "I've never had much direction in my life, nothing I wanted to devote myself to until you held my hand and sat with me when I prayed I would die. You gave me reason to want to live. Just wanting to hear your voice made me fight to get through the hell of each day. I loved you before I even saw your face. I loved you for your strength and compassion, because you cared for me so selflessly. Your beauty was an added blessing. I've never felt so close to anyone as I felt to you in that stinking little room, and I knew I didn't want to lose that."

"But you did."

"No. I abused it but I don't believe I won't have it back. I'm too stubborn or maybe just too vain to believe that." His arms tightened but she didn't resist the embrace in this charmed hour of truce.

"What would it take for you to fall out of love with me?" she challenged quietly. Her hand absently rubbed the broad golden chest. He felt so good, so strong, so male.

"I don't know. I don't think you could ever hurt me that badly. Could you?" He raised her chin so she could meet his questing eyes.

"I don't know that either" was her simple reply.

"Do you hate me being here so very much?"

Smiling, she smoothed back a stray lock of blond hair, letting her fingers glide through the untidy strands to enjoy the feel of it slipping through her fingers. "Not tonight, at least. I needed you tonight, Skyler. I cannot promise you I ever will again."

He shrugged and smiled. "I'll take that risk."

She accepted the warm press of his lips without reservation and had no complaint as his hand began a slow caress down the length of her body.

And when, much later, they slept, it was curled together in an intimate tangle of arms and legs. Like lovers. Like man and wife.

170

Chapter Thirteen

He would never get used to the brightness of the Carolina sun. It seemed to penetrate his eyelids, indifferent to his desire for more sleep. With a grumble, he rolled away from the window, pushing off the covers that had somehow gotten over him.

Skyler opened his eyes in alarm to search the unfamiliar room, not certain where he was. But then he'd been too preoccupied to notice decor last night. Smiling to himself, he settled back on the pillows and let his gaze roam over the room. It spoke totally of Savannah.

Everything was in pleasing shades of pink, cream, and grey. It was feminine but not so much so that a man would feel unwelcomed. There was no abundance of lace or frills or flounce, Savannah's tastes more simple and practical. A hand-sewn quilt covered the tester bed. A wedding ring pattern, he noted with a smile. Sheer drapes hung at the windows and a few basic toiletries were neatly arranged on a bureau top. There was no dressing table to preen at, only a full-length cheval mirror. He raised a brow at his own image appearing there, long, well-proportioned, and naked amid a tangle of sheets. And quite alone. He regarded the signs of his virgin bride's initiation with a bittersweet remembrance. Thinking of her made the thought of lingering in bed by himself unappealing.

He dressed quickly, humming a cheerful tune, then went out into the hall to brace the Russell household. Rising Sun was a magnificent home from its upper floors of warm heart pine to its entrance of parquetry. Murals covered the walls of both upper and lower halls in a continuous hunt scene. Upstairs, there was a line of bedroom doors, and Skyler could imagine guests being asked to stay for weeks at a time to enjoy the splendid hospitality. He hoped his would last that long.

The freestanding staircase was made of deep mahogany, with elaborately turned balusters and gracefully sweeping handrails. Two elaborate parlors paved with squares of black and white marble faced each other across the hall, which ended at the dining room. He glanced briefly inside each, noting the identical fireplaces ornamented with large half-sun medallions. That carving was repeated above the arch of the doors and in each of the main rooms.

Supposing he would find the family gathered over breakfast, he proceeded to the dining room. Savannah sat with her back to him, with Hillary across the wide table. At the head of the table sat a delicate older woman.

"Good morning," he called softly, placing a hand on Savannah's shoulder. He couldn't miss the stiffening of her body.

Hillary straightened, all sunny smiles. "Why, Lieutenant Reade, what a surprise. Don't tell me you were the cause of all that commotion last night." She gave a naughty giggle, lowered eyes sweeping between him and her sister. She had puzzled over the mysteriously closed door and Savannah's flushed, edgy manner. Now she knew why. Her gaze swept down the tall, rugged Yankee, then drew up in surprise at the broad band on his finger. Married? But surely he hadn't been.

172

In bewilderment, she looked at her sister, seeing the slight wink of gold on her tightly clenched hand.

"Oh my," she cried in shock and delight, then skipped around the table to fling impulsive arms around Skyler's neck. Her kiss was hardly proper for a welcoming sister-in-law, falling warm and moist nearly full on his mouth.

"Hillary! Savannah? What is going on here?"

Laughing gaily, Hillary held up the large hand to display his ring. "Oh, Mama, look."

To clarify the matter before her mother's befuddled gaze, Savannah said emotionlessly, "Mama, this is Skyler Reade, my—my husband."

"A pleasure, ma'am," he began formally while untangling himself from Hillary's clutches.

Adelaide Russell rose slowly, eyes assessing the handsome, fair-headed young man. She came around the table to face him, the stranger who was now family. Small hands rested on his shoulders to bend him down so she could press a soft scented cheek to his rough one. "Welcome to our house," she said with a sincerity that made him flush.

"Thank you, ma'am."

As she seated herself again, she gave him a quizzing glance. "You've a peculiar accent, Mr. Reade. Are you perhaps from New England?"

"Pennsylvania, ma'am," he answered cautiously.

"My husband and I visited Newport one year. Beautiful country but a bit cold. Perhaps we'll go there when he returns." Her eyes took on that wistful glassiness.

Skyler gave Savannah a quick look of puzzlement. Seeing her distress, he said smoothly, "I think so too, ma'am. You'd be most welcome in my family's home should you decide to journey North."

He continued to stand a bit awkwardly behind

173

Savannah's chair until she made a motion with her hand. "Delilah, set another place for Mr. Reade. He'll be joining us for breakfast."

A slender black girl bustled in with a place setting of china, laying it out efficiently on Savannah's left. She couldn't keep her gaze from curiously gauging this Northerner who would join her mistress's table.

"When will you be rejoining your troops, Lieutenant?" Hillary asked sweetly. Her eyes were warm and subtly predatory.

"I chose not to renew my commission. I didn't think Savannah cared much for the color of my uniform."

Savannah frowned at the glib reply but Hillary cooed, "I think a man in uniform is so handsome."

"With any luck, you won't see any around here," he said with a dry smile.

"I'd have thought you'd want to go North to see your family and be among friends," Savannah suggested with frigid civility.

"Perhaps I will but I had more immediate family to see to first."

His eyes moved over her caressingly. Hers rebuffed him with a cold fury, her hand stirring sugar into her tea so vigorously most of it filled the saucer. She took a taste of it then wrinkled her nose, returning it to the saucer. When she stood, Skyler rose politely.

"The morning is going to waste and I have much to do," she announced tensely.

"You do way too much, child," her mother chided. "Perhaps Skyler will lessen that burden for you."

Her glance went to him cuttingly. "I don't think he'll be here that long. Please excuse me."

To her annoyance, Hillary followed her to her room. When she saw the unmade bed and its revealing stains, she gave a gleeful shout and danced about her glowering sister.

"Oh how wonderful," she exclaimed excitedly. "Was it fabulous? Was he a marvelous lover? Did you enjoy every minute of it? Don't be mean and stingy, Savannah. Please tell me."

"Yes, now will you go away," she growled irritably.

Hillary sank down on the foot of the bed, eyes alight and lips pouting. "I think I hate you and am terribly jealous. Such a positively gorgeous man. It must be heaven to be lost in those big strong arms." She hugged hers about herself in rapture. "And you married him. What fast work. How wonderfully romantic."

"Stop it, Hilly," she snapped. "No more of your drivel. I married him because I had to. He was our only means of escaping Beaufort and freeing Darcy. For no other reason, so don't go making any up. I don't care anything for Skyler Reade."

"Excuse me."

Savannah started guiltily at the low voice behind her. She whirled to face the cool grey eyes, wondering how long he'd been listening. Long enough from the twist of his lips.

"I didn't mean to interrupt but I seem to have lost my cufflink somewhere up here in the heat of the moment last night."

Blushing furiously, she searched the floor until she found the piece of gold beneath her discarded drawers. She thrust it at him, ignoring Hillary's smirk. He simply extended his wrist and waited patiently for her to fasten it with an angry, stabbing motion.

"Could you spare the time to show me about?" he asked hopefully.

"No" was her short reply. "I'm sure Hillary could give you a most enlightening tour. Wouldn't you, Hilly?"

"Oh, yes," she agreed quickly. "I'd be happy to."

175

Without waiting for his response, Savannah stalked from the room and retreated to the sanctity of her office. Try as she would, she couldn't keep her mind on the elusive figures, especially after seeing Skyler and Hillary strolling arm and arm along the rear porch. They were laughing together, fair heads bent close. Her eyes lingered over him, conjuring the image of him at her bedside, all golden and virile. Unconsciously, her breath had deepened with remembered passion.

With a disgusted snort, she shook her head to clear the nonsense from it. She was beginning to think like her sister. She forced her thoughts to return to the pages spread out before her with a fierce concentration. For the rest of the morning, her attention span was fractured at best, which added to her bad temper. A visit from Ben Tyree was the last thing she needed.

"You look mighty peeved there, Missy," he began from his lounging stance against the door frame. He turned his head to spit a huge wad of tobacco outside.

"I have cause, Mr. Tyree," she said crisply. She tossed her pen down on the blank page in aggravation.

"A pretty thing like yourself shouldn't have such worries."

Savannah frowned, tired of his crude overtures. He had been dropping poorly veiled hints for some weeks now. "If you have something on your mind, come out with it."

He advanced into the room with a rolling swagger. "It just don't seem natural, a right comely female like you doing a man's work when there's one around to take care of it."

"Darcy will take over when he's ready," she began in terse defense.

"I weren't talking about that useless piece of gentry. I meant a real man." His beefy hand lowered to touch a stray curl.

176

"You mean someone like you."

"I mean me. I could take care of all this busy stuff for you. It wouldn't be no problem. A lady like you wants for a man to look after her, to see to her business and other—umm—needs she might have. And iffen I was to move up to the house, I could see to all that right fine."

Savannah stared at him coolly, refined brow delicately arched. "I'm sure you would like to, but be assured that my needs are being very well met at the present time."

"What you need is a man."

"She has a man."

The low voice startled them both. Ben Tyree scowled darkly at the interruption but Savannah angered him by looking mildly amused.

"Mr. Tyree, my husband, Skyler Reade. Mr. Tyree is our overseer."

The silver-grey eyes narrowed lazily. "I appreciate your concern for my wife's well-being, but as she's told you, she's being well tended."

Ben Tyree recognized the threat in the smooth words. The tall, handsome Yankee wasn't bandying idle talk. He was staking property and the lady wasn't objecting. With a tight twist of his thick lips, he pushed past the new master of Rising Sun and stormed down to the slave quarters to relieve some of his frustration. And to think he had wasted a new shirt on the ungrateful wench.

With a relieved sigh, Savannah slumped back in her chair. "Why is it that every man who walks upright thinks he knows just what a woman needs? What conceit. Why can't they believe that not all women are helpless creatures who need to be looked after?"

Skyler touched her cheek with a long forefinger, eyes warm and admiring. "You are a very capable woman,

177

Savannah. You just don't have much sense some-times."

She slapped away his hand impatiently but couldn't help the pleasure his remark stirred. "I assure you, I do very well for myself, Mr. Reade."

"I'm sure you do, Mrs. Reade." He ignored her dark look. The silvery eyes droped meaningfully. "And do I meet all your needs, Savannah?"

She turned away, not favoring him with an answer. Her posture was stiff and unyielding. He viewed that straight back and graceful neck in appreciation.

"Well, you certainly met mine and I thank you."

She picked up her pen and tried to immerse herself in the work at hand, but all her senses were attuned to the big man who stood behind her. She jumped when his hands rested on her shoulders.

"You look tired, Savannah," he said kindly. The long fingers began to gently ply her knotted muscles. "You're not invulnerable, you know. It has to be difficult handling all this alone. Let me help you."

She twisted away from the soothing massage to glare up at him. "Oh, and you know so much about running a plantation, do you, a city-bred boy like you? You think you could be the master of these books?"

"The books are not what I want to be master of," he warned huskily. He pulled her to her feet with a quickness that allowed no reaction. When her mouth opened to register a complaint, his was upon it, sealing in her argument most effectively. Her fists flailed at him, then she was holding to those broad, sturdy shoulders with a sound of helplessness. She enjoyed the domination of his kiss, the way it weakened her will and frightened her with its power to confuse. Before she lost herself completely, she pushed away and turned so he couldn't gloat over the flush of longing in her expression.

Once her features were composed, she looked up at him proudly. "I need no master, sir, and if I did, it would not be you."

"Of course not," he replied with a grin. "You would select someone like Mr. Tyree and you could be lost in his big, strong arms."

His mimicry of Hillary coaxed a reluctant smile. "And how was your tour with my sister?"

Making himself comfortable on the corner of the massive desk, he chuckled softly, "Oh, very enlightening. She showed me all the highlights, the pond where she received her first kiss, the tree she carved the names of all her beaus. Not much bark left there. The gazebo where she heard her first proposal, the terrace where she had her coming-out party."

"You must have been intrigued," she said wryly.

"The best part was seeing the rail you pushed your first suitor over when he tried to kiss you and—"

"No more, please," she laughed. It was a light, musical sound, the first of pure enjoyment he had ever heard from her. "I'll strangle her for telling you that."

Their eyes met and for a moment they both experienced a warm communion of closeness. Then Savannah grew somber, remembering who she was, and the distance returned like a barren wasteland between them.

"When are you leaving, Lieutenant?"

"Leaving?"

"Returning North where you belong. Surely you don't plan to remain among your enemies." The chill of her glance told him he might be wise to consider her one.

"If I went North, would you go with me?"

She blinked incredulously. "No, of course I wouldn't. My home is here. I wouldn't leave it for you."

"Then I'll remain as well. You are my wife. Our home

179

is together. It doesn't matter to me where it is."

"Skyler, we have no marriage. I do not think of myself as your wife."

"Then what exactly were you last night?" He waited with raised brows while she blushed and searched for words. "Our vows are legal and became binding upon your bed. We have a marriage, Savannah, and I am not inclined to release you from it."

"You are odious," she groaned miserably. "If you cared for me as you claim, you wouldn't wish me in a position I find intolerable."

His eyes darkened to a smoky pewter. "Is it? Parts of it you seemed to enjoy well enough." He caught her hand deftly and held it in a firm, imprisoning grasp. She tried to wrest it from him, then gave up the struggle with an angry frown.

"It's lunchtime. Come up to the house with me. Your books can do without you for a time but I cannot."

He allowed her no argument, hauling her up from the chair and holding her hand in the crook of his elbow. She had no option but to walk beside him or be pulled along.

On the wide veranda, Jeffery lay waving his chubby arms contentedly next to Caroline's momentarily vacant chair. After peering curiously into the cradle, Skyler's face split with its broad grin as he scooped the infant up in large, gentle hands.

"Hello, little fellow. And who might you be?" he asked warmly. His spontaneous delight made Savannah look at him closely. Most men showed little interest in children other than their own.

Jeffery gave a gleeful squeal as he was swung up to such a great height. Those chortles turned to wails of fright when he was roughly snatched up and crushed to his mother's bosom.

Caroline Russell was flushed with maternal fury, eyes black and burning with hate. "What do you think you're doing? How dare you! Don't you ever touch my child. How could you think I'd let you put your blood-stained hands on my baby? You stay away from him, do you hear me?"

Breathing hard with upset and child protectively smothered in her arms, Caroline spun and ran into the house, leaving Skyler and Savannah staring after her.

Voice soft to cushion the fierceness of the other woman's attack, Savannah placed a light hand on Skyler's arm and said, "She had no reason to react like that."

The glassiness of shock finally leaving his eyes, he glanced at her briefly. His mouth twisted in a sad smile. "No, she had every reason. I shouldn't have intruded." He shifted slightly so her hand slid from him. "I don't expect her to love her enemy." Silently, he went into the house.

Savannah couldn't explain her feelings. Though she had treated him more harshly herself, Caroline's words filled her with anger and an odd protectiveness. She had hurt him with her cruel words and Savannah found she resented that. More strange was her wont to comfort him and his unwillingness to accept it. Unsettled by her own inconsistency, she followed him in to a strained and quiet meal.

Skyler's belongings arrived in a huge shipping wagon late that afternoon. In addition to his trunks of personal belongings, there were crates of impossibly priced or impossible-to-get items that had Hillary exclaiming like an excited child at Christmas time. There was flour, salt, refined sugar, smoked meats, writing paper, coffee, liquor, and a tin of chocolates that had his pretty sister-in-law in ecstasy. She and

Adelaide made much of his addition to the nearly depleted larder, all the fuss accepted with modest shrugs. The proceedings were watched by a suspicious Savannah and from the veranda by an obviously drunken Darcy. That was his usual state by dinner time, increasing his air of self-pity and cynicism.

"Trying to buy your way into the family, Yank?" he called out sneeringly in the heavily slurred voice.

Skyler turned a cool eye to him, brow lifted. "Not at all. I'm only seeing to my own comfort. You don't have to benefit from them if you choose not to. I won't be offended. I'm not making any gifts to you."

Darcy frowned petulantly, mind too slowed by perpetual drink to verbally spar with him. Instead, he grew nasty in his insults. "I think you're getting a mite too comfortable here. Your welcome has already been overstayed. Just because my sister momentarily lost her sense of loyalty doesn't mean we're going to bed down the enemy. You might as well pack all that back on the wagon and take your blue-clad butt with it. I run things here and I didn't ask you to stay."

Skyler still maintained a polite attitude but the grey of his eyes became crystalline ice. "I was under the impression that Savannah ran all the affairs." When Darcy flushed darkly, he continued frigidly. "She is my wife, and as long as she lives here, so will I. Unless of course you wish to turn her out. If so, you'd better be prepared to take on all the tasks she's been doing so you can wallow in your self-destructive revelry."

"Skyler, enough," Savannah interceded crisply, torn by the opposing sides. She wanted to protect her brother but was gratified by her husband's stance. She turned to the fuming drunkard who bore so little resemblance to the brother she had admired all her life and said indiscriminately, "Like it or not, I am married to him and he has a right to lodgings in my home. You don't have to welcome him but you might want to consider that without him you would still be locked in that prison having never seen your son. He didn't do it to gain your indebtedness, so you don't have to thank him, but he is going to stay as long as I allow it. I'll hear no more arguments."

Expression stiff with outrage, Darcy returned to the house and his bottle. With a heavy heart, Savannah turned to one of the house servants and instructed, "Take those things up to my room."

His presence officially established, Skyler sat at the dinner table to a fare richened by his generosity, but the atmosphere was subdued by the pointed absence of Darcy and his wife. That tension increased when Savannah followed him to their room as the late day's shadows lengthened into evening. She stood warily at the door while he opened his trunks and pushed her gowns aside to make room for his wardrobe. The intrusion of his personal effects into the privacy of her room was as disturbing as he was. They mingled with her things to form an intimate link. His choice of attire was substantial, varied, and richly fashionable. Seeing the expensive assortment, she wondered about his circumstance. He had said little about his financial standings nor had her pride succumbed to curiosity enough to ask. Her brows lowered as he tucked several small bottles away in a dresser drawer. Laudanum?

Her puzzlement was diverted when he extended a package to her.

"Some things for the baby I asked my sister-in-law to send down. Maybe she would take them from you," he explained with a quiet awkwardness.

Taking the parcel, she said his name softly.

"No, don't apologize for her or your brother," he

interrupted. "They've a right to their hatred."

Feeling the stirrings of deep sympathy, Savannah followed him out onto the gallery. Looking up at his strong profile against the blooming stars, they could have been back in Nassau.

"They're not going to accept you," she told him as kindly as she could. "To them you represent all the hurt and loneliness they've suffered. Darcy wasn't always like this. He used to be full of life and fun until—"

"Until the Yankees crippled more than just his leg," he finished astutely. "And your mother? Do they blame me for that as well?"

"You're an outsider. You don't belong here. Can't you see that? It will only get worse."

Ignoring her observation, he asked, "What's the baby's name?"

"Jeffery."

He smiled a wistful, faraway smile. "My brother has three children. Seeing that little boy made me think of how much they must have grown since I last saw them. Do you like children, Savannah?"

His intense gaze made her wary. "Yes, I do."

"Good. I want us to have lots of them. I want you to be the mother of my children. I want us to have a big family with lots of love and happiness." He took up her hands and pressed them to either side of his face. Firmly, she pulled away.

"You want too much," she told him bluntly and returned inside. When he remained out on the balcony, she took advantage of his absence to quickly slip into her faded nightdress and burrow beneath the covers. Lying with her back to the windows, she forced her breath to be steady when she heard him come in and latch the doors. That breath stopped when he blew out the light. Every muscle in her body stiffened when the bed dipped beneath his weight. After a few moments of rigid tension, she heard him say softly, "Good night."

It was some time later, when his breathing had grown deep and even, that she realized he intended to remain on his side of the bed, choosing sleep over the battle for her favors. With a sigh of odd disappointment, she let herself search for slumber.

Chapter Fourteen

After spending the night in restless agitation, Savannah slept in much later than was her custom. Finding Skyler up and already gone puzzled her, but finding him nowhere in the house, she became uneasy. She approached Tyree with some reluctance when she saw him loitering around her office.

"Have you seen Mr. Reade this morning?" She couldn't bring herself to call him her husband.

"He was poking around in the office for some time, then got his horse. Heard he asked directions to Columbia."

Frowning, she swept past him into the paneled room. Everything was neatly arranged and looked suspiciously untouched, but knowing he had been there plagued her throughout the day.

It took several hours to get to Columbia, but when Skyler hadn't returned by early evening, Savannah's annoyance with him took a subtle twist to gnawing worry. He was a Northerner and a stranger. Even if he weren't in uniform, his accent alone could force him into harm's way. When he strode in unconcerned and laden with packages, her anxiety sharpened her tongue like a honed blade.

"Where have you been? Don't you know how dangerous it is in the city for you? What madness would make you risk your foolish life to go there? These roads aren't safe after dark even for those of us who've lived here all our lives."

Skyler simply grinned at her, his tone mocking her concern. "If I'd known you'd miss me so, I would have waited until you decided to rouse your lazy bones this morning." Realizing her stony stare was the only answer he would receive, he handed all the parcels but one to Delilah. Holding a large bandbox by the ribbons, he asked, "Is Hillary somewhere about?"

Like an actress waiting in the wings for her cue, the pert blonde waltzed into the hall, dimpling flirtingly. "Were you looking for me, Skyler?" When her eyes fell on the box, they grew round as blue marbles. "Is that for me?"

"It would look rather ridiculous on my head," he teased.

She snatched it from him with a greedy delight. Savannah gave a sharp hiss of recognition as she drew out the hat that had caused such trouble between them. She tied the frilly confection atop her fair curls and pirouetted on tiptoe.

"How do I look?" she asked him coquettishly.

"Beautiful, but I'm not the first to tell you that," he laughed, eyes warm and pleased.

"Thank you, Skyler. You are so sweet," she declared. She hugged him dramatically and showered his smiling face with kisses. "Wait until Mama sees me."

She scurried off in a rustle of taffeta, leaving Skyler to face her scowling sister.

"I got something for you, too. Are you going to be as grateful?" he cajoled expectantly.

"It takes more than a silly hat to placate me, Skyler Reade," she told him sternly.

"I'm sure it does," he mused, then took a bulky packet from inside his coat. "Maybe this will earn me at

188

least a smile."

She took it gingerly, and under his expectant gaze, opened the ties. There was no change in her expression as she scanned the contents. He didn't expect the same exuberant display he'd gotten from Hillary but hadn't planned on the fury in her eyes when they lifted. Without a word, she flung the papers in his surprised face and ran up to her room.

"Savannah, what's wrong?" he asked in bewilderment, shutting the door to insure their privacy. "I thought you'd be pleased."

"Is that what you thought?" she railed at him. "I have sweated blood to put food on our table and to keep the creditors at bay, and you stroll in with a snap of your fingers and pay off every one of our debts. How dare you do such a thing! This is my home, my responsibility. Did it ever occur to you that you were making a mockery of everything I've worked so hard to do? You flash your Yankee greenbacks and have everything at your feet. Did you think these slips of paper would buy my affection?"

"No. I just wanted to make things a little easier for you. I wanted you to be able to take a few hours away from those books to spend on yourself. I wanted you to be able to use the money from your crops to buy something nice for yourself because I knew you wouldn't take anything from me. Savannah, I just wanted to help you."

"I didn't ask you to. I don't want your help or need your patronizing. I can take care of my own affairs. I don't need to waste money on the frilly things Hillary dotes on."

"Why not? Are you afraid of looking like a woman?" He intercepted her slap and continued, holding her hand in check. "Are you afraid that if you looked like a female no one would take you seriously? You don't have to prove yourself to me or anyone here. There's nothing wrong with needing help, only in not knowing how to ask for it."

"But I don't. I was doing just fine by myself. I don't need your charity. And I don't want your interference. You have no right. I can take care of everything myself. There is nothing I need you for."

He observed her flushed face and fierce combative stance, then pulled her close, securing her with an arm behind her back. "You're wrong, Savannah. I will not interfere with your business affairs again, but there is something you need me for, something you can't do alone."

"What?" she demanded hotly.

"Make your own babies."

His kiss was sudden and powerful, bending her back over his arm while his mouth slanted over hers. For a moment she almost submitted, then with an angry mutter began to twist in an attempt to wriggle free. He suppressed her struggles easily and swept her up to bear her to the bed. Her circle of hoops and layers of petticoats conspired against her, trapping her in an awkward tangle.

"Save your fight for a battle you can win, my fiery little Rebel. This one is lost to you already. I'm going to make love to you, Savannah. You might as well surrender gracefully."

She lay still, panting with the force of her fury. There was no sign of weakening in the depthless blue eyes. "How can you call it making love when you know I hate you?"

"As I told you before, your hate doesn't bother me," he told her with a grin.

"I never surrender. I may have to concede but I never give up and I'll never be willing in your bed. Doesn't it bother your pride to take your own wife by force?"

Her goading jeer had no effect. His weight shifted slightly so he was partially above her, chest heavy on the fullness of her breasts in their constraining corset. It was far from comfortable and impossible to move.

"If not willing, I must have held some other eager creature in my arms the other night." Her groan of outrage produced a soft laugh, gentle and teasing in the face of her anger. "I don't think I'll ever have to use force, do you? I would never hurt you, Savannah, and you'll never intimidate me with your claim of hatred. I know better and so will you. You're too passionate to deny me for long. Now, I want these clothes off you. Are you going to do it or do you want me to?"

"I'll do it. Get off me," she ground out through clenched teeth.

He sat back to give her room enough to manipulate the fastenings of her plain gown but not enough to attempt anything as foolhardy as trying to escape him. Under his amused glance, she began to divest her clothing, movements jerky and defiant, until she sat before him in her brief underthings. The teasing light had gone out of his eyes by then, leaving them smoky and dark.

He caught her hands as they pushed at the straps of her chemise, preferring to remove it himself. She couldn't control a gasp at the feel of his hot mouth as it tasted the sweet bounty of her bosom. Hands on her satiny shoulders, he laid her gently back on the coverlet.

Savannah squeezed her eyes shut, the battle now with herself and the traitorous weakness that urged her to clasp the fair head close and beg for the pleasure he held for her. She tried to concentrate on her hate, on the rocket trail of his betrayal, but her resolve trembled as his lips nibbled down to her trim waist, tongue laving wetly over the quivering plane of her belly. Her fingers

191

clenched in the sheets so they wouldn't seek him out. She bit her lips to keep them from moaning his name. The exquisite torture ended and his mouth came up to move upon her narrow resisting lips. When he couldn't persuade her to soften them to him, his kisses branded a circle about her throat. His hands joined in the assault on her will by gliding over her supple flesh, gently plying and encouraging the response she would deny him.

Try as she would, Savannah couldn't stave off the insistent waves of sensation stirred by his relentless touch. Her hands rose to grip his strong shoulders, her body pressing up against his hands with an ache of need. And when he ceased his subtle attack, she moaned in frustration, distressed by her frailty and more so that he had stopped without fulfilling the urgent desires he had kindled.

"Now can you tell me that you don't want me? Tell me you want me to stop and I will. You have only to tell me you want no part of what I've started. Can you do that, Savannah?"

"You know I can't," she panted, a simmer of hate and passion. The smug confidence in his sultry eyes made her emotions take a bitter turn. "You're stronger. I cannot fight you. I'm bound to you legally, so I cannot flee you. You have weakened my body, but want and love are not the same thing. You can make me want you but you cannot make me love you. I will never love you."

"For now I am content with the wanting."

His kiss was deep and possessing. Only the discomfort from the chill of his coat buttons made her rebel.

"You're scratching me," she complained irritably, temper still not subdued by her desires. "Take off your jacket."

He sat back, eyes teasing and warm. "You take it

off," he challenged boldly.

Scowling at him, she tugged the dark coat from him, sending it flying across the room.

"And the rest," he prompted with a raise of his brows.

She jerked his shirt free of his trousers, then gripping either side of his collar, gave a fierce pull. Shirt studs and buttons scattered across the bed and floor as the garment separated down the front. With a lusty rumble, Skyler crushed her up against him. His mouth plummeted down to seize her startled lips with a hungry fervor. Her resistance collapsed beneath that blazing onslaught and she returned the kiss with equal intensity. Her palms moved restlessly over the warm golden chest, the feel of rapid thunder beneath them only building her excitement.

The sound of breaking glass brought them apart. Without a backward glance, Skyler was off the bed, pistol freed from the holster beneath it.

"Stay here," he ordered, already rushing to the door.

The front yard was cast in eerie shadows and light from a dozen torches. Stepping onto the veranda, Skyler recognized some of the illuminated faces as men he had seen in Columbia. Even the banker who had smiled while taking his money was among them, only he wasn't smiling now. The light glinted off the barrels of shotguns and rifles.

"We've come for you, Yankee," called an angry voice. "We don't much care for the likes of you in our heartland. Aiken convinced us to warn you first, but most of us are for shooting you down where you stand. You got five minutes to get your things or we'll take you without them."

There was a swish of fabric as Savannah came to stand before the half-dressed man. She wore a softly feminine robe but the rifle in her hands was as deadly as

193

her stare.

"Jamie, Abner, Mr. Aiken, Mr. Thompkins, what brings you out calling at this time of night?" Her voice was cheery and light but became deadly serious when she hissed behind her, "Skyler, go back inside."

"This ain't no social call, Miss Savannah."

She smiled prettily at the mob, all the while easing backward, using her body to try to push Skyler out of danger. "Why you all had me scared nearly senseless. I thought we were being set on by a passel of Yankees."

That brought a couple of uneasy chuckles but a loud voice cried out, "The only Yankee here is the one you're protecting. Step aside, Missy. You've no part in this."

"No part?" She laughed with forced gaiety. "Why, Tom Lester, this man is my lawful husband. True, he's from the North, but he's no Yankee soldier. You all know better than to think I'd hide one of those filthy swine in my house after what they've done to my family."

"It's one and the same, Savannah, and we mean to have him."

Their forward movement was cut short as the rifle she cradled took a more defensive pose. "Now if you boys think you're going to just waltz up here and snatch my husband out of my bed, you are sadly mistaken. I'm already mad enough at what you interrupted to pepper the lot of you."

There were some muffled laughs but the mood of the group was still hostile. Sensing they would not be easily swayed, Skyler stepped from behind Savannah, ignoring the clutch of her hand, to face them. The flickering torch light turned his hair and eyes to silver and his bare chest to bronze.

"This is not my fight, gentlemen," he claimed earnestly. "It's not my war any longer. I've made my home here with my wife and I just want to live it in peace. I'll take arms against you if you threaten her or her family, but not in the name of something I don't believe in." There was a startled mutter as he tossed his revolver down at the foot of the steps. His hands spread wide. "I just want to hold onto what's mine, not tamper with what's yours."

More discussion murmured between the men. Taking advantage of their indecision, Savannah stood at Skyler's side, looking courageous and beautiful in the artificial light. That as much as her argument changed their minds.

"You all know me and know where I stand. I give you my word as a citizen of the South that he will be my responsibility and that I will see he remains neutral. If I find he's betraying that trust, I'll give him to you myself." She spoke so vehemently that Skyler gave her a quick look.

Without waiting for their reply, Savannah took Skyler's arm and led him into the house with her. His back prickled anxiously, but by the time they closed the door, most of the men had turned to their horses. He leaned against the door, expelling his breath noisily.

"Tossing that gun out was like standing there naked," he confided to a silent Savannah. "Thank you."

She said nothing, her eyes going past him to where Darcy lounged against one of the windowsills, a bottle in his hand instead of a gun.

"I appreciate your support," she snapped acidly.

"I'm not risking my life for him. I would have let them have him," he told her bluntly. "Take him and good riddance."

"Instead of your drunken contempt, you should be thankful he didn't feel the same about you." She turned on her heel and ran up the sweeping stairs in a flurry of robe and bare legs. She brushed by a pale Hillary without a word. Skyler followed, ignoring his sister-in-law's upset features and her plea for him to tell her what was going on.

When Skyler touched her shoulder, she turned into his arms to hold to him tightly. She couldn't control her shivering, mind full of images of Beaufort.

"It's all right. It's over," he soothed. "They're gone."

"But for how long?" she cried. She wrenched free to look up at him. Her eyes were large and fearful. "Skyler, you have to promise if there is any threat to my family, you'll leave here. You have to promise me you won't put them in any danger. Promise—"

His large hand stole behind her head, bringing her mouth to his with a bruising force. The robe slithered to the floor with a sigh to echo her own. He took her down to the bed with a tender savagery. His demanding claim on her body made her cry out in helpless want, the soft sounds asking him to chase away the fears of the night with his loving. And he did, wonderfully so, until the power of their mutual pleasure made the world apart from them cease to exist.

As they lay together in drowsy satisfaction, Savannah looked at his forceful profile, admiring him while his eyes were closed and he couldn't see her. He was so handsome. When under the spell of his passion it was difficult to remember exactly why she tried so hard to hold herself from him. No man had ever loved her so totally, so consumingly. She couldn't help but be moved by the tenderness of his touch, the persuasion of his mouth, or the devotion in his eyes. It would be so easy to love him. But the euphoria of their moment together would soon ebb to the distrust and doubt and bitterness of a past she could not dismiss. But perhaps she could.

The lazy grey eyes turned to her when she said his

name softly.

"Skyler, you arranged for Darcy's freedom. Could you do the same for my uncle?"

The softness of his expression was gone. "No" was his flat reply.

"But why? Skyler, can't you do this for me?"

"No, Savannah. No, I won't," he told her with a firm finality. "The man deserves to be where he is. He's no better than a pirate and he betrayed your trust. I won't help free him."

She rolled away from him but not before he saw the hurt and unforgiving coldness in her eyes. When he touched her shoulder, she flinched away, pulling the covers up in a defensive barrier. He withdrew his hand with an unhappy frown, sensing he had missed something very important.

Whether they liked it or not, as the weeks became months, Skyler Reade became a member of the Russell household. Caroline and occasionally Darcy found their way back to the dinner table, the initial tension becoming a grudging hostility. Skyler took their pointed commentary on the Confederate victory at Chickamauga and their general contempt for the inferiority of the North's military leaders. Little news of any of the Federal accomplishments reached them. All stories of the shifting battlefield were colored a conspicuous grey.

Skyler was true to his word not to intrude in the running of Rising Sun. He left Savannah to her books and spent his days in Hillary's or Adelaide's company, but the nights he claimed. He endured his wife's avoidance during the day but in the privacy of their room he demanded her attention. Though the physical side of their marriage was frequent and vigorous and well-enjoyed by them both, Savannah never relaxed her unwilling pose. What ended in mutual satisfaction always began as a clash of wills. She never once surrendered to him without a fight. Each night was approached as a new battle, waged valiantly even though the outcome was assured. She never let him think her compliance would last more than the moment and he never took her submission for granted. Though frustrated by it, her resolve impressed him and, contrary to her wishes, made him care for her all the more. He lived for those few minutes in the aftermath of their loving when she would lay contented in his arms, talking quietly with him as lovers did, recognizing he had won the night and able to bear it without bitterness. His one regret was he never woke to find her beside him, the sheets always cool and empty. And when they met, her expression gave no hint of the pleasures they had found. The wall was reinforced between them by her cool determination, leaving him to hope one day she would not have the strength or inclination to rebuild it.

While he idled away the days, Skyler became fascinated by the institution of slavery. In spite of Tyree's grumblings, he rode out to inspect the cotton harvest, watching the mechanical black machine move through the fields with untiring precision. The workers weren't sure what to make of his forthright overtures, shying away from his direct curiosity and crisp, rapid speech. His questions often granted him blank stares but the occasional answer confused him even more.

He never voiced an objection to the unnatural servitude until he came upon an enraged Hillary lashing a cowering Sally with a leather belt. When he caught her wrist, the blue eyes flashed up in bright fury, only to dissolve into her typical flirtation.

"Why, Skyler, I didn't know you were there," she cooed, shooting the whimpering girl a sharp look.

"I'm sure you didn't," he replied coolly. He pried the strap from her. "Why don't you go downstairs and let me finish here."

She hesitated, then with a forced smile did as she was told. By this time, she was sure she was madly in love with her sister's husband and didn't want to fall from his favor.

Tossing aside the belt with distaste, Skyler knelt down beside the trembling girl. He touched one of the welling stripes that rose up on the unprotected arm. Sally cringed away, eyes rolling whitely until he realized she was more afraid of him than of her angry mistress.

"I'm not going to hurt you, Sally," he assured her softly. "I just want to make sure you're all right."

"I's just fine, Missa Sky. Missy Hillary didn't hurt me none."

Skyler repressed a frown, for the welts said different. "What did you do to deserve this punishment?"

The dark head hung in shame. "I was mightly bad. Miss Hilly was right to whoop me."

"What did you do?"

"I done laid out the wrong dress for her. I's so stupid. I should a knowed she wouldn't want the taffeta on a day like this. It were my fault, Missa Sky. Cain I go now please?"

He stood with a nod and the girl scurried away to put the offensive garment back and see to the proper replacement. He was still musing over her complacent acceptance of the brutal treatment when he found Hillary in the parlor. She was quick to try and placate him with pat excuses. Sally was lazy and needed

199

occasional guidance to improve her attitude. She didn't really mind, Hillary assured him with a blameless smile. They were just simple children who needed a firm hand. Skyler said nothing but the incident stayed in his mind.

Even the suspicious field hands warmed to Skyler after they heard of his intercession in Sally's beating. The housemaids were shy and giggling around the tall, fair Yankee once convinced he had no ulterior motives to his teasing. The tiny dark children always dogged his heels in hopes of treats that he smuggled from the house for them. The men began talking more freely and ventured to ask him about the North. They saw him as strange and different but not threatening, and responded to his friendliness with wary smiles. Unless Ben Tyree was around.

Savannah's acceptance of slavery bothered Skyler. Though she had no personal maid, she took their service for granted, something he was more and more reluctant to do. And she condoned Tyree's bullying. It didn't make any sense to him, knowing what a tender heart she had. He couldn't quite believe she saw them as subhuman chattels. At least he didn't want to. Seeing his place as an outsider in the Southern home, he was careful not to overstep his bounds by making unwelcomed observations or criticisms. He knew Savannah tolerated him reluctantly and didn't want to jeopardize his position by challenging something he didn't quite understand. If she was forced to choose between him and her way of life, he was certain he would be shown the road. So he walked a tentative path until he was thrust into making a stand on the subject.

One of the house girls approached him with huge, frightened eyes. He didn't know her name but he had seen her often near the kitchen. Her panic and indecision battled as he waited for her to speak, then in a teary rush, she blurted, "Please Missa Sky. I knows you be a good man. Cain you help my Caleb? Missa Tyree be beating him something fierce. He been sick. He ain't lazy. Please Missa Sky. I be afraid he gonna kill him."

Chapter Fifteen

Ben Tyree was a fierce, angry man. With no accomplishments of his own, he relied on his meanness to give him a sense of worth and power. He had no compunction about using the lash to encourage respect or, better yet, fear. To him, the dark workers were beasts of burden to be driven firmly. His white skin gave him the authority to do whatever he pleased in the black community and he thrived on that superiority. The only threat to his reign was the sharp-eyed Yankee. He was careful to keep his more unsavory dealings quiet, but when Skyler Reade interfered with him, it was a threat to his standing and he struck out viciously to protect himself.

He turned on Skyler fiercely when his arm was gripped in a viselike hold. The downward stroke of his heavy rod was stilled in midair.

"That's enough, Tyree," the Yankee said harshly, an order before all the wide-eyed field hands.

"Git your nose out of this, Yankee. It's none of your business," he snarled. He tried to pull free but the grip was like iron.

"It is now. Drop that switch."

When Tyree's arm began to fall, Skyler relaxed his hold. He never saw the quick upstroke that caught him across the temple, felling him in a stunned whirl of blackness. Tyree was instantly atop him, jerking his arm up behind his back and forcing his face into the newly turned soil.

"Don't you ever come out here with your high and mighty ways a preaching and a socializing with the nigras. We don't need that kind of trouble. Do you hear me?"

With a supreme effort, Skyler tossed himself on one side, upsetting the weight on his back. He rolled and scrambled, outstretched hand seizing the heavy staff and ramming the end of it into the paunchy middle of his opponent. He straddled the barrel chest, barring the switch across the thick neck until Tyree's eyes bulged.

"Skyler, let him up."

There was no concealing his surprise at the sharp crack of Savannah's voice. She sat on the back of her yellow horse, expression as severe as a cold winter.

"I said let him up."

Slowly, Skyler obeyed, head ringing and too muddled to comprehend her anger at him. He stared up at her blankly, awaiting some explanation for her fury. When it came it dazed him even more.

"Get on your horse and get back to the house. You have no right to interfere in how things are done."

"But, Savannah, he was—"

"I don't want to hear it. That's why I pay Mr. Tyree to take care of things. Let him do his job and stop meddling in things you don't understand."

"I understand cruelty," he argued. He was shocked by her indifference to the man who had crawled off with the aid of his wife. She seemed so distant and heartless, and it scared him to see that in her.

"Your ways are not ours. I won't have you interfering with Mr. Tyree again. He doesn't have to answer to you. Do you hear me, Skyler?"

"And just who the hell do you answer to?" he

204

challenged coldly. Their eyes fenced briefly, then Skyler swung up on his horse and kicked it into a hasty gallop.

Savannah looked after him, expression still stony, and said to the amazed Tyree, "Carry on with things, Ben. Forgive my husband. He doesn't understand. If he bothers you again, let me know. I'll deal with him."

"Yes, ma'am," the overseer muttered, thanking his luck for whatever quirk had made her take his side.

Savannah rode back to the house more slowly, spirit dashed within her by the look on Skyler's face. What must he think of her? What kind of perverse monster did he see? The disbelief and hurt in his eyes haunted her. How could she make him understand that the ways they had to employ weren't her ways. She hated them. She hated Ben Tyree but she needed him as much as she needed the institution he preyed upon. The cruelty of it sickened her as much as it did him. Ben Tyree, whatever his methods, was the man who kept the workers in the fields when neighboring plantations were being deserted. If Skyler weakened his hold of fear over them, they would be lost. If only she could make him understand.

Skyler made no appearance at dinner. When darkness came, Savannah finally donned a nightdress and waited by the cooling air of the window. She dreaded their meeting yet worried over its delay. She left the lamp off because she didn't want to see her reflection in the glass, afraid of seeing what Skyler saw there.

It was late when he finally arrived. He cursed low and meaningfully as he stumbled over a chair and the edge of the bed.

"Skyler?"

"Were you expecting someone else?"

The belligerent tone made her frown. Was he that

angry. She crossed the room to light the lamp but he intercepted her, hands rough and hurting on her upper arms. The smell was immediate and overwhelming.

"You are drunk," she accused distastefully. "Let me go."

"You don't give orders in this room. Drunk or sober, what does it matter to you? It's not as though you'd welcome me either way."

"Skyler, you're hurting me. Let go."

"I'm hurting you? Bruising that pure, snow-white flesh? Should I care? Should I care more than you did about that man in the field?" She was glad she couldn't see his face for his voice was hard enough to bear.

"Skyler, you don't—"

"Understand? What's there to understand? Simple human decency? Or don't you think of them as human? Is that how you do it? Tell me. I want to know. Is that how you sleep nights?"

"Please. Let's talk of this in the morning when you're more rational," she urged. His fingers were cutting into her arms.

"I don't want to be rational and I don't want to listen to how you explain away the vileness of what you are. I love you, Savannah, but by God, I don't like you much right now."

"Skyler—"

His hard kiss sealed off her words, forcing them back with the unfamiliar discomfort his gesture caused. He swung her around so she struck the wall and pinned her there. He forced her lips apart with the thrust of his tongue. She gaged at the harsh intrusion and began to fight him in earnest, out of fear. When his hand rose to squeeze her breast, she twisted enough to free a hand and slapped him with all her strength. He seized her wrist and jerked it up behind her back so she was pressed closer.

206

"That's how you people deal with everything, isn't it? You'd probably enjoy having your friend Tyree put a few dozen notches in my back like he does to the field hands. Is that what you think it will take to put me in my place?"

"Damn you, let me go. How dare you treat me like this?" she spat, outrage overweighing her fright.

"Oh, I dare. Your laws give me as much right over you as Tyree has over those unfortunates in the field. I can do anything to you I like. As my wife, you are my slave. Would you have me treat you the same way Tyree does the poor, terrified women out in those cabins? Would you like to feel as helpless as they do? Maybe I should show you what it's like to be violated and have no say in it."

She was shivering in fury and fear but her words were bold. "I do know. I know how they feel every time you come to me in the night."

He called her a vicious name, then kissed her with a violence that drew blood—his or hers, he didn't know. All he knew was his want to drive the fire and rebellion from her, to silence the cutting power of her words to wound him. But when he felt her tears, his touch gentled and his kisses scattered over her face, foul, clumsy, and apologetic. He had frightened her badly and she was in no mood to accept his tenderness now.

"Just take what you want and leave me alone," she bit out tightly.

"What I want?" he echoed, staring at the shadow of her face in frustration. "Do you think this is what I want, to be forever raping my own wife?" He was panting hard, giving his voice a breathless quality of despair. "What I want is for you to come to me. I want you to kiss me. I want you to hold me. I want you to tell me that you love me, that you care about me, that you want a future with me. Is that so much? Can't you give me any of those things? Can't you spare me the slightest smile or the simplest touch?"

She remained rigid in his arms, her breath a soft hiss in the sudden silence.

"Have it your way then," he growled. "Keep your frigid, rebel bed. If you want me, you'll have to come to me. I'm tired of the fighting. I hope that pleases you."

He shoved her away with an abruptness that made her stumble. By the time she'd recovered, he was gone. She stood, panting and hugging her arms about herself, for a long moment. How badly she must have upset him to provoke such a reaction. How he must despise her in the role of slave abuser. His anger was unfair and unjustified. She had to find him and explain that to him. She knew she'd have no rest until she righted that picture he held of her. In sudden determination, she pulled on a robe and hurried down the stairs.

The main floor was completely dark. She glanced quickly into each room, pausing when she heard the harsh, uneven rasp of his breathing. He was lying on the sofa in the parlor, knees drawn up to his chest while he moaned softly to himself. With an exasperated sigh, she started to withdraw, to leave him to the misery of his drunkenness, when the desperation of his plea stilled her.

"Savannah, help me."

Lighting a lamp, she came to kneel beside him, asking worriedly what was wrong. It was some time before he could answer. His teeth were tightly clenched, flushed face all jutting angles from the tension in his jaw. Sweat glistened on his brow. Between the gulping breaths, he managed to force a choppy sentence.

"My arm . . . I can't bear it . . . Savannah, please . . . help me . . . stop the pain." His arm was hugged to his chest, fingers gnarled in an odd fist. Frowning, she put

208

a hand to his cheek. It was cold and wet.

"Skyler, I'll be right back."

The glazed eyes rose in alarm. "Don't leave me," he panted brokenly.

"I'll be right back," she soothed.

"It hurts, Savannah," he moaned, eyes closing tightly.

"I know it does." She brushed back the sticky hair in a tender gesture. "Hold on for me. I can make it better."

He nodded jerkily, head rolling away in a fog of agony.

Savannah ran up to their room and returned with a bottle of laudanum. She uncorked the top and reached for a glass to measure it into. He snatched it from her hand and tipped it up for a long, deep swallow. Shivering helplessly, he lay back, praying for a quick release into oblivion. Seconds seemed like hours of excruciating waiting. He clung to the awareness of her gentle voice but the words were lost to him. Then, thankfully, it began to ease and his body lost its tension inch by inch.

"Oh, Skyler, why didn't you tell me what the laudanum was for? How long has this been happening?"

"Just once in a while. Nothing to worry about. Be fine in morning." His words began to slow and slur as his eyelids drooped heavily. "Didn't mean to upset you before. I just love you so much."

"Can you get up? Do you think you can make it upstairs?"

"Sure."

She lifted him into a sitting position. His head fell back, lolling on a boneless neck. Carefully, she eased him back and draped her robe over him. When she bent to kiss his damp brow, he mumbled and shifted, pull-

209

ing the robe under his chin.

"Don't, Rhea," he muttered thickly. "Too tired. Let me sleep."

Savannah sat back on her heels so fast she nearly toppled. A stab of jealous hurt lanced through her heart. Rhea? One of his past loves? A special one that he would call her name at such a time. She wanted to question him, but the opiate held him in its smothering embrace where he would lull away the hours until dawn.

Skyler woke with a groan, legs cramped from the unaccommodating sofa and arm aching dully. His head was the worst, throbbing and humming with the aftereffects of the drug. He sat up slowly, Savannah's robe still about his shoulders. Seeing it, he smiled with the fuzzy remembrance of her concern.

"Delilah," he called hoarsely as the girl passed the door. "Some coffee please."

When she returned with the silver service, she responded to his question by saying Savannah had been up for some hours, leaving orders that he not be disturbed. Gauging his unsteady state, she poured for him, nodding at his thanks.

"Can you sit and talk with me for a minute?"

She looked startled at his request, eyes flashing to the door. "What you want to talk about, Missa Sky?"

"Please sit. It makes my head hurt to look up."

She sat gingerly on the edge of the chair, nervous and wary, not of him but of those who might overhear. She, like the other house servants, liked the talkative Northerner but there were other things to be considered.

Skyler looked more awkward, fidgeting with his cup until the coffee sloshed over the edge, burning his hand. He sucked on it, then asked bluntly, "Is Savannah good to you? I mean, does she treat you well? Does she

210

ever—umm—ever strike you or the others?"

He looked so uncomfortable with the questions that she chuckled softly. "Miss Vannah? Gracious no. That child be the soul of kindness. I never seed her lay a hand on anyone or order it be done, not like the other one."

Hillary, of course. Skyler nodded in understanding.

"There ain't a one in this here house that doan love Miss Vannah."

That proclamation brought confusion to his expression. "How can you say that when she holds you in bondage? How can you love your keeper?"

"Missa Sky, you doan know the Missus a tall. No sir. I's free because of her. You didn't know that? Dat's right. A lot of us folks here in the house be free. Ever since she be a little one, she been a arguing with her daddy about holding slaves. Course he wouldn't hear of it and there was nothing she could do. Then one Christmas she be asked what gift she wanted and she say all solemn like that she wanted the papers of one of us. The Massa he fussed and fumed but he gave in to her, and every year since, one of us be granted our freedom cuz that's the only gift she'd have."

He stared into his coffee cup for a long while, then said, "Thank you, Delilah."

The dark blue eyes rose from the sheaf of paper, registering surprise but not displeasure. "Skyler," she said quietly. "How's your arm?"

He flexed his fingers for her. "Fine. Thank you for seeing to me."

She gave a squeak of surprise as he lifted her from her chair to plant a firm kiss on her lips. She didn't resist nor did she respond until his mouth gentled, caressing hers with a sweetness that broke her will. A hand came up to touch the fair head, then she moved

211

away, wary and unsettled.

"I wanted to tell you I was sorry about yesterday," he began. "You're right. I didn't understand about a lot of things but I think I do now. My words must have been very hurtful to you."

She looked down, saying nothing, but the stiff line of her shoulders made a clear statement.

"Would you come up to the house with me for a little while?" he coaxed unexpectedly as he gathered her into his arms.

"Why?" The word was brittle with suspicion.

"To thank you for being there when I needed you," he murmured. His eyes smoldered warmly with suggestion and invitation.

Savannah met that hopeful gaze coolly, her emotions smarting because of a name he had called in his distress. "You don't need to thank me. Really, you don't."

Normally, he would have cajoled and teased her until she gave in, but today his arms fell away and he stepped back.

"Of course not. I forgot. You don't need anyone, do you?" Expression oddly sad and troubled, he touched his thumb to her cheek briefly. "I'll let you get back to work."

Savannah puzzled over Skyler's change in mood over the next weeks. He seemed bothered by a new restlessness that had him edgy and short-tempered. She sensed a growing dissatisfaction with his surroundings, as if he were finally feeling how isolated he was from his own people. She caught him watching Jeffery scoot along the floors, a wistful half smile upon his face. Though he never dared pick him up again, she could see the longing in his eyes. He spent a lot of time reading the sketchy accounts of Grant's assumption of the military in the Mississippi and his victory at

Chattanooga. She knew his thoughts were on his brothers. Hearing him ask casually about the state of the railways, she began to wonder if he were planning to leave. And for better than a month, she had to confess, there was nothing to hold him.

Since the morning in the office, Skyler had made no attempt to touch her. Their bed was shared in sleep but not in intimacy. At first, she was relieved when he slipped beneath the sheets in his drawers, offering a polite "good night," but the passing of time wrought a subtle change. Their chaste bed became one of unbearable loneliness for her. She missed the excitement of his loving, but more than that, she longed for the demonstrations of his love. He treated her with a cool reserve and the alienation frustrated her. She missed the emotional closeness they shared after their physical needs were sated. She never realized how much she depended on him, on his being there, on his receptiveness to her moods, on his tenderness that made the stress of the day unimportant.

More annoying was that he didn't seem to mind the new state of their relationship. She noticed sullenly that Hilllary was often with him, walking, riding, or simply sharing conversation on the veranda. He wasn't stingy with his smiles around her nor with his pocket money. She was forever showing off some gift he'd made her. But for Savannah there was nothing, no smiles, no trinkets. Not unaware of the situation, Hillary made herself readily available as a cheery companion and Skyler easily returned her flirtations.

Savannah was in a turmoil, fearing she was losing her husband to his home in the North or to the charms of her sister. She didn't know how to compete, so she retreated glumly into her paperwork.

The cotton crop was more than plentiful, and with new hope, Savannah sent it off to Charleston. All the amassing debts were pinned to the successful run through the blockade. The news reached her on a rainy December afternoon. She stood staring out the streaked windows in a fog of panic and upset when she felt his presence behind her.

"What happened?"

"It's gone" was her numb reply. "All of it. The ship was sunk. We've nothing left to start again. I don't know what I'm going to do. I have no more jewels to sell, nothing more to barter with."

How wrong she was there, he thought with a faint smile. He lifted her slack hand and curled her fingers about a wad of notes. "Is that enough? I could get more if you needed it."

She looked down blearily at the money. "Thank you," she whispered faintly. Her shoulders slumped with defeat and crushed pride. "Skyler, would you please hold me?"

He turned her into the broad haven of his chest, cradling her there while she trembled in helpless fatigue. His lips brushed the dark coronet of curls and his large hands massaged the weary shoulders, slowly moving down to press her to him.

The sudden awareness of him brought an end to her grieving. She closed her eyes in ecstasy as his mouth trailed down her temple and cheek to feast gently on her throat. The effect of that gesture on her starved passions was frightening. Holding his head to her, her breath came so quick and shallow her thoughts spun in a giddy whirl. Then he stopped the erotic play and simply held her, oblivious to the devastation he had begun.

"Skyler," she began faintly. "Do you still care for me?"

"You know how I feel about you," he answered with

214

a quiet reserve.

"No. No, I don't. How could I when you spend all your time courting my sister." Her voice sounded peevish but she couldn't help it.

"Hillary's good company, which is more than you've ever tried to be to me."

She winced at his bluntness and pulled away. He didn't try to hold her. "Take her then," she pronounced stiffly and fled the room.

When Hillary peered in the open door and saw Skyler standing at the window, she gave in to an unworthy impulse. He looked so alone and she knew how badly his relationship with Savannah had deteriorated. He must be in need of someone and it would be her, she concluded selfishly.

When the slender arms encircled his neck and kisses nibbled against it, Skyler's heart melted. With a soft cry, he turned and swept up the supple figure in a desperate embrace, never expecting it to be other than his wife. His mouth moved against the moist, parted lips with a hunger that clouded all else. By the time he realized something was not right, a choking sound from the door made his eyes fly open. With a shock of confusion, he thrust Hillary from him to face a very pale Savannah.

"Forgive me for interrupting but there's a Union messenger for you downstairs. I—I thought it might be important." She whirled and hurried down the hall in a clatter of slippers.

One look at his shattered expression told Hillary everything. She'd never had a chance with Skyler Reade. It was only her ego that encouraged her to think so. He left the room without even glancing at her.

The courier exchanged a few pleasantries with Skyler, then had to rush off. He hadn't known how good the sound of a solid New York accent could be. He looked at the letter sent via Beaufort with a growing uneasiness. It was in Leslie's hand and the fact that his sister-in-law was writing seemed ominous. He broke open the seal and scanned the contents. Then he went upstairs and began to mechanically pack his belongings.

Chapter Sixteen

"Skyler?" That simple question trembled with many things.

"I have to go home," he said tersely while stuffing his shirts in a random disarray into a trunk. "The letter was from my family. My mother is very ill. It was posted over a month ago." He paused and took a deep, steadying breath.

Savannah stared at him for a long minute, then made her decision. She stepped up to push him gently aside. "You're making a mess of things. I'll pack for us."

He stared at her blankly. "Us?"

"I'm going with you," she concluded as if it were the only possible answer, then began redoing the crumpled heap of his clothing into neat, orderly piles.

He looked at her profile, a ghost of a smile etching his face.

While Skyler readied their transportation, Savannah made the announcement to her family. With an emotional wail, Hillary cast her arms about her sister in a flood of repentant tears.

"Oh, Vannah, don't go. It was all my fault. I've been chasing him shamelessly. He thought it was you. He doesn't care a whit for me. I've been so jealous and mean. Can't you forgive me? Please don't go."

"Hilly, you're being a goose. Stop this nonsense. It

has nothing to do with you. There's an illness in his family and he has to go home."

Hillary sniffed noisily and allowed herself to be put away.

"He has to but you don't," Darcy said quietly. He looked surprisingly lucid for the time of day. "Don't go with him, Vannah. The North is no place for you."

"My place is with my husband. He'll need my help to get through our lines. I need to know you'll see to things here. Will you do that, Darcy?"

His nod was reluctant but she was grateful for it. Her mother's embrace was warm and comforting, the same as she had felt in her girlhood.

"When will you be back?"

"I don't know, Mama. It depends on Skyler," she added a bit shyly.

Adelaide stroked her dark hair lovingly. "He's a good man, child. He'll look after you, I know, but come back to us. Your Papa will be home by then and we can be a family again."

"Yes, Mama," she answered with sudden tears. She wiped them away quickly, hearing Skyler's approach, then turned to him. "I'm ready."

"Skyler, you see to my little sister, you hear?"

Skyler looked to Darcy in surprise. It was the first time he'd ever used his name or, in fact, addressed him directly. He took Savannah's elbow in a possessive grasp. "You can count on it."

They started down the drive in the buggy, Skyler looking ahead with anxiety and Savannah behind with longing as her family gathered under the sheltering porch to see her off in the chilly drizzle. She waved until they became a distant blur and Rising Sun just another sprawling red brick home, then she turned and settled with a sudden uncertainty beside her husband. Was she doing the right thing? Doubts crept up with a subtle nagging. All she knew was that she couldn't let him go North alone, leaving her behind with the way their relationship lay between them. The thought of him not coming back to her was more frightening than what waited up North. Her fears were laid to rest when warm fingers fell over hers, enmeshing and squeezing slightly.

They traveled the Southern rail as far as they could. Savannah was grateful to transfer to a carriage, for the rails were in dreadful disrepair and the ride dirty and treacherous. She made all the arrangements for them until the sound of the surrounding accents lost the pleasant drawl to become a twangy curtness. Skyler did the talking for them after that point, booking them seats on an eastbound train.

Skyler was a silent, distracted companion and Savannah left him alone with his thoughts. In spite of the war, rail accommodations were crowded due to the holidays, Christmas less than two weeks away. There were no sleeping berths available, so they made themselves as comfortable as possible in the unyielding seats. Skyler held her loosely against his side so her head could pillow on his shoulder. If he slept at all, she never saw him.

Savannah slept through their arrival in Philadelphia. The first thing she was aware of when Skyler shook her shoulder was the chill even in the heated interior. The windows of their car were all steamed so there was no seeing into the darkness beyond. When she followed him sleepily into the station, it was like stepping into an uninviting void of strangeness. People were all about swaddled in bulky wraps, speaking in tart, quick voices while the hissing haze from the engine clouded them with the fogginess of a dream. Skyler located a dark-skinned porter and paid him well to see their bags were sent on, then led her to the crowded street. When he saw her shivering in her inappropriate

219

mantle, he bundled her in the heavy coat he'd been carrying. He didn't see her grateful smile, too busy looking about the familiar dirty city.

The conveyance whisked them down an endless gridiron of streets. Savannah's first impression of the North was it was cold and it smelled funny, the oily, smoky perfume of industry. She was thankful when they sped from the busy streets into plots of parklike grounds and palatial homes. She was speechless when they turned into a wide brick drive. His home? It was a huge, overwhelming structure like everything else she had seen in the burgeoning city. The two and a half stories were of rubblestone covered with stucco and scored to look like the more refined ashlar. Simple symmetrical wings spread out on the sides of the flattened front. A large three-part Palladian window looked down on them haughtily from the second floor, the other windows long, mullioned, and simply dressed. To her eyes, the effect was one of reserved elegance rather than welcomed hominess.

After helping her down, Skyler for once forgot his manners and hurried ahead, leaving her unescorted. He was met at the door by a plain-faced woman all in black. She had no time to say anything to him before he gave a low, pain-filled wail of grief and loss. The woman embraced him easily and guided him inside, shutting the great door without having seen that he wasn't alone.

After he'd recovered from his initial shock, Skyler leaned away from the comforting shoulder and tried to find his voice. "When did it happen, Les? What happened?"

"She's been gone almost a month, Sky," his brother's wife told him gently. She steered him to a low sofa where she continued to hold him loosely. "It was her heart. She complained of not feeling well, then she was

220

"gone within the week, the day after I sent word to you."

"I should have been here," he mourned heavily, eyes filling with blame and sadness.

"You couldn't have gotten here in time even if we'd known where to find you," she soothed. She held the fair head to her bosom as she would with one of her children who was hurting.

After a few minutes, he asked, "How's my father?"

"He's doing well. You know how he lived for your mother. It was very hard for him at first. Seeing you will make it better."

"And Palmer and Brent?"

"Both here, thank the Lord. They're at evening service. I stayed home because Bobby was running a bit of a fever."

"I'd forgotten it was Sunday," he mumbled, then straightened with a steadying sigh. "You're a good woman, Les. I'm sure you've kept everything together."

"What is it, Sky?"

He looked about with a puzzled alarm. "Where's Savannah?"

"Who?"

It was the same question Brent Reade was asking himself as he observed the beautiful woman stomping back and forth on their front walk. He could see little of her other than a reddening nose, flushed cheeks, and intriguing eyes of darkest blue. He assumed a courtly pose and approached her with a smile.

"May I be of assistance, ma'am?"

She looked at him in obvious surprise, then smiled, a warm enduring gesture that sparked the lovely eyes. "You must be Skyler's brother."

It was a redundant statement, for Brent was Skyler in younger years. The only difference was in the dark eyes. Those widening eyes flashed to the house hopefully.

221

"Is Sky here?"

"He's inside. I fear he's forgotten me."

Hearing the slightest upset beneath her joking tone, Brent grinned gallantly. "I don't know how he could possibly do that but I shall take him severely to task for his carelessness. Or should I just be grateful I found you? I'm Brent Reade."

"Savannah Russell. Reade," she added a bit awkwardly.

Brent goggled at her, mouth unhinged, but before he could draw any conclusions, the door opened.

"Savannah, forgive me," Skyler began repentantly.

"She's already keeping bad company."

He turned to the man beside his wife and grinned hugely. They came together with a crushing hug and much enthused backslapping. Side by side the likeness was uncanny. Eyes warmed with affection, Skyler stepped back and rumpled the other's fair hair.

"It's good to see you, little brother. Let's get inside. It's freezing out here." With one arm about his brother's shoulders and the other about Savannah's, he lead them inside, where Leslie waited with a bemused smile. She eyed the strange woman curiously. Before Skyler could affect a proper introduction, Brent rushed through them with a mischievous smile.

"Leslie, this is Savannah Reade."

"How nice to meet you."

Leslie took the extended hand in a daze, doubly shocked by the combination of title and accented voice. "I don't understand," she began uncertainly, looking up at Skyler for the answer.

"Savannah is my wife. We were married in Beaufort this spring." His gaze rested on the dark-haired beauty, growing soft with emotion. It was a look Leslie didn't miss and she began to smile. "Please make her feel welcomed, Les."

222

"Of course I will. What a dunce you must think me, standing here with my mouth open, but this is such a surprise. Of course you're welcomed, Savannah." Her embrace was as genuine as her words, making the shivering newcomer relax her reserved stance gratefully. "How cold you are. Come upstairs with me at once. I'm sure the boys have much to talk about and they don't need we women hanging about."

"Thank you, Les," Skyler said with quiet meaning, then turned to smile at his wife. "She'll take good care of you. I'll see you later."

Savannah nodded and reluctantly followed the other woman upstairs. She cast an anxious glance behind her to the security of her husband's presence before being swallowed by the shadows of the big house.

"I'm sure you'd like a hot bath after your trip. Train travel is so abominable and filthy. Where are your bags? Is someone bringing them from the station? I'll have them brought right up to you so you can change. What a surprise! Skyler's wife. If you need anything at all, my room is the second one across the hall."

Savannah was relieved to only have to nod while Leslie kept up a cheerful chatter. Her mind was too agog with the somber surroundings to return the banter. The heavy paneling and plush, muffling carpets seemed to loom dark and engulfing all about her. All was stiffly correct and formally forbidding. Skyler's room was such a relief she heard her breath expel weakly.

"I'll order you up a bath. It will take just a minute or two."

Alone in the strange room, Savannah looked about, totally mystified. How much she learned about the man she'd married in that single surveying sweep. Before, Skyler had always blended into her surroundings, but this was his essence and it was like seeing a new side of him. Unlike the parts of the house she had seen, his quarters were light, airy, lived-in, and completely without order. On every available surface there were books with broken spines laying face down, half read, projects started and left incomplete, letters ending mid sentence. His closets held half a summer wardrobe and half a winter, as if he had never finished the transition. She thought it oddly inconsistent that so faultlessly neat and organized an individual could cultivate such clutter but it made her smile at such a human failing. How little she knew of this man she called her husband.

The hot water arrived to fill the metal tub in their dressing room and she spent a glorious twenty minutes soaking off the stale city smells and the stiffness from her bones. By the time she emerged, lost in Skyler's robe, the trunks had come from the station. There was a calming domestic pleasure in sorting through their clothing and hanging them together. She selected a sober gown of charcoal grey watered silk and a simple cameo broach to adorn the bosom ruching, then decided to brave the austere halls in search of Skyler. She found she wanted very much to be with him, to feel the warmth of his gaze and wide smile in this cold mansion. Following the route Leslie had brought her took her back to the main hall. The sound of masculine voices drew her to the parlor doors left half open to invite her listening. They weren't the happy voices of a family joyfully reunited.

"I don't understand you, Skyler. You don't have the decency to appear at your own mother's funeral, then you show up on the doorstep with some Southern tart on your arm and expect a red-carpet welcome."

"I got the welcome I expected, sir. And Savannah is my wife, not some whore I'd allow you to defame. I would have been here for the burial had I known of it in time. You know I would have."

"That doesn't change the fact that you chose to desert your position, useless though it was, in order to chase that woman across the South and take up housekeeping with her and her traitorous family. Nothing has changed, has it? I thought the military would point you in some direction but you're as shiftless and irresponsible as ever. I'm not surprised that you would turn your back on your country but I didn't think you would so betray your family, especially the memory of your sainted mother who loved you in spite of your weakness. How could you have so little regard for the sanctity of our grief to come to our house so unforgivably late with that woman—I can't bear to call her your wife. You didn't even have enough mettle to tell us of your infamous choice of bride. How could you think we'd accept you or such an outrageous match."

Savannah pushed open the door to survey the four Reade men gathered there. Considering the hotness of the words spoken, the atmosphere was surprisingly subdued. Skyler and the tall, commanding figure of his father, Fletcher Reade, stood before a huge fireplace, brandies in hand. Brent was lounging in an overstuffed chair, long legs carelessly draped over its arm, looking bored and restless. Palmer, Leslie's husband, sat on an opposing sofa, expression set in disapproving lines. His dark brown hair and eyes and undistinguished features mirrored those of the portrait above the mantelpiece—his mother, Mary Reade.

"Excuse me, gentlemen."

Palmer and Brent rose instantly and all looked to her in surprise. Not one to be put off by a roomful of unsettled men, Savannah swept in with an air of dignity to stand at Skyler's side, her hand resting easily on his arm. He raised a questioning brow at her cool,

225

arrogant expression and repressed a smile at what he knew was to come. She began in a chillingly formal tone not softened by her gentle drawl.

"If my name is to be so bandied about, I'd as soon have it done to my face and not by gentlemen I have not yet had the pleasure of being introduced to. I am Savannah Russell Reade, Skyler's wife. I understand a good wife is to maintain a silent shadow behind her husband. If so, forgive me, for I am not a good, proper wife.

"I had wanted to greet Skyler's family with the same open-mindedness that he met mine, and expected to be received with like politeness and respect. It was not my intention to brazen my way into a private conversation, but I cannot bare unfairness of any kind and what I heard in this room was intolerable."

She paused, drawing a deep breath, and regarded each man in turn. Brent looked amused, Palmer appalled, Fletcher stoic, and Skyler regarded her with eyes that simmered and warmed with admiration.

"Perhaps you don't understand your son, Mr. Reade. Perhaps it's because you don't know him. Do you know he nearly drowned with the rest of his crew when his ship sank. Did you know he withstood pain that would kill many a man in order to save his arm. He married me, not caring that I was from the South, and accepted my family because they were a part of me. He didn't turn his back on all of you to hide in the South. He stayed because I was needed there and couldn't leave. He didn't make a choice between you and me nor did he think he'd have to. The very moment he heard of any problem, he packed and disregarded any danger to come North. I wanted to come with him. He told me so much about his fine family I was looking forward to meeting them. Because of what I know of him, I expected him to have come from a home of impeccable breeding. But I see hospitality is something that stops at the Mason-Dixon line. I would no sooner spend a night in this house than I would in one of your military prisons. You need not worry about accepting me because I wouldn't have any of your snobbish, narrow-thinking lot. I will be on the next train South and you needn't trouble yourself to call a carriage. I would rather walk than force one ounce of courtesy from you. Good evening, gentlemen."

There was a stunned silence as she turned on her heel, but before she took three steps, Skyler seized her up for a long, demonstrative kiss, unmindful of who looked on. When he set her back all breathless and flushed, he said emotionally, "How I love you, my fiery little Rebel, but you needn't fight my battles for me. Do you think I'd let you walk out of here. Not alone, anyway." Holding her close into his side, he turned to face his father. "Well, sir, what's it to be? Do you throw us both out or do you apologize to my wife for being such an insufferable bigot?"

Fletcher Reade looked between them for a long moment, eyes of pale icy grey calmly gauging, then unexpectedly he smiled that broad grin that blessed two of his sons. "I am a bit of an old fool. I may go on about what a disappointment he is, but I love my son and wouldn't lose him so soon. I would be grateful if you would accept my regrets that I spoke so hastily with such an uninformed mind. This past month has been a trying one and I've seen little call to use manners. I've let my grief give me an excuse for rudeness. I need my family about me, and that includes Skyler and his new bride, who I'd like to have the opportunity to know better if she'd allow it."

Savannah took the large hand he extended with a suddenly shy smile. "I'd like that too."

"Would you please stay and let us show you the

North can rival you for hospitality?"

"Thank you, sir. I came down to say good night and fear I said much more. Perhaps we can start tomorrow as a new beginning."

Skyler saw her to the door and kissed her cheek tenderly. She leaned into it, a sweep of longing weakening her senses, but he moved away all too quickly.

"Can you find your way up? I want to spend some time with my family now that you've taken the poison from their bite. Do you mind terribly?"

"No, please go ahead. I'll be fine. I'm very tired anyway." Could he hear the disappointment in her voice? She hoped not.

"Good night, Savannah. Thank you for being here."

She hoped he'd kiss her again but he merely brushed her cheek with his fingertips, leaving an aching void of feeling she wanted him to awaken. Chafing in the sterile environment she'd insisted they maintain, she climbed the stairs and fell asleep in the large bed, alone and lonely.

The sound of movement in the dark, unfamiliar room woke her with a moment's panic until a filtering of moonlight through the parted drapes glinted on the fair hair. She watched for several minutes as he stood motionlessly at the window staring out into the darkness. His breath escaped him in short, hiccupping gasps. When her arms slipped about his middle, his hands clutched her tightly.

"I can't believe she's gone," he said slowly to the night. "This house is so full of her I expect to see her in every room. How do you get over that?"

She laid her head against his broad back, remembering the pain so well. "Don't try. Keep the memories alive and she'll never be gone."

"If only I had been able to see her one more time. I

should have—I should have . . . done a lot of things but it's too late now." He turned in the circle of her arms and held her to his chest. "I can see now how you must have hurt losing your father. You don't still blame me for that, do you?"

"No," she whispered against his shirtfront. "Come to bed, Skyler. It's very late."

He offered no resistance when she led him from the window. He shed his clothes, leaving them in a careless heap, and slipped beneath the covers with her. They burrowed close in the chill, Skyler cuddling her in the crook of his arm. His cheek lay gently atop her head.

"I love you, Savannah," he told her simply. He expected no response and there was none as she lay near him, engulfed by his heat and secure strength. He smiled wistfully into the ebony waves and closed his eyes.

Chapter Seventeen

To wake and find his wife still asleep at his side was an unexpected pleasure. It had happened only once before, after their second night together. He felt that same strong stirring of contentment just watching her, admiring her beauty, so serene and vulnerable when not on the defensive. He liked her being here tucked beneath his covers, the midnight cloud of her hair spread across his pillow. He felt the warming glow of love deepen and flame into an uncomfortable reminder of how long it had been since that love had been demonstrated. The decree he had made in a fit of anger had been a torture to keep but never so much as in this quiet moment. She was here because she wanted to be with him, for reasons he didn't understand and she hadn't explained. She had come to a bristling defense of him before his family. Would she have done either of those things if she didn't care for him? If that wasn't proof enough, how long would he have to wait for a definite answer? He found he didn't want to let another second pass.

Her hair was a ripple of silk between his fingers and the flesh of her nearly bare shoulder the warmest satin. All soft and perfumed from her evening bath, the sensual invitation she offered was too much. His mouth hovered over her innocently parted lips in a moment of hesitation, then lowered to move upon the willing cushion of softness in a lingering caress. No nectar of heaven could taste so sweet and satisfying.

He didn't withdraw when he felt her wake beneath his kiss. Her breath caught, then her lips yielded to his persuasion, drinking deeply of the love he longed to share as if she too had been thirsting. When he finally lifted his head, she gazed up at him with a question in those dark, depthless eyes.

"I love you, Savannah," he said huskily, the emotion of his words making her quiver, "and I want you. If you say you want me, it will be enough. I won't ask for more of you again."

Savannah said nothing for a timeless moment, studying the strong, handsome lines of his face and lost in the smoky passion of his silvery eyes. When she spoke, her tone was hoarse with the constricting force of her own desire.

"Oh, Skyler, I—"

That thought was never completed. The door to his room burst open and two small bodies hurdled like projectiles onto the bed. High juvenile voices clamored for their Uncle Sky. When they saw he wasn't alone, the two imps sat back on their heels in a suddenly shy silence.

"Don't look as though she's going to gobble you up," Skyler chuckled. "This is your Aunt Savannah. Now where are my hugs?"

Satisfied by his brief explanation, they were instantly upon him, thin arms about his neck in a flurry of excited giggles. He crushed them fondly to him, a large hand atop each of the dark heads. Savannah sat back smiling to herself. He hadn't looked so happy since the day of their wedding.

"All right. Loose me, you little monkeys, so I can

introduce you properly."

Brother and sister obediently sat still and smiled tentatively at the woman in their uncle's bed. Michael was seven, all lean and lanky with the promise of the Reade height and his father's coloring and bone structure. Five-year-old Jennifer was her mother's child, pleasant, amiable features promising warmth if not beauty and still stubby with a childish roundness. They regarded Savannah with open curiosity when she exchanged greetings with them.

"You talk funny," Michael proclaimed.

"I'm from South Carolina," she told him seriously, repressing a smile. "To me you sound funny too."

Eyes wide and guileless, Jennifer asked, "Are you a damned Reb?"

"Jenny, where did you hear such a thing?" Skyler scowled. "I don't want to hear that again."

"From Michael," she admitted, eyes clouding with teary confusion at her uncle's anger.

"I heard it from Poppa and Grandpa," Michael piped up in his own defense.

"Well, I'm sure they weren't speaking of your aunt. Now get on with you so we can get up and have breakfast before your Uncle Brent eats it all."

Giggles restored at his good-humored grin, they scampered out.

Savannah folded her arms across her bosom and pouted fiercely, "I wonder if they would like to be called damned Yankees."

Skyler laughed and took her down to the mattress, pinning her there with elbows on either side of her head. "Isn't that how you still think of me?" he teased. When she petulantly refused to answer, his voice lowered throatily. "How do you think of me, Savannah?"

Her eyes began to drift closed in anticipation of his kiss but they sprang open at a rap on the door.

"Skyler, Savannah, breakfast is on," Leslie called cheerily.

"Now you see why I called it crowded," he grumbled.

Savannah laughed and rolled beneath his arm to escape his dangerous proximity. While she dressed, he lay on his back, arms folded behind his head to watch her through veiled eyes. That heavily lidded stare made her oddly shy. Perhaps it was the strange room, the uninviting house, the new wary family, or just her nervous awareness of him and how much she had wanted to answer his question. If he asked again, she wouldn't hesitate.

"Come along, you lazy brute. They'll be waiting for us," she insisted, tossing him a clean shirt.

"They're used to waiting for me, but all right."

The dining room was filled with all but the youngest Reade, who Leslie was keeping in bed as an extra precaution. The noisy gathering made Savannah think of her own family before the war had taken the joy out of it. She sat quietly observing them and discovered much about her new relations.

Fletcher was the unquestionable head of the group, with his lionlike mane of silver hair and strict grey eyes. He was an established surgeon, one of the finest in Philadelphia, and now split his time between his lucrative practice and exhaustive rounds at the area hospitals. Serious-minded Palmer followed in his professional footsteps. He had joined his father in a large office in the city, but since his enlistment that office stood empty, too much for one man to run. Fletcher maintained a well-stocked clinic in the home's

234

rear wing, with Leslie serving as a capable assistant.

Plain, cheery Leslie seemed complacently maternal, but Savannah sensed a deep, quiet strength in her, a strength she would need to rear three small children while her husband was away in the makeshift field hospitals. Her easy acceptance of the Southern woman was typical of her want to keep harmony in the family. The role of peacemaker was one she had inherited from Mary Reade and she was often put to the test in the midst of such strong-willed men.

Brent was an outrageous scamp. Savannah liked him immediately, seeing in him how Skyler must have been. The same age as Savannah, he'd been in medical school, plodding along unenthusiastically with barely passing grades, when the war broke out. He had rushed to join up in a flurry of excitement, much like her brother Darcy, but had been spared as yet the tarnishing of his idealism. He was a free spirit, in love with living a reckless life with singular selfishness. At the same time, he had such an endearing manner one couldn't help but begrudge him his indulgences.

In her husband's case, that recklessness had tempered to an idle disinterest. He had no burning desire to fight in this war or to take any chosen direction. She felt his father's resentment at that flip attitude and realized Fletcher blamed his middle son for much of his youngest's straying ways. The fact that Skyler had considered consignment, hiring another for three hundred dollars to take his place in the fighting, had caused a severe rift through the family that still left unpleasant eddies. Though Skyler held an unaffected pose during Fletcher's frequent jibes, Savannah wasn't convinced that he didn't feel their sting.

Most of the talk at the table revolved around the family medical practice, Skyler's desertion of it, and

235

the assurance that Brent would do the right thing after the war. While the silver-haired patriarch expounded on family loyalty and duty, Brent rolled his eyes in comical dismay until Leslie gave him a discreet cuff to the head.

Finally Skyler gave a heavy sigh of aggravation and announced, "Medicine is not the only endeavor a man can undertake without feeling he's gone against some great biblical directive."

"Don't blaspheme at my table, Skyler," the older man warned, heavy brows lowering in a disapproving scowl. "Medicine is a fine, noble cause and I won't hear of your mockery."

"But it's not everyone's cause. It wasn't mine and if it's not Brent's, I hope you'll treat him better than you did me. You'd have thought I'd broken some sacred commandment handed down through the generations."

"Tell me what great cause you've chosen to apply yourself to," Fletcher challenged with a raising temper. "Don't lecture me when all you seek to do is escape any responsibility. Name one thing you've ever completed, one commitment you've ever stood by. A politician." His snort was derisive. "Another lazy dreamer. Perhaps you'll make a good one. You've all the right qualities." The way he said it left no question that he felt they were useless ones.

The grey eyes came together like steel on flint. Skyler's voice was cool and firm, intending no disprespect.

"My choice for my own future is not open to discussion, not at this table or anywhere else. You've a right to your opinion but I don't have to defend mine."

"Of course not. Back away. You don't feel you have

to defend anything. You don't even feel obligated to defend your country. While your brothers are risking their lives in the field, you sit safe and secure. You found the first way out, then betrayed everything we hold sacred to sleep with the enemy."

Savannah's eyes dropped quickly to her lap, where her hands clenched in upset. She hated the warming flood of color that rose in her face as the silence at the table grew long and stilted. Skyler broke the echoing stillness with words as brittle as ice.

"I realize that this is your table, sir, and you can say whatever you like, but if you continue with these sentiments, my wife and I will not return to it."

"Sit down, Skyler, and smooth your feathers. I've every intention of apologizing," Fletcher began contritely. "You come by your outspoken foolishness quite naturally. Again, I ask your forgiveness, Savannah. I don't speak ill of you personally but of a sector whose rash thoughtlessness brought us to the brink of disaster."

The dark blue eyes came up to meet his unblinkingly. "I accept your apology and will not argue politics at your table, but do not expect me to be ashamed of what I am or where I come from or to make apologies to you for a war that has taken my father and ruined my brother."

The heavy brows rose, impressed by the eloquence of her straightforward speech. "Fair enough. I declare this table neutral ground for the sake of all our digestions."

Savannah gave a smile of agreement but her fingers were cold and unresponsive when Skyler squeezed them. Forgiven but not forgotten, that stiffness told him.

As the meal came to a close, Jennifer turned to her

mother and tugged her sleeve. "Mama, now that Uncle Sky is here can we get a tree and have a real Christmas?"

Leslie started to shush her in dismay but Fletcher interrupted, coming to place a large hand on the dark head.

"No, Leslie, the girl is right," he said quietly. "Christmas is a time for children and family. Mary wouldn't have wanted her passing to take that away. She would have wanted us to celebrate being together in such unpredictable times. This is a time to rejoice in the birth and in life not to dwell on death. I want all the black trimmings put away. I want the most beautiful tree we've ever had in the front room. I want you children to put aside your grief and go out and visit your friends, make merry and accept the invitations you've had to parties and such. You'll be gone away all too soon as it is. Do this for me and for your mother."

Leslie hugged the elder man with a soft cry. The three sons exchanged somber looks but none of them would challenge their father's wish. Christmas would come as usual without Mary Reade.

As the room cleared, Skyler caught Savannah's arm, detaining her until they were alone. The seriousness of his gaze gave her uneasy pause.

"Savannah, if things are too uncomfortable for you here, we can stay in a hotel or return to Rising Sun, whichever you want."

She eyed him with disbelief but his expression was as sincere as his sentiment. "They are uncomfortable but not impossible. You survived my family. I can weather yours."

His hug was sudden and strong, stopping her breath and her heart with a jolt of emotional response.

"Thank you. It's important for me to be here,

238

especially now. We may not always like each other but there's a lot of love in this family. It would mean a lot for you to share that with me."

He held her back by the shoulders, eyes intent and warm. She leaned toward him.

"Skyler!"

He turned in time to receive an onslaught of plum-colored taffeta and plumes. The exclamation of surprise was never uttered as his mouth was fully and passionately claimed. Slender arms trapped him in that fiery embrace while Savannah looked on in stunned embarrassment.

"Oh, Sky, Sky," a throaty voice whispered between the hungry kisses. "I just heard you were home. Why didn't you let me know? Why haven't you answered my letters? Do you have any idea how I've missed you? How I've longed for you? How I've dreamed of us being together?"

"Rhea, enough," he said awkwardly, untangling himself. The formal distance in his tone finally reached her in warning. "Rhea, there's someone I want you to meet."

Rhea Sherwood stepped back, large tawny eyes going past him to the woman who stood in his shadow. They studied each other with dissecting thoroughness, neither liking what they saw.

Rhea Sherwood was a handsome woman, not pretty but striking much the same way Savannah was. She was tall and willowy, with creamy skin, a sharp triangular face, lush red lips, and a mass of heavy chestnut hair. She was no winsome girl. Savannah guessed her to be closer to Skyler's age than her own. Her vivid hazel eyes contained a shrewd perception that was immediately threatening.

"Rhea, this is Savannah, my wife. Savannah,

Rhea Sherwood."

He didn't need to describe Rhea's position. That much was obvious. Knowing that she had been her husband's lover, Savannah couldn't help but admire the other woman's calm dignity as a slim white hand extended.

"Skyler's wife. What a surprise. How nice to meet you. It explains much and I am feeling very foolish."

Savannah took the cool fingers to exchange an empty gesture.

"It's my fault, Rhea. I should have written you but you know what a coward I am," Skyler murmured.

The golden eyes lifted to his for a moment of lingering appraisal. "Yes, I know you very well." She said it silkily, surely, almost possessively, then turned to Savannah with a smooth smile. "You've managed quite a feat, my dear. Skyler has been very wily in eluding the snare of matrimony. You're a fortunate woman. But then you know that."

"I hope she does," Skyler agreed with an easy smile. He was relieved at how well the meeting was going. With Rhea, one was never too certain. "How have you been, Rhea? You look wonderful."

"How nice of you to say so." She took up his arm in casual fondness, seeming to forget they weren't alone. "Actually, I came to invite you to a political luncheon at the Regent. You would do well to be seen there. It's too easy to forget faces in Washington. The congress-man will be there, and the mayor and many of our friends. I know it's dreadful short notice but it could be quite a coup. Say you'll come." Seeing him hesitate, she added quickly, "Bring your wife, of course. I'm sure they'll all be charmed to meet her."

"Don't be too certain, Miss Sherwood."

Rhea's face stiffened on hearing Savannah's voice.

She didn't need to say any more. It was plain in her narrowed eyes. Southerner. Traitor. And worse.

"Skyler, please go," Savannah urged diplomatically. "I'd be quite out of place with all those stuffy, bureaucrats and frightfully bored. Go with Miss Sherwood and have a pleasant afternoon."

Before he could reply, she swept by them, fearing her generosity wouldn't withstand his scrutiny. Unsure of what emotions she was feeling, her first instinct was to retreat to their room. Never the coward, she determined to seek out some company in the huge house, partly because Skyler's room was too personal a reminder of him and partly because she was bored.

"Forgotten again?"

She turned to smile ruefully. "So it would seem."

"I saw Sky leaving with Rhea." Brent looked at her quizzically until his unspoken question prompted a crisp response.

"They're attending some political luncheon and I was in no mood for more sectional arguments."

"He told you about Rhea?"

"Oh, yes," she lied smoothly.

"You must be very sure of his love to trust him so easily with her."

"Yes, Skyler loves me," she replied without any doubt.

"Trust him, but you'd be wise not to trust Rhea, not after all she's lost. In her mind, you've snatched the ring from her finger. She's been planning her engagement and wedding for a long time now."

Savannah shrugged with feigned indifference to this new information. "He's my husband, not hers. There isn't much she can do."

Brent raised a brow at her bravado and grinned. "I never fancied her as a sister-in-law. Too pushy for my taste."

"And do you approve of me?" she asked dryly.

"Wholeheartedly. Enough to offer my service as an escort while you're in the lurch."

She frowned at his choice of words but took his arm in acceptance.

Savannah retired early, worn out by the day of sightseeing with an exuberant Brent Reade and done in by pretending Skyler's absence didn't bother her. His luncheon had extended into the evening without word and what she felt about the situation had sharpened into a confused jealousy. As she donned her nightdress and combed out her glossy hair, she told herself it was only because he wore the title of her husband and not that she cared what he did. Wounded pride was easier to accept than bruised emotion, especially when her feelings were in such a turmoil.

She wanted Skyler. She wanted to share the benefits of his love but could not bring herself to give in return. So much had changed since that day on the beach when he had shattered her naive hopes. Was she wrong to continue to hold him and her own emotions at bay or would surrendering them be a shameful compromise of all her standards? Could she envision a life without him in it? If he was to be her future, was she cheating herself even more than him? Did she want her marriage to be a battlefield of wills over a nearly forgotten principle? Was it more of a moral wrong to betray her family or the sacred vow she spoke to him? Was she afraid of her own weakness or of the strength of what he awoke in her?

Being with Brent was so easy and fun, for he was Skyler without the damning taint. She enjoyed being with him in a way she couldn't be with her own husband, relaxed and laughing and yet aware of a part of her that wished it could be that way with Skyler.

His arrival interrupted further thought. He paused inside the door to appreciate the sight of her standing before his small bureau mirror, black hair loose about her shoulders. When her eyes met his in the glass, the deep blue depths were guarded and waiting.

"I'm sorry I'm so late," he began as he took off his coat and pleated shirt bosom. "These affairs have a way of going on forever and are impossible to escape from."

"What affairs are you referring to?" she asked coolly, but he sensed the submerged anger in the question.

"Is there something you wish to ask me?"

"Is there something you should have told me?" was the curt counter.

Skyler sighed. Perhaps it wasn't going to be so easy after all. "You mean about Rhea?"

Savannah turned to face him, expression impatient. "I assume she's one of your past attachments."

"Rhea has been a friend for a long time."

The simple answer brought her anger to a head. "You dismiss her easily for one who was almost your wife."

"Who told you that?"

"Why didn't you?"

He spread his large hands wide in resignation. "Because it wasn't important."

That made the dark eyes snap even fiercer. "To whom? To you or to her?"

"Savannah, I don't want to argue about Rhea with you. It's really none of your concern. She was a friend of mine long before I met you. That's all. I'd like her to remain a friend."

"How convenient to have your mistresses as

friends." She heard the spiteful pettishness of her words but didn't care. She was hurting. The situation was forcing feelings from her that she didn't want to face—jealousy, possessiveness, fear, desire—and her only recourse was to strike back to deflect that hurt.

Skyler crossed to her in three great strides. He seized her by the arms and held her firmly when she would pull away. "Enough, Savannah. What an impossible woman you are sometimes. You want to know about Rhea and me, I'll tell you. We were lovers. I like Rhea, I always have, and probably always will. She wanted to be my wife, and at the time, I couldn't think of a reason not to marry her. She's bright, clever, beautiful, and she loved me. And then I met you. I knew then that I didn't want to marry Rhea or be with anyone other than you. I married you. I gave you my name. For me, there can be no other woman. I don't care what reason you might give me or how frustrating what we have might be, you are my wife and I would never be unfaithful to you, not with Rhea, not with any other woman. As long as you have my name, you have me and that's the end of it. No more foolish tantrums about Rhea, for she ceased to exist in my heart the moment I saw you."

The passion in his voice made her feel childish and embarrassed. And afraid. She couldn't allow herself to believe him so easily after being burned by his lies. "And when your interest in our marriage commitment fades, what then?"

Skyler flushed angrily at her use of his father's sentiments and shook her roughly. "You don't listen, do you? You prideful, stiff-necked—" He broke off his categorizing to draw her up tight to his chest. The feel of her drove away all complaint.

Savannah held herself rigid as he kissed her. The

244

heated perusal of her lips shocked through her system with a delicious preview of what she had long wanted. She had wanted to feel the crushing strength of his arms about her, had wanted him to dominate her rebelliousness so she could enjoy him without the shame of surrender. Realizing what a sham her protest was, she redoubled it in an attempt to fortify her waning reluctance.

"Not this time, Savannah," Skyler warned as she struggled against his gentling touch. "No argument. If you're determined not to provide me with the comfort of a good marriage, I won't let you deny me its pleasures. I am your husband."

"Not by my choice. Never by my choice. I don't want you. I hate—"

Her epithet was silenced by another hard kiss until she was breathless and dizzy. Taking advantage of her momentary concession, Skyler carried her to the bed where her fight returned twofold. He had to nearly rip the nightdress from her, then sit astride her twisting figure while he removed his own clothing. Her fierceness prevented any tender overtures and her violent objection kept him busy fending off sharp nails and viciously wielded knees. Instead of being deterred by her savage protest, he was made more determined. The thrashing contact of her supple nakedness excited a dramatic reaction. The fiery stab of her fingernails served to heighten the other sensations, sensations too demanding to restrain while trying to woo a wild cat bent on claiming a pound of his flesh.

Abandoning his plan to coax her from her anger, he vowed to force her passions and overcame all her denials with a quick, claiming thrust. Her soft cry almost made him relent, then the fingers that had been so intent on shredding him began to ply and twist in his

245

hair. The sounds she made had nothing to do with anger or hurt.

The sweetness of the reunion she had tried so desperately to prevent proved as crippling to her will as she feared. Each provocative movement was welcomed by her body with an eagerness that urged them closer to the promise of rapture. Knowing she was lost to him didn't stop her from trying to suppress the pleasure he was giving her. She tried to turn her focus from the silvery silkiness of his hair, from the hard unyielding weight of his big body, from the rasps of his breath as it brushed shakily past her cheek, ever quickening, and from the tightening spirals of tension he was building within her. But it did no good. Shivery waves of delight swamped over her, drowning her protests with a quelling satisfaction. She heard herself whisper his name in that euphoric daze, then bit back the tender claim that would follow.

Skyler was kissing her gently, warmly, gratefully, but she wanted no part of his graciously accepted victory or of the tenderness he would grant the conquered.

"No," she moaned, turning away and pushing at his hand. "No. I hate you. I hate you."

He captured her face, holding it so she could not evade his eyes. In a low, breathless voice, he insisted fervently, "You will love me, Savannah. I'll make you love me. I'll thaw that Rebel heart of yours."

"No," she urged faintly, squeezing her eyes closed to block out the intensity of his, the desperation and frustration she felt as well.

"I'm your husband. You have to love me. You have to forgive me. You can't continue to punish me forever. Tell me you love me. Damn your cold heart, tell me you love me."

His grip tightened, unintentionally pinching her

cheeks between his large hands. In a guilty dismay, he felt the wetness of her tears upon them. When released, she rolled onto her side, back to him to sob in ragged misery. Wearily, he stared at the ceiling, the sound of her weeping teething on his heart until he could stand the torment no longer. He rose to hurriedly dress and left her alone to her unhappiness.

Chapter Eighteen

It was nearly dawn when he returned, slipping quietly into their room and undressing without light. He slid under the covers cautiously, his efforts to keep from waking her unwarranted. Savannah hadn't been able to find rest in the large, empty bed. It was cold and unwelcoming as the temperature dropped outside. She huddled, shivering beneath the chilly sheets, too tired to dwell on immediate concerns. Instead, she let her thoughts drift wistfully to Rising Sun and the blissful contentment of her childhood. Skyler's arrival tore that pleasant picture from her. She was resentful and unwilling to speak to him as he settled some distance from her.

The silence in the room stretched out and Savannah's fitful trembling returned. Skyler's obvious comfort only stoked her misery.

"I'm cold," she complained pettishly.

Without a word, he tossed his portion of the down comforter over her and rolled unobligingly onto his stomach.

Frowning, she tried to arrange the extra covers about her but the chill persisted. "Skyler, I'm still cold."

Muttering in annoyance, he scooted over until his hip and shoulder brushed against her, offering a re-

249

luctant, teasing warmth. When he showed no intention of moving any closer, she nudged up against him so he could feel her shiver. With a sigh, he put his arms around her and drew her back to him until they lay back to front. The heat of his body covered every inch of hers like an encompassing blanket. He smelled pleasantly of brandy and cigars, and that familiar odor carried her back across the years to a dimly lit study.

"Better?" he asked softly.

She nodded, snuggling contentedly until her comfort was assured. She smiled to herself at the feel of his lips upon her hair and was able to sleep soundly.

The morning shone with an unnatural brightness, drawing Savannah to the window. She wrapped a patchwork quilt about her to insulate against the nip in the air. When she looked out over the yard, she gasped in childlike wonder.

"Oh, Sky, it snowed. Everything's so beautiful. Just like a fairyland."

Not too enthused about the blizzard he had trudged home in, Skyler grunted from beneath the covers.

"Oh, come look. You have to see this," she persisted excitely.

About to grumble that he had seen snow on each of his thirty-one winters, he peered over the blanket sullenly. And stared. Savannah stood before the blinding glitter at the window, ebony hair tossled about the coverlet that didn't extend to her bare feet. Her toes were tightly curled under. Her eyes sparkled with animation, warming him like a summer day. With a marvelling smile, he swung out of bed and tugged on a pair of flannel drawers before joining her at the mullioned panes.

The front trees and picket fence were liberally coated

with a powdery glaze, and a blanket of muffling white hugged the ground, making everything so pure and brilliant he couldn't help but share her awe.

"It is beautiful," he agreed. "It almost hurts to look at it."

Nestled in the curve of his arm, Savannah beamed up at him. "I wish I was a child again so I could run outside and roll about in it."

He grinned at her energetic words and cautioned, "If you decide to, you'd better dress more appropriately."

She returned his grin, eyes mellowing to a warm simmer that set his system tingling with unintentional allure. His hand rose to stroke her hair, the gesture shocking her back from the magical fantasy of the morning. She flinched away, startled that she had allowed her defenses to drop so low between them. Feeling her recoil, Skyler retreated a quick step, his expression tightening. A slow flush colored Savannah's cheeks when she saw the weals that liberally marred his shoulders from their conflict of the night before. Awkwardly, her defenses quickened.

"Where did you go last night?"

Skyler frowned and walked away. He began to dress as if he'd forgotten the question, then answered heavily. "I don't want to fight with you this morning, Savannah, so please don't start."

"I don't want to fight either. I was just asking."

"I went out for drinks with some friends."

"Friends?" His reluctance made her suspicious. "Do I know any of them?"

He was buttoning his shirt, his broad back to her. "Rhea asked me to go earlier but I said no."

"But you changed your mind?" she goaded.

"Yes." He said it with a cold finality as he turned. His eyes were as cold as the ice outside. "About many things. Get dressed or we'll miss breakfast." The

251

sharpness of his tone set her back in startled silence, so he continued brusquely. "I'm going to ask Leslie to take you into the city for some proper clothes. You'll freeze if you don't get some warm things before you return home."

Her insides froze. Until *she* returned home not *we*. "Aren't you coming with me?" she ventured hesitantly.

The silver eyes pierced through her. "Do you want me to?"

The question hung between them, a two-edged sword. When she didn't answer either way, he tugged on his coat.

"I'll see you downstairs."

When she entered the dining room, she found Skyler's mood had taken a radical swing as he sat bouncing his youngest nephew on his knee. The precocious four-year-old was a beautiful child with white blond hair, wide smile, and merry pale eyes, the image of his uncles. Savannah's heart gave a tender twist. Would her children look like this?

As if reading her thoughts, Skyler's eyes rose to meet hers above the fair head, warm and speculative, lingering only briefly so as not to invite rejection. He hadn't forgotten their chilly encounter of moments ago.

After the meal, at the children's insistence, Skyler and Palmer shouldered their heavy coats and gloves to see to the cutting of the tree. Savannah watched them march down the walk, Palmer carrying the toddler in his arms and holding Michael's hand, and Skyler with Jennifer riding on his shoulders, sharpened axe beneath his arm. The fresh snow blew about them like an upended liquid paperweight. The feeling that swelled in her bosom was odd at first and she didn't recognize it. It was a welling of pride for the tall, blond man, a pride in his goodness and his capacity to show love even when it was undeserved.

"He dotes on those children."

Savannah smiled at Leslie. "Of course he does. They're beautiful children, Leslie. You're so very lucky."

The plain face warmed with appreciation. "They can be a handful but Skyler is so good with them. Palmer is a wonderful father but sometimes I can't help but wish he had a bit more of his brother's giving nature. He's a good man, your husband, and he'll make a fine father."

Savannah blushed awkwardly but was not offended by the gentle encouragement. "He wants a big family but these aren't exactly the best of times to begin one."

Thinking she meant the war, Leslie nodded sadly. "I don't know what I'd do without Palmer. He's my strength. I wish somedays he would have agreed to take a consignment and stayed home. There's so much work to be done here and it would have been no disgrace. I wish we could keep them all home."

At that moment, Savannah had never envied anyone as much as the mousy Leslie Reade who had everything and every blessing life could offer.

The return with the fallen fir was a noisy affair announced by the bitter rush of December air through the open door.

"Uncle Sky chopped down our tree," Jennifer crowed. "It was the one I picked."

"No mine," Bobby howled.

"It was the one we all decided on," Skyler ended diplomatically as he shook the diamond drops of moisture from his fair head. With cold-stiffened fingers, he took the steaming mug of coffee Savannah offered.

"Thank you," he murmured softly, holding her gaze

for a lengthy minute. He took a cautious sip and let the heat warm his face before setting it aside. "Let's get this green monster inside and see if we have to cut a hole in the ceiling to fit it in."

With the tree trimming set for after dinner, Leslie and Savannah set off in the early afternoon in an open buggy. The sun was high, melting away the ice and snow and tempering the crisp air. To Savannah, it felt invigorating even though she shivered in her light-weight wrap.

Her bag nearly bulged with the wadding of notes Skyler had pressed upon her with a lengthy list of what she should purchase. Shopping for a wardrobe had never delighted her the way it did Hillary, but she was excited on this bright day, perhaps because she had someone to dress for.

Leslie saw her to the best shops, having been instructed by her brother-in-law on what he wanted to see her return with. Savannah was overwhelmed by the selection, with clothing so scarce in the South. Prices reflected the war effort. Many factories had converted to produce military wear. There were several gowns of brocade, satin, and velvet made to withstand the temperature as well as two evening gowns. Savannah would have settled for one but Leslie insisted. Then they added a cashmere shawl, woolen mantle, and plush velvet Talma cloak for braving the outdoors. The one thing she bought without Skyler's direction was a fine linen sleep dress with delicate handwork and a standing ruffle. It was the kind of gown a new bride should have for a wedding night. Leslie gave a tiny smile but said nothing.

Parcels strapped on the buggy, the two women lingered in the mercantile, buying candies for the children and admiring a selection of imported toys. As they laughed and talked together, three men began to mutter between themselves. They were rough-looking laborers. Some of the phrases Savannah was meant to overhear were crude slurs about her and her birthplace. It was with difficulty that she ignored them but inwardly she seethed. Leslie hadn't heard them, so Savannah pretended she didn't either as they returned to the street. As Savannah climbed into the buggy, Leslie exclaimed in sudden remembrance over something Palmer had asked her to pick up. She begged Savannah's patience and dodged across the busy street.

While she waited, Savannah let her thoughts wander ahead to the Christmas she would spend with her new family. Intent on that, she failed to see the buggy approach on her side. She barely had time to cry out before her arm was roughly gripped and she was jerked from the seat to the slushy gutter.

"See how proud you are now, you stinking Reb bitch," one of the men from the mercantile growled low and menacing.

"Let go of me, you—"

The fact that he hit her was almost as stunning as the blow. She spun, falling hard on the street next to the buggy wheels, skirt dragging in the melting sludge and palms skinning on the cobbles. It couldn't be happening, her mind screamed in panicked disbelief, not in the middle of the day on a busy street.

Before she could struggle to her feet, she was flung back down, wrists gripped and pulled up behind her back until she cried out in pain and fear.

"Don't hurt me," she wept hoarsely. "Please don't hurt me."

"Is that the way your niggers beg before you take a whip to 'em?" snarled a raspy voice. "Now you're going to know how that feels, you arrogant slut."

Held on her knees in the icy cold run-off water, she shut her eyes as one of them smeared her face and neck with an oily muck, coloring her skin from fair to darkest black. The taste of it filled her mouth, gritty and foul.

"Did that humble you a bit, Missy? Take a little chunk outta your pride? Maybe you'll have better sense than to strut your Southern tail around our streets. Traitor. Whore. Do you understand now? We don't want your kind around here."

There was a sharp crack and a wail of distress. Her arms were suddenly freed. Savannah lurched forward, gripping one of the wheels to drag herself up. Leslie stood in the buggy, whip in her hand. One of the men held crimson fingers to his cheek.

"Get in, Savannah," Leslie called crisply. She eyed the muttering trio while the shaken woman crawled into the seat beside her. "Lay a hand on this buggy and you'll lose some fingers," she warned before laying the whip across the horse's flanks. They started away from the side of the road with a jolt, slush splashing up on their assailants.

Breathing in broken sobs, Savannah took one last look behind them. She saw one of the men reach down and heft a chunk of dirty ice. His arm blurred. There was a stabbing pain to her head then nothing as she slumped down on the seat.

Awareness lapped back with the fuzzy edges of remembered terror. With a cry, she tried to sit up but strong hands and a flash of agony through her temple held her still.

"Don't try to move, Savannah. Lay very quiet. You're all right."

It was Palmer's low, professional voice and she obeyed unquestioningly. She kept her eyes closed to the too-bright lights in the room. A warm, wet cloth moved gently over her face, cleaning away the filth from the street, then something cold and stinging touched her head. At her sharp gasp, the cloth was lifted.

"You've got a nasty gash there. I know it hurts but it has to be cleaned."

Drawing a deep breath, she nodded. She made no further sound as the burning returned, though her eyes leaked helpless tears.

"A little something for the inside too, I think."

She drank from the glass he held, choking on the biting liquor but braced by its immediate warmth. She ventured a look about her, things swinging dizzily at first then becoming steady. From the austere walls and sparse furnishings, she assumed she was in the clinic at the rear of the house.

"Just lie still. Leslie's gone for Skyler. He'll be here in a minute."

Again she nodded weakly and closed her eyes. Her consciousness seemed to wax and wane in rhythmic pulses.

"Where is she? Oh my God. Is she all right?"

He had been cutting balsam for the garlands and the hand he put to her cheek held the pungent smell of pine, crisp, woodsy, and pleasant. Her eyes flickered open to focus on the sharp, worried features.

"Savannah? Savannah, can you hear me? Good God, what happened?"

She said his name in a pitiful whisper, arms reaching up for him. He scooped her up to his chest with a tender roughness and held her there while Leslie told him a sketchy version of what she'd seen. He turned on her with an impotent fury, words sharp and cutting.

"You left her. You left her and let this happen? I told

257

you to stay with her. Is this how you keep your word?"

"Skyler, please," Savannah murmured fraily, looking up at him with huge, dazed eyes. "It's not Leslie's fault. She couldn't have known. She saved me from them. Please don't blame her."

He looked at his wife's savaged face in a frustration of anger and upset. Black smudges still discolored her skin in blotchy patches. Her jaw sported an egg-sized lump. The gash on her head looked tender and raw. She looked more like a battered brawler that his sheltered wife. The dusky eyes rose in awkward apology. It could have been much worse and he owed Leslie more than he could say. "I'm sorry, Les."

Leslie only put a comforting hand on his shoulder and said nothing.

Skyler's gaze returned to the woman he loved and he winced at the sight—the cut head, the ruined dress, all signs of abuse to one he held so dear. His insides still ached from the clutch of fear when Leslie told him she had been hurt. The hand that touched her dirty cheek was far from steady.

"Is she all right, Palmer?" he asked without looking up.

"She took a pretty hard knock. She should stay off her feet and get lots of rest. I don't think it will be more serious than a headache and a tiny scar. If the discomfort gets too severe, I can give her something for the pain that will help her sleep. I just wish we could return a little of that discomfort to the thugs that did this."

That harsh sentiment won a nod from his brother.

"Did you recognize any of them, Leslie?" Palmer asked. "It would give me great pleasure to go calling with the sheriff."

"No. There are so many new faces these days and it

258

happened so fast. I didn't know them."

Skyler smoothed back the tangled hair and asked softly, "How do you feel?"

"Dirty and angry. And scared."

He cradled her gently, trying to hide how badly he was shaken. He felt the same helpless tremors of rage and panic that had possessed him on the steps of her home in Beaufort. Knowing she had been threatened and vulnerable to hurt and he had been powerless to prevent it was only made worse by the knowledge that he had brought her to the danger. He lifted her carefully and carried her through the maze of halls and up the stairs to their room.

Having removed her soiled and torn clothing, he saw her into the bath and washed the grime from her with a caring hand. She barely moved, sagging with weariness and shock until he placed her beneath the sheets on their bed and watched over her until she was asleep. His expression was set and unreadable, concealing thoughts that spun in an agitated whirl.

By evening, Savannah felt well enough to insist on being present at the tree trimming. While she reclined, covered and fussed over on the sofa, the large twelve-foot tree was draped in an arrayal of popcorn, cranberries, candy, and molded wax ornaments. When pronounced suitably dressed, Fletcher solemnly lit the multicolored candles that nestled in the short-needled branches. The tree shone with a flicker of light that reflected in the awed faces of the children. While Leslie served slices of hearty fruitcake and spiced cider, Skyler sat on the floor in front of Savannah's couch. The children clustered about him while he read from Dickens's *A Christmas Carol*. Their rapt faces mirrored a delightful horror as he read the words of the spirit Jacob Marley in a gravelly timbre.

Savannah smiled as she watched him entertain young and old alike with his rendering. Absently, her hand reached out to touch the back of his head, fingers running through the ashen locks of hair. Without pausing in his recitation, he turned slightly to press his cheek into her palm. She was asleep long before Scrouge met the Ghost of Christmas Present, and the candles on the tree were snuffed out one by one.

The terror was so stark and real it woke her with a cry of alarm. She was trembling weakly, body damp with a sheen of perspiration. Before she had even opened her eyes, Skyler's arms were tightly about her.

"Hush now," he whispered in the darkness. "It's all right. I'm here."

She clung to him frantically, face buried in the warm pulse of his throat. The weeping came softly without control as he rocked her in the safe haven of his embrace.

"Do you want me to get you something to help you sleep?" he asked in quiet concern.

"No," she sniffed. "I just need you."

"I'm right here."

"I was so afraid," she cried tremulously.

"It's over. Nothing will ever hurt you again. You're the bravest woman I know and I love you so very much. I should never have brought you here. If they had done anything to you, I'd have lost my mind. I'll take you home tomorrow if you want to go. Just please don't cry any more and don't be afraid."

Her tears had stilled during his husky speech and her fears as well. The hands that clung to him in search of comfort began to rub along the line of his shoulders. When the silence weighed between them, she looked up at him, seeing the dim shadow of his angular features, seeing them better through the gliding touch of her fingertips.

"Skyler," she whispered, "make love to me."

He was motionless, even his breathing seeming to stop.

"Skyler?"

Slowly, with infinite care, his lips came down to meet hers, encountering an eager acceptance that gave him pause. Her light touch smoothed over the planes of his face in a sensuous caress, then slipped into the spun silver of his hair. Her mouth parted to receive his deepening kiss and to return the featherlike dance of his tongue. With a small sound of wonderment, Skyler withdrew, kisses teasing across her face and neck. She returned them with equal fervor, marvelling at the different textures of his skin, from rough cheek to warm sensitive throat, and at the shivery tremors she elicited with tiny nibbles of her teeth.

When his large hands moved reverently over the creamy satin of her body, hers touched him with an innocent exploration. She admired the hard swelling contours, from taut leanness to firm muscles, in a way she had never quite dared before. She had always revelled in his strength but the explicit power of his long, large build awed her with a new awareness of how easily he could have taken anything he wanted from her. She let the half-realized and barely under-stood emotions run freely, feelings of want, of safety in his arms, of desire for the man he had come to be to her, tender, possessive, loving, protective. The warmth of those feelings loosened all restrictions that had governed her in his bed. She feasted on the sweet, unyielding flesh, delighted in the feel of him, gave voice to the moans of sensual gratification his purposeful handling of her provoked.

And when they came together to strive for the ultimate reward of their passion, she cried his name, weeping with the strength of her joy and the beautiful sense of oneness with the man who had been lover and enemy but never her beloved. She lay in his arms in a languorous fulfillment, still holding to him in a reluctance to surrender their physical closeness or this new attitude of emotional truce. Hearing him whisper of his love, she let the peaceful lull of contentment steal her gently into the realm of dreams.

Chapter Nineteen

The morning was grey and somber but not so her mood when Savannah awoke to find herself resting on the golden plane of Skyler's chest. With memories of their night together playing wistfully upon her mind, she smiled and burrowed against his solid heat. Her fingers teased through the downy covering beneath her cheek.

"Good morning."

The throaty whisper of his voice evoked none of her defenses. Selfishly, she wanted to savor this time with him, willing the worry of consequence to wait. "Good morning," she returned in an equally hushed voice.

"How do you feel?"

"Marvelous," she purred, purposefully mistaking his question.

His large hand cupped her chin, tipping it up so he could delve into the sultry mystery of her eyes. He could read her simple happiness in them but was hesitant to believe it would last. Her enthused participation in their lovemaking had been a delirious heaven and this warm compliance a dream come to life, but he didn't trust it. The mood was too fragile to pin any hopes to. He vowed to enjoy it as long as it lasted, then not to be disappointed if nothing more followed.

Savannah's palm rubbed over the stubble on his

cheek, then she stretched up to sample his mouth, moving over the generous fullness with a slow deliberation. His hands ran up the gentle curve of her back, spanning her torso while his thumbs circled the tightening tips of her breasts. With a sigh, he pushed her back, looking at her with a cautious, searching glance. The way she returned his look, all inviting and soft, made his heart want to believe things his head warned him not to.

"What now?" he asked.

"Now?" she echoed with the lift of an arched brow. Her fingertips traced the shape of his lips.

"Do you want to leave? I promised I would take you back if you wanted to go." Neither his quietly spoken words nor his expression betrayed his own hopes.

"Leave?" She fell silent, mulling it over carefully. The nightmare of the encounter on the street seemed far removed from the safe harbor of Skyler's cluttered room. "No," she said slowly. "I don't want to leave. I don't want to spend Christmas on some dirty train."

"Savannah, I'll do my best to keep you safe, but the mood in the city gets uglier by the day. Keeping you from harm means more to me than plum pudding with my family."

"Thank you for that but no. I won't be run off by some bullying roughnecks. I won't be intimidated. They frightened me, Skyler. They had me begging for my safety. To beg the likes of that vermin makes me ashamed of my weakness. Never again. I won't be helpless like that again."

The angry conviction in her tone impressed him but was upsetting as well, with its hint of her careless stubborn streak. Her pride wouldn't let her admit she had reason to fear, so he had to worry for her.

"I'm proud to have you for a wife, you impossible woman, and I do want to stay here a bit longer. If you feel uncomfortable, we can go at any time. I won't have you living in fear again."

"I won't. I have you."

Her kiss was warm with the beginnings of passion, stirring his emotions and encouraging him to think of pleasant ways to spend the rest of the morning that wouldn't involve leaving their bed. She seemed more than willing.

"Sky, are you decent?" Brent called through the door. He opened it almost without a pause, then grinned as Savannah sunk below the covers, still very much in his brother's arms. "Glad to see you're feeling better, Sis."

"What do you want, Brent?" The low, gruff timbre told of his bad timing.

"Sorry for the interruption but Rhea's downstairs."

"So?" His belligerence stemmed from the delightful shivers Savannah caused him as her nails grazed up and down his ribs. The mention of his former love prompted a sharp jab that made him wince.

"She said she had to see you and would wait. You know Rhea. She'll just put up her feet and stay there all day." Brent's grin widened in amusement.

"Let her," Skyler grumbled then, with an apologetic look at his wife, added, "Tell her I'll be down in a minute. Do you mind?" he asked Savannah after Brent had gone.

"No," she lied bravely. She lay back silently as Skyler slid out of bed to dress. Her eyes devoured the sight of his sleek masculine physique but there was a twinge to her jealous heart, knowing Rhea Sherwood had appreciated the view as well. Her lips were decidedly cool when he bent to kiss her.

"Wait for me?" he suggested hopefully, seeing their closeness slip away.

"I think I'd like to have some breakfast" was her

smooth rejection.

Frowning slightly, he nodded and left her to join his past.

Depressed and restless, Savannah got up, instantly regretting the movement for the cannon fire it touched off in her temples. She tottered unsteadily into the adjoining room to splash water on her face and received an unpleasant shock when she looked into the mirror. The cut at her hairline had swelled to an unsightly purple bruise and was matched by the discoloration on her determined jaw. The marks were a reminder of her vulnerability, and her anger with her assailants, Skyler, and Rhea, returned rekindling her independent pride. No, she would not cower in her room. No, she would not hide from the woman who shared her husband's background and his bed. It had never been her way before and it would not be now.

They were talking in the parlor when she came downstairs. Savannah hadn't planned to eavesdrop, but when she caught a few words of their topic she could not easily walk away. Rhea was speaking in a tight, angry voice.

"You can't do it, Sky. It would be political suicide. To go to such an affair with a Southern tart on your arm would ruin your name and your future, a future we plotted so carefully together."

"I am quite capable of plotting my own future, something you never wanted to accept. I only followed your lead because your ideas were sound and pleasing, not because I couldn't walk a straight path without someone to guide me. If you thought you held the strings for a nice political puppet, I'm sorry to disillusion you."

The sharp tone was instantly softened to a coaxing plea. "You know my interest in you isn't political. We were so good together. I wanted the best for you, for us.

266

Would you fault me for that now?"

"No, Rhea. I'm grateful to you. We can still be good together but not the same way."

"Because of her." The spite was back with a brittle snap. "How could you do this to me, Sky? How could you hurt me so?"

Surprisingly, he laughed. "Oh, Rhea, I doubt that I've broken your heart. Bruised your pride perhaps. You can replace me with any one of several dozen men without compunction."

"But I don't want any other man."

In the suspicious silence, Savannah peered around the door and felt her blood heat with a surprising violence. The comely auburn-haired woman was standing toe to toe with her husband, ruby lips attached firmly to his. Had she not seen his quick reaction of protest, she might have been provoked to snatch up the first available pistol and put an end to both of them.

"Excuse me," she drawled, deriving a smug satisfaction from the shock in the other woman's face and the panic in Skyler's. She let him fret uncharitably while turning a cool smile on her rival. "If I were a man in my county, I'd be asking you to choose a weapon, but I understand things are much more civilized up here. I'll merely warn you that I don't appreciate trespassers. Because Skyler values your friendship, I will allow this one indiscretion, but don't mistake my intentions or think me soft and easily deceived. I am neither, Miss Sherwood. Don't assume that you can toy with my husband at your leisure. You had your chance with him and he did not marry you."

Skyler stood very still as she reached up to rub the lip rouge from his mouth. Its corners twitched in a smile he didn't dare let escape. Her possessive jealousy couldn't have pleased him more but he didn't want to risk the feel of her palm over it.

267

Rhea's momentary alarm was absorbed by her unshakable poise. The sharp chin rose defiantly. "You may be Mrs. Reade, but what good can you do him? Your presence is a blight on everything he has worked for. Skyler has a brilliant future in this state and you are destroying it. You'll be a black mark he can never erase from his reputation as a statesman. No one will trust or vote for a Republican who is tied to a Southern—"

"Tart, I believe you said." Savannah made light of Rhea's observations but inwardly she was shaken with doubt. Was the woman right? Was she a poison to Skyler's career. She looked at him, the question phrased in her deep blue eyes. His response more than reassured her.

"Rhea, you mistake my priorities. A Washington office was your dream. I merely didn't object. Savannah is my wife. I won't go where she's not accepted. This war is not going to last forever. When it's done, I think people will be in a forgiving mood. Until then, who knows. I just might become a cotton planter."

Rhea shuddered in horror but Savannah chuckled, placing a hand on his arm.

"I'm afraid you'd starve, city boy," she teased.

"I'm overwhelmed with everyone's confidence in me. Is it my fate to sit on the veranda and live off our money?"

His wry question brought a sparkle of mischief. "That and one other thing you've said I can't do without you."

His smile widened to show he recalled the reference.

The intimate exchange was not overlooked by Rhea. Or underestimated. She would not be foolish enough to lay down an open challenge again. She would launch her attack with more subtle ploys.

"I'm sure you know what's best for you. I should be off. Will I see you tonight, Sky?"

"Perhaps."

She repressed a frown of annoyance at the vague reply but had no option but to bid the couple a polite good day.

"Tonight?" Savannah asked pointedly.

He pulled her into a close embrace, surprised and pleased when she didn't protest. "Not a rendezvous, I assure you. It's a Christmas ball, a rather grand affair that's a tradition among our neighbors. We take turns hosting it. We usually go as a family but this year—" He shrugged in uncertainty.

"Skyler, I truly don't want to be a hindrance to you," she began softly. Her eyes lowered with uncommon sensitivity. He tipped her head up with a thumb beneath her chin.

"You are a joy to me, Savannah. Never forget that. I meant what I said to Rhea. You are all that matters to me. I wish you'd believe that."

"I guess I do," she answered in a timid voice.

"Are you up to braving the chilly winter of Philadelphia society?

The challenge brought back her plucky arrogance. "I've a new set of clothes made for the occasion."

As it turned out, the family's barouche was full with the exception of Fletcher, who declined but wished them all a good time. The party was held in a neighboring mansion, neighboring being some ten miles of travel. Squeezed between Brent and Skyler, Savannah found herself as excited and prickly with nerves as a debutante at her coming-out ball. She tried soberly to remind herself that these were Yankees but she continued to view it as a chance to meet Skyler's friends. She couldn't fathom why it was so important

269

for her to make a good impression but her care in her appearance testified to it. Perhaps it was the way Skyler looked in his full black outfit of evening tails, white vest, and tie. The sight had stirred her emotions with a giddy mix of pride and desire. The formal wear was so sleek and elegantly draped on his large, well-proportioned form, sophisticated yet undeniably sensual. Shamelessly, she anticipated being held to that starched shirtfront and, even more privately, taking it off him.

The home of Jacob and Abigail Prescott was ablaze with light, indoors and out, illuminating the well-dressed couples in attendance. Except for a light sampling of blue and braid, there was no evidence of a war. With Lee's Gettysburg Campaign dissolving in the summer and the Confederates driven from Pennsylvania, war seemed far removed. Ample food and drink were in evidence, as were high spirits. To Savannah the gaiety seemed to have a false ring, as though everyone were desperately trying to pretend it was just another holiday celebration.

In the large entry foyer, Skyler removed her cloak and handed it to one of the servants along with his own overcoat. His silvery eyes lingered over her with an impassioned thoroughness. An embarrassed but pleased color rose in her face. That bold stare told her he was thinking along the same lines for the end of their evening.

"You're beautiful," he whispered as his lips brushed her temple.

The looks she received when she entered the spacious room told her the same thing. She had chosen a dress of deep blue velvet and ivory lace to accent her dark coloring. The pointed décolletage plunged deep, leaving bare the creamy slope of her shoulders and swell of her bosom. Small puffed sleeves were adorned

270

with the same pleated frill of net and threaded black ribbon. The huge sweeping bell of her skirt consisted of a lush lace-edged overskirt and trained underskirt of ruched and puffed net that made a delightful sigh as she moved. Her raven hair was styled in a high-set chignon with a spill of inky ringlets and loose tendrils that concealed the marring bruise. Knowing the fate of her own jewels, Skyler had presented her with a complimentary set of drop earrings and heavy classically styled necklace of triple pendants. The effect was visually stunning and feminine, and Skyler's possessive arm about her tiny waist stated clearly that she was his.

He escorted his wife about with pride but, even so, was careful of who he introduced her to. He steered away from the Democrats who would punish the South even at the cost of women and children. He didn't want the evening to turn into a political forum, remembering too well the fiasco of their last appearance in Beaufort. He wanted it to be an enjoyable night for both of them, one in which they could represent man and wife not North and South. He kept to a circle of family friends and liberal Republicans who shared the President's view of rejoining the country without the avidly sought retribution of his opposing camp. They found his bride as charming and witty as she was beautiful, and Savannah relaxed in their company. She was on her best behavior, the sharpened wit softened to a gentle humor and the fiery flash of her eyes warming to a heated glow whenever they lifted to his.

From a distance, cold amber eyes watched them dispassionately while the shrewd mind behind them plotted.

At Savannah's assurance that she would be fine, Skyler left her for a moment to fetch them some refreshment. When he was cornered at the punch table by a group of former friends, Rhea slipped up next to

Savannah with a watery smile, her arm linking the other woman's with a companionable ease.

"Good evening. Are you enjoying the company?"

Savannah looked at the other woman coolly. It was on her mind to say, "Until now," but she settled on a smile and a nod.

"I thought you could use some advice on being a politician's wife. I could be of help to you. It was a position I almost held."

Savannah stiffened at the reference and cast a quick glance about for Skyler. She had no wish to be taught a lesson in etiquette by his former love but could see no way to discourage her without making a scene. She held her temper with difficulty, the mild smile affixed to her face.

"Why thank you, Miss Sherwood. It is kind of you to consider my education."

"You must call me Rhea. After all, Skyler and I go way back. We're practically family." The golden eyes glittered above the silky smile. "He's quite a man, our Skyler. He has a great future ahead but you must be willing to do your part to help him get there. We worked long hours, sometimes all night making plans for his campaign. I dedicated myself to him totally. Even if he hadn't been such a wonderful lover, I would have helped him because he's going far. He has the makings of a senator, at least. He has the face and the voice and the presence. All he needs is the push to achieve. That's his one fault. He has to be pushed along very carefully. Why there were nights when he didn't want to discuss politics at all." A little smug laugh. "Well, you know how he can be. It's hard to say no to him once he's undressed."

Savannah gritted her teeth. She wished she had a glass of the ruby punch. It would have clashed beautifully with her yellow brocade gown. "I am

272

intimately acquainted with my husband's habits. Get on with it, Miss Sherwood. You had a point to make, I assume."

Rhea's smile curled. The other woman had grit. It would be hard to provoke her. In other circumstances, she might have even liked the bold Southerner, but Skyler stood between them and Rhea was determined not to lose sight of that goal. She had to handle things discreetly. Skyler had to be shown what a liability the woman was. She had to turn his thinking around to match hers before she lost him completely, and with him gone, so were her ambitious plans.

"What are you going to do to see to your husband's success?" she asked bluntly.

"I wasn't aware he needed my help. Skyler is a capable man. I think you underestimate him. I'm not even certain a career in politics is what he really wants."

Rhea gave a tinny laugh. "Of course it is. It's what he's suited for, it's what he's always wanted."

"Or is it what you've wanted, Miss Sherwood?"

She drew a hissing breath and let it out slowly. "What I want is no longer the issue, Savannah. As you said, he is your husband. If you want to keep him, you'd better learn something of his world. He may be satisfied with a pretty playmate for his bedroom for a time but you have to have a means of holding him when he's ready to move on. You have to show him how much you can do for him."

"I'm not sure you're the one to be teaching me how to accomplish that."

Rhea swallowed her pride to reply, "Skyler didn't love me. You have that advantage but it may not be enough. I'm not doing this for you. I'm thinking of Skyler and the benefit he can be to our country. If you are a loyal wife, you'll want to see he gets where he should be. You can either help him or be a stumbling block he'll grow to resent."

Savannah considered her words. She didn't trust the woman's motives. Rhea Sherwood coveted her husband but seemed sincere in her desire to see him succeed. The thought of holding him back and creating a future tension between them was one she wanted to avoid. Like it or not, Rhea knew what she was talking about. She knew the mechanics of lobbying for a man in office. She knew the right people, how to make the right connections. Above all things, even above her jealous distrust of his ex-love, Savannah wanted to make Skyler proud of her. She wanted to show him that she could fit into his world and be of service to him there.

"All right, Miss Sherwood. I'm listening. What is it you propose?"

Rhea's smile was genuine, a smooth cat-in-the-canary-cage gesture. "You show uncommon good sense, Savannah. Few women would be willing to take help from their husband's old friends. That takes considerable bravery."

Savannah gauged her coolly. She couldn't be sure the edge of mockery was in the other's voice.

"Come, Savannah. Let me introduce you to some people."

Chapter Twenty

From the refreshment table, Skyler peered over the head of one of his companions to see Savannah in a conversation with Rhea. Frowning slightly, he tried to excuse himself but was caught up by the arrival of Tony D'Angelo. They exchanged warm greetings, and for a moment, Skyler forgot his plan to rescue his bride. Tony was full of news from the Tennessee front and Burnside's relief from duty. His colorful oration drew a crowd of those who had thought to put aside the war for an evening but couldn't resist hearing of it. He and Brent got into a discussion of field commanders, and eventually the curious filed away and Skyler began to search the room once more. He saw Rhea coolly sipping champagne with an elderly statesman but there was no sign of Savannah.

Rhea looked up at the tall, blond man, an innocent smile curving her lips. She could hardly keep her eyes from scorching down the length of him in ardent appreciation. Soon, she thought, soon.

"Where did Savannah go? You were talking with her just a moment ago."

"Have a glass, Skyler. Have you met Thomas Thorogood?"

Skyler exchanged a short greeting but his restless gaze was scanning the room for the familiar figure of his wife. Rhea's hand curled warm and possessive about his elbow.

"You haven't danced with me yet this evening, Sky. You aren't still angry over that scene this morning, are you?" Her voice was a soft, chiding croon.

"No, of course not. I really must—"

"Dance with me," she concluded. "Everyone is looking at us. Don't be mean and make them all think you've thrown me in the lurch. We're still friends, aren't we?"

He gave her an easy smile. "You know we are, Rhea. You know I wouldn't tarnish your reputation."

He took her in his arms for the spinning steps of the waltz. She felt comfortable and familiar there, leaning slightly toward him. She followed him with practiced grace, knowing his steps and anticipating each turn. They looked good together, moved well together, and he enjoyed the ease of leading her about the crowded floor. The golden eyes were lifted to his and the full, inviting lips were close and eager.

"Sky, I love you," she said suddenly. Before he could object, she went on casually, "You didn't expect that to change, did you? We've been friends for ever. I want you to be happy, Sky, and I want you to know that I'll always be there for you if you need me."

The words brought a bittersweet smile. Oh, if he could only hear them spoken from other lips. "Thank you, Rhea. That means a lot to me. You mean a lot to me."

As he spoke, his eyes drifted over the crowd of faces and froze. His concentration was so absorbed that he missed a step and crushed the slippered foot beneath his unthinkingly. When Rhea gave a gasp of hurt and surprise, Skyler released her with a hastily murmured, "Excuse me."

"Sky?" Before she could reach out to him, he was

276

pushing his way through the dancers. She frowned darkly, not needing to see his destination.

From his position on the dance floor, Skyler saw Savannah in a secluded alcove surrounded by a group of political reporters. Wondering how they had managed to single her out, he rushed to serve as her buffer. They could be a savage lot when dealing with people they liked and he didn't want them preying on his wife for her unpopular background and ideals. As he drew closer, Savannah's eyes lifted to meet his briefly. There was no sign of panic or need in the dark midnight gaze. He slowed, then hesitated. She was speaking easily, fielding the direct questions with a cool adeptness that he envied. He remained outside the fringe of the group and listened. Slowly, the tension left his features, to be replaced by a warm, admiring smile.

"You own slaves, Mrs. Reade?" she was asked pointedly.

"My family does. We have a cotton plantation near Columbia and it requires a large work force to make a profit. Profit is hard to come by when forty cents out of every dollar goes North to factor's commissions, interest charges, freight, and insurance. In a way, you gentlemen have grown prosperous off the institution without being accused of perpetuating it."

"What does your husband feel about being linked to a slave holder?"

Savannah handled the question without hesitation. "Skyler was appalled by it as any moral person would be."

"And you, Mrs. Reade?"

"Slavery is an evil I have never condoned. The men in my family did not go to war to protect their right to own other men but to protect our home from unfair invasion. Would any of you have done any different?"

That raised a few brows but the mood was hard

277

to sway.

"You see it as an evil yet you do nothing to stop it. Isn't that hypocrisy?"

She faced the man who spoke directly, eyes calm and voice level. "Sir, there are nearly as many black people in the South as white. They are untrained in all but the most menial of tasks and are frightfully ignorant of the world outside the plantation they live on. You propose to free them into a world they don't know how to live in. It is a noble cause but an ill-conceived one. Where are all these poor people going to go? North? And are you going to welcome them with open arms and train them to compete for the same jobs held by whites in your factories? Look at your protest in New York where white objectors tortured and lynched black men, women, and children. They don't want slavery abolition and equality."

"So you propose to keep them shackled to serve you?"

"I know our peculiar institution is wrong and must be changed, and I am not alone in that. Seventy-five percent of the South doesn't even own slaves. The greater wrong is in your rash solution to the problem. It will collapse our entire economy and send millions of people adrift. We are an isolated people raised in stagnation and ignorance and in fear of the very work force we need to survive. The South doesn't need to be punished. It needs to be helped into the nineteenth century. We are a proud people opposed to change but we can learn. We can't be taught by intimidation and violence, but with understanding and patience. With men like my husband and his friends in positions of power, this country can be brought back together. Excuse me, gentlemen. I've enjoyed our talk, but my husband is here for an evening of celebration not soapboxing. I mustn't ignore him."

Skyler took her hand, leading her from a spattering of applause and murmuring to the quiet hall. He turned her easily into his arms.

"Foolish of me to think you needed rescuing," he teased. "Are you trying to make Southern sympathizers of us all?"

"No, just lessen some of the ignorance. On both sides. Do you think they'll listen?"

He shrugged his elegant shoulders. "Some, perhaps. Some are deaf to all but the drum and cannon fire. Were you doing campaigning for me?"

She studied his shirt buttons intently until he lifted her chin with his thumb. "Are you angry?" she asked in a quiet voice.

"At myself for letting you get into such a situation. Savannah, those men can be ruthless."

"I can hold my own, Yankee," she claimed boldly.

His smile was loving. "I know you can, little Rebel, but why would you want to face those jackals?"

"I wanted to make you proud of me. I wanted them to meet me and get to know me so they wouldn't judge you so harshly for having married a Southerner."

He was wordless for several seconds, searching for a way to tell her how much the gesture meant to him. "Savannah, you don't need to do my politicking for me. I don't care what they think of you or of me for making you my wife. All I care about is what you think, and right now I am very proud and very pleased."

"Was it wrong of me to speak to them?"

"Not wrong. What I heard was very right but the risk was unnecessary. I don't expect you to work at furthering my career. I didn't marry you to make my speeches or pave my way. I married you to be my wife and share my family. If you want to do more, it would make me happy, but I don't want you to feel pressured into doing anything you don't feel is right for you. It's

279

not that important to me. Not as important as you feeling comfortable and happy when you're with me."

"What's not right about setting a bunch of arrogant Yankees on their ears?" she countered. "Let's just say it was to make up for the last time you took me into public. Hopefuly, I left a better opinion of myself this time." She looked up at him, seeing not the young naval officer on a dirty beach but a statesman who could heal a nation, starting with the ravaged ground of her heart. "Skyler," she began in a hushed tone.

She never got the rest out as they were spied by a jovial Tony D'Angelo. He tottered to where they stood and snatched up full glasses to fill their hands.

"To old friends," he cried in an animated toast.

"Old friends," Skyler echoed, clinking his glass. "And new," he added, touching the rim to Savannah's.

She was spirited off to dance with the swarthy captain, and in their short conversation, she did much to amend his first impression of her. By the time he handed her back to Skyler he was thinking what a lucky man his friend was. The rest of the hours of the evening were spent mostly on the dance floor, dividing the time between Skyler, Brent, and the new friends she was beginning to like in spite of their accents and politics. The only other disturbing note to the night was an odd conversation she had with the wife of a well-known businessman.

The woman approached her and drew her aside while Skyler was distracted. She introduced herself as Faith Wilmington. Her accent was pure Georgia. As they spoke, Savannah couldn't help but wonder over the woman's skillful questioning and finally grew blunt.

"What is the purpose of this talk, Mrs. Wilmington?"

A smile creased the older face. "Why you, my dear. Are you planning to return to South Carolina?"

"After the holidays, yes. Why do you ask?"

"Are you a patriot of your country, Mrs. Reade?"

At first, Savannah bristled at the question, but then it didn't seem so odd considering the company she was keeping. "I love my state, Mrs. Wilmington, and I love my home."

"And are you willing to take some risks to prove that love?"

"What kind of risks?" She had begun to draw away in suspicion. Who was this woman to be asking such questions of her?

"Risks that would help ease the suffering of men like your brother and those he fought with."

"What do you know of my brother?"

"I've asked about you, all very discreet of course. I know you are a compassionate woman, Mrs. Reade. I was just wondering if you were a brave one as well."

While Savannah frowned apprehensively, the woman pressed a slip of paper in her hand and folded her fingers over it.

"If you are in Washington on your way home, stop at this address. Go alone. You'll be doing humanity a great service." She said a quick good-bye and hurried off as Skyler rejoined her. He smiled down into her troubled eyes.

"Skyler, who was that woman?"

"Her husband is a clothing manufacturer. I believe she's from Atlanta. They were married years before this mess started. They live a few miles North of us. Why?"

She gave him a nervous smile and peered after the mysterious woman. "Just curious about meeting someone from my homeland so far away." She tucked the piece of paper into her tiny bag, dismissing it and the odd conversation as her husband took her into his arms for a dance.

The hour was late when a weary Leslie sought them

281

out and suggested they begin home. Her feet aching with the unaccustomed miles of waltzing, Savannah was eager to agree. As they found their wraps, they were approached by a wobbly Rhea Sherwood who clung precariously to Skyler's arm.

"Oh, Sky, I seem to have shared one toast too many to the New Year. Could you be a good friend and see me home? My wretched driver has gotten himself into similar straights and I am quite stranded. I'd be most grateful and surely Savannah wouldn't mind."

The bleary golden eyes turned to her hopefully. Not wanting to appear clinging and heartless, Savannah was forced to be charitable. She cursed Brent for having found himself a pretty escort at the last minute and her own pride that refused to let her suggest accompanying them.

"Go on, Skyler. I'll wait up for you."

As good as her intentions had been, she couldn't keep the frown from her face as Skyler assisted the helpless woman into her buggy, then took up the reins.

A light snow was falling as Savannah stood looking into the night. Leslie's private words to her as they mounted the stairs remained in her thoughts. They created a nagging worry as she recalled them.

"Rhea Sherwood is rich and spoiled and used to getting everything she wants," Leslie told her not unkindly. "She's known Skyler since they were children and she wanted him ever since she saw his potential. Rhea wants power and she sees politics as her way to have it. She wants to be a first lady, of a city, of a state, of a country. She's groomed Sky to make that happen for her. She pushed him into politics with her own ambition and considers him her creation. She sees his good nature as a weakness and feeds on that. He is not a fool but he is a man. He doesn't understand how deceitful a woman can be and how she'll use and bend friendship. Savannah, if you want to keep him, you'd better see he learns that lesson. Rhea was never right for Sky. I think you are. Don't let him be misled. If you love him, keep him safe from women like Rhea."

If you want to keep him, she said. If you love him.

She turned as the door opened and Skyler faced her cautiously. His smile of apology was offset by the wariness of his eyes. He checked his pocket watch and grimaced at the suspicious lateness of the hour.

"The roads were treacherous," he began to explain but she only nodded in noncommittal silence. "I couldn't just abandon her, Savannah."

"I know" was her quiet reply.

"I'm sorry. Please let's not fight."

She approached him slowly, the velvety bell of her skirt rustling on its stiff ruching of net. Standing close, she reached up to wipe away the smears of bright lip rouge that stained his mouth and cheeks. Still she said nothing.

"She kissed me. She was very drunk. I didn't encourage it. I had to practically drag her out of the buggy. She's been a friend for a long time. I can't expect you to make allowances for her bad behavior but at least trust me, I—"

The rest of his hurried reasoning was unnecessary. Savannah's hand caught the back of his head, drawing it down so she could reach his lips in an urgent kiss. Recovering from his astonishment, his arms encircled the supple figure. Velvet crushed against his immaculate evening wear.

Without a word, she stepped back, fingers busy with the buttons on his shirt, opening it so her palms could slide over the heated plane of his bare chest. When she did speak, her words were low and rough with emotion.

283

"Love me, Skyler. I don't want to lose you. Please love me."

The velvet gown fell heavily from its own weight, followed by the layers of undergarments, until the borrowed jewels gleamed against her fair skin.

Slowly, Skyler turned and blew out the light.

Chapter Twenty-One

The days before Christmas were ones of hurried cheer laced with the hint of melancholy. The Reades remembered the loss of their beloved wife and mother, and Savannah thought of Rising Sun. She helped ready the house for the festivities, hanging garlands of greenery, making colorful paper chains with the children, and working in the kitchen to prepare sweets. The house was filled with a continual influx of people, the main two being Tony D'Angelo and Rhea Sherwood. Both of them disturbed Savannah for different reasons. Tony closeted himself with Skyler to talk war and strategy, urging him to rejoin the rank this time in the cavalry, where he served under Pleasanton. Rhea was carefully inoffensive, even making a grand apology to Savannah for borrowing Skyler on the night of the party, but her subtlety was not unnoticed. She sought every minute to be alone with Skyler. While they talked politics, she found innocent ways to touch him. Though privately simmering, Savannah kept her composure but managed to be present whenever the scheming female was on hand. Leslie's words remained with her.

On Christmas Eve, the entire family attended an evening service at their church. The minister's prayer for peace in the new year had tears in many eyes including Savannah's. Even in the sacred pews, she could feel the hatred of burning stares. Though she said nothing of it, it weighed heavily on her mind for the rest of the evening.

It was a family custom to stop at the homes of various friends after the service, where they drank spiked cider and talked of times past. On the last stop, Skyler suggested they walk the few remaining blocks home. Though tired and depressed, Savannah agreed, hoping the snowy silence of the night would give her troubled mind some ease.

It was a crisp and cold night that settled about them but almost pleasant without a wind to make it bitter. A featherlike snow powdered the walk and lay glistening atop Skyler's bare head. Occasionally harness bells and carolers' voices drifted on the still of the evening, but for the most part, it was as if they had the world to themselves.

"Cold?" he asked. At her brief nod, his arm went about her shoulders to draw her close into his side. She could sense there was something on his mind and waited until he found the right words. "I know you'll want to return home after the holidays."

"There's no hurry," she answered quietly.

"Savannah, do you want me to go with you?"

He stopped her and turned her by the shoulders to face him. His expression was grave, betraying no pressing of emotion.

"That would be your decision," she replied in a constricted tone. Caught unprepared, her heart fluttered nervously in time to the swirl of her panicked thoughts.

"No," he disagreed. "It's yours. I'll only go if you ask me. Things can't go on the way they have been. I can't pretend your wishes don't matter to me. I need to know, Savannah. I need to hear it from you. Do you want me to go with you?"

Suddenly all the clutter of confusion was gone and she answered him simply. "Yes. Please come with me."

A smile of monumental relief flickered across his face, then he was serious once again as he reached into his coat. He fished out a small box. Using his teeth to tug off his gloves, he presented her with the gift.

"Merry Christmas. I know it's early but I couldn't wait." He snapped open the box, hearing her quick draw of breath. "It was my mother's. It would mean a lot to me to have you wear it on your hand."

While he waited anxiously, she stared at the ring, a beautiful fantasy of gold and diamonds that sparkled as breathtakingly as the crystals of ice all about them. Slowly, she drew the glove off her left hand and extended it to him. He took it reverently and slid on the band so it fit next to her wedding ring. Savannah swallowed the lump of emotion that lodged in her throat along with the silly urge to weep. Her acceptance made this ring a symbol the first had not been.

"I didn't get you anything," she mumbled awkwardly.

"Yes you did," he countered, bringing her chilled fingers up to his lips to kiss them warmly.

"I mean a gift. I wanted to give you something but I didn't have the means."

"Yes you do. The greatest gift would be the words I long to hear, but if you can't afford them, give me a child, Savannah."

A shy smile trembled on her lips but the deep dusky eyes warmed to the thought. "It's not a gift I can give alone."

His grin was wide and brilliant. "But it's one I can enjoy giving as much as receiving."

While he fetched them some hot spiced grog to warm them from the walk, Savannah changed into the virginal nightdress she'd had no chance to wear. It seemed right for this night somehow, for it was more like the wedding night she'd cheated him from so many months before. She felt like a bride, nervously awaiting her chosen.

It was the approach of the New Year, she told herself, the time for starting, for beginning again. Was it time she gave them that chance? Were they even the same two people of nearly a year ago? So much had changed. The way she saw Skyler had changed. The terrible trap she felt caught in had become a tender snare she was reluctant to seek a release from. Gradually, her objection to the situation had worn away, blurring the reasons for holding so zealously to it. When recalling that betraying event, she found herself making excuses for his actions. The only concession she had not made, could not bring herself to make, was in her failure to respond to his nightly statement to her. When she tried to visualize or form the words, a hard knot of protest choked them back. But he was patient, sure some day they would come. Why couldn't she be so confident?

Skyler shut the door to their room with a boot heel, balancing the steaming mugs in both hands. His gaze swept down her with a lingering appreciation before he came to hand her a glass and curl up beside her on the bed pillows.

"A toast?" he proposed, raising his glass. "To our families. May they have the opportunity to meet and become friends. And to our family, the one we'll start between us."

The glasses clinked together and they both drank. Then purposefully, Skyler took hers and set it beside his on the dressing table before turning to take her in his arms.

What little sleep they managed to find that night was

288

interrupted early by excited whispers from the hall outside as the children hurried to peep through the railing for a glimpse of what Santa Claus had left them. Groggy but smiling, the adults were roused so the procession downstairs could begin. The children were kept out until Fletcher had the tree aglow with light, then they were ushered in to exclaim and goggle over the stacks of brightly wrapped gifts. Skyler found the two of them a sofa safely beyond the gleeful destruction of paper and ribbon, and held her close while they watched the children's delight. Knowing his thoughts, Savannah shared his wistful smile, her eyes going to the two rings on her hand.

With the children crowing over their prized gifts, a metal-cast set of toy soldiers for Michael, a doll house for Jennifer, and a rocking horse for Bobby, Savannah looked at the odd one she'd received. It was Frederick Douglass's *Narrative of the Life of an American Slave*. Though the publication was not new, copies of it couldn't be found in the South. Seeing her uncertainty, Fletcher was quick to explain.

"I meant no offense, Savannah. You're a bright young woman. It would be a shame for you to see only one side of things."

She looked at the volume thoughtfully, then said, "Thank you. I will read it and see my family does as well."

Fletcher bent to give her a fatherly kiss that made the gift more precious in her eyes.

As the women prepared the table, the boys wrestled on the paper-strewn floor, their ages not limited to the youngest two. Even Palmer was drawn into the roughhousing, riding his sons like a bucking horse. Savannah shook her head at such foolhardiness when she came to call them to dinner. With a smile, she watched Brent and Skyler wrestling like a pair of children until her husband was sent tumbling. There was a loud clunk as his elbow struck the edge of a low marble table. He stayed down on his knees, doubled over, clutching his arm to his chest.

"You're getting old, Sky. Have I wounded you or just your pride?" Brent teased.

Feeling uneasy, Savannah bent down and put a hand atop the fair head. "Skyler, are you all right?"

"Fine. Just winded me is all."

His hoarsely uttered laugh didn't convince her. She shooed the rest of them away to the table, then lifted him back onto his heels. His face was flushed darkly and wet with sweat. The fingers on his favored arm had already drawn up tightly into his palm.

"Skyler, you're not all right. Let me get your father."

"No," he barked harshly, then seeing her distress, said more softly, "Please. I'll be fine in a minute. Go back to the clinic and get me some morphine just to cut the pain. Savannah, please don't argue. Just do it."

Leaving him reluctantly, she paused in the dining room to tell the family to start without them, that Skyler had bruised his elbow and she was getting him some ice to put on it. Uncomfortable with the lie, she hurried back to the office. She rummaged through the cabinets until she found the opiate.

Skyler had managed to pull himself up onto the sofa when she returned. His eyes were tightly closed and his lips clenched into a thin line. That he was suffering greatly, she didn't question. He didn't open his eyes when she fed him a spoonful of the liquid. Nor did he move when she held him in a close embrace until the drug began to soothe his hurt.

They joined the table with apologetic smiles. No one noticed how glazed Skyler's eyes were nor that he used only one hand to eat scant portions of what Savannah served to him. It was an elaborate meal of thick mock turtle soup, turkey, tart cranberries, mince and pump-kin pies, fruit from a large platter for those who had room, and a hearty coffee. Savannah tasted little of it, watching covertly as Skyler began to weave in his chair. She was grateful for the end of the meal so she could hurry him out and up to their room. He sprawled out on the bed fully clothed and slipped deep into unconsciousness. She adjusted his clothing to make him more comfortable, then sat at his side to watch over him in worried indecision.

She must have fallen asleep herself some time in that late, lazy afternoon, for it was well after dark when she awoke feeling stiff and rumpled. Skyler was still stretched out beside her. She lit the lamp and gave a frightened cry.

He was lying on his back, eyes half opened in a vacant, silvery stare. His pale face was cold and clammy to her touch and slick with sweat. When he didn't respond to his name, she gave in to her fears and raced down the hall to pound on Palmer's door. He answered clad in a brocade dressing gown, rubbing unfocused eyes.

"Please come quick. It's Skyler," she cried. The panic in her voice prompted him to run ahead of her. While he bent over the alarmingly still figure of his brother, she blurted out all she knew.

"What did he take?"

"Morphine. Just a spoonful. He was in such pain," she explained faintly.

"Damn him. He knows better," he muttered, then slapped the colorless cheeks methodically. "Sky. Sky, wake up. Come on, Skyler." He gave another terse oath. "He's in shock. Leslie, wake up my father and take Savannah down for a cup of coffee. Go on now. I'll take care of him."

"He's not going to—" Savannah couldn't make

291

herself finish the thought.

Palmer squeezed her hand tightly and gave her a calming smile. "He'll be all right. Go on with Leslie now."

It was a long tense night for the two of them as they sat seldom speaking over a pot of strong coffee. For Savannah, not being with Skyler was the worst part. The second was looking into Fletcher's eyes when he came into the study to pour himself a cup of the black, steaming brew. She was instantly on her feet but the elder man waved her down.

"He's sleeping, Savannah. He needs the rest. How long has he had problems with that arm?"

Just the one time that I know of but there have been others. He wouldn't talk to me about it. What's wrong? Will he be all right?" She couldn't help the fear that trembled in her voice.

"I don't know. There's a lot of swelling. It should go down by morning. What's wrong I won't know until I take a look inside."

"You mean surgery?"

"Anything else would be guesswork. Something painful enough to put him into shock isn't something to take as lightly as he has been. If you have any influence with him, convince him he doesn't have much time."

Those words haunted her when she sat at his bedside hours later, relieved to see the grey eyes flicker then focus. He gave her a groggy smile of recognition, then drifted until things sharpened enough in his dulled mind to make him concerned. That deepened into upset when she told him what had transpired.

"Your father wants to operate as soon as possible," she concluded.

"He wants to take my arm just like the rest of them. The answer's no. Don't badger me, Savannah. That's the end of it." His expression was tight and closed but she knew there was more churning behind it.

"Then you tell them yourself," she said quietly. "They're waiting downstairs."

"Like vultures, no doubt," he said acidly as he stood on wobbly legs. He waved Savannah off when she tried to help support him. "Let's get it over with. Then be ready to pack. We'll leave on the next train."

"Skyler—"

His sharp look silenced her. She followed him downstairs with a heavy heart, dreading the confrontation to come and afraid she would be called on to take a stand on one side or the other.

Palmer, Skyler, and their father exchanged wary looks as if preparing to do battle. Skyler seated Savannah on the sofa but he himself stood on guard and defensive for the first volley from his father.

"Whatever possessed you to do nothing about this? Skyler, you had to have known how serious it could be. There's every possibility of a bone fragment that could cause nerve damage or even paralysis. Why didn't you have it taken care of?"

"Taken care of?" His voice was strident and strained. "Do you know how they'd take care of it? About right here." He made a savage chopping motion just below his shoulder. "That's what your learned colleagues told me. Their knives were hanging over me if I chose to stay in the service of my country. The price was too high. My answer was no to them and it is no to you."

Fletcher reddened, thinking of his harsh slurs to his son about disloyalty and cowardice when they were so far from the truth. "So what do you plan to do? Keep treating yourself with opiates until your arm is as useful as a chunk of wood or kills you?"

"At least I'd fill a sleeve with it" was the belligerent reply.

Fletcher sighed and cast a glance at Palmer, who

began a reasonable argument.

"Sky, at least let us take a look. It can't do any harm. It could be something simple, something we can correct."

"Or I could wake up without an arm. No thank you."

Feeling the sway of persuasion go to her, Savannah stood and placed her hands on the tense shoulders. "Skyler, no one fought harder to save your arm than I did and I will again. But I just cannot watch you suffer so when it could be helped. Please don't be stubborn about this. Let them help if they can. Trust them. Trust me." He turned to her at that gentle plea, eyes shadowed and uncertain. "Please."

She could see him battling within himself, then with a heavy sigh, the fight was done. "All right." He looked to his father, expression unyielding. "But you have to promise me that if it's something you can't fix, you won't make any decisions with my life. I want you to close me up and leave things alone."

"Skyler—"

"I want your word."

The older man nodded ruefully. "You have it."

Skyler swallowed hard on that decision. "When do you want to do it?"

"Tomorrow. The swelling should be gone by then."

It was late but Savannah could tell by the rapid tempo of his breathing that Skyler wasn't asleep. He had withdrawn into a distant, pensive silence throughout the evening and even now lay on his back on his own side of the bed, not touching her. As the clock in the foyer below chimed out three times, she crossed his isolating barriers and rolled close to give him a gentle caress. Without a sound, he turned into the welcoming cushion of her bosom, his arms drawing her even

294

closer. She held him, willing him her strength and support until finally he relaxed in sleep.

Fletcher had everything readied by nine o'clock when he approached his stoic son. Surprisingly, the older man caught him up in a strong embrace, then held him back with a firm shake.

"I'll do my best for you. Remember those military shams weren't dealing with their son."

Skyler nodded, a bit heartened, then followed Palmer back to the clinic. Savannah started after him but Fletcher detained her.

"Savannah, I need to ask something of you, something difficult, something I want you to give a lot of thought to."

She braced herself, summoning the courage to meet his steely gaze without betraying her reluctance. "What is it?"

The large hand ran through silvery hair in a distressed gesture. "I've given Skyler my word and I won't break it. I've promised to take no drastic action without permission. I'd like you to give me that permission."

She stared at him blankly, hoping she didn't understand. To her dismay, he laid it out with stark clarity.

"If what we find is inoperable and a danger to his life, I want your authorization to remove his arm."

"I can't give it," she told him hoarsely. The dark head shook from side to side in numb denial. "I gave him my word as well. He trusts me."

"Even if it means his life. He can survive with one arm. Is the price of two worth more to you than having him at all?"

"That's not fair. This has nothing to do with me or what I want. It's what Skyler wants." She sat down heavily, mind whirling in horrified confusion. It rang

295

with the memory of Skyler pleading with her to save him from James Ambrose's saw. He had vowed he would rather be dead. But could she let him make that sacrifice? Could she give him up when she had the means to save him, even a part of him? It would be difficult, but Caroline managed with Darcy. Given the choice, she wouldn't let him go in preference to the way he had been before. But did she have that kind of courage?

"Do whatever you have to do to save his life," she stated with a conviction less firm than it sounded. "Take his arm if it's the only way."

"What are you talking about?"

That shrill demand came from the doorway where Rhea had overheard part of their discussion.

"This is none of your concern, Rhea," Fletcher told her crisply.

"Yes, it is. Someone has to think of Skyler. You can't maim him and ruin any chance he has of a future. Who ever heard of a one-armed congressman? You can't do that to him. You can't turn him into half a man, a cripple, a freak."

Savannah faced her coldly, voice shaking with an outraged fury at her narrow, selfish outlook. "Even with only one arm, he'd still be all man to me. You have no right to judge. Skyler's future doesn't hold a place for you and lucky he is that it doesn't."

Leaving the other woman stiff with indignation, Savannah accompanied her father-in-law to where her husband lay on the table. His eyes warmed in groggy pleasure when he saw her.

Taking up his slack hand, she pressed it to her lips and then to her cheek, tears beginning to burn in her eyes and throat. He licked his lips as if they were dry and murmured something low. She had to bend to hear it.

"I love you, Savannah."

The drug he'd been given to relax him had Skyler's thoughts moving sluggishly. He smiled up at the lovely face that filled the entire field of his blurring vision. Her words were long and distorted and it was hard for him to grasp them.

"I need you, Skyler. Please don't leave me. I'm sorry. There was no other choice. Please forgive me and know I'll be here for you."

His brow furrowed slightly at that but realized he probably misunderstood. He smiled vaguely. He had no worries now. Savannah would watch over him. She was still speaking to him but the words were lost. Something in the solemn nature of her expression made him want to hear her, knowing he missed something important. He tried to focus his concentration, tried to follow the movement of her soft lips, but all was fading into a warm, foggy haze.

"Savannah, we're going to put him under. You'll have to go now," Palmer urged gently.

"Can't I stay with him?" she protested, reluctant all at once to let him out of her sight fearing, yes, fearing she would never see him again.

"No." Fletcher's word was final. He lifted her up with a firm hand.

She searched the strong, lined features with a desperate need for assurance. Her convictions crumbled when the slack fingers slid from hers. "Please take care of him." Her words were small and frail.

"Don't worry. We're not without a stake in this ourselves." His slight smile gave her the strength to return it. The large hand was supportive as it took hers up and pressed something into her palm. "Hold this for him until afterwards."

She didn't look to see what it was until later, bending to place a quick kiss on her husband's cheek before Leslie shepherded her out. Her heart gave an uncomfortable skip when the door closed between them.

The last thing she wanted as she moved mechanically through the big house was another confrontation with Rhea Sherwood. The sharp-faced woman awaited her in the foyer, eyes reddened and angry. Before she could speak, Savannah held up a restraining hand.

"Please go home, Miss Sherwood. There is nothing more you can do here."

The amber eyes narrowed with menace. "Perhaps not now but there will be. When Skyler finds out about your disregard for him—and I intend to see he does—it won't be you he turns to. Skyler should be mine. He will be mine because he's going to hate you for what you've done."

"Just leave, Miss Sherwood."

The women eyed each other in open challenge and dislike until Rhea finally backed down in concession to Savannah's position in the Reade household. Her venomous glance as she went out the door said clearly that nothing was settled.

Alone in the haphazard room she shared with Skyler, she looked down at the small object she held in her hand. It was Skyler's wedding band. Praying he would have a finger to wear it on, she clutched it tightly and began to wait.

Chapter Twenty-Two

Swallowing seemed to take a ridiculous amount of time, but once he managed it, the arid feeling left his mouth. His vision was more difficult to master. The vague grey shapes focused only after repeated blinking and a studied effort. Hazy figures became Savannah and Brent. He puzzled over their presence and their smiles for several minutes until at last the cloaking fog lifted from his brain.

With a gasp, he tried to sit up but the strength wasn't there to support the movement. His left side felt numb, too numb.

"No," he wailed in bitter anguish. His eyes squeezed shut against a world he no longer wanted to see. "My arm is gone."

Brent gave a soft chuckle and lifted his hand to place it over his left wrist. "Everything is right where you left it."

"It went fine, Skyler. There was a splinter of bone that pinched the nerve in your elbow. Your father took care of it. He can explain it to you better when you're not so groggy."

Skyler nodded absently, touching his hand with near disbelief.

"He said it would be a week or two before the pain and stiffness give you full movement, but after that you should have no problem at all," she continued happily.

Patting his knee, Brent stood and announced, "I'll go tell father you're awake. He'll want to come and admire his handiwork."

Skyler exchanged a wobbly grin with him, then turned his attention to Savannah. She met his look with a tender smile.

"It's all over then," he murmured, voice still a bit slurred.

"All over. Now all you have to do is get stronger."

"I was so afraid, Savannah," he admitted quietly. "I couldn't bear the thought of not being able to put both arms around you. Nothing will get in the way of that now."

"Don't be so sure."

Savannah turned to glare at Rhea Sherwood. Outrage as well as alarm fueled her harsh tone. "Get out of here. Can't your petty vengeance wait until he's better?"

"So you'll have time to soothe him with lies and excuses? No. He needs to know now."

Looking between the two women in bewilderment, Skyler demanded, "What do I need to know?" He raised an unsteady hand to quiet Savannah's protest while he looked to Rhea for explanation.

"About this Southern slut's treachery," Rhea began. When she saw Skyler's face darken in anger at her words, she hurried on to build the gallows on which she could joyfully watch her rival hang. "How could you defend this woman when her hatred for you is so clear? While you lay trustingly on that table, she was telling your father to amputate your arm. Do you really think she is happy to see you whole? She was hoping for a fitting revenge to have you maimed and dependent on her."

"Rhea that's nonsense and I don't want to hear it.

300

Savannah would never have gone against my wishes like that."

She couldn't meet the confident grey eyes that rose to her in unquestioning faith. She could feel them linger in a curious doubt as hers remained downcast.

"Savannah? Tell me what she's saying isn't true."

"Yes, Savannah. Tell him," Rhea sneered.

"Only to save your life. That was the condition," she said softly.

"What?"

Her eyes came up then, dark and filled with anguish. "Skyler, I had no choice. I couldn't risk your life for a limb. I know you're angry now but please understand."

"Understand?" His tone was incredulous. "No, I don't understand. Why? How could you do such a thing to me?"

"Skyler, please."

He wouldn't hear her excuses or reasonings, eyes large and dazed with hurt. "You lied to me. Savannah, I trusted you. You asked me to believe you and I did. I believed you."

"Please listen to me, Skyler. Let me explain."

"No. There's nothing you could say that would explain what you've done. Rhea, get her out of here. I don't want to look at her."

Obligingly, Rhea gripped the other woman's arm and propelled her toward the door of the anteroom where Skyler lay recovering. Savannah was so stunned she went without a struggle, pleading eyes on her husband. But he had turned his head away, dismissing her.

"There's a train tonight at six," Rhea hissed with a nasty gloating. "You consider taking it because you'll have no place here. He'll never accept you back and I'll see he doesn't miss you."

With a hard push, Savannah found herself in the

301

hall, barred from her husband's side by his lover's twisting words and his own mistrust. She was vaguely aware of Fletcher passing her and of the harsh, angry words that emitted from the room. Minutes later, Fletcher emerged, face mottled with impatient rage.

"That fool," he growled to himself. "Stubborn, unbending fool." He saw Savannah sitting in a daze and placed a kind hand on her shoulder. "Don't let him upset you. Give him time to think and he'll see reason. Eventually he'll forgive us both for what needs no apology. Give him time, Savannah. He'll realize what we did was best for him."

She sat long after he'd gone in a stupor of doubt and despair, haunted by the accusing eyes. Forgive her? Not easily. Not any time soon, said that impassioned glare. If she could get him away from Rhea's subtle influence perhaps she could calm him and get him to give her fair consideration. After all, she was his wife. Her place was at his side not on the other side of a door.

Bolstered by that, she started back inside the room but the scene she encountered halted her with an icy shock. Rhea sat on the edge of the bed, one hand rubbing his bronzed chest and the other teasing through his ashen hair. His own large hand lay familiarly on her thigh.

"Forget her, Sky. She'll only hurt you more. You know that now, don't you?"

"I—"

"Of course you do," Rhea interrupted silkily. "You're not a simpleton, even though she takes you for one. You can see through her clever schemes. She's never loved you, Skyler. Never. Not like I do."

"No, she doesn't love me."

His sad, heavy words stabbed through Savannah's conscience. She wanted to burst into the room and deny it but she couldn't, held by the same bonds of

302

honor that had kept her from him all along.

"Then good riddance to her. Skyler, you have to get on with your life. She was only using you, trading on your generous heart to clothe and feed her traitorous family. That's all you ever were to her. She was never a real wife to you. Divorce her, Sky. She's no good for you. It would be one betrayal after another. Don't let her ruin you."

"I don't know, Rhea. I know you're right," he mourned gullibly, willing to trust her bending of the truth in his hazy state. "What am I going to do?"

"Divorce her, then we can get on with the plans we've made. They were such good plans. I will never desert you, Sky. I'll be at your side just like always. I'll see you to Washington. It's what we've both wanted. Don't deny yourself a future. Share it with me."

She bent to kiss him, red lips moving over his with a hungry encouragement. Slowly, his hand came up to tangle in her hair, surrendering to the power of her seduction with a weary resignation.

He slept for most of the day with Rhea at his side. Occasionally on waking, he wanted to protest her presence in favor of another, but his exhaustion and the draining effects of the chloroform kept his objections unvoiced. By nightfall, he was strong enough to want to be in his own room. Between Rhea and Brent, he managed to stumble up the stairs with minimal discomfort. His brother's uncommon silence puzzled him, but before he thought to ask after it, he stared about his room in dumb shock.

Everything Savannah had brought with her from the South was gone, her gowns, her toiletries, the small portrait of her family that had stood on the nightstand. In glaring contrast, all his gifts remained. The closet was full of the dresses she had purchased with his coin. On the bureau top lay two rings, one a plain gold band

303

and the other a sparkle of diamonds.

"Where is she, Brent?" His voice was odd and constricted.

"I took her to the train depot. She should be out of the state by now," he replied coolly.

"You took her? Why?"

"She asked me to. She didn't give any reasons, though she looked like she had plenty." He gave Rhea a meaningful glance.

Skyler didn't notice. He picked up the rings with a trancelike concentration, examining them as they lay cold in his palm, empty of the warmth they held when circling her finger. For the first time, he realized that she had taken his ring as well, symbolically severing the link between them.

"Let her go," Rhea pronounced with unfeeling pleasure. "It's what we want, isn't it, Sky?"

He made no respone, curling his fingers about the pieces of gold and lifeless stone.

Days and miles away, Savannah sat rigidly on the unyielding seat as yet another group of Federal soldiers searched the train and some of its passengers. She knew this stage of the journey was the most dangerous, that grey contested area between North and South. So far, she had passed through these inspection points without problem, her papers showing her to be the wife of a former Naval officer. She used them without compunction, vowing not to think about what she'd left until safely at Rising Sun.

What made her more apprehensive on this stop was the extra padding in her petticoat. She'd picked it up in Washington. On impulse, she'd sought out the address Mrs. Wilmington gave her. She'd been received warmly and told the difficulties of what she was

304

attempting as well as those she would contact in Charleston, where she would deliver her smuggled pouches of quinine. She staunchly refused payment for the risk she took, feeling a proud surge of patriotism for the first time since Skyler Reade had clouded everything in blue Atlantic waters. It was good to be doing something for the cause again, something her father and brother would approve of. Runners of every kind of drug were common between the North and the South, some like Savannah doing it out of compassion and love for their country and others out of greed for the price they could command.

Savannah let out her breath as the car jerked and began the slow shuttle southbound once more. Weak with relief, she shut her eyes and tried to relax, hoping the ache of tired muscles and a troubled heart wouldn't keep her from sleep yet another night.

She spent a restless night in Charleston. It was a city of constant uncertainty, its populace under siege and wary like those in Richmond. The owner of the rooming house she stayed in told her of the Yankee shell that had burst in the neighbor's parlor, destroying every piece of furniture but miraculously leaving the mirrors unbroken. Most of her uneasiness was due to the evening spent in a shadowy room after delivering the quinine. She had spent over an hour divulging all the information of spring troop movement she had overheard in the rooms of the Reade home. Telling herself she was doing her duty didn't lessen the tinny taste of guilt or the stench of spying from what she had done. Wryly, she understood what Skyler must have felt when lighting that rocket on the beach. She could force it all behind her now. She was going home. Skyler Reade was out of her life. Hadn't that been what she wanted for so very long?

She was lucky to find the rail between Charleston

and Columbia in operation, at least for the day. The Union army was forever ripping up the tracks and hindering their repair by heating the iron and twisting it like grotesque ties about tree trunks. The trip was faster but not much more comfortable than the flight from Beaufort. How long ago that seemed. Her stay in the North was like a hazy dream now that she was surrounded by thick drawls. Talk was buzzing about John Hunt Morgan's troops blowing up the bridge at Muldraugh's Hill, Kentucky and the Confederate clash with the Federals at Chickasaw Bayou. She only half listened, glad she had no one involved that would keep her waiting in anxious dread for the lengthy, sometimes inaccurate lists of the missing, dead, and wounded.

From Columbia, she was able to hire a buggy to take her and her single trunk to Rising Sun. She was thankful for the leisurely pace and the sweetness of the day that allowed her to breathe in the beauty of her homeland. While flowers had yet to bloom, their greenery was a palette of shades from fragile yellowish to deepest emerald. Live oaks spread interlacing branches to make airy tunnels of shadow and light. She let her thoughts wander back along those shady lanes, imagining she and Darcy racing on horseback, hearing her mother instruct her daughters on decorum as their carriage spun toward a neighboring plantation, hearing her father's booming voice as he argued secessionism with Robert Barnwell Rhett and other Carolina fire-eaters.

With those fond memories playing gently on her mind, the warm red brick of Rising Sun appeared and the hurts and worries of the past weeks were absorbed by the welcoming sight of home. She felt a wave of love and joy when she saw a tall, lanky figure limping from the office to the house.

Darcy Russell looked well. The pallor of sickness and futility was replaced by a healthy color of industry. The gaunt frame had filled out to its former wiry strength. Apart from the awkward roll of his gait and the single crutch, he looked like the brother who had gone cheerfully off to war. Until she got closer. His features were as handsome as ever, with the classic chiseled beauty Hillary shared. His lean cheeks were not shaven and his pouty mouth strengthened by a lush drooping mustache. His eyes were what gave Savannah a nasty turn. They were the same clear blue but the light in them was hard and old and empty. Only a spark of warmth intruded in that opaque stare when he turned to see her jump down and run toward him. He endured her embrace with a half smile and loose circle of one arm.

"Hello, Sis. Back home to stay?" he asked flatly.

"Yes. I'm home."

Darcy looked around, then gave her a curious glance. "Alone?"

"Yes."

He interpreted the chilly reply with a lift of one brow but refrained from sermonizing. He knew her too well not to see the pain she tried to conceal with a narrow glare. "The Yank's not coming at all?"

"No, he won't be coming." She turned to see to the handling of her trunk, composure firmly set when she turned back to him. "How is everyone?"

They began to walk toward the house slowly, because of his condition and her weariness.

"Good, I guess. Hillary's in a state cuz there's no beau to court her. Mama's still setting a place for Papa at the table. Caroline and the baby are fine."

"And how are the finances?" Did she imagine it or

307

did he stiffen slightly.

"Good. We're managing. Ben's getting good work out of the nigras. We don't have near the runaways of other folks. There's food on the table and money for seed, so I guess everything's good."

Savannah cast a sidelong glance at him gauging his refined profile suspiciously. Why did his answer leave her cold with misgiving? Perhaps it was just his strangeness. Or was it the careful evasive wording? Either way, she was determined to get a look at the books as soon as possible.

The rest of the family was not as reserved in its welcome. The tears and happy laughter lifted her spirits momentarily, only to be dashed by Hillary's eagerness to see Skyler. She ended the discussion with one crisp statement.

"Skyler and I have gone our own ways. He won't be joining me. Now or ever."

Those brutal words sank home with brutal clarity as she sat alone in her room, lost in the bed that seemed half full. Even with no reminders, the room seemed full of Skyler, as if it were no longer hers alone. Irritable at her melancholy, she got up to pace the darkened shadows, restless and aimlessly moody. When her bare foot trod on something small and hard, she picked it up to examine it in the dim light. It was one of Skyler's shirt studs.

The flood of emotion surged up so fast and with such unexpected power that she had no defense against the weeping. It racked her with a bitter fervor until she clung to the bedpost, weakened by the rattling sobs. Her chest ached and burned raw with the passion her pent-up feelings wrought. Deeper, harder to bare, was the emptiness in her heart when she realized how alone she was. Skyler was gone. For all her protestations and claims of hatred, Skyler Reade had made a place in her life, one he had carved out diligently while she fought his every move, one he cushioned with the depth of his love and lit with the heat of his desire. That place lay vacant now and she knew no way to fill it.

The weeks with his family had lulled her into a not unfavorable acceptance of her fate as his wife. In fact, she had come to welcome it, finding comfort in its secure embrace. But once again, he had cheated her out of knowing happiness. He betrayed her yet anew when she should have known better than to be vulnerable to his meaningless promises of love and commitment. Apparently, their marriage would be another of his attempts that slacked in interest and lay unfinished. Rhea would see to that. Well, let them have each other, she told herself, forcing up a strengthening anger. She didn't care. She didn't want the future he offered. He was the enemy. Hadn't he proved that?

Only the heavy hurt in her breast told her different.

The night was long and lonely. Savannah welcomed the light of day in hopes of finding distraction in the mechanics of running the plantation. Dressing quickly, she hurried out to the office, then frowned at the unkempt state of things. She found scraps of paper with amounts owed but no paid receipts and no books. She searched the entire room but could find no trace of the ledgers.

Puzzled and a bit angry, she waited impatiently for Darcy to come down to breakfast, putting her question to him without the courtesy of greeting.

"Don't get riled, Sis. I've got the books. I was going over something late last night."

His smooth answer only fueled her distrust. "I'd like to see them."

"There's no need, Savannah. I'm taking care of

everything. You don't have to go grey worrying anymore."

"I worry more when I don't know what's going on. Are you hiding something from me?"

He laughed but there was no amusement in the sound. "Really, Vannah. Did your stay in the North make you suspicious of all Southerners?"

His voice was so sarcastic she stared at him in bewildered hurt. Was this her older brother, the teasing hero of her younger years who had no meanness in his heart? He sounded almost as if he despised her. That realization upset her deeply and she hurried to make amends.

"Darcy, I don't mean to sound as if I didn't trust you."

"Didn't you?" The hard fierce look held for a brief instant, then he smiled again, the slick meaningless gesture that was more disturbing because of its falseness. "I'm handling things now. As Papa's oldest and only male heir, that is my position. If I need your help, I'll ask, but until then the books are my business. You stick to the running of the house and leave the man's work to me. Unless you think my mind is as crippled as my body."

She flushed at his insinuation. To challenge him now would affirm it, and as obnoxious as he was being, Savannah didn't want to hurt him. "All right, Darcy. I'll stay out of your affairs," she promised. "But this is my home and I won't see it go to ruin because you're too proud to ask for help."

"Everything's fine, Sis. Trust me."

She eyed him coolly, having no recourse but to accept him at his word. Perhaps he could manage without her and it was only her vanity that made her feel that Rising Sun held her invaluable. She owed him a chance to prove himself and maybe it was just the chance he needed to feel whole again.

As the weeks passed, she began to doubt the wisdom of her decision. Darcy was a constant companion of Ben Tyree, and when they weren't out in the field, they were indulging in chummy drunkenness in the office. Muddy boots and empty bottles stained the papers beneath them in careless disregard. Whispers of the treatment of field hands reached the big house, doubling Savannah's concern. They were stories of undeserved cruelty. Zane Russell had believed firmly in the institution of slavery but had never been unfair in his measure of punishment. She could hardly believe Darcy would condone such vicious behavior, but then he had returned home from the war a different man, one who saw things through a cold, bitter slant. And Savannah was afraid for and of that man he'd become. Even Caroline noticed the change. She would never be disloyal enough to say so but she could see the haunting unhappiness in the brown eyes, as if she had lost the man she loved.

But none of those things were as bad as the visit from Philip Aiken, their family banker. Savannah received him graciously in the parlor.

"Darcy's gone into Columbia, Mr. Aiken. I fear he won't be back for some time."

"I know. I saw him there. It's you I want to speak to, Miss Russell—er, Mrs. Reade."

"Savannah," she insisted, to relieve the confusion of explanation.

"Savannah, I wanted to make sure you were aware of the situation here at Rising Sun, though it may already be too late." He took the glass of blackberry wine with a hollow smile.

"What situation is that, Mr. Aiken? I've been away and my brother has been seeing to those matters."

"Not very well, I'm afraid."

"I don't understand," she murmured, fearing she did all too well.

He laid a stack of obligatory notes on the marble-topped table between them. The seriousness of his expression warned of their gravity.

Trying to control the trembling in her fingers, she began to sift through the notes, fifteen hundred dollars for a blooded stallion, four hundred dollars for a pair of boots, six hundred dollars for imported champagne, three hundred dollars for rum. The nightmare went on and on, the ridiculous excess making her want to laugh hysterically. Then she came to the gaming debts and her blood chilled. The amounts were staggering. She listened in mute horror as the banker's quiet words spelled out the fate of Rising Sun.

"These notes have been presented to me over the last two months as lien holder on your properties. If they cannot be met, I'll have no choice but to foreclose on them to pay these off. With prices the way they are, even the land and the house may not meet the debt."

Finding her voice, she asked faintly, "How much do we owe?"

"Two hundred seventy-five thousand dollars."

Savannah felt as though she'd been struck in the middle, the air driven from her in a forcible gasp. When she remained still and pale, Aiken went on uncomfortably.

"I can give you until the first of April. I wish it could be longer."

"Thirty days. I don't know if thirty years would be enough time."

"What of your husband, Mrs. Reade? Could he be ap-

312

pealed to?" Aiken suggested hopefully.

"No. He has no interest in these properties. No, Mr. Aiken, I fear our luck has run out. I thank you for your courtesy."

The little man nodded unhappily, hat crushed in his hands. "I'm truly sorry, Mrs. Reade."

"So am I, Mr. Aiken. So am I."

Chapter Twenty-Three

Darcy returned late, reeling drunk. Savannah listened dispassionately to the irregular thump of his crutch in the foyer, then called to him from her seat in the parlor. Her brother swung into the room, grinning foolishly at her. He looked so much like the mischievous Darcy of her youth that it took her a moment to begin. Even in his intoxicated state, he could read the dire consequence in her face and the grin faded.

"Why didn't you tell me, Darcy?" she began with surprising evenness. "Why didn't you tell me when there was a chance we could save some of it, at least the house, for Mama's sake?"

For once there was no belligerence in his tone, just a futile frustration that quickened his sister's sympathies. "What was I to do? Come crawling to you? Isn't it enough that I can't walk like a man but to have to crawl for help like a useless failure."

"Stop the self-pity," she snapped in weary irritation. "Haven't you hidden behind that excuse for long enough? There's nothing wrong with your mind. How could you get into such troubles? Didn't you even know you were drowning in debt?"

"I don't have to listen to this," he said petulantly. "It was none of your business."

"It is my business when you're pulling the comfort of

my home out from under me. How could you be so stupid and careless? Can't you ever think of anyone else but yourself? Without the land, we have nothing. What are you going to give your son? Your pitiful excuses for an inheritance?"

Darcy sat heavily, head dropping into his hands. To her dismay, Savannah realized he was weeping. "I don't know what happened, Vannah. I wanted to pretend everything was the way it was before, that there were no worries, no limitations, no scrimping from day to day. There was just so much presssure. I didn't know what to do. I just didn't know when to stop. What am I going to do now? How can my family forgive me for my foolishness?"

Savannah laid a gentle hand on the fair head, anger spent and no heart for any further recriminations. "We have to look forward now. Rising Sun is gone. We have to make plans."

"I'm no good to you. I'm no good to anyone," he moaned. "I wished they'd let me die."

She shook him hard enough to make his teeth snap together. Squatting down so their eyes were level, she said fiercely, "Don't you dare say that, Darcy Russell. Not ever. Not after all the worry and prayers we spent on you. None of us is perfect, not me, not you. We can only do our best. We have to go on."

"I can't, Vannah. I'm so tired."

"Then I'll do it for all of us," she said with a tough conviction. "I'll see to everything."

But what she saw was her precious home slip away from her day by day. Only Caroline and Darcy knew the truth. She saw no need to alarm her mother or Hillary until all hope of a miracle was gone. Privately, she made arrangements for them to move to Charleston, where Jonah kept a house. How they would live once they got there, she didn't know. Charleston was far from safe but there was no question of returning to Beaufort. And there was nowhere else for them.

In a helpless depression, she wandered through the grand house, revelling in its memories while her heart and spirit ached. She strolled the terraced gardens with its grassy ramps connecting the flower beds, herb garden, grape arbors, and small fruit orchard. Already, it was in sad disrepair. What would it look like after abandonment? There was little hope of finding a buyer. She had seen the sad remains of other neighboring estates left empty when the family was forced out by the cruelty of the times. The thought of Rising Sun fading into forgotten decay broke her heart. But there was no hope of keeping it. Telling herself that didn't make the letting go any easier.

And when word came within a week of the deadline that an offer had been accepted for the purchase of the land and house, Savannah gave way to the tears of loss and failure, mourning the way she would the death of a loved one. When she reached the bottom of that great well of hurt, she began dry-eyed to prepare for the task of telling her family.

Heavyhearted, she moved across the veranda, phrasing in her mind the words to tell her mother she could no longer wait for her husband's return within these walls. The sound of buggy wheels distracted her from that grim duty. She paused, putting a self-conscious hand to her untidy hair and wishing she had worn something more presentable to meet Philip Aiken and the new owner than the plain ankle-length skirt and cotton overblouse that belted at the waist. The welcome froze on her lips as Aiken stepped down, followed by a tall man with hair the color of palest ash and eyes that glittered like polished steel as they rested on her.

Oblivious to the looks the two of them exchanged,

317

Aiken began cheerfully, "Imagine my surprise to find the identity of your buyer. I confess, I sent him a message advising him of your trouble, but I didn't expect it to get through in time. A good thing he thought to leave me his address should you ever have any difficulties."

"So you are the new owner of Rising Sun," Savannah said stiffly.

"Of the land and everything on it," advised the crisp Northern voice while the silvery eyes grew heavy lidded with the meaning of his words. "I thought it was a good way to assure my welcome."

In a daze, she offered the cooler hospitality of the house, leading the way to the parlor. As the guests entered, there was a shriek from the stairs and a hurried rustle of petticoats.

"Skyler," Hillary cried, casting her arms about his neck in tactless enthusiasm. Her scattering of kisses brought a wide grin.

"At last, a proper greeting," he murmured, glance sliding to Savannah's rigid figure.

"Savannah said you wouldn't be coming but I knew you would," she gushed, clinging to his forearm excitedly.

"Why wouldn't I come when I'm given such a welcome," he teased.

The four of them sat in the parlor sipping a light claret while Aiken spelled out the transfer from Russell to Reade. Savannah listened to the proceedings from a fog. She couldn't force her eyes to lift above her clenched hands, staring at the vacant finger on her left one as a disbelieving fury began to build. Skyler had purchased Rising Sun. Was this his vengeance to toss her and her family out so he could move in with his Northern bride? How ironic and cruel a justice. She couldn't quite believe he hated her so much. She couldn't look at him, afraid the feelings of longing and loss would be too much for her to contain within the silent dignity of her pose. In her mind, she could see him in Rhea Sherwood's arms. Or was it Reade now? Her insides ached with a heavy numbness and a hatred that blinded her to all else. She managed to smile at a jovial Philip Aiken as he took his leave, then froze at Skyler's quiet words.

"Hillary, could you give us a moment alone? I wish to speak to Savannah. Close the doors please."

With the click of the doors, Savannah swallowed her cowardice and raised her head. The sight of him was a pain akin to death. He looked magnificent, the fair hair cut short and swept aside with the rake of careless fingers, skin still warmed by the Carolina sun, eyes clear and keen and reading of many things, wide, generous mouth touched with a slight smile. She noted with a traitorous gladness that his left arm moved easily and with no sign of discomfort within his travel-stained coat. His hand bore no ring.

"Hello, Savannah. You look surprised to see me. Weren't you expecting me?"

His calm question provoked a flash of annoyance and her tone was brittle with it. "Why would I, sir? I would hardly think your wife would approve of such a venture."

"My wife is why I'm here."

She looked at him in some confusion, then summed up crisply, "Are you having trouble with the divorce?"

"Divorce?" Now he looked perplexed. "From you? Why would you think that?"

The guileless bewilderment was more than she could endure. With a snarl of hurt and humiliation, she slapped him, palm stinging in satisfaction from the fierceness of the act. He held his cheek, staring at her as if she'd gone mad.

319

"Why, indeed," she raged at him. "How big a fool do you think me? I saw you, Skyler. I saw you with that woman, making your plans for your future together. She seemed eager enough to dispose of me and you had no objections. I trust my rings were her size. She already knew the rest of you fit well enough."

He had begun to smile, a broad gesture of relief and amusement as he watched her pace and fume with seething emotion. "Savannah," he began softly to placate her, but the momentum of her anger carried her on.

"How dare you come back here to flaunt your infidelities. Well, I don't care. Do you hear me? Have your Northern cow. I hope you'll be very happy. I hope you both get everything you deserve. I hope she'll love you and give you the children you want." Her voice broke off with a sobbing catch. To her added anguish, tears began to trace down her flushed cheeks. She knocked them away with the back of her hand. The humored look had left his face but the contrition that replaced it fueled her upset.

"Savannah, I may have been stupid but never an adulterer."

"But I heard you agree to set me aside. I saw you kissing her," she accused hotly, the pain she'd been carrying in her heart bursting forth in outrage.

Skyler made an impatient gesture with his hands. "Good God, woman, I was out of my head with pain killers. What Rhea told me took me by surprise. You can't know how it hurt me. I didn't even understand what had happened until the next day. You ran off without even giving my mind a chance to clear."

"To what purpose?" she railed. "So you could believe more of her lies? You don't think that hurt me? After I—oh, never mind. Why did you have to come here?"

His reply was maddeningly simple. "I love you."

"I don't love you. When will you see that? It won't work between us. You can't keep running after me, trying to buy me and my love. I don't want you. I don't want you here."

"Would you have rather I ignored the letter telling of your troubles? Would you have preferred me to let you go homeless? Would your pride have you live on the streets instead of accepting what I can give you? Go ahead." He dropped the deed to Rising Sun at her feet, his eyes a steely challenge. "Tear it up. Throw it in my face. Prove how much you hate me. Go on, Savannah."

She bent to retrieve the paper, bosom heaving passionately. For a moment he feared she would rip it to pieces to spite them both in the heat of her anger, but she couldn't force her hands to make the defiant motion. Instead, she clutched it reverently, dark eyes filling with frustration and helplessness. Her words to him were low and shaken.

"This is the one thing I value more than my pride. I can't let it go even if it means accepting it from you. I hate you for using it to trap me. Let me go, Skyler. Please. Can't you see I'll never be yours willingly? Do you plan on tying me to you with clever snares I can't escape? Give me the deed. Release me from this torment."

He stood very still, smoky eyes beseeching her to understand. "I can't. I can't lose you. As long as I have it, I have you. I have no pride where you are concerned. I'd do anything to keep you—rob you of free choice, endure your hate, anything. I love you, Savannah. You're all I have."

"But that's not love," she cried in desperation. "If you loved me, you'd let me choose, you wouldn't chain me to you against my will. Skyler, I can't give you what you want. I can't love you in return. I can't make you happy and be the wife you want. You have to accept that. I don't care for you."

"You're wrong," he vowed hoarsely. He gripped her arms and pulled her up against him, claiming her lips with an insistent kiss that sought to prove her objections false. His mouth seared across hers in an urgent hunger, trying to draw from her an answering passion. But there was no sweet response, no yielding to his desire. She was wooden in his arms, her tender lips without life or warmth. Breathing hard, he released her, searching her stony face for any sign of softening. His disappointment was crushing. She turned away from him, deed crumpled in her hand, the body that had given him so much pleasure rigid in its denial. The sight wounded and alarmed him, for he didn't have time to begin again, chipping away the ice that encased the loving woman within.

"Savannah, I've reenlisted. I'm leaving tomorrow. I don't know when I'll be back."

That brought a sharp reaction. She spun to face him, eyes huge and bright with sudden fear.

"No," she whispered, voice faint and strickened. All she saw was the endless lists before her eyes.

"Would you send me into battle without even a kind word?" His fingertips touched her cheek hopefully.

Only a stronger emotion could overcome the numbing shock his announcement had given her. With a surge of determination, she thrust away his hand.

"Do you think I would send you out to kill my friends and neighbors with my blessing?" she spat rebelliously. "Perhaps our troops can succeed in doing what I have been unable to and rid me of you forever."

The sentiment sliced through him but he bore it without a flinch. With a slight smile, he told her, "Perhaps they will."

They regarded each other tensely for several long

seconds before he spoke again, tone cool and emotionless.

"I have something to take care of. I want to see you and your brother before supper. I've something to discuss with both of you."

He strode past her, not sparing a glance or seeing the way she crumpled on the sofa with a silent sob.

Ben Tyree looked up at the sound of an approaching horse. He'd expected Darcy or even his brash sister but never dreamed of coming to face the cold-eyed Yankee who'd bested him once before. He fingered the butt of the heavy revolver he carried and waited until the horse drew abreast of him.

"I want you out of here, Tyree," Skyler began without amenities. "Get whatever belongings you have together and come up to the house for your pay. I want you off this property by nightfall."

Tyree gave an incredulous laugh. "Who the hell do you think you are to order me around like I was some shiftless nigger?"

The grey eyes were unblinking. "The owner of Rising Sun." He gave the stocky man time to digest that, seeing the reluctant belief in the tiny eyes. The man's next laugh was shrill and nervous, then a slick smile twisted the thick lips over tobacco-stained teeth.

"Now, Mr. Reade, you got no call for this. I know we don't cotton to one another, but I'm a good overseer and you're not likely to find another. You need me, Mr. Reade. Just ask your missus."

"What you are, Mr. Tyree, is an animal herder, not a worker of men. I've seen you beat and bully these people and now I can put an end to it. I won't allow that kind of thing and I won't allow that kind of man to work for me. Get out, Tyree."

Tyree's chin squared belligerently. "You's making a

323

big mistake. Do they know what you're doing up at the house? You can't run this place without a whip and a willingness to use it. How else you gonna get that lazy bunch to work? They got to be scared of you. They got to know if they run off, you'll come after them, and when you finds them, they'd wished they'd minded their manners. Are you going to do that? Hell, they probably bless you every night along with Mr. Lincoln. You're a fool, Reade. A dammed fool. You don't know nothing about these people."

"I know they're men. That's something you never realized. Now get on your horse."

Indignantly, Tyree clapped his flat-crowned hat over the greasy hair and shook his fist in warning. "Just you wait until I tells Darcy and Miss Savannah what you're up to."

"Tell them anything you like," he said coolly. "Just tell them on your way out."

Savannah and Darcy sat stiffly in the library, eyeing the tall Yankee with hostile stares. Ben Tyree had already told them what had happened in the fields but they weren't prepared for all that he had done. Savannah listened in a stunned silence and Darcy with a mounting rage.

"I'm sure you heard of Ben Tyree's dismissal," he began.

"You're crazy, Yank," Darcy proclaimed. "We'll never be able to replace him. The man may have been a brute but he always got results."

"I have no intention of replacing him" was the startling reply.

"Are you going to let the fields lay fallow? Do you think if you ask them nice, you'll get a day's work out of the nigras?"

"There are no more slaves at Rising Sun."

That brought a gasp from Savannah, but before Darcy could launch a tirade, he continued smoothly.

"I've given them all their papers. The ones who'll stay can work for a fair wage or a parcel of land they'll hold title to. The ones who wish to leave are free to go."

"Skyler, do you know what you've done?" Savannah asked faintly.

"The man is crazy. He's just buried us," Darcy raged as he poured himself a stiff drink.

"Caleb will be setting up work details," Skyler went on, unperturbed. "He's a good man and the others respect him. I trust him to do the work."

"But he's a nigra!"

"He's a good man and the others will follow him. That takes care of the fields. Now for matters closer to home. Caleb will answer directly to me, or Savannah in my absence. At no time do I want you to touch the books or the purse strings," he told a livid Darcy. "Your name will not be taken on credit against this plantation. It took a great deal of trouble to dig you out of debt and I'll not have you burying Rising Sun and your family out of your own weakness again. Philip Aiken will dispense a monthly allowance to you and to Hillary to spend or waste as you please, but you won't touch a penny of the estate's money. Savannah and Aiken are the only ones who can use it."

"This is an outrage," Darcy seethed. "I'm not going to live on your damned charity."

Skyler met his eyes with a straight, chilling gaze. "Fine. No one will hold you here. You and your family can go anytime and anywhere you like, but my generosity ends at the door. You will not be missed by me."

Darcy cast a helpless glance at his sister but she was sitting pale and wordless, expressionless eyes on her husband. She was no help to his cause. He looked back at the hated Northerner who held their future in constricting hands. His features worked in frustration and rage but he couldn't satisfy his pride by spitting in the smug face. He stood awkwardly, leaning on his padded crutch. Never had he hated his infirmity so much as now.

"You're a bastard," he stated impotently and hobbled from the room.

Skyler watched him go dispassionately, then turned to his wife, awaiting her reaction. It was surprisingly mild.

"That was a heartless thing to do," she told him flatly. "You unmanned him."

"He did that to himself long ago. Would you prefer I give him free reign again. The man is a fool and a wastrel, and I won't have him throw my money away on his own vices. He failed you. I won't give him the chance to do so with me. If that makes me heartless, it can't be helped. Better heartless than homeless. I won't have fools or slaves in my house."

Her chin squared defiantly. "What, then, am I?"

His eyes lowered, heating to a simmer. "You're no slave, Savannah, but you are mine by a different bond and I will never release you from it."

"I am surprised you would trust such a lowly bond servant with your wealth," she said dryly. "Aren't you afraid I'll be a poor steward as well?"

His chuckle was warm and flattering. "Never that. I would trust you with all I have to the extent of my life."

Pursing her lips, she gave him a narrow look. "Perhaps you would be wise not to trust me so much."

He extended a hand to lift her to her feet. "I never claimed to be a wise man."

He kept her hand clasped in his, drawing it against his chest so she had to stand close. His eyes stared down into hers, dusky and full of promise, until hers dropped

326

away uncomfortably. She pulled her hand purposefully from him, concealing her confusion with a cool disdain. His wolfish grin was far from encouraging to her shaken senses, as if he could feel her weakness and was eager to put her resolve to the test. She feared it was one she would fail yet again.

They sat down to a bland meal made up of their dwindling larder. Even Darcy and Caroline were present to effect a hostile front. Adelaide was thrilled to see him and was full of questions about his trip North since Savannah had been reluctant to speak of it.

Savannah was disturbed at how easily Skyler sat at their table, speaking familiarly with Delilah and assuming the role of host with a casual air. Most unsettling was how right it seemed for him to be there and how relieved she was to have a man of strength heading their table once more. He may not have been her choice, but he was capable of the task, pulling Rising Sun again from ruin. And then there was the covetous joy of looking at him. She could deny him with her words but she couldn't deny the way he stirred her heart with his bold, angular looks and superbly fashioned form. She reasoned that this silent lusting was a sign of her female failing and not one of character weakness—as long as she didn't surrender to it.

Hillary sat fidgeting and frowning until she finally confronted her brother-in-law, phrasing her question with a pert smile and pretty dimples.

"Skyler, I hear you freed the field hands. Sally has some ridiculous notion that she doesn't belong to me anymore. Isn't that silly?"

"No, Hillary. It's the truth. It applies to everyone at Rising Sun. There are no slaves and masters here," he explained kindly, as if to a confused, rebellious child.

"But, Skyler, I can't manage without her. What am I going to do?"

"Learn to ask instead of demand. Offer her a wage

and a little respect. We have servants at my home and they enjoy their work."

She looked at him doubtfully, mouth a petulant bow, but her eyes were thoughtful. "I don't know if I can think of her that way."

"It will take time," Savannah supplied. "Either that or learn how to comb your own hair."

Hillary made a face.

Delilah hurried into the room and hovered indecisively between Savannah and Skyler.

"What is it, Delilah?" she asked.

"Miss Vannah, there's a passel of Confederate troops a coming up the way," she blurted out nervously, eyes going to Skyler.

Chapter Twenty=Four

Savannah was very calm, mind racing ahead to the blue Federal uniform in Skyler's bag. "Skyler, go with Delilah. See he's out of sight and make sure you take all his belongings with him." As she spoke, she was removing his table service with quick efficiency. She gave him a stern look. "Go on. It's your hide they're after."

With a nod, he followed the black girl from the room and Savannah turned to her family.

"Not a word about him being here," she instructed, meeting Darcy's plotting gaze. "It would go just as badly for us. Skyler is a Union officer and they wouldn't treat us kindly for harboring him. Not a word. Go on and eat. Act normally."

Savannah went out on the front steps to greet the dusty grey-clad officers. The three had ridden up to the house, leaving their weary troops near the road. The plumed hats were quickly doffed to her.

"I beg your pardon, ma'am, for the untimely interruption," the senior officer began in a courtly voice. "Might we have your permission to encamp for the night on your property?"

"You're more than welcome to the land, Colonel, and to any extra provisions we can spare," she replied calmly. "My family and I were just sitting down to supper. Would you care to join us, sir?"

He declined quickly, apologizing once again for the intrusion.

"Would you and your officers come up to the house for a cordial once you're settled in?"

"That would be right kind of you, ma'am. Thank you."

"I'll have some biscuits and stew prepared for your men and brought down with some cool refreshments."

"You're too kind, ma'am," he repeated with a formal bow, and the three of them retreated down the drive to see to their encampment. She waited until they were a safe distance before spinning in a bell of skirts to ready all for the evening.

Colonel Ruffin, Major Berow, and Captains Croft and Payne sat in the parlor enjoying the fine brandy and the company. Tim Berow was from a neighboring county and remembered the Russell girls, particularly the beauty of the younger. Seeing them again, it was Savannah who caught his eye with her graciousness, cultivated poise, and intelligence. He noted with pleasure that she wore no ring and he turned his attentions to her. He addressed her with a warm charm and subtle hints of his attraction to her. His intentions didn't seem to fluster or upset her and he was encouraged.

While Hillary flirted like she had been a hermit for years and Darcy voiced an interest in the movement of the war, Savannah sat back observing the soldiers, not unaware of the handsome young major's lingering glances. As the evening wore on and the glasses knew many refills, she casually suggested that he might enjoy the night air and he was eager to comply.

"What are you doing so deep in Carolina, Major?" she asked smoothly as they strolled along the terraced lawn. "I wasn't aware of any troop movement in our

330

state. Should we be alarmed?"

His laugh was low and pleasant. "Don't fret, ma'am. You're in no danger." His arm looped through hers in a casual assurance, drawing her closer to him as if offering protection.

Savannah made sure they kept walking, carefully plying him about his mission. She was surprised to learn they were following up on one of the pieces of information she had fed them. Having gleaned all she could from him, she guided him back up toward the house but he halted her in the yard.

"Miss Savannah, I'm not usually a bold man but these aren't normal times. Might I ask a token of you to see me through the battles to come?"

She gave him a soft smile. He looked so young and swaggering, reminding her touchingly of Darcy and Brent Reade. "What would you like, Major?"

Without leave, he pulled her up against his dress uniform for a kiss. Her surprise let it go on longer than the circumstances would warrant, and well encouraged, Major Berow took advantage of her seeming compliance to move his hand over her snug bodice. That brought an immediate response. Her hands came up between them in protest.

"Major, we'd better go inside," she said stiffly.

"I'm sorry if I alarmed you, ma'am. Might I beg the honor of calling on you?"

She gave him a sad smile. "I'm sorry, Major. I can't make promises in these uncertain times. It wouldn't be fair. Let's go in."

Her room was shadowed in darkness when Savannah readied herself for bed. She was weary from the tension of the day and the glasses of brandy that had eased her through the evening. As her linen nightdress slid over her head to the floor, a movement near her window brought a gasp of fright.

"Did you see your Rebels safely bedded down?" The Northern accent seemed to have a harder edge than usual.

With an annoyed gesture, she straightened her gown and began to brush out her heavy hair. "They'll be moving on in the morning at first light."

His silhouette shifted, leaving the open windows to advance into the room, where he loomed large and uncomfortably close. His voice was low and silken, making her wary of his mood.

"And do you plan on seeing them all off the same way?"

"What way is that?"

"By letting them kiss you and put their hands on you as if you didn't have a husband to whom you deny those pleasures."

"Were you spying on me?" she snapped and turned away, but his hand closed over her arm, holding her in place.

"You're my wife, Savannah," he growled in warning.

She glared up at him, temper flaring hotly in the aftermath of all the shocks and humiliations of the day. "Do you know what being your wife means to me?" she demanded fiercely. "It means being forced to sleep with a man I hate, an enemy to me and my country. It means I have to suffer your arrogance and live as a servant where I once walked proudly. You own me and can claim me whenever you please, but you can't demand my affection. You can't make me give my heart to you. It's mine to bestow on whomever I choose. You own the land and everything on it, but what you want most I'll never give you. I won't love you, Skyler, and you can't dictate where my affections lie. Now release my arm before I scream and you spend the rest of the war as a guest of the South."

His fingers opened and she moved quickly away.

"Do you love him, Savannah?" he asked flatly.

"Who?"

"That officer."

He sounded hurt and resigned, and she was angered by the gentle reassurances she wanted to give him. Instead, she made her words coldly cutting.

"That's not your concern, is it? You never cared about my feelings, only your own selfish ones. Content yourself with knowing I cannot act on any feelings I may have. Good night."

Savannah curled under the single sheet, her rigid back a barrier toward the center of the bed. For a long while she could feel Skyler's intent gaze as he stood unmoving, then she heard him undress in the darkness. He lay full length on the bed but she could tell by his tension that sleep was a distant stranger to him as well. Frowning to herself in the awkward bed she had made, she closed her eyes and tried not to be so aware of his long frame beside her.

The major's kiss troubled her, not because of what it stirred but because it did nothing. It was pleasant enough but she felt no desire for a reoccurrence. His embrace had been strong and hopeful but it woke no spark of response within her. She recalled that first kiss she'd shared with Skyler and how it had shaken her very soul. In his arms she had found comfort and rapture. She had never been unmoved by his touch no matter how angry or determined not to show it. If she weakened her resolve now, she knew it would be just as devastating.

His return had thrown her into a panic of confusion, laying bare emotions she had hoped never to confront again. The stay up North had warped her perspective, making her vulnerable to him and willing to be persuaded to yield her heart. But here, back in her own home, the old rebellion returned. But it couldn't quite crush the memory of how she had relished their closeness. All she knew was she had to let him go without succumbing to those feelings or she would be lost. In his absence, she could gain back her objectivity and subdue the flutter of uncertainty that made her breath so short and difficult when he was near.

Cautiously, she rolled toward him. The slow rise of his chest told her he was asleep. Unbidden, her hand rose to stroke along his arm. She could feel the raised thickening of scars near his elbow. When he didn't stir, she grew more bold, rubbing the golden mat of his chest. Longing assailed her with a poignant twist. She wished he were a man she could come to in unqualified love, a man she could be a true wife to instead of an enemy she had to deny.

With a sigh, she turned away from him and the temptation he presented. She didn't see his eyes open, a glimmer of silver in the dimness as he stared at the ceiling for a long while.

The brightness and gentle stir of the breeze woke Savannah from her sleep to face a waking dream that made her chest tighten in painful need. Skyler stood at the open window watching the Confederate troops withdraw. She hated him for the way he looked standing so straight and unintentionally exciting in thin cotton drawers, powerful, virile, and achingly attractive. Her eyes caressed the length of him in appreciation.

Catching herself in that blatant leering, she sat up. The movement drew the silver-grey eyes.

"You should't be standing there in plain sight," she cautioned sensibly, but he only shrugged.

"I'll probably be seeing them soon enough as it is." He glanced back out the window with a reflective frown. "Strange. I can't hate them even though I may be killing them in a few days time."

334

"In Beaufort?" she scoffed. "Not likely."

"I'm not going to Beaufort," he told her quietly.

She watched in puzzlement as he took out his new uniform. It was different from the Naval issue he had worn when courting her. He drew on an officer's frock coat of dark blue cloth. The breast front had a double row of seven brass buttons. On the shoulder straps were gold maple leaves and a circlet of embroidered silver on yellow cloth, stating a regimental number. His dark blue trousers bore the yellow piping of the cavalry. He wound his crimson sash twice about his lean waist to tie at his left hip. It wasn't until he added a heavy sabre belt and revolver holster that she became alarmed.

"Skyler, what is all this?"

"Probably sheer madness," he joked with a wry smile. "I've joined the cavalry. I'm going to a real war."

Savannah stared at him in horror. The cavalry meant continual fighting on the front lines. "Whatever possessed you to do such a thing?" she cried faintly, heart in her throat to constrict the words.

"Seeing my brothers go back so willingly. Tony D'Angelo arranged for my commission in his unit. I'm meeting up with them this afternoon."

She looked blank. "This afternoon? Where?"

"Here, in South Carolina. I figured if I was going back into the thick of things, I'd jump in with both feet." He'd finished dressing and was regarding himself critically. He looked dapper and handsome, and with the sidearms, dangerous.

"Skyler, what are Yankees doing here?"

"We're not officially. Tony's on some raiding expedition along the Confederate railway. They're out to capture and destroy an arms depot. I take command tomorrow but I thought I'd ride along."

Savannah was swept by a dizzying chill. The raid he

335

described was the one Major Berow's men were anticipating. Skyler was riding into a trap she herself had set.

Skyler continued on, not seeing how pale she'd become. "From there, we'll swing North to Virginia. I don't know where I'll be or when I'll be back. It could be a long while. Aiken will take care of finances for you. You have complete draw on the account I established, so don't be stingy with it if there's something you need or want. Even a silly hat. Take care of your family. If I'm killed, everything reverts to you, so you might think of that when you ask your maker for deliverance." Again the wry smile. "I hope your Rebel brethren left enough for my haversack. If it doesn't compromise your stiff-necked sense of loyalty, I'd like you to see me off. I'd like you there. You needn't pretend any sentiment or spare me a smile. I just want to see you."

He paused, awkward with that hopeful plea, chagrined that he would have to ask it of her. She hadn't moved or spoken but continued to stare at him oddly, out of relief or reluctance he didn't know. Picking up his white gauntlets, he turned and started downstairs to see to his departure.

As if in a dream, Savannah rose and dressed. Unconsciously she chose her loveliest, an uncommonly soft and feminine gown of aniline-dyed magenta. The wildness of the color accentuated her dark beauty and the pallor of her face. Doing her hair up in a heavy knot, she rushed blindly down the stairs, not wanting to miss him. Seeing him off to his death, a death she arranged.

Skyler was already outside, checking the new cavalry equipment on Beauty. Even the blued iron buckles and lead-backed brasses on the black leather bridle bore the same relief eagle that repeated on his shirt buttons.

Attached to the saddle was a double holster and a new Henry repeater. In a daze, Savannah passed a smug-looking Darcy and Caroline as she swept out onto the wide veranda. His eyes lit with an unrequited warmth when he saw her standing at the top of the steps.

"I didn't think you'd come out," he said softly. "Thank you. Now I have the memory of your beauty to take with me."

He came slowly up the stairs, sabre bumping his calf at every step, until he stood one below her so their eyes were almost even. Hers closed in anguish as his large hand cupped her cheek, then stroked lingeringly down to her chin and slender throat. Her heart clutched in agony as his lips touched hers, pressing against them briefly, fully, lovingly.

"Good-bye, Savannah," he said simply, and while she stood in stunned dismay, he swung up on his fancy mount. That trance didn't break until he reined about and started down the drive in an easy canter.

Savannah gave a sudden sob and flew off the porch, skirt lifted high so she could race after him. He pulled up when he heard the cry of his name and waited for her to reach him. She clung to the hand he held down to her, uplifted face wet with tears.

"Skyler, please. Please don't go," she wept brokenly.

Confused and moved by her emotional entreaty, he smiled slightly and bent to kiss her hand. He was nearly unseated when her arms went about his neck, drawing him down so she could catch his mouth in an urgent kiss.

"Don't go," she begged him. "Stay another day. Skyler, don't leave me yet. I need you so much. Don't leave with things the way they are between us. Love me, Sky. I need you to love me."

As easily as if she weighed no more than a mite, he brought her up to sit in front of him in the saddle, ruched petticoats crunching noisily in protest. Arms tightly about her, he guided his horse around in a half circle. Savannah held to him, shivering fitfully and weeping with the force of the emotional catalyst that had shaken her. Nothing mattered but keeping him at Rising Sun another day.

She was vaguely aware of him sliding down, then catching her in his arms. Her feet never touched the ground as he carried her up to the house, past the scowling faces of her relations, and up the sweeping stairs. Even when he set her down in the privacy of their room, she couldn't bear to release him. Her arms were twined about his neck and her face was pressed into the stiff, new-smelling flannel of his shirt. When he spoke her name in question, she lifted her head to look at him through eyes that glistened like deep shimmering seas.

Wordlessly, he kissed the dampness from her cheeks, then took her parted lips with a sweet tenderness. That brought the tears anew, falling silently to bathe both their faces. He brushed them away as well, then simply held her until she had control of her shivering fears.

Skyler held his breath as her fingers moved over the brass buttons of his uniform. The coat slipped to the floor followed by the clatter of his sabre belt. His eyes squeezed closed as her mouth did tempting things to his throat and chest. This unexpected play of passion confused his thoughts and enflamed his body but he didn't question it. He wanted it too badly. And when she guided his hands to the fastenings of her gown, he complied with unusual clumsiness until it mingled with the dark blue cloth at their feet.

"Skyler, love me."

The huskily spoken words of encouragement were hardly necessary as her thinly clad breasts grazed him with wanton allure, breaching his anticipation with a surge of desire that saw them quickly to the bed. In the

338

glow of midday, the uninviting pallet of the long night became a receptive haven for their shared kisses and urgent hands. As flesh covered flesh, Savannah pulled him down to greet her open mouth, the wild plunging motion of her tongue purging his mind of its wont to linger. He was pitched into an excited maelstrom of urgency that demanded a swift, fiery satisfaction. Her guttural moan of desire as he thrust within her only heightened that fervor.

Savannah hadn't believed such intensity possible. Passion burned like a fever in her blood, pounding in her head and boiling in her loins. The feel of him imbedded inside her with a firm, powerful claim touched off a swirling madness. The want, the fear, the relief sharpened every sensation to a crisp, almost painful clarity. Her body shook with the raw extremes of pleasure. She couldn't have enough of him, of the hot taste of his mouth, of the masculine scent of his excitement, of the driving pulse of his body. In her desperate striving, she bit his shoulder, clawed his sweat-slicked back, kissed him hard enough to bring the taste of blood. All the while, the sounds of her passion tore from her in whimpering cries and urgent growls. She was fighting not against him but with him, struggling for something to relieve the terrible pressure that had begun to bind her, torturing her with sensations too shattering to be absorbed within the realm of sanity. Her whole world burst with a searing brightness, the tension arching her body like a bow. Then she fell into darkness.

The drumming of her heart filled her head, bringing awareness back with a sweaty dizziness. Her mouth was dry and her body ravaged by chills. A soft mewling sound of bewilderment brought an immediate comfort.

"Shh, Savannah. It's all right." It was Skyler's voice spoken tenderly against her hair.

Her arms knotted about his neck in uncertain panic, frightened by her loss of consciousness and the torrential emotions that had brought her to it. The solid head of his damp body restored her warmth and reassured her that all was well. Slowly, her shivering ebbed and she was able to loosen her frantic hold on him. Embarrassed by her excessive passion, she couldn't look at him, keeping her face hidden in the pulsing hollow of his throat. What had alarmed her, he accepted with an awed welcome.

"That was incredible," he murmured softly as he stroked her tumbled hair. "I've heard of such things happening but I've never been a part of it. Are you all right?"

"It was like dying," she whispered. "I was afraid until I found you with me. Oh, Skyler, I never dreamed it could be like that, like perishing from sheer delight."

He continued to hold her as the breathless exertion of their union gave way to a sated peace. Then he told her quietly the same tender, caressing words he always did after their intimacy.

"I love you, Savannah."

"I love you, too."

Skyler stiffened as if he'd received a mighty shock, then his breath spilled out, low and shaken. "Do you mean that?" he asked with a fragile hope.

Savannah looked up at him, meeting his searching gaze with a timid smile. "Do you mean, do I love you? Yes. Yes, I do. I love you, Sky. I have since we left Nassau. I thought I was fighting you but it was me. I can't fight anymore. I love you. I want to be a wife to you in more than just name. I want your love. I want your body. I want your children. I want your future to be ours. I'm sorry I've hurt you but I didn't understand. There's never been anyone for me but you. I accept that now and I beg you to forgive me my stubbornness."

340

"Forgive you?" He closed his eyes briefly and gave a strained laugh. When he looked at her once more, his eyes were a liquid quicksilver. "I never thought anything could be as sweet as this moment."

His unsteady hand stroked down her cheek, then rubbed up with his knuckles. She kissed them, then offered her lips to him, sighing when his mouth cushioned against the throbbing bruises left by their thoughtless hunger. She gave herself to that kiss, letting him taste the full bounty of her feelings in it.

"If I'm to keep you only until morning, I'd like to spend that time here," she suggested shyly. She sidled a coaxing glance to see if he was in agreement.

Skyler gave her a lazy smile. "We can do anything you like."

She touched his damp, swollen mouth with her fingertips, tracing its generous line. "You said some day I would want to share with you. I want to please you. I want to make you forget how stingy I've been with my loving."

"You've always pleased me, Savannah," he said simply. "I have no complaints."

"Then let me love you this time."

She rose up on her elbow so he was on his back beneath her. The cascade of her ebony hair brushed him like a silken caress. For a long moment, she studied his face, taking in every line and angle, as if for the first time, while he stared up in bemusement. Her fingers followed the path her eyes had taken, smoothing over the lean contours. His mouth opened in anticipation of her kiss but he wasn't prepared for the lazy flirtation of her tongue, teasing him into a light breathlessness. That impudent tip darted to his ear to earn a hard shiver and a rash of gooseflesh before flickering down to one of his flat brown nipples. With a teasing persuasion, it rose tightly against her provoking lips.

An attentive suckling brought a soft groan and loud crack from his toes as they flexed and curled under. He pushed gently at her head when the splintering sensations likened to pain but she was satisfied to move on.

Laying her head on his shoulder, Savannah watched her hand trail down the hard plane of his stomach. She could already see she claimed his interest, but to awake him from passivity to full arousal with her questing touch gave her a strange elation. She continued the intimate exploration until every curiosity was met.

Wanting to see what effect her play was having on him, she lifted her head to find his half-closed eyes upon her, bright and unfocused. When he reached for her impatiently, she caught his hand and whispered, "Not yet."

At her prompting, he rolled onto his stomach, tensing briefly as her thumbs dug into the base of his neck, then sighing with grateful relief as the firm massage eased the strain of overtaxed muscle. He lay unmoving at the mercy of her kneading fingertips, moaning as her palms revolved in small circles down the curve of his spine to the firm plateau of his buttocks. They lingered there for a moment before ascending by the same route. By the time she turned him, he was in a tentative state between languorous relaxation and acute anticipation.

He stared up at her in dreamy wonderment, puzzling yet reveling in her taunting seduction. When he would have the feel of her lips on his, they sketched maddeningly about his features. When he would embrace her, his hands were held away in playful discouragement.

"Lay still," she breathed upon his anxious mouth. "Let me love you."

In lieu of an answer, he caught her tempting petal-soft mouth in an urgent press, eager for an outlet for his mounting ardor. She refused to let the kiss deepen, tantalizing him to a frenzied frustration with the featherlike dance of her tongue that continued to elude capture. Only when he groaned, "Savannah, please," did she relent and give him the hot, devouring kiss he wanted. But even that had no duration as her kisses moved up to the tip of his nose to his forehead to the mussed bristling of his hair. His fractured breathing scorched her throat, and as if in sympathy, she returned to seek his mouth once more.

While their kisses grew intense, Savannah's soft white thigh rubbed casually across his tortured hips. With an easy movement, she was astride him, then before he recovered from the feel of her, she lifted slightly and sat back until their hips met, taking him fully within the velvet heat of her body.

"Oh Sweet Christ," he cried hoarsely, holding himself rigid in a fight to gain control of the tremors that would spell quick ruin to her plan. When he had gained a tenuous hold, his eyes opened wide and glittery.

Without moving her lower body, she bent forward to exact a kiss, then arched in ecstasy as he cupped her dangling breasts in eager palms to draw them one by one to his lips. The flashes of delight as his tongue circled and rolled the swollen tips made her struggle to remember her purpose. A subtle shift of her hips was enough to reclaim her power. The enticing rhythm she began had him tossing restlessly until she stilled his flushed face between her hands. She wanted to see him, to gauge his pleasure and exult in being its source. As she watched his features tighten in taut expectation, she realized how much he had given to her, how selfishly she had taken of his love without return.

His large hands clasped about her waist to assist her

movements, urging them to a fierce tempo that defied continuance. He tried to prolong that fevered pace, wanting the splendid searing of icy heat to last just moments longer, but the sweet friction shattered his restraint. With a soft cry, he reached up for her, hands tangling in the mass of her hair, pulling her down so his face could press into her shoulder. The feel of her slender body convulsing above him broke his will and he poured himself into her with a great shudder of relief.

They lay joined together, too spent to move, bodies trembling in exhaustion and hearts beating a like rhythm. Voice a frail whisper, Savannah said his name.

"Sky?"

"What?" he managed with difficulty.

"I love you."

A deep chuckle vibrated beneath his cheek. "I think you've proved that well enough. I've finally won that unyielding Rebel heart but it feels as though I'm the one who surrendered."

"A truce then," she suggested. "No more battles."

"Done," he muttered. Smiling, he drifted into an appeased sleep.

Chapter Twenty-Five

Without thinking, Skyler answered the light tap on the door with a muffled "Come in." It opened part way, then closed abruptly to a nervous giggle on the other side. Fully awake by then, he frowned at the unencumbered nakedness of him and his drowsy wife before calling testily, "What is it, Hillary?"

"Mama wanted to know if you'd be down for supper" was the tittery reply.

"Supper?" he grumbled irritably. "Hell, no."

Savannah covered his mouth with her hand, scolding him with a glance. "Have Delilah send up a tray. And a bath," she added, feeling the sticky heat of her body.

"I surely will, Vannah" came the cheerful response. "I could even bring it myself."

"That won't be necessary," her sister said tartly. She tried to keep in a laugh as Skyler grinned up at her roguishly.

"Have a good evening" was followed by a regretful mutter of "I wish I were."

Eyes sparkling with sultry amusement, Savannah laced her hands atop her husband's chest and propped her chin on them so she could gaze in lazy happiness upon him.

"Hello," she murmured huskily.

"Hello," he answered with equal gruffness.

"Are you hungry?"

He smiled languidly. "My appetite has been whetted for the moment but don't go away lest I feel the need of a snack." His fingertips grazed along the curve of her rib cage to rest fondly on her backside.

"An appetizer, perhaps?" she offered. The pink tip of her tongue touched his mouth.

"An appeteaser, you mean," he growled. She laughed as he caught her lithe form to him and rolled so he was above her. Their eyes fenced in an intimate challenge before he relented and kissed her soundly.

Side by side, they cuddled close despite the uncomfortable heat, dozing pleasantly until they heard the slosh of water filling the tub in the adjoining room. When the outer door clicked shut, Skyler raised a questioning brow.

"Who gets the first bath?"

"I do," she claimed, leaping from the bed with a squeal as he tried to catch her. She paused at the door, lush, glistening body making a breathtaking picture, and promised saucily, "I won't let the water get too cold." His menacing expression prompted her to disappear with a very uncharacteristic giggle.

Smiling to himself, Skyler closed his eyes and let himself nap lightly until another knock urged him to draw up the sheet. A smiling Delilah bore in a covered tray and set it down on the nightstand. She surprised him by taking up his hand and pressing a grateful kiss to it.

"Thank you for what you done for my people here. You're a good man, Missa Sky, and none of us be forgetting that."

He flushed in awkward pleasure as she hurried out. A rumble of his stomach coaxed him to investigate the tray.

346

"You're not eating everything, are you?" Savannah called petulantly.

Smiling, he flung back, "I'll leave you some coffee."

There was a sound of complaint and a splash, and Savannah appeared in the doorway within minutes, wrapped in a revealing white robe. Her chilled breasts formed hard points in the fabric. Skyler ogled the sight contentedly until she came and slapped his hand.

"Pig. Beast," she declared poutingly. "You've eaten the best already. You are no gentleman."

His eyes drooped in a mercurial simmer. "I always keep the best for myself." She slapped at him again when he tugged at the belt of her robe.

"Go take a bath," she urged. "You're spoiling my meal."

With a rumble of warning, he seized her and jerked her to him, playfulness replaced by a surge of duskier emotions as he nuzzled her clean-scented skin.

"The water's getting cold," she cautioned, and reluctantly, he released her to seek the tub. She grinned as she heard his curse.

"What did you put in the water?"

"A little perfume," she said innocently. "You liked it well enough on me."

"I didn't want that kind of welcome from my troops," he remarked in surly humor.

His casual mention brought a pensive frown to Savannah's lips, darkening her mood with an uneasy guilt. It brought back the reason for this afternoon of unequaled bliss. As she toyed with her food, she wondered if even now his troops were preparing to ride into a well-planned ambush. She couldn't have saved them all, her conscience cried out. If she had warned him, Skyler would have ridden to stop it and the confrontation would have been inevitable. The thought of his blood on her hands was unbearable. And if he

347

discovered her part in it, would he be as unforgiving as she had been? She could plead duty as he had. Would he believe it or would he construe it as a bitter act of vengeance by a jilted woman? Would he be wrong if he did?

Those damning thoughts preyed upon her features when he emerged clad in a towel swaddled about his lean hips. His smile faded in concern when she rushed to him, clinging with a desperate shivering.

"Savannah? What is it?"

"Oh, Sky. Please hold me."

He did, cradling her close to the dampness of his chest. "What's wrong? Tell me."

"Please don't go," she pleaded miserably. "Stay here with me."

"I can't, love, no matter how much I want to," he soothed, gratified by her fears.

"Haven't you given enough already?" she argued pettishly. "They almost had your life and your arm. I won't give them more."

"But they never had my loyalty," he explained gently. "Not until now. It's what I should have given to begin with. I laughed at it because I didn't understand it. I owe it now."

"You owe me," she demanded. "I'm your wife. You owe me a husband, a father, a future."

"And I want to give you those things so much I hurt, but I can't back away now. I've made a commitment and this one I have to see through."

"But why start with this one? Oh, Skyler, I'll simply die if anything happens to you."

"Shh. None of that." He held her back, hands on either side of her dark head. "When I heard Leslie say that to my brother, it felt as bad as hearing you say it. Please sit with me and try to understand."

Eyes large and teary, she bravely complied, curling

348

into his side on the edge of the bed. She held in her sobs as he spoke quietly to her.

"Savannah, I've never done anything in my life to be proud of. Everything I've begun I've found too hard or tedious and have given up on. You're the one thing I wanted to work at. I couldn't give up on you. It made me think of other things, important things that I've avoided for too long. I need to know I've done something worthy of having you." He waved off her protest and hugged her close.

"After you left me, I spent a lot of time with my family, really listening to them. They had values that made me ashamed because I held none. That troubled me a lot of nights alone without you, and what I discovered was that I wanted a good place to raise our family, a good, decent place. That place wasn't here, Savannah. Slavery is wrong. It's an evil I have to help end if I'm to bring children to live in this world. I can't have them growing up like Hillary or Darcy or even you, my love. It breaks my heart to oppose you on this but wrong is wrong. I can't just hide here and close my eyes to it anymore. I know there are lots of other reasons for this conflict—some I don't understand, some I don't agree with—but the cause is just. I can't live with you when our worlds are torn apart. We couldn't survive it, not forever. When the country is one, so can we be. I love you, Savannah. I'm doing this for us so we can have a future. Please say you understand."

She raised her shimmering eyes to him and cried, "Oh, damn you, Skyler Reade, I do understand and I love you for it, but don't you dare die to prove it. You have to come back to me. I've lost you and found you too many times to suffer that again. You promised nothing would ever come between us."

"You promised you'd wait for me."

"For as long as I have to." She repeated that long ago vow vehemently.

The night slipped away to a pastel dawn as they slept in each other's arms oblivious to the hours they were missing. Savannah murmured sleepily as a warm hand slid up from thigh to rounded breast and remained there to fondle gently. She lay still, eyes closed and pretending sleep while stirring shivers woke her languid body. A gasp escaped unintended when his mouth claimed that aching pinnacle with tender savagery until her hands rose to twine in his fair hair. She could feel his smile.

"I thought you were asleep."

"I am," she purred. "And what a wonderful dream."

"I'll see it has a happy ending," he promised.

And it was a most pleasant dream, soaring on his inspired touch and lingering kisses. It lacked the earlier frantic passion and urgent intensity but its sweetness ran subtle and deep. He built her excitement slowly, purposefully. His hands molded her emotions like malleable clay, shaping, bending, but never breaking. His mouth rained urging kisses between her breasts, his soft panting growing deeper to share her hurried breathing, tasting and delighting in her joy. Her hushed words only increased his satisfaction.

"Come to me, Sky. Share this dream. It's so beautiful."

They moved together as one, unhurried, savoring each plateau of fulfillment they experienced and forging a binding permanence in their intimate dance. And when they fell away repleted, it was more a beginning than an end and all that he had promised.

"I love you, Savannah" came the expected claim, then he waited almost anxiously.

"I love you, Skyler."

His breath expelled in a shaky rattle. "I was afraid

350

you said that before because I was leaving and you knew it was what I wanted to hear," he confessed a bit shyly.

"I said it because I wanted to bring you back. And because it's true," she added.

He rolled onto his stomach and reached into his shirt pocket from where it lay on the floor in dismissal the day before. He made a satisfied sound and sat up, presenting his open palm to her. Nestled in it were her two rings.

"Will you wear these now without seeing them as a symbol of a trap I caught you in?"

"Yes."

He slid them on her finger. They felt completing and good. While he admired them and the slender hand that bore them, she reached the other into her night table and displayed his simple band.

"And will you wear this as a symbol of a marriage of give and take?"

Smiling, he nodded and let her push the ring on his finger. Their kiss was long and thorough, restating the words they had spoken and those that lay silent on their hearts. Skyler gave a grumbled curse as a knock on the door ended the tender exchange.

"Missa Sky, there be a soldier downstairs to see you. He say it mighty important he see you now."

"Tell him I'll be right down, Delilah."

Skyler was mildly annoyed by the interruption but Savannah was terrified. She caught him about the neck in an urgent embrace, hugging him fiercely as if physical closeness could melt them into one.

"Oh, Sky, I love you so. I need you so very much," she cried in a low desperation. Her hot kisses pressed to his throat and cheek until he held her away.

"Save some of this until I come back up," he suggested warmly. He chucked her under the chin and began to dress once more in the blue uniform.

From her huddled position on the tangled sheets, Savannah watched him, chewing her lip in dread, fearing what awaited in the meeting downstairs. Had their time together created a strong enough bond to see them through what lay ahead or had she been foolish to lay bare her soul to him? Just looking at him made her heart swell with the ache of loving him, love all the more powerful because she had denied it for so long.

"It's probably Tony here to rail at me for not showing up yesterday," Skyler was saying, grinning slyly as he shifted through her discarded petticoats to find his shirt. "What shall I tell him? Smelling like some kind of rose garden, he'll probably assume I spent the time wallowing in a brothel."

When he saw she returned none of his teasing amusement, he came to sit next to her on the bed, caressing her worried features with a gentle touch of his fingertips. Wet crystals sparkled on the dark fringe of her lashes and fell like perfect diamonds on his hand.

"Where's the little Rebel who cursed me from her front porch?" he cajoled with an encouraging smile. "Don't make me hate leaving you any more than I do already."

She gave him a shaky, tight-lipped smile and rubbed her palms lingeringly beneath his open shirtfront. That sensuous massage woke a smoky passion in the grey eyes that grew more apparent as his fair head dipped and his open mouth crushed her masterfully. That searing twist conveyed his desire for the woman he'd given his name and his love. Resolutely, he pushed away, gaze heated and happy. Giving her cheek one last touch, he scooped up his coat and went to see to his obligations.

Savannah waited for as long as she could, taut with uncertainty. Then she quickly dressed and went below.

352

She paused outside the library doors, bolstering her courage, then stepped in.

"Skyler?"

He stood at the long windows, back to her as if admiring the view of the garden, but his posture told her he was looking in rather than out. When he spoke, his words were faint with disbelief.

"They're dead, Savannah. All of them except the boy who brought the news to me. All dead—Tony, my entire troop." His head shook in a dazed fashion.

Savannah stayed in the doorway, conscience torn and bleeding at the sight of his grief, but she said nothing, letting him slowly, ponderously gather his thoughts.

"It was an ambush, you see. They never had a chance to even fire. The Rebs knew. How could they have known about the raid? I should have been there with them. Why wasn't I there?"

She must have made some sound, for Skyler turned to her. He looked terrible, stunned, shaken, face etched with the pain of loss and guilt. She couldn't bear to see him hurting so badly.

"Oh, Skyler, I'm so sorry," she blurted out hoarsely. "It wasn't supposed to happen that way."

He stared at her. Knowledge, unwanted and undreamed of, began to dawn. With a tortured moan, he whirled away. "Oh God, Savannah, please tell me you had nothing to do with this. Please tell me."

Her silence was damning.

In angry frustration, his fist pounded the window frame. The violence made her insides shiver as fragilely as the glass panes. It took him a moment to control it before he could face her. She shrank beneath that cold, emotionless gaze. She could see him piecing everything together behind that frigid stare.

"You killed them," he said tonelessly. "You killed

them as surely as if you'd pulled the trigger. You knew they were dying while you were upstairs making love to me. You made me think it was because you loved me." A jagged edge of pain flashed in his eyes.

"No, it was because I loved you," she explained in anguish, hands stretching to him beseechingly. "I had no idea you would be involved. I couldn't let you go. I couldn't risk that."

His laugh was harsh and jeering. "So you played the whore to keep me here. You used your body and your lies to assure I'd stay in your bed. Do you expect payment for those services now? Do you expect me to thank you for saving my life, sparing me so I'd have to suffer the knowledge of your treachery? It would have been better to let me go and die with some scrap of dignity than to let me spend my life weighing the blood of my friends against my foolish trust in you. I trusted you, Savannah. I brought you into my home to meet my family and friends. I loved you."

That broken wail brought her to him with a sob. It was like casting herself upon a statue. He was rigid in her embrace, making no move to touch her or yield to her tears that fell in a frantic stream.

"I love you, Skyler. Please don't condemn me," she wept forlornly.

Steely hands gripped her by the upper arms, prying her away. His expression was sharp with loathing. "What else did you tell them, you spying little bitch?"

His words cut her like the slashing edge of his sabre but he had no sympathy for her distress. Desperately, she pled her case, throwing open her soul in hopes of mercy.

"I never thought I'd see you again. I left you believing our marriage was over, that I had no more ties to the North, no loyalty to you. They told me it was my duty to our cause. I was hurt, Skyler. I wanted to

354

put it all behind me, so I told them. I never thought you'd come back to me. I never thought there'd be a chance of any harm coming to you because of my words. I told them about enemy soldiers, not about my husband and his friends. I never thought I'd love you so very much, that we'd have a chance for a life together. Please believe me."

"Stop it," he snarled, shaking her hard enough to scatter her tears in a salty spray. "Stop the lies." His breath hissed fiercely between clenched teeth as he struggled with the impulse to either strangle her or take her roughly to the sofa in hopes of driving away all the hot, choking emotions that seared his mind and twisted his heart. The deep liquid eyes that lifted to his made it more difficult, the red parted lips unbearable. Unable to stop himself, he caught her face between ungentle hands, trying to search out the truth in her anguished look. But he knew the truth. It had been shown to him in a stark, grisly demonstration he couldn't ignore. His voice shook with strain.

"I always believed you'd care for me. I always told myself that given time you'd love me. I convinced myself that my love was enough. I didn't want to accept how much you hated me but, oh, how you proved it. You pushed my face into it. God, how much you must hate me. Well, I believe you now. You couldn't have made it more plain. You had it written in blood."

"But I don't. I love you," she cried frantically, hands clenching over his. "And you love me."

He repelled her grasp, hands falling heavily to his sides. He looked weary and empty. "You found a way. You finally found a way to hurt me enough to destroy my love for you."

"No," she sobbed in denial, but something in the deadened eyes told her it was so.

"Good-bye, Savannah. I never meant to hurt you.

Even now I can't bring myself to pull your home out from under you. Take it. Keep it. I won't be back. I guess you've earned it." When she caught his arm, he pushed her away. "Don't follow me out. Just let me go with a little self-respect. You've stripped me of everything else."

Giving her one last look, he turned and walked away from her, away from Rising Sun and a life he had wanted to share with her, without a backward glance.

Slowly, Savannah moved through the room and down the long hall, feet unconsciously leading her on a fatalistic path to the front porch. It was a bright, baking hot morning, sunlight reflecting off the packed earth drive and the gleaming brasses of the two horses. One was ridden by a boy of about Hillary's age and the other Skyler swung up on. If he knew she stood there, he gave no sign of it. The strong profile never turned her way. With a low word to the youthful private, he kicked his stallion into a showy canter. The boy followed until both riders disappeared down the drive.

It can't end here like this, Savannah told herself with a shaky certainty. He wouldn't stay away. He would come back to her. She knew it. She could feel it in the aching heart that shared the same love his did. He would find, as she had, that such a love couldn't be denied. And even if he couldn't forgive her, he could never forget her and that helpless attraction would draw him back to where she would be waiting.

"I love you, Skyler," she whispered to the dissipating cloud of dust. "And I will wait for as long as I have to."

Chapter Twenty-Six

Two dozen field hands and their families came up to wait uncertainly before the big house. They knew the blond Yankee had gone. Only the question of whether his word would remain in his stead remained to be answered.

So small a number, Savannah thought anxiously, but some had stayed and were looking to her for direction. Quietly, with authority, she told them that if they stayed and worked the land, they would be assigned parcels to tend themselves to grow whatever they needed and with the right to sell the surplus. The dark heads nodded in wary acceptance of that, further encouraged by her vow to supply lumber for homes they could build on those plots with clear deed after seven years. She spent the morning with them, listening to their grievances and needs with an understanding air that initiated trust. Afterwards, she spelled out what would be expected of them. One hundred acres had been broken, and with men and women working diligently, the seed could be sown in time but only if all cooperated.

Fortified with satisfaction that the new arrangement might work quite well, Savannah was able to face the events of the morning with a calm, detached composure. Skyler had gone and she refused to dwell on the reason for the rocky parting. There would be another time for that. She needed to channel her energies into maintaining his home so it would make him proud when he returned. She concentrated on when, not if. She shed no more tears over the bitter words he'd spoken. They served no purpose now. She never told her family of them, and if any of the servants knew, they said nothing. She conducted the affairs of Rising Sun as Skyler had directed and would listen to no dissension from anyone. They may have grumbled but she wasn't challenged, and things continued on the sprawling plantation.

Balmy April gave way to a scorching summer. News of the war reached them thirdhand on visits to Columbia. Lists of Confederate dead and captured read like a directory, with page after page of names. There was no information on Nothern casualties, so Savannah tried not to dwell on it, sharing her prayers between the soldiers of the South and her husband and his family. Though Darcy ridiculed the Union's new General-In-Chief of the Army, she was chilled by what she heard of Grant's bold, relentless daring. "Unconditional Surrender" Grant they called him. News was grim for the Confederacy. The thirteenth Amendment was passed to abolish slavery. Arkansas and the Nebraska Territory joined the Union. Sheridan bedeviled Richmond. Terrible tales drifted back about the Battle of the Wilderness and Bloody Angle. Loss of irreplaceable leaders was devastating. The South mourned its flamboyant champion as J.E.B. Stuart succumbed to his mortal wound and was outraged by the burning of the Virginia Military Institute.

Though Skyler had left them an ample sum of gold, supplies were growing so scarce that unavailability, not cost was the problem. Staple goods were hoarded whenever they could be found, in fear that the war would linger another year. The Union continued to divert shipments from the South and the states grew lean and ravenous from the deprivation.

Savannah forced an optimistic face, refusing to be discouraged by the setbacks in the field or loneliness in her room. She filled her evening hours with memories of the half day she'd spent knowing the full benefits of love. The ony time she came close to weeping was on discovering that blissful interlude would bear no fruit. She kept that and all other heartaches locked away, and forged on with a single determination. Skyler would be back and she would be waiting.

One late June evening Savannah was sitting on the veranda staring wistfully up into the deep-starred night when she was startled by a low voice.

"Mrs. Reade?"

She stood in wary surprise, for the rider seemed to have materialized out of the darkness without a sound. He wore no telltale coat of blue or grey.

"Yes, I'm Savannah Reade."

"I have a message for you."

She took the thin envelope and before she had time to offer thanks or hospitality, the horse was reined about and disappeared in anonymity. The letter was light but it weighed heavily on her heart. No one paid the fearful prices of a special courier to bear news unless it was bad. Her immediate thought was that it was from Philadelphia saying Skyler had been killed. Like a sleepwalker, she drifted into the house to find light enough to read by. For several minutes she turned the travel-worn missive over and over in her hands, then ripped it open.

The origin brought a puzzled look. Charleston. The name deepened her frown. James Ambrose. She hadn't seen or heard from him since the capture of the *Harrier*. The message was brief and cryptic.

"I've come across something you once held very dear. If you are still of that mind, come at once."

It was followed by an address but no further explanation.

Skyler. That was the only thing it could mean. Skyler was in Charleston.

Four nights later, repressing an irritable yawn, James Ambrose shuffled to answer the soft knock at his door. He hadn't slept for close to forty-eight hours and he was phrasing a choice epithet for whoever pulled him from it now.

Jerking open the door, his surly growl was stilled by a shadowy figure in the hall, a woman enigmatically garbed in a hooded cloak.

"Dr. Ambrose, you sent for me?"

Over brandies, Ambrose explained to his guest how he happened on his present position as surgeon in command of the makeshift hospital established in one of Charleston's empty warehouses. There he oversaw treatment of both Confederate soldiers and Union prisoners.

"And Skyler is there?" Savannah asked faintly, both excited and anxious at that knowledge.

"He came in with the wounded from Spotsylvania, so many of them. His wounds saved him from interment at Libby but he's due to be sent to Andersonville at month's end."

Andersonville. The name of the notorious Georgia prison sent a chill like death through her. Stories reported the death rate of Federal prisoners had risen from three hundred to three thousand men per month. If Skyler were sent there, she knew she'd never see him again.

"How badly is he wounded?" she asked to distract her thoughts from that tented hellhole.

"He's healing—a miracle in itself in these conditions—but he's weak and fevered."

"Why?" The question came out softly. "Why would you do this for him. Did he ask you to write to me?" She couldn't believe that somehow.

"No. I don't think he even knew who I was. I saw the ring and took a chance on it being you."

"But why? He put you in prison."

Ambrose shook his head. "The Union Navy put me in prison. A certain Lieutanant Commander Reade arranged for my exchange and release. I owe him a chance at freedom.

"I want to see him." That was said quietly but was nonetheless a command.

"In the morning I'll arrange it. Until then, I have a fairly comfortable sofa."

The presence of a tall, handsome woman moving among the prisoners with a bucket of cool water aroused no suspicion from the guards. She wore the crisp uniform of the Ladies' Auxiliary who had insinuated themselves into the hospital to see to the ease of suffering. Untrained as nurses, they made themselves useful by writing letters for the patients, reading to them, cleaning the wards, and performing small humane tasks. Most of the guards begrudged such service to the enemy but the head surgeon saw the ladies were not prevented from their merciful rounds.

She had dippered water to nearly two dozen bandaged, ragged men when she came to a stop, hand rising to her eyes as if in weariness. To Skyler, she was just another passing shape in his grey, uncertain world of fever. On better days, he exchanged pleasantries with the soft-spoken angels but today he couldn't find the strength for it. He wanted to sleep, to search for ease to the torment of his body, but the woman lingered. Her hand came down to touch the heavy shackles that chained his ankles to the metal bed frame. She moved up to stand beside him, hand laying across his hot, sweaty brow. It was cool and he sighed with relief, eyes closing.

"Is there anyone I can contact for you, Major? Your family? Your wife?" That last was said a bit hopefully.

The low, quiet words woke a new agony, for surely he was delirious to think it so familiar. "There's no one," he rasped with difficulty.

The soothing hand stroked lightly down his bearded cheek, the tenderness of that touch surprising him with its intimacy.

"I'll be back for you, Major. Rest easy."

The strangeness of her words brought his foggy gaze up but she was gone and he was left alone with his dirty discomfort.

Savannah collapsed in Ambrose's office, face pale and voice shaking. "I can't let him spend another day in there. You said he was all right. He looks awful. I almost didn't recognize him."

"War isn't kind or pretty, Miss Savannah," Ambrose said with typical bluntness. His curt expression no longer offended her. "He's better off than most. Better off than he'll be at month's end."

Savannah's lips tightened and her eyes took on that thoughtful concentration. "If you can get him out of his chains and up here, I can get him out. You must have been willing to take the risk or you wouldn't have sent for me."

Ambrose gave a wry smile. "With or without me, I'm sure you'd try and you'll have better luck with my help. But not today. We've got ward inspections and he would be too easily missed. Tomorrow I'll have Major Reade brought to my office for further interrogation. That's not too irregular. What you do after that I don't want to know about, but you'll have less than two hours to get him out of Charleston before they start searching all the public conveyances and main roads."

"Don't worry. They won't find us and no one will connect you."

Something in the somber blue eyes convinced him.

Skyler spent a restless night, unable to find any comfort on the hard, narrow cot. The warehouse was a furnace, holding in the heat of the day with a suffocating intensity. There were no windows, no fresh air to relieve the scorching stagnation of filth, disease, and suffering. The weight of the shackles pulled his foot at an awkward angle, awaking a dull throb to echo in his temples. The visit from the Southern woman had upset him, filling his head with thoughts of another he swore to banish from his mind and heart. He cursed the feebleness of both that would have him send some word to her. But then, he told himself bitterly, she would probably rejoice to hear of his incarceration. Besides, it didn't matter. He knew his destination. It would be easier on his family to think him missing or dead than to know his fate was to be meted out at Andersonville.

Despite the heat and sweat, he was plagued with continual chills, from fever or infection he didn't know. They hadn't bothered with his foot, probably willing to let starvation or the flux run a close race with blood poisoning. Would they be going by train? Surely not in the two-wheeled ambulance carts. The joggling torture device had tossed him about unmercifully from the battlefield to his first stop in Richmond.

When he felt the pull at his chains, he raised himself on his elbows to look at the Rebel guard in blurry question.

"Dr. Ambrose wants to see you, Yank."

Ambrose. The name was familiar but his hot brain

couldn't make the connection. "What does he want with me?" Was that his voice, so hoarse and cracked.

"Maybe Jeff Davis wants to see you've been well treated." The sneer was accompanied by a jerk on the chains.

It was a supreme effort on Skyler's part to contain the cramping spasms of pain and nausea the cruel punishment woke. The guard had no patience with his condition, hauling him up to his feet by the tatters of his coat.

"Come on, Yank. On your own hind legs. Now move."

Ambrose's office was down two steep flights of stairs. At the continual prodding from the guard, he managed the steps by leaning into the wall for support. By the time he stood wavering in front of the doctor, he was soaked with sweat and too dizzy to focus his eyes. The disorientation made him appear docile.

"Sit down, Major," came the gruff voice. Was he going mad? Even it sounded familiar.

Sagging into the straight chair, Skyler's awareness lapped like a rhythmic tide, giving him only fragments of the doctor's words as he spoke to the guard. Groggily, he looked about the small room, surprise making his hazy eyes pause at the figure of a woman sitting in the corner. Her dress had become a symbol of the South, black silk trimmed with deep bands of crape. Only the cut of this one flared in front to accommodate the child she was carrying. Instead of the white widow's cap, she wore a stylish hat, its heavy veil obscuring her face. His vague curiosity didn't last and his stare dropped away.

"Sergeant, I would speak to you outside for a moment. I will be right back, Mrs. Stevens."

Skyler heard the rustle of stiff crinolines. A cool

364

touch on his cheek woke his heavy eyes.

"Skyler, can you hear me?"

He stared, sure his fever had snapped his senses. But no. There was no mistaking the serious dark blue eyes behind the black netting.

"We've got to go now. We haven't much time."

He continued to stare at her blankly, gaze lowering to her distended middle in confusion. Surely she hadn't been with child when he left her.

Chuckling softly at his bewilderment, Savannah turned away and fumbled beneath her skirts. When she revolved, her figure was trim and enviable. What she had delivered was a tightly wrapped bundle she quickly untied. It held Darcy's uniform.

"Get your clothes off," she instructed crisply as she amended her own costume by adding white lace cuffs and collar, a broad colorful belt, and a brilliant array of paste jewels, a socialite sans the mourning.

Skyler's movements were slow and awkward, prompting her to come to his aid. She stripped the soiled coat from him, followed by the strong-smelling shirt. Her breath drew in at the sight of the long, poorly healed gash that ran from his collarbone to the center of his chest but she didn't pause. She tugged down his trousers with a careful deference to his bandaged ankle, then dressed him in the faded grey with equal efficiency. Thankfully, he had lost enough weight to make the fit plausible. Finally, she could ignore the question in the dazed grey eyes no longer.

"Why are you doing this, Savannah?" he asked tonelessly.

She met his gaze, then returned it coolly. "I owe you for Darcy" was her explanation. That was enough to appease him without becoming complicated. "Can you walk? I have a carriage outside but you have to manage that far."

"I can manage."

"They'll be looking for a pregnant widow and a Union officer. We don't look the part but I can't risk you being recognized. This isn't going to be pleasant but you're just going to have to trust me until we're out of Charleston."

He looked wary but nodded. He eyed the heavy length of gauze she held suspiciously, flinching back when she put a round pad over one of his eyes.

"Hold these in place while I wrap," she ordered.

Apprehensively, he kept the pads over his eyes while she wound the bandages about his head. Panic rose up quick and stifling as all his sight was erased by shadowless black. He fought the urge to tear at the wrappings, her voice giving him a focus to cling to.

"That should do nicely. Just remember not to speak. I'll lead you out. Skyler, we're going home."

The guard was absent from outside the door, just as Ambrose had promised, and Skyler's betraying uniform was safely tucked in a basket of filthy bandages on their way to be burnt. No one noticed the passage of an attractive woman leading a blinded Confederate officer down the hall. Savannah walked slowly, unhurriedly. Skyler's arm was heavy about her shoulder and the grip of his hand claimed his tension.

"Steps. Just one flight then we're out. Can you make it?"

A brief nod.

Balancing him on the steps was no easy task. She felt Skyler recoil as his other arm was taken by one of the guards who assisted them to the front walk. She turned her sunniest smile on the man.

"God bless you, sir," she said in all sincerity while the soldier flushed and shrugged.

The only vehicle she could rent was a ramshackle buggy and tired horse but it would get them as far as the train. She pushed her husband into the seat, then climbed in to handle the reins. The streets were in bad repair from the constant shelling and the buggy bounced about the ruts on unsprung wheels. She glanced beside her to the partially hidden profile. His jaw was taut and his mouth thinned into a white line. She couldn't help his discomfort so she concentrated on his life, and much would depend on making the train in time.

It was still in the station when their winded horse wheezed to a stop. A belch of black smoke obscured the platform amid clouds of steam.

"Where are we?"

"Quiet," she hissed as they mingled through the crowd. Thankfully, she had their tickets safely tucked away. She didn't try to hide, remembering his lesson from the cafe in Nassau. She talked freely to those they passed and took a seat in the center of the car with Skyler next to the window. She lifted his injured foot to the opposing bench, hoping to discourage anyone from taking the spot across from them. Unfortunately it didn't deter a slickly dressed merchant who settled in opposite her. He glanced at the sightless man, then gave her a silky smile. Her frigid look made him pout sullenly.

The train jerked forward, straining and snorting until it gained momentum. Unconsciously, she had taken Skyler's hand. In his limbo state, he clung to it gratefully. She gave it a slight squeeze and settled in for the journey.

It was hard to relax in the suffocating darkness filled with bodiless voices and startling sounds, but Skyler's exhaustion would no longer support him. He leaned

367

his forehead against the vibrating glass, the hot achiness returning now that the tension had passed. He had no protest when Savannah's arm slipped about him, guiding his head to her shoulder. A wave of nostalgic longing swept him at the scent that lingered in her clothing, another bitter ache to bear. He hadn't the strength to consider his rescuer other than to be glad their destination was other than Andersonville. Pushing aside the fears that had haunted him for the past weeks, he was able to sleep, dreams soft and teasing like that familiar scent of stirred memories.

Feeling his weight slump against her, Savannah let down her reserve with a shaky sigh and hugged him tightly. He smelled. He was filthy. He was probably crawling with things she didn't want to consider but he felt so good in her arms. How gaunt he was. Beneath the borrowed grey shirt, his ribs were like the rails they rode on. When she got him home she would see to him properly, but for now she was content with his foul, sweaty heat. She had him back. Now to keep him.

His sudden cry woke her and most of the car. In the darkness she could hear his frantic breathing as his hands rose to his bandaged eyes. She caught those unsteady hands and pulled him to her once more to whisper words to calm him.

"It's all right, Sky. We're almost there. It's Savannah."

"I can't see," he moaned in bewilderment.

"Shh. Don't speak. I know. Just a little bit longer."

His fingertips rose to touch her face, searching over its contours in uncertainty. There was no mistaking the tender mouth, chiseled cheekbones, and strong chin. He made a soft sound of wonder.

"It is you. I wasn't sure," he whispered huskily. "I can't believe you came for me."

"Did you think I wouldn't?" was her gentle reply. His

368

cheek was oddly bristled under her palm. She drew him to her slowly until their lips met, tentative at first then with urgent rediscovery. It was a bittersweet reunion shortened when he turned his face away in confusion. Silently, she held him, hopes swelling on the tide of emotion that brief union inspired. Perhaps things would be all right.

Chapter Twenty-Seven

It was daylight when Savannah woke, stiff and feeling unrested. Skyler was sitting beside her, alert posture telling her he was awake. She straightened from the pillow of his arm, bringing his head about in question.

"Good morning," she murmured quietly, then frowned when he turned back toward the window. Refusing to allow his rebuff to wound her, she made quick reparations to her untidy hair. Across the aisle, she noticed a trio of Confederate infantry men observing them with interest.

"Spotsylvania?" one of the men queried, gesturing to Skyler's wounds.

"Yellow Tavern," she amended, voice low and conspiratorial. "The same day we lost J.E.B. Stuart."

"We was at the Bloody Angle," said another, proudly displaying his sling like a banner. "What unit was you in?" he asked, leaning past her, but she intercepted the question, tone pained and mournful.

"I'm afraid my husband hasn't spoken since that dreadful day. The doctor was hopeful. He said it was because of his head wound. I'd rather not discuss it anymore. I don't want him upset."

The grey-clad soldiers nodded in unison, and with sympathetic looks, they returned to their own conversation.

Savannah settled back, satisfied, and repressed a smile when she saw Skyler's mouth twist wryly at her improvising.

Once outside Columbia in a hired buggy, Savannah turned and began to unwrap the yards of gauze. Finally freed, Skyler's eyes screwed up tightly against the brightness of the day. He blinked rapidly, then looked about the lush, colorful South Carolina countryside, senses dazzled after the grimness he'd endured. Slowly, cautiously, that gaze shifted to the woman beside him, that sight more blinding than the rest. That unsettling reaction made his tone unnecessarily brusque in his own defense.

"Thank you for what you did."

Savannah regarded him unblinkingly. "As I said, it was a debt owed, and as you know, I always pay them."

With that cool rejoinder, she slapped the reins down on the horse's bony flanks and they traveled on in a tense silence to Rising Sun.

Though he would have preferred to walk in on his own, the ride had stiffened his leg to the point where it wouldn't hold him. Reluctantly, he accepted Savannah's help to hobble up the front steps. They were met in the hall by the Russell family. For once, Hillary didn't rush to embrace him but stood back, handkerchief delicately at her nose. Only Adelaide showed any welcome, coming forward to kiss his scraggy cheek.

"Welcome home, my son," she said warmly. That greeting won a fierce glower from Darcy.

"Thank you, ma'am," Skyler mumbled, awkward with the affection more than the hostility.

"That's Darcy's uniform," Caroline cried in dismayed recognition. "Savannah, how could you?"

"Get that off your filthy Yank," Darcy began to shout.

But to Skyler the angry words faded into a dull roar

in his ears. A sweat as cold as melting ice bathed his face and hands as the elegant stairway began to writhe like a living thing before his eyes. He heard Savannah's voice, oddly distorted calling for assistance, then a blackness deeper than behind the bandages swallowed all.

He gave a sudden start as a cool wash covered his forehead and temples. The soft voice made him relax.

"Easy. It's all right. Don't try to move."

He lifted a feeble hand to push aside the cloth. The pastels of Savannah's room swayed and blurred, then all came into focus on the woman sitting on the edge of the bed.

"Feel better?" she asked in gentle concern. She took the wet cloth and sponged it over his face and neck. The chill revived him.

"Feel awful. What happened?"

"You fainted. I had you carried up."

He gave an embarrassed groan and closed his eyes. After a moment, his nose wrinkled. "What's that horrid smell?"

Admirably, Savannah didn't laugh. "You, I'm afraid. I've had a bath drawn for you as soon as you feel up to it."

"Now. I can't stand myself," he muttered.

With her help, he managed to stand and totter into the adjoining room. When she began to unbutton his shirt, he pushed her hands away in bruised dignity.

"I am quite capable of bathing myself," he snapped harshly.

Savannah's dark brow arched. "Excuse me." She retreated huffily into the bedroom and waited several seconds. His call was right on time, chagrined and reluctant.

"Savannah, I can't manage."

Taking a deep breath, she composed her features and

373

went back in. As emotionlessly as she had at the hospital, she undressed him, this time to the skin, and helped him into the metal tub. His injured foot was propped on the rim to keep it from getting wet. She couldn't resist a touch of sarcasm as she flipped him a clean cloth.

"See if you can manage this. I want to get a look at your foot."

Contrarily, he was content to soak in the hot water while she carefully unwound the dirty linens from his ankle. When the wrappings became darkly discolored, the stench from the wound was nearly gagging. She had to stop when the dressing pulled, bringing a cry of protest. Skyler's fingers clutched the edge of the tub, white-knuckled with strain.

"All right," she soothed. "I'll leave this for now. Let's concentrate on getting you clean."

He had no objections to her taking over the task, eyes closing as the soapy cloth scrubbed away the layers of grime and sweat. The exercise was relaxing and oddly sensual as the cloth moved the length of his long body with a lingering care. With a jolt of surprise, he realized how aroused he was becoming by the simple charitable task. To flush those thoughts from his mind, he plunged his face beneath the water and began to vigorously lather his hair.

Savannah smiled to herself as she washed the lean sinew of his back. He might pretend disinterest but his distress told her otherwise. His reaction said clearly that he was not unaffected by her, and that small concession fueled her optimism. Skyler Reade was still a man and she could make it difficult for him to resist that basic fact. And fully intended to.

Clean and shaven, Skyler stretched warily on the bed as she bent to examine the slash across his chest. The clinical set of her features made him uneasy.

"A sabre?" she questioned, and at his nod Savannah poked the edges of the scabbing cut until he winced. "It's ugly but there's no infection. I'll put some ointment on it to keep it soft so it won't tear open. I've got to get those dirty bandages off your foot and that's going to hurt you. I'll be as careful as I can."

He sucked in a breath and braced himself, but when the cloth pulled on the noxious wounds, he reached down to grip her wrist.

"Leave it," he panted.

"And have you lose a foot?" she countered levelly. "I'll wet the wrappings and hopefully it will come free."

He waited apprehensively for her to bring up a steaming basin. Using tongs, she dipped a cloth in it, then neatly flipped it over the crusted linen. He jerked at the sudden scalding, teeth clicking shut. When the hot cloth was removed, Savannah peeled the bandage back neatly.

Breath hissing noisily, Skyler propped up on his elbows to watch her.

"What did this?" she asked, examining the twin punctures on either side of his foot.

"A bayonet," he told her tightly. "It went clean through. Didn't even notice it for hours then I looked down and my boot was full of blood. It ended up killing my horse, passing through my boot, and into a lung. That horse carried me all day. Must have been its stubborn Southern breeding."

She responded with a slight smile, hearing the admiration and pained regret in his voice. Serious once again, she asked, "How long has it been since this was looked at by a doctor?"

"I don't know. A couple of weeks, I guess. Why? How bad is it?" Her stiff manner gave him warning.

"It's bad. Infections running all through it. I might be able to draw it out if I start a poultice right away.

Are you willing to let me tend you?"

Their eyes met and held, Skyler's warming unconsciously. "There're no better hands I'd rather be in."

She rubbed his toes, then smiled faintly. "All right. Let's get started."

Savannah kept the poultices up around the clock for the first two days, working against the infection while she was feeding his resistance with frequent nourishing meals. Both seemed successful, and on the second night, she felt secure enough to let the dressing cool on his leg as she burrowed beneath the covers for some much-needed sleep.

Skyler lay awake listening to her breathing, trying not to think of the pulsing ache that rivaled the one in his ankle. He tried to think of Tony D'Angelo and the slaughtered men she'd led to their deaths. He tried to concentrate on the viciousness of her lies. He tried to cool the sudden heating of his blood when he thought of her slightly clad figure curled beside him, of the scent of her glossy hair, of the paradise she could bring him so effortlessly. Restless and trapped in that torturous proximity, he tried to sleep, tried to summon a saving weariness, but his senses were keenly alert. With a futile moan, he half turned toward her, drawing her relaxed body to his painfully tense form. She sighed in her sleep, face nestling into the hollow between his neck and shoulder. Unbidden, his hand stroked along the curve of her ribs, rising to knead one heavy breast until its sleepy crest hardened in innocent temptation. That temptation made him groan aloud and his arms encircled her tightly, holding her close while he mourned the distance between them. A distance he feared could never be bridged.

He awoke with the pounding demons back in his head, searing his thoughts and burning in his blood. His eyes felt hot and dry, opening them a labor, focusing them an impossibility. He turned his head slowly to the side but the blur of white sheets was unobstructed. Licking his parched lips, he made a croaking call.

"Savannah?"

When there was no answer, he pulled himself up. The movement caused the floor to teeter wildly. He stood with the aid of the bedpost and hopped awkwardly to the door. He leaned against the wooden frame, giving thanks for its coolness. The hall was a dark twisting ribbon, its walls seeming to breathe, the hunt scene coming to life on those painted strips.

"Major, what are you doing up?" came a voice full of censure. He tried to find a face amid all the distorted visions but everything melted into a blur of color and texture.

"Savannah?" he called into that seething mass, hoping for rescue.

"You're burning up with fever. Get back to bed."

Burning? He shook his head in denial. "Cold," he mumbled. "So cold."

A wrap was draped about his bare shoulders and he was steered firmly back into the room. Everything took a dramatic dip as he was laid back on the mattress.

"You rest, Major. I'll get Savannah."

He reached out frantically and caught a soft feminine hand. He pulled it close, pressing it to his hot cheek. "Savannah, don't leave me. Don't go."

Caroline struggled distastefully to draw her hand away but his grasp was strong. "Please, Major. Release me. I'll get her for you."

But he was beyond reason, clinging to her hand, kissing the tense knuckles, rubbing them against his cheek until she felt a surprising dampness. His voice was even more alarming, a low, tortured moan.

"Savannah, please love me. I know you've every

reason for your hate and I've told you I feel the same, but can't you please care for me just a little. Just a little. I love you so much. What can I do? What do you want? What would make you care? Why can't you love me? I've done everything I know how. Why isn't it enough. It's never enough."

With a softening of compassion, Caroline bent and stroked the damp hair. "Shh, Skyler. It's all right. Just lay quiet. Everything will be all right."

The glazed silvery eyes searched vaguely but couldn't find her. "Savannah?"

"I'm here," Caroline soothed. "Close your eyes. Rest now. I won't leave you."

"I love you, you know."

"I know. Close your eyes."

He obeyed weakly, letting the dizziness suck him down into darkness.

The fever lasted nearly two days, raging high with bouts of delirium but never as clear as the words he spoke to Caroline. Savannah remained at his side, cooling his hot face and keeping him covered to fight the chills in defiance of his thrashing. When the fever broke, it left him drained and in a deep sleep that lasted twenty-eight hours. After that, his strength seemed to surge back. He slept a great deal of the time and, when awake, devoured everything on his tray. Within a week, Savannah caught him up hobbling about the room.

"What are you doing?" she demanded, setting down the tray she carried to hurry and grip his arm.

"I'm fine. I just couldn't stay abed any longer." At least alone, he added to himself. "I want to go outside and get some fresh air on my face."

She looked skeptical, eyes gauging him critically. "I think you need more than your drawers on if you're going for a stroll."

He assented to that, surprised to find all his clothes still sharing her closets as if she'd been expecting his return at any moment. Refusing to don more than trousers and a linen shirt, he accepted her offer of a shoulder.

The terraced lawn in the rear of the house was a blinding green, its flower beds an artist's palette in comparison. The thick bladed grass felt cool between his toes as Skyler looked about with a smile.

"This must have been beautiful."

"It was. My father proposed to my mother here. I always thought it was the most romantic spot on earth." Suddenly awkward with that confession, she bent and began to gather an armful of the fragrant flowers while he watched her among the graceful blooms, a rival for any one of them. She would have been bewildered by the fierce expression on his face had she looked up. "Looking on all this makes it hard to imagine a whole other world of war not so far away."

"Another world," he echoed, sounding so strange that her gaze lifted. His features were taut and distant.

"What was it like in battle?"

He looked down at her kneeling in a pool of colorful blossoms, eyes wide and innocent of that horror. How could she ever understand? "It was loud and it smelled," he said tightly.

"Skyler?"

Her concern made him angry for not knowing how he felt. "It's done," he snapped. "I don't wish to dwell on it for your morbid interest."

She frowned as he limped back to the house. Would she ever know the secret he and Darcy now shared?

The days passed uneventfully, Savannah busy with ledgers and plans and Skyler hobbling about in a solitary cloak of silence. Even Hillary was put off by his gruffness and preference for his own company. At

379

night, the tenseness between husband and wife as they shared the same bed made sleep nearly impossible. Once she managed to find slumber, Savannah was often awakened by Skyler's restless tossings. She made no complaint, fearing he would find another place to pass the night. Strained as things were between them, she didn't want to be separate from him, taking a martyred pleasure in his presence. Her pride held her back from seeking his arms with admissions of her loneliness and love. That and a fear he would reject her and close all doors forever. They never spoke of their arrangement, conversations limited to his occasional question about the state of Rising Sun. What hurt the most was the way he looked at her, grey eyes veiled and cool, never warming at the sight of her as they once had. Sometimes he looked almost angry and other times as if he saw something he despised. If he hated her, why did he stay? Each day she feared he would announce his plan to return North. Alone. She was thankful for every night she could lie on the silent bed beside him, hoping the next day would lend her some sign of what he was feeling, some hope that they could yet have a future.

For Skyler, it was just as difficult. Being near Savannah without enjoying the intimacy of that closeness had him constantly on edge. Only her aloofness kept him from tumbling over it. Each casual rebuff reminded him that she hated him. He was frustrated and confused in his position as unwanted guest, constantly wondering why Savannah had gone through the trouble of rescuing him. He knew he should go and be done with it but was fatalistically held, hoping she would convince him that he was needed, that she cared. His own feelings were in like turmoil. He wanted to hold her in contempt but was unable to shake the deep admiration he held for her. He wanted to remain cold but warmed with love whenever she was near. He refused to give her the satisfaction of knowing how helpless he was to her, refusing to utter the first words of reconciliation, refusing to yield to the passion that simmered unstoked but eternal within him. It was hard to be with her but impossible to think of being without her, and he writhed in that ever-tangling net. She was his wife but the joys of marriage were kept from him, and he was never so aware of that as the morning he came upon her in the gardens.

The morning was yet cool when Savannah spread a quilt upon the lawn for she and Jeffery. She could scarcely believe how the child had grown from plump infant to lanky toddler, all blond curls and blue eyes like his father. Distracted from her melancholy by the child's gleeful giggles, she lay stretched out on her stomach pointing out the different colors in the patchwork. A whisper of intuition caused her to glance up. Skyler stood watching them with a wistful expression.

"Good morning," she called to him. "Come join us. There's room."

Skyler hesitated, then dropped down on the coverlet, crossing his long legs but looking far from comfortable. He offered his wide-eyed nephew a tentative smile.

Jeffrey gauged the tall, fair-haired man curiously. He knew his name but had always been kept at a distance by his uncle's unwelcoming looks. The smile was all he needed as an invitation to scramble up on his knee.

"How big you've gotten," Skyler mused, indifferent manner thawing rapidly. "You must be a year and a half old now. It seems so long ago. I remember the night you were born. It was the night I asked your Aunt Savannah to marry me." He glanced up but Savannah was pointedly studying the tiny stitches on the quilt. He frowned slightly, taking her lack of response as a sign she remembered as well, remembered how he had used her distress to force her into a situation she hated. And apparently still did. Sighing to himself, he looked back at the cherubic face and smiled. "I'd like a whole house full of little fellows like you. I bet you'd like some playmates, wouldn't you, some little cousins to share your games and adventures with? I don't think I'd like to grow up alone."

"He doesn't have to."

The quiet words brought up the silver-grey eyes in wary question. His response was equally hushed.

"Children aren't conceived miraculously."

She didn't drop his intense stare. "As you said, it's not something I can do alone."

Testing the ground before he put his feet on it, Skyler said, "I wasn't aware you wanted children."

"I told you I liked them."

The cool counter forced him to advance slightly. "Even my children?"

"You are my husband. How else would I get them?"

The caustic edge to her words made him draw back defensively, his gaze growing distant and chilled. "You aren't naive, Savannah. There are other ways I suspect you would find more appealing."

Only the presence of the child kept her from slapping him. She looked away, struggling to suppress the tears of hurt and outrage that prickled behind her eyes. She forced her words out brittlely.

"I am not a whore, sir."

"You're not a wife either."

That stinging summation cried out for an angry reply, but before she could speak it, Caroline came upon them. Immediately, Skyler set Jeffery away from him and got to his feet, tensing for the tirade he was sure would come. But Caroline only smiled and picked up the boy, hugging him warmly.

"It's time for your nap, young man," she told the pouting child. "Perhaps your Uncle Skyler would take you up to Minnie."

Stunned, Skyler took the eager child she extended. He didn't know why but Caroline's attitude toward him had gradually warmed since the morning he had found himself wrapped in her robe. They were far from friends but the cautious overtures had him nonplused and grateful.

"I'll take good care of him," he said somberly.

"I know you will," Caroline answered with an easy smile that coaxed one in return. "Don't keep Minnie waiting too long."

Lifting the boy onto his shoulders, Skyler started up to the house. Caroline looked after them for a moment and turned to meet Savannah's incredulous gaze.

"He's the boy's uncle. I see no reason to deprive him of that because of our prejudices," the dark-haired woman announced staidly as she took a seat on the quilt. "Savannah, this may be none of my concern but a blind man could see how miserable you are. If this marriage is so intolerable, end it."

The strickened eyes glistened before she looked away. "I don't want to end it. He's my husband, Caroline. And I love him."

Caroline stared at her sister-in-law in surprise. "I don't think he knows that."

Savannah sniffed wearily, dabbing her eyes with her sleeve. "It wouldn't make any difference. You don't understand."

"Perhaps I do. More than you know," she said sympathetically. "I know Skyler loves you and I know for some reason he believes you hate him." Savannah turned in astonishment, but she continued. "I also know that he's different now just as Darcy's different. I can't guess at what changed him nor will he tell me. All I can do is accept him and love him. I do love him and can only hope that some day he'll be the man I married again. If not, I'll love him for the man he is. I'd better tuck Jeffery in."

Savannah sat in the warm morning sun long after Caroline returned to the house, mulling over her words. When she finally stood and folded up the coverlet, her face was etched with a determined smile.

Chapter Twenty-Eight

Skyler gave a start as light fingertips trailed across the breadth of his shoulders, brushing the nape of his neck in passing. He turned, stared, then stood. It took a moment for his senses to return enough to seat his wife beside him at the dinner table. Savannah had not only changed she'd been transformed, and his riveted eyes were full of that delightful transformation.

Savannah had searched through her closets until she found just the dress for her purpose. It was dramatically styled in emerald and black plaid tafetta. Its low scooped neckline was edged with a bertha of jet beaded black lace and the snug curved lines of the bodice molded her figure into hourglass perfection. Everything about it was made to tantalize the senses—the crunching rustle of the belled skirt, the flirting winks of the beading, the slippery sumptuousness of the fabric, and the wafting of seductive scent that lingered in its sweeping folds. If a gown had ever been designed to lure a man, this was it, and Savannah meant to see it did.

Even her family gawked in amazement, but Savannah's attention had only one direction. She spent the mealtime plying her charms so subtly only Hillary was aware of it. The blue eyes glimmered with approving amusement. Savannah's fingers brushed over his when passing serving dishes. She leaned over him to get the pepper mill, so the delicious perfume would tease his nostrils. She dropped her napkin and had to bend to retrieve it, a balancing hand on his thigh while the bounty of her creamy bosom was displayed in seeming innocence.

And at meal's end, when she slipped out into the night to sip her glass of wine, she smiled into that fruity elixier when she heard him follow. She slowed her step to allow him to catch up, then continued to stroll as if unaware of his presence.

"I regret my words to you earlier," he began quietly. "They were unkind."

Savannah tilted her face toward the deep heavens as if she hadn't heard, eyes reflecting the glow of the stars. "The nights here are so inviting, so mysterious. The moon seems close enough to touch, especially tonight because it shines in your hair."

She turned, brushing against him as her hand lifted to his head, fingers sifting through that fair moonlight. He stood very still as that lingering touch stroked down his cheek, then repressed a shiver of desire as she began to walk again. He fell into step, hand lightly resting on the small of her back.

"I regret many things as well, Skyler," she said softly. "I've put those things behind me. I want to look to the future as if it were one of those distant stars. Sometimes it seems impossibly out of reach but I will have it. I will get what I want."

"And what is that?"

She stopped him with a hand on his chest, bringing him around so they faced one another. She didn't speak but looked long and deeply into his eyes. She could see the desire there but also the confusion and distrust. He would have to choose between them.

"It's late. I'm going back in," she announced in that

same hushed voice, the throaty timbre playing havoc with his system. "Good night, Skyler."

She stretched up to brush his cheek with a fleeting kiss, then pressed hers against it. When she felt the sudden quickening of his breath, she stepped away and, with a small smile, returned to the house.

Purposefully, she didn't light the lamp in their room, opening the balcony doors so the moonlight spilled in incandescently along with the fragrant evening breeze. She paused in the bathing glow until she felt him close at her back.

"Could you unfasten my gown for me, Skyler?" she asked, then drew in a rapturous breath as his fingers worked deftly down the row of buttons. Her insides quivered as warm hands parted the fabric to glide over her smooth back without obstruction. She wore nothing beneath the gown. He gave the shoulders a slight push and the gown slipped to the floor, leaving her naked to the silken touch of the night air. His large hands spanned her waist and she revolved in the circle, arms lifting to rest on his shoulders and mouth opening for the intoxicating taste of his. In spite of the cool breeze, her body was flushed with sudden heat as she pressed to him. The roughness of his coat excited hard peaks on her nipples and the cloth of his trousers did little to conceal the massive increase that strained against it.

Still savoring the hungry passion of his kiss, she began to undress him, slowly, seductively, letting him feel the sleek satin of her body as each piece of his clothing fell away. She gave a soft moan of need as his hands cupped her rounded buttocks, rubbing her starved loins against the urgent heat of him.

Easily, he bore her to the bed, seeking entry to that honeyed pleasure denied him for so long. She guided him there, leisurely manner discarded as a wave of desirous longing trembled through her. The juncture was a fiery paradise neither of them could delay for long. Limbs entangled, breaths shared in plunging kisses. They urged each other at a fevered pace toward a rewarding climax that released the tension of long abstinence in great shuddering sighs of ecstasy.

Lost in that heavy feeling of fulfillment, Savannah lay against his damp chest, delighting in the circling strength of his arms. She waited in breathless anticipation but he was silent. He never said the words she wanted so desperately to hear, words he gave so freely when they were unwelcomed but withheld when they would make all complete for her.

The sweetness of their reunion taking a sour turn, Savannah wept soundlessly. Feeling her distress, Skyler frowned into the darkness, reading her regret that she had surrendered to her body's weakness in those faint spasms. The physical needs between them may have been soothed but the emotional ones were still lacking. Nothing had changed.

He woke with a hoarse gasp, sweat drying on his face and cold on the back of his neck. He lay still in the darkness until the frantic pace of his heart slowed, but he was far from calm. Even Savannah's slumbering nearness brought him no comfort. Shaken and too edgy to seek sleep, he rose so not to wake her with his restlessness. Pulling on trousers and an unbuttoned shirt, he wandered the dark halls, ending downstairs.

The marble of the parlor floor was cold against his bare feet but not as cold as the persistent chill of terror that pricked at his spine. The remembered nightmare haunted even his waking hours. He paced the floor in weary agitation, hoping the fragile shivering would subside.

"This will help."

Skyler whirled, drawing a startled breath, then

forced his strained muscles to unknot. It was only Darcy sprawled in one of the chairs. A goblet dangled from one hand. The other gestured to the French crystal decanter, where amber liquid glistened invitingly behind green etched glass.

"It won't make them stop but it will make them easier to bear."

"What are you talking about?" he growled in annoyance, unsettled by his state of clammy breathlessness beneath the hard, cynical eyes of his brother-in-law.

"The dreams," Darcy summed up with an astuteness that made him all the more alarmed. "I've heard you roaming the halls since you've been back. I used to, too, though not as gracefully as you."

"Dreams?" he echoed faintly.

"You don't still hear them? The drums, the cannons, the screams from horses and men alike? Haven't you ever woken up with the burn of powder in your nose and the creep of fear crawling all over you?"

Skyler stood frozen, staring at him in an awed shock. Darcy only gave him that wry smile and clinked his glass against the decanter.

"Help yourself."

Slowly, he poured himself a glass, the rim clattering noisily on the crystal. He took down the contents in two great swallows, eyes watering at the choking burn.

"Pour another. You need it."

And he did. His stomach was a jiggling mass of nerves, palms so wet he could barely hold the glass. While he sipped the bolstering liquor, he eyed Darcy suspiciously.

"They don't understand, the women don't," he was saying casually. "Caroline always wants me to talk about it but how could I tell her about the things I saw? I was there and it still is like some nightmare. Then

389

there was Lookout Point. Nothing in battle was as bad as that. I used to be afraid to close my eyes at night for fear I'd open them and find myself back there."

"And can you sleep now?" he asked softly.

Darcy laughed tightly. "With one eye open. Sit down, Yank. I hear it was mighty bad in Spotsylvania. You were in the middle of that blood bath?"

Skyler took another long swallow to wet his dry mouth, then sat heavily. As he spoke, his eyes took on a glassy, dazed shine. "When the Wilderness caught fire it was like marching into Hell. Some men broke and ran just at the sight of it. The smell of the dead and the wounded." He closed his eyes tightly and moved on quickly in his narration. "It was all fog and rain when we met again. Between us we lost twelve thousand men on one square mile of that miserable ground. The Bloody Angle they called it. I don't see the fighting any more but I can't forget a single face. A lot of the fighting was hand to hand for hours on end. It was madness and everyone was lost to it. There was no time to think, just this crazy scramble to strike first, to kill to survive, and I survived it." He nodded to himself, as if in assurance of that fact, but the viciousness he'd found in himself that day made him tremble.

Darcy had fallen silent, eyes staring into his glass but seeing other things there—faces of the men he'd killed, faces of the starving at Point Lookout. Hearing the other speak of his fresh wounds made his own seem old and distant. It still wasn't a comfortable feeling.

"It's the train I see in my nightmares," Skyler continued in a low voice. "The train from Charleston. I wake up on that train with Savannah sitting beside me in the dark. She smiles and holds up a lantern. The other passengers are all the men I've killed. At first I could see all their faces and recognize every one, but now they're just skeletons in bloody uniforms, all turned to grin at me. When I ask where the train is going, Savannah just smiles and says, 'Why to Andersonville, of course. All your friends are there waiting. I sent them on ahead.' Then it gets dark again and I can hear the rattle of bones moving about in the darkness. When I wake up, I'm never quite sure where I am. I'm always afraid I won't wake up in time and the train will get to that destination."

Darcy sloshed more liquor into the tipping glass and nodded. "I know the ride well." He looked for a long moment at his brother-in-law and gave a wry smile. It was easier to think of him as family than it was to envision him in the blue uniform. His sister's fault, of course, for insisting they take him in. "Savannah is one hell of a woman and I don't say that because she's my sister. She's very loyal to her family and to her country, and when you made her feel that loyalty for you as well, you put her in the middle of a lot of pain. She's never said anything to me. She keeps those things inside, thinking she's strong enough to handle it all. But she's not. She's just a woman. Hell, she's just a person like you and me. We aren't meant to carry the world and all its problems. Her problem is we all depend on her and expect her to devote herself to us alone, as if none of the other things was important. We're jealous and spiteful if she gives any attention away. We're pushing her to make a choice she can't make because we're all an equal part of her. I think it's time we stopped being so selfish and gave her a little back of what she's given to us. And, Skyler, she'd never let you get off that train at Andersonville. As long as she's beside you, she'll always see you get home."

Skyler stared at him in a thoughtful silence until Darcy's glass touched his in a toast of grim camaraderie.

"To the men who make these wars," he called. "May

391

their sleep be just as troubled."

Savannah paused in the doorway, expression bemused as she looked at the two men snoring obliviously in the none too comfortable chairs. Quietly, she crossed to them, taking the glass from Darcy's slack hand and slipping her robe about her husband's shoulders. She puzzled over what had brought two so unlikely companions together in the middle of the night to share a drink and doubted she would ever have an answer. Satisfied as to the question of Skyler's whereabouts, she returned to her room to spend the remaining hours in restful sleep.

She was just as surprised to find the two of them up in the morning before her, having breakfasted together before going their separate ways. Darcy had ridden into Columbia and Skyler was out somewhere in the fields. She took a handful of buttery biscuits and went to her father's office, hoping to relieve some of her plaguing emotions that marred the beauty of the day. Her plan of the night before had only partially succeeded. She had her husband as a lover, but without the feeling behind it, it was an empty satisfaction. It only proved he wanted her physically. She still hadn't reached to the heart of him to find if he had forgiven her. Morosely, she toyed with a column of figures but might just as well have been trying to decipher Greek for all the sense they made to her.

"Good morning."

The longed-for voice brought her daydreaming thoughts into sharp focus. She glanced up, then gave a bewildered smile at his outrageous looks.

"What on earth have you been doing?"

"I wanted to look at the irrigation system and thought I'd dress practically," he answered with a grin.

He stood in the spotless office dressed in baggy overalls of blue canvas. They rose to mid chest, then fastened with buttoned straps over his bare chest. He wore them as a solitary garment instead of over clothing the way the field hands did. The pant legs were rolled up to his knees and were dripping on muddy bare feet. With his broad, browned shoulders and tangle of ashen hair, the effect was oddly stirring.

"So you've been out wading in the muck," she observed with a disapproving arch of one fine brow.

Undaunted, he came to sit on the corner of the desk, dangling feet splashing mud and water on the polished wood floor. "I was thinking of becoming an engineer once and I seemed to remember a waterwheel in one of your streams. Tobias told me it hadn't worked in some time, so I thought I'd see if I could fix it."

As he went on proudly and in enthused detail to describe his method of attack in the muddy stream, Savannah found herself watching him in a fanciful daze. Her eyes lingered over the expanse of his chest, down the line of the unconstructed overalls to the filthy calves, one still bearing its vivid scars. The sight of him aroused her senses. She let her gaze wander the prominent angles of his face, those bold features that were so compellingly handsome, the face of her husband, her love. In sudden decision, she rose, catching him in mid sentence as she came to stand between his straddled knees. Now was the time to find out if she still had a marriage.

Meeting the startled question in his eyes, Savannah held his lean cheeks between her palms and leaned forward to kiss him. His mouth was slack with surprise, then quickly firmed as her attention became more pronounced. Her tongue traced the generous curve of his lips, then slipped between them to stroke over his in velvet invitation. His posture was no longer one of ease, straightening and growing tense. But he didn't reject her.

393

Her kisses moved upward, grazing his temples and flickering over his closed eyelids.

"Savannah." It was a hoarse protest.

"Shh."

Her lips returned to tease his, small hands rubbing the warm bronzed flesh of his shoulders and body leaning nearer until she languished upon him. She was all fluid availability, sensuous, feminine, beautiful. It was too much.

With a low groan, Skyler's arms bound her to his chest, a willing captive of his strength. His mouth slanted across hers, demanding, possesssing, yearning, and she gave back to him with like passion. After several minutes of the heated exchange, they broke away, breathless and panting, but stayed in the circle of each other's arms.

Skyler searched her rapt expression in anxious doubt, seeing only the reflection of emotions to match his own simmering in the deep blue eyes.

"Savannah, I don't know if I can take another chance with you," he mourned sadly. "It hurts too much knowing I'm the only one who cares."

She only smiled, moist lips curving up in sultry allure. "It's no risk, Skyler. I love you."

She felt him recoil slightly, his breath rushing in rapid uncertainty against her face and hair. She reached up to touch his cheek, fingertips splaying across that taut plane encouragingly.

"I don't know how I can make you believe me other than to tell you it's so. So much hurt has passed between us but so much good as well. You're the man I want, the man I've always wanted. I have your name but I need your love. Skyler, I need you. I need to know our lives will be forever entertwined. I need to know I can love you without reservation. Can I, Sky?"

He was silent for a long moment, hesitating, trying to

find a reason not to yield all to what he wanted. But he could think of none that would rival the soft, pleading look in her eyes. "Yes," he said quietly. "Yes, you can, because I can't help but love you. I've tried and failed miserably to cut you from my life and have been miserable. Even in your hate, I loved you. Through your betrayal, I loved you. I'm tired of these endless things that conspire to keep us apart. Come to me, Savannah, and let's start again."

With a sigh, her arms curled about his neck, eyes shimmering with a happy glow. "Shall we try to make it a life for three, husband?"

The warmth seeped back into his gaze, basking her with the heat of his emotions. "Here?" he suggested huskily.

"Upstairs. After you wash," she added primly.

He pulled her closer, overwhelming her with his masculine aura of power and virility. "Are you sure you want to wait that long?"

Her eyes grew heavy lidded as she considered that. "Forget the bath," she purred.

As they lay side by side on their large bed, Savannah in the brief tangle of her chemise and Skyler in his muddy bare feet, she turned to him with a sigh of contentment, stroking the firm, golden chest with possessive admiration.

"What do you want, Sky?"

"You mean now, this minute?" he asked, catching up her hand to nibble her fingertips.

"I mean for us. Is this to be our home or would you prefer to go North to be with your family?" Her eyes lowered so he wouldn't see her prejudice.

He thought of the conversation he and Darcy had shared and smiled. "This is our home, Savannah. Pennsylvania is not so far that we can't visit."

She looked up at him, eyes shining with a glad

wetness. "And my family?"

"This is their home, too. I'm used to living in a crowd. I wouldn't have it any other way." He smiled at her obvious relief, turning her hand so he could place a kiss on its palm.

"Then you'll want to assume the management of Rising Sun."

His smile widened at her self-sacrificing tone. "A city-bred boy like me? No, thank you. It's in much more capable hands now. I'll find something to be useful for, if nothing else than filling you with our children and watching them grow."

"I love you."

"Only because I let you have your way."

"I loved you even when you were being a pushy, brash Northerner."

"Me?" His brows rose in an innocent sweep. "I was doing what was best for you, you stubborn, prideful little Rebel."

"And I do so enjoy what you do," she murmured. Her wrists locked behind his neck as he moved atop her, settling his weight comfortably along the delightful cushion of her body. "And what you do, you do so well."

The intermingling of their lips was interrupted by a brisk knock.

"If that's Hillary, I'm going to tear out every one of her pretty blond curls," Savannah promised savagely. She pouted when Skyler rolled away and pulled on a pair of trousers, then tossed her a robe with a roguish grin.

But it was Darcy who stood in the hall, expression somber and strangely concerned.

"A letter for you, Yank. Aiken was holding it. He hadn't heard you were back. It's from Philadelphia."

Skyler took the envelope gingerly, eyes noting the

bold lettering, smeared though it was, on the travel-soiled paper. It was from his father.

Darcy put a hand on the other man's shoulder in awkward compassion. "I hope it ain't bad news," he offered gruffly and hobbled off.

Skyler stared at the envelope for a timeless minute, eyes wide with a superstitious dread.

"Sky, would you like me to open it?" Savannah asked gently, feeling the anguish of his indecision.

"No, it's all right. I'll do it." He gave her a weak, false smile. "It's probably nothing."

He tore open the stiff paper, eyes moving slowly over the single sheet inside. There was no change in his expression as he handed it to her and walked slowly to the open veranda doors.

"My dear son," the letter began. "Since we've heard nothing from you, I'm sending this to your wife in hopes it will reach you through her. There is no easy way to tell you of Palmer's death."

Savannah gave a small gasp, eyes flying up to her husband's broad back. Through a haze of tears, she continued to read.

"He was killed during the siege of Petersburg by a sharpshooter, as he was tending the wounded in a forward trench. He would have wanted to give his life serving others but I can't help but feel the waste. I wish I had better news to tell you of Brent. He has been listed 'missing presumed dead' under Sherman's command in Georgia, but we haven't abandoned hope."

"You have often been in our thoughts. Leslie and the children send their love as I do and pray you, your wife, and her family are well. Come home when you can or send some word. Your father."

Savannah wiped her eyes and carefully folded the letter, replacing it in the envelope. Then she went to Skyler. He drew a deep, shaky breath when she touched his arm.

"I was just thinking of those little children with no daddy," he said woodenly. "It just isn't fair, Savannah. It isn't fair to lose them both. It just isn't fair." His composure broke, and with a low moan of grief, he turned and let her hold him wordlessly until his quiet weeping stilled.

"Are you going home, Sky?" she asked gently when she felt him wipe his damp face on the silken shoulder of her robe.

"No," he answered, voice low and gravelly. "Not home. I can't do any good there. It's too late. I'm going to help put an end to the war that killed my brothers."

The evening meal was a sober occasion. The Russell family had rallied to console Skyler, seeing his loss not as two less of the enemy but as losing members of a family, and they weren't strangers to that grief. He accepted their condolences with a quiet gratitude but his eyes were on Savannah. She had barely spoken to him since he told her of his plans. She stayed by his side, clinging to his arm, but her eyes were glassy with shock. Only when they lay together in the aftermath of their urgent lovemaking did she begin to sob softly.

"Skyler, I can't lose you," she lamented, trembling fitfully in his tender embrace.

"You won't. I have to go."

"I know, but I just can't be brave about it."

"Of course you can. You're the bravest woman I know. I'll come back to you. I promise. Have I ever broken my word? Have I?"

She shook her head, sniffing loudly.

"I won't this time either. I'm going to be with you when you have each of our half-dozen children, and I'm going to sit on the porch and watch them grow along with my grandchildren after that. No one's going to deprive me of that joy."

"You're going to make such a fine father," she told him with a loving smile.

He kissed her thoroughly. "I'll write you." Another kiss. "I'll think of you every day." Another kiss. "I'll dream of you every night." Another kiss. "And I'll be back to live all those dreams."

"Can we live one of them now?" she asked huskily, then sighed as his mouth came down on hers in answer.

At breakfast, the family received another shock as Darcy hobbled in freshly groomed in his faded uniform. He observed them with a cynical grin as they stared.

"If Hood can go into battle minus a leg and strapped to his horse, I reckon I'll do fine. The Yank was right. This war's got to end and the South needs every man."

Caroline flew to him with a wail, just ahead of Hillary. From around the two weeping women, he took Skyler's extended hand.

"Let's hope the next time we meet, it'll be here as friends," he offered, then reeled as Savannah joined the group, hugging him about the neck.

Supplies and food were gathered by a quiet household, then all came together on the veranda. After accepting teary kisses from the females of the family, Darcy hobbled to Aurora. Savannah insisted that he take the fleet yellow mare for luck. Hugs were equally given to the tall Yankee, even by Caroline. Savannah walked him to the leggy gelding he had chosen because it was bred in Virginia.

"Remember your promise," she ordered sternly. She refused to let tears spoil her last look at her husband.

"Remember I love you," he replied.

Their kiss was long and bittersweet, the effort it took to step away monumental. With a trace of his broad smile, Skyler mounted his horse and turned to Darcy with a crisp salute. The Southerner returned it smartly.

Together, they cantered down the long drive, each taking a different turn. Darcy went East and Skyler North, neither imagining the circumstances of their next meeting.

The ladies stood, eyes straining for the last glimpse of their men, then wordlessly returned to the house.

Chapter Twenty-Nine

The fall and winter months at Rising Sun were lean and hungry. Food was scarce, and their table consisted of vegetables from the garden with a biweekly sacrifice of a hen or occasional hog. There were no complaints from the war-weary women, veterans now of deprivation. Their only relief was in the infrequent letters from Skyler and Darcy that they shared together in the evening—with the exception of the more intimate passages. A surprise parcel from Leslie Reade did much to raise spirits when it arrived by special courier close to Christmas. It contained coffee, sugar, sweets, and best of all, writing paper. They had been using strips of bleached wallpaper from a spare bedroom as paper was impossible to find in the South. Savannah kept up a steady correspondence with the Reades, paying terrible prices for the illegal delivery of mail to the North. She kept them informed of Skyler's good health and his whereabouts when she knew of them.

With the help of "The Confederate Recipe Book," the women were able to make do or provide substitutes for their needs. Published in '63 and bound in wallpaper, it told of how to make cosmetics, dyes, medicines, and foods from common plants and vegetables. Coffee substitutes were made from parched sweet potatoes and even parched okra seed, which they found to be the most palatable. Dried raspberry leaves, as well as blackberry vines and huckleberry bushes, made tea. Candles were made by dipping string in a mixture of mutton suet and beeswax. Clothing was so scarce it was fashioned from mattress ticking, sheets, and old draperies, bonnets from cornhusks, palmetto leaves, and straw adorned with dried flowers. Hillary wore these as proudly as she had the one Skyler bought her in Columbia.

With no market for cotton in the blockaded South, the women spent evenings picking seed out by hand. Caroline and Adelaide then carded it to spin and weave into homespun cloth. As she worked, Caroline's high, reedy voice was often heard carrying the South's most popular war song.

> "My homespun dress is plain I know,
> My hat's palmetto too;
> But then it shows what Southern girls
> For Southern rights will do.
> We have sent the bravest of our land
> To battle with the foe
> And we will lend a helping hand—
> We love the South, you know."

She continued to work toward the war effort, soaking scrap iron in brine and vinegar to produce copperas dyes, the new color of the Confederacy. She sent simply sewn garments to Darcy and the men in his unit, along with the crudely made knit mufflers Hillary worked at so painstakingly.

Savannah had no talent or patience for the tiny stitches. Instead, she worked the fields behind an old pony and helped plant corn, beans, potatoes, and enough peas to fatten their few hogs. With Hillary, she cooked their meals over an open fire. In the soft candleglow, Adelaide read each night from the Bible to encourage their spirits. Her voice was gentle and soothing to their individual fears. And so they survived those bitter months until a letter from Skyler shook their security.

From reading his letters, Savannah was certain her husband would make a great politician. They were long and flowing, full of colorful oratory. He painted a picture of excitement, well-being, and ease, and knowing him, Savannah knew how untrue it all was. His words weren't his feelings but what he felt they needed to hear. Reading between the lines and from his short, personal closings, she knew how disturbed he was by what he saw. She could feel his loneliness, frustration, and anger in the amusing tales he related. And she loved him for wanting to spare her the truth.

His letter of late January was terse and stripped of rhetoric. It told her bluntly to get out of South Carolina, to leave Rising Sun as soon as she could pack. Sherman had given Savannah, Georgia to Lincoln as a Christmas present, and now the general was moving north into the Carolinas with a vengeance, planning to lay it to waste for breeding the nest of secessionists. His march would lead him to Columbia and they lay directly in his path. He didn't need to elaborate. Sherman's march to the sea was a tale of waste and destruction carved sixty miles wide. The South was dotted with Sherman's Sentinels, the skeletal chimneys of plantation houses he put to the torch. Skyler pleaded with her to go North with her family to seek refuge with his own, vowing the carnage would soon be at an end and he would come for her. Included with the letter was another sheet of paper that flared her temper hotly when she read it. She forced herself not to tear it up. She might have need of it.

At dinner, she calmly announced the contents of

403

Skyler's letter to a mixed reaction.

"Yankees," Hillary shrieked in near hysteria, remembering well the invasion of their Beaufort home. "We have to go. We have to get away before they get here."

Caroline's voice was derisive. "Really, Hilly, that beast will never get this far. Hood will save the Carolinas."

"I fear he's already deserted us in favor of Tennessee," Savannah amended softly.

But she was undaunted. "Our boys will turn that virulent blue tide and crush them soundly."

Savannah kept her doubts to herself but her mother's quiet comment ended discussion.

"I will not leave my home, not without your father."

"But Mama—" Hillary whined.

"And I won't leave you here alone," Savannah said staunchly. "We'll weather the sweep of the blue tide."

But as the days passed, the situation grew more ominous. Lines of ragged butternut-clad men stole by in columns of four, the ghostly remains of the pride of the South. They were dirty and starving and weary of war. Some wore blood-stained bandages, some had feet wrapped in rags or shoes so full of holes they were held together with twine. When told to fall out many sprawled on the ground, too weak and exhausted to move, while others crept up to the house begging for food and water. Savannah made sure a huge pot of hominy was kept simmering, and she and Caroline dished it out to the pitiful troops who ate from their broken hats or dirty hands. Some were full of thanks and blessings, some stared silently, eyes full of tears.

Seeing the tired, broken men left no illusion that Sherman could be stopped. Having them stream by daily in retreat sapped Caroline's sympathies until one day she began to scream and taunt them for their

404

cowardice, for deserting the women of the South, for failing to live up to their bold pledges. Aghast, Savannah dragged the angry wailing woman from the porch. There were no more handouts from Rising Sun after that, and Savannah began to plan the move to Charleston.

Then the line of Confederate troops dwindled to a fearful silence, the dreaded calm. Sherman was coming. In a flurry of panic, Hillary dashed about the house, snatching up her belongings and vowing to flee on foot rather than face the raping hordes. Savannah's assurances that few instances of that kind of abuse happened did little to calm her. Her hysterics bloomed full on the quiet night when they saw an unnatural glow on the Southern horizon. She stood in the parlor trembling from head to foot and faced her mother with fear-inspired hostility.

"We're all going to be killed. Is that what you want, Mama? We've got to get away from here," she shrilled.

Adelaide regarded her with pale, gentle eyes. "Hillary, everything will be fine."

"How can you say that? Can't you see they're already putting the torch to our neighbors? You can stand there while they burn the roof over your head but I'm not. I'm not."

"Your father will be here soon and—"

Hillary pounced on that oft said sentiment, eyes bright with frustration. "He will not be here," she began, pushing away her sister's hands that would pull her out of the room. "He won't be here because he's dead. He's dead, Mama. He's been dead for years. He's never coming back. Never. You can wait until the angels come for you but Papa's never coming home again. He's dead. He's dead."

The only sound was Hillary's strained weeping. Pale and silent, Adelaide Russell rose from her chair. Eyes vague, she went to embrace her sobbing daughter, then pressed light kisses on the cheeks of her other child and daughter-in-law. Then with her graceful dignity, she mounted the sweeping stairs and climbed slowly to her room.

Eyes red and swollen, Hillary glared defensively at the two others. Pettishly, she wailed, "Don't look at me like that. I just told the truth. Somebody had to. We couldn't leave her here with her fantasies. Papa's not coming but Sherman is. We have to leave. I said it for all of us."

Savannah halted Caroline's harsh retort and said wearily, "In a way, you're right. We can't stay. Pack your things. We leave in the morning for Charleston."

Savannah spent most of the night making arrangements for the journey. Together with Delilah, she carried all the family's remaining heirlooms of jewelry, silver, and crystal away from the house and buried them in the ground. Treasured paintings and knick-knacks were wrapped in burlap and stored in an unused root cellar. The food supplies they couldn't carry were divided between those who would stay, including the faithful Delilah who vowed she'd see no Yankee trash, Skyler excepted, set foot in her family's home.

Finally, exhausted, Savannah composed a short note to Skyler telling him where he could find her and left it in their room. That done, she was able to get several hours of deep, much needed sleep to dream of Skyler standing at the foot of the stairs at Rising Sun, warmed eyes lifted to her.

She rose with the sun, anxious to get on the way. Carrying her carpetbag stuffed with just those things she would need and Skyler's letters, she sent Delilah to wake her sister while she spoke to her mother. Hopefully, she could convince her of the necessity of their flight.

Adelaide's room was cool and dark. Speaking cheerfully, Savannah went to open the drapes to let the sun spill in.

"Mama, time to wake up. I have to talk to you about last night, about what Hillary said."

She turned toward the bed and hesitated. Adelaide lay on the coverlet, fully dressed. One of her father's favorite jackets was held in a loving embrace. Her eyes were closed as if in sleep, but a sleep so deep Savannah felt a prickle of fear.

"Mama?"

She touched the fragile hand and its chill brought a rush of tears. With nothing left to wait for, Adelaide Russell had gone quietly, peacefully to meet her husband.

Adelaide was put to rest in the small family cemetery. Daughters and servants all wept as Jeffery placed a spray of early jonquils on the freshly spaded earth. Then silently the three women and boy got into a loaded down buggy, with only Minnie to accompany them, and headed East to Charleston.

Savannah didn't look behind her but knew Delilah would be posting the notice Skyler had sent her on the front door of Rising Sun. Simply, it declared the land and house property of Major Skyler Reade of the United States Army of the Potomac and invited Sherman's officers to have a comfortable stay, to help themselves to whatever they needed, but to leave the house untouched out of courtesy for a fellow officer. If it could save her home, she could bear the disgrace of welcoming the enemy. As long as she didn't have to see it happen. Nor would her child witness that humiliation.

The road to Charleston was crowded with refugees fleeing ahead of the Union forces. Savannah kept a steady hand on the reins and a primed pistol across her knees, but they weren't disturbed. The city of Charleston had endured terrible shelling, exploding bombs leaving craters in the streets and fire-gutted skeletons in the fashionable North Battery District. Fort Sumter had been reduced to rubble, but even after continuous bombardment from land and sea, Charleston remained scarred but proudly defiant. The Federals were resigned to the fact it could not be broken by direct attack and waited for the deterioration of the Confederate cause to take its damaging toll.

Jonah Russell's modest house was untouched by the repeated carnage. Like many of the city's homes, his was a long, narrow single house with its gabled end facing the street and its side housing an enclosed piazza for inviting privacy from the busy traffic. Wrought iron gates opened through the high brick walls, but the weary travelers didn't pause to admire the extravagant landscaping with its tailored shrubs and miniature fountains. Even in sad disrepair, the lush tangle of overgrown foliage held an exotic beauty. They were too eager for rest and repast to notice much of anything. The home's interior was hot and musty and, sadly, its larder empty. Though exhausted and aching, Savannah offered to see what the city yielded in the way of supplies while the others settled in.

Knowing no one in the city, Savannah went where she knew she could find a friend. She waited in the small office for nearly an hour until he arrived, still wearing a blood-splattered apron from surgery. His annoyed expression at being called away was replaced by a surprised smile when she stood.

"Mrs. Reade, a true pleasure to see you. What brings you to Charleston? Not another daring cause, I trust?"

She explained her situation briefly, then came to the point of her visit. "We have no provisions and I was

408

wondering if you knew where some decent food might be purchased."

"Decent?" He raised a heavy brow. "That is relative. There's little to be had even if you can afford the cost. What is available is difficult to get to. When word travels that supplies have come through, you can plan on a veritable stampede, and if you don't mind me saying so, you don't look in any shape for such rigors."

Savannah considered that. She had anticipated as much. Calmly, she suggested, "But I am capable of working. If you've need of three capable sets of hands, my sisters and I will work for our meals."

Ambrose smiled admiringly. "It's hard, gruelling work, Savannah."

"I'm not afraid of work, Doctor."

He pursed his lips thoughtfully. "Of course not. Report to me in the morning. Early. For tonight, I'm sure I can arrange an advance in pay."

Savannah's relief made her sag briefly, the lines of strain and weariness appearing fleetingly on her face, but Ambrose knew she wouldn't appreciate his sympathies. Instead, he grinned and glanced at her long-lost waistline.

"I see your Yankee survived," he commented, bringing a quick warming to her eyes as she placed her hands on the distended belly.

"Very well, thank you," she returned with a smile.

"I take it he's back in the army."

The animation faded, replaced by a tightening of anxiousness. "He's riding with Sheridan. I haven't seen him since July, though I do get letters." Her lowered eyes said it was hardly the same thing.

"I'm sure you won't have long to wait. It's just a matter of months before we can all go home and I'm sure he's anxious to be with you in your condition."

She said nothing to that.

"The child is due in May?"

She nodded.

"Then good, vigorous work will be good for you as long as you don't push too hard. I'll see you don't," he concluded in warning. "Now go home and rest. You both need it."

Leaving Jeffery in Minnie's care, the three women began work at the warehouse hospital. Pleading a delicate nature, Hillary escaped duty in the wards and worked with other young women scraping old sheets and worn cotton and linen garments to obtain lint for dressings and charred rags for substitute sponges. Silk for sutures was nonexistent, so they measured out cotton or flax thread and even boiled horsehair to make it pliable. Even in this sheltered work, there was no escape from the screams and weeping of the wounded and, worse yet, the smell.

Caroline and Savannah worked the wards, rewetting water dressings on amputated limbs and gently bathing the upper bodies of the filthy men brought in from the field. Savannah spent part of each day assisting Ambrose in surgery. No sign of her earlier queasiness remained as she witnessed the barbarity of operations with little or no anesthetic. Crude drugs like opium were saved for the worse cases and the medicines in their pill form were often insoluble and did nothing to ease suffering. In minor cases, folk remedies were used out of desperation. The women of Charleston grew poppies in their walled gardens. Tinctures of jimson and maypop root were used to relieve pain, yellow jasmine to control fever, the inner bark and pith of the alder for making salve for suppurating wounds, and slippery elm bark and prickly pear leaves were pounded to use as emollient poultices. Infection was nearly certain since cleanliness of wounds wasn't

410

considered important. Sponges and instruments were used on consecutive patients, conveying blood poisoning, gangrene, and lockjaw from one unfortunate to the next. Sterilization was unheard of and most measures used to relieve suffering only increased it out of ignorance.

Common sense told Savannah to keep things as clean as possible. Her extra efforts may have saved the lives of many in her section. She was one of the few women willing to aid the Union prisoners. She volunteered for the duty, repressing her upset when Caroline refused to help the enemy. She saw her husband's eyes in those tortured faces and had no trouble finding the compassion to treat them equally.

Ambrose had been right. It was wearying, spirit-crushing work but it supplied them with two meager meals a day from which they hoarded enough to take home to Minnie and Jeffery. They were too tired to speak much. The hardest to bear was getting no letters from their loved ones. The news they did get was all bad, the end of the Confederacy a certainty that its generals prolonged like a lingering death. Sheridan ravaged the Shenandoah Valley with cold, brutal strategy while Sherman raped the South with his idea of total warfare, taking everything his army needed from the land and destroying all else. When he reached Columbia, a desperate decision was made in Charleston. Its defending army was gathered for a forced march in hopes that an enmassed Confederate front could turn Sherman from his inevitable entry into North Carolina. On February 17, 1865, Sherman reached Columbia. February 18, Charleston was evacuated of troops. On February 19, Columbia was burned.

The citizens of Charleston reeled in shock, realizing

411

they had been abandoned to a ruthless army impatient to reap vengeance against their long-defiant city. In a panic, those who could fled on the tails of the Rebel army as the blue tide advanced into the conquered streets. Looting, burning, and destruction was inevitable, and rebellion quelled mercilessly by the war-hardened men in blue.

With Sherman bound North, Savannah was anxious to return home—if they still had one to return to. They gathered all the food they could to await the opportunity to escape. Only Savannah braved the streets on a final visit to the hospital, leaving the others to pack what they could in the shabby wagon. Clutching her shawl about her, she dashed along the streets, never letting her eyes wander to the atrocities on either side in the lurid, flaming shadows. By the time she reached the hospital, she was damp with the sweat of fear, but that hampering emotion didn't show in her serious blue eyes.

Union officers had taken over the hospital. Too valuable to replace, Ambrose and his staff were allowed to practice under supervision. James Ambrose greeted her with a vague, defeated stare that upset her more than the carnage in the streets.

"We're leaving to go home," she told him in a quiet aside. "I wanted to say good-bye and wish you well."

"You've been a God send to me, Savannah, and you'll be missed, but a safe journey to you. Be careful of the wolves on the road." He spoke of the bummers, deserters from both armies who traveled in lawless bands behind Sherman, destroying what was left them with a gleeful indifference. He would have said more to her but an urgent tug on his arm drew him back to where he was needed the most. Savannah's last sight of him was calling crisp orders while tying an apron about his middle.

She slipped back into the dangerous streets carrying a bundle of foodstuffs one of the workers prepared for her. Tension made her body ache, fear lending a furtiveness to her eyes as she hurried along the edge of the alleyways hoping to go unnoticed. As she turned a corner, she didn't retreat fast enough to escape the bleary eyes of several drunken infantry men. Hearing them call after her as if she were a street woman plying her wares, she fled in panic as the sound of their boots grew closer. The parcel of food fell as she clutched her awkward middle, exertion waking a protest there as well as in her burning lungs. Like a pursued hare, she dodged down a dim side street and burst onto the next. Panting and gasping, she pulled up short and stared in shock at the back of a Union officer who was about to swing up onto his horse.

With a strangled, breathless cry, she ran forward with all her remaining strength. The name she tried to call was a hoarse whisper of raw effort. But he must have heard her graceless approach, for he turned and she had yet another shock.

"Skyler," she whimpered faintly but her eyes deceived her. The blond hair and tall, well-proportioned build were his. Even the face was the same. One eye was covered by a leather patch and the other was impossibly brown. With a confused moan, she sank to her knees, head swimming in a dizzy fog of disappointment and discomfort. Gentle hands lifted her and held her close to the unfamiliar yet disturbingly identical form.

"Savannah. My God, it is you. Let's get you out of here. Tell me where."

From the pommel of his saddle, she gave directions as best she could, then leaned weakly against the sturdy shoulder. Her thoughts were spinning madly. The sharp twinges in her abdomen took all her concentration, making her weep in terror that the baby had come to some harm. Not Skyler, the ache in her heart pounded in a frantic rhythm. Not Skyler but Brent. Somehow she had found Brent Reade.

Chapter Thirty

By the time he sat her down on one of the benches in the private garden and wet his handkerchief in the fountain to cool her brow, Savannah was sufficiently recovered to look at him. The pains in her belly had eased to an occasional dull spasm and she ceased to fear for her child now that the fearful episode was over.

"Better now?" he asked in concern, sitting close beside her.

"Oh, Brent, you gave me a start. I thought—I hoped—"

"That I was Sky," he concluded. "Sorry, but you'll have to settle for me for the moment. What put you in such a rush and what are you doing here?"

Slowly, laboriously, she told him of the events leading to her anxious flight while he listened, arm about her shoulders. When she'd finished, it was her turn to question him.

"Your father wrote that you were missing, likely dead."

"Almost," he vowed, touching the eye patch. "Took a nasty gash but I'm still here. They must have gotten the names mixed up in the field hospital. They're always doing things like that. I was out of service for several months and it will be several more before I can take this thing off. The doctor promised I would have some vision left, at least enough to eye a pretty skirt."

Savannah laughed. It was the first time she had made that sound since Skyler left and it was odd to her ears.

"Skyler's all right then?" he urged. "You've heard from him? I've been cut off from everything for almost a year."

Then he didn't know. Slowly, she told him, "As far as I know, Skyler's well. I had several letters from him before coming here. He's with Sheridan. It's impossible to find out information on a Union officer through our channels."

"I gather he managed to see you at least once," he chuckled, placing his hand happily on her rounded middle. "He must not know or he would have deserted to be here with you."

Savannah looked down awkwardly. "How could I tell him, Brent? He has enough to worry over with times so uncertain." She didn't voice her main reason for silence—the knowledge that he would insist she go North to safety. Stubbornly, she wasn't prepared to leave her homeland or her family as long as both needed her.

"So I'm to be an uncle again. That's grand news. I'm glad you both worked things out between you."

"So am I," she agreed. "I love your brother very much."

"The rest of the family? Any news?"

"Leslie and I wrote regularly. The children and your father are well."

"And Palmer?" He searched her face hopefully, expression stiffening when he saw the wetness in her eyes.

"I'm sorry, Brent. Palmer was killed at Petersburg."

He winced as if she'd struck him, shaking his head in a daze of disbelief. With a hard swallow, he knuckled his good eye fiercely. "Then we'll have to get Sky back, won't we? Until then, I'll apply for emergency leave and take care of you for him. We have to keep our family together. I won't lose any more of it."

"Skyler!"

They both turned at the sudden shriek and Hillary drew up in amazement, staring at Brent in uncertain alarm. He quickly rose, courtly smile erasing all signs of grieving.

"A frequent mistake today," he said smoothly. "I'm Brent Reade. Skyler's my brother. And you?"

"Brent, this is my sister Hillary."

Cursing the shabbiness of her dress, Hillary dimpled prettily. "Savannah, shame on you for not mentioning your husband had another at home just as handsome. I declare, I would have defected North in a hurry had I known it was twice blessed. And I thought my sister got the last good-looking man. You aren't married, are you, Colonel Reade?"

"If I was, I'd look for a way to remedy it." He bowed over her hand, the perusal of his gaze saying he didn't mind the tattered state she was in.

Smiling to herself, Savannah looked between the two smitten young people with a flash of optimistic intuition. Things would be all right for the Reades and the Russells.

They left the smoldering ruins of Charleston behind them, Brent happily wedged between the two sisters while Caroline, Jeffery, and Minnie shared the rear seat with the luggage. Relieved of the burden of leadership, Savannah dozed frequently, head pillowed on Brent's shoulder. Waking several times, she was given an awkward turn of confusion, mistaking the fair-haired Yankee officer at her side. If only it had been Skyler, she grieved to herself. Hillary didn't mind the substitute, happier in the practice of her rusty coquetry than she had been since they left Beaufort. Silently, Savannah envied her enjoyment, then chided herself for her meanness. Hillary was entitled to a taste of the same excitement she revelled in. And Skyler would return.

Throughout the last few miles of the journey, all were silent. The ruin of South Carolina was all around them. Homes and barns were blackened rubble, croplands set to the flame, railroad lines ripped up with formal iron bows dressing the scorched trees. Sherman destroyed well wherever he went. They didn't need to see Columbia to know its fate. Though the Federals denied striking the match, it lay mostly in ashes. Columbia wasn't what concerned the women in the wagon. What if Rising Sun had suffered the same fate? As the miles drew them closer and the scarred foundations of many of their neighbors were passed, the tension grew almost unbearable.

"Look," cried Hillary. "There it is."

The ladies were in tears as Brent drew in the reins at the front steps. It stood soiled by drifting soot, windows broken out here and there and half the veranda charred by a short-termed blaze. But it stood—their home.

Delilah advanced onto the porch, dropping the massive shotgun she held to race down with a glad cry, embracing the women as if they were family. She eyed Brent's face and uniform with suspicion but hugged him as well when he was introduced.

Over a scant dinner, Delilah explained how Rising Sun had managed to survive. Only Skyler's notice had saved it from the similar fate of others on the thousand-mile path of blackened chimneys. Though careless, the Union troops had done no serious damage during their overnight stay. They had taken the few remaining animals and all the meal that hadn't been hidden, but they had respected the property.

"What about the porch?" Caroline asked. She felt a bit awkward with the black woman sharing a place at the table instead of serving at it, but then she had already welcomed a Yankee, now two. Times were changing.

"Some of that bummer trash did that. Rode up just as bold as you please on them dirty mules and asked for the valuables. Tobias and me met 'em with guns and the others had pitchforks, so they got a mite discouraged. They done throwed rocks and torches after dark, the cowards, but no real harm was done."

"You saved our home, Delilah," Savannah said quietly. "It's a debt we can't repay other than to tell you it's your home as well for as long as you like."

"I like that fine, Miss Vannah."

And so they settled in once more to make Rising Sun a home. Brent proved invaluable, providing the knowledge and a strong back to rebuild the porch. It lacked only the whitewash to restore it to its former glory. He saw to the cultivation of the fields in an ambitious plot of ground. Tobias had hidden the seed from the marauders and his foresight would see them through the next winter. With Columbia destroyed, they were on their own, completely self-sufficient, and they survived it if not prospered. And they were happy.

Hillary pursued Brent Reade just short of being shameless and he showed no sign of minding the attention. His eye patch was gone, revealing a thin scar that ran from brow to cheekbone. Hasty stitches had closed the gash in his eyelid but he had only a hazy vision from that bloodshot eye. He never complained. It was better than the permanent patch.

Caroline and Savannah spent many a sociable hour on the veranda watching Jeffery grow as quickly as

419

Savanna's girth. Their amiable talk concealed their worry over their husbands. Sherman roared through North Carolina. Sheridan laid waste to the Shenandoah. Grant was enveloping Lee at Petersburg. All they prayed for was a quick end to it. The South was in ashes and they were anxious to rebuild.

And then it was over. They heard the news from a raggedy man dressed in the remains of his uniform as he made his way home. Lee's hopes of escaping Grant and joining Johnston failed, and in early April, while the weary refugees of the Army of North Virginia camped near Appomattox Court House, the two generals met and agreed on terms. Within days, Johnston surrendered and the war that had torn a nation asunder was at an end.

On one cool afternoon as April warmed into May, Savannah stood awkwardly as a single rider approached. Her hopes sank when the face was an unfamiliar one but she advanced to meet him with a determined smile.

"Mrs. Savannah Reade?"

"Yes." Her thoughts catapulted back to a summer night and her chest tightened in panic.

"A letter for you, ma'am."

She took it in trembling hands, not even noticing when the rider took his leave. The address was Charleston. Ambrose? She broke the seal and took out the two sheets of paper the envelope contained. The warmth of the day chilled abruptly into an iciness that gripped her heart. Wave after wave of sickening dizziness swept her until she had no strength to return to the house or call for assistance. The thunder of her pulse was like hoarse cannon fire. She swayed in the empty drive, sheets of paper clutched in her hand. As she tried to cry out Caroline's name, her abdomen contracted painfully. Sudden wrenching pressure brought a surge of wetness to stain her petticoats, and with a shock of alarm, she realized the baby was coming. She managed several stumbling steps before she saw Brent at the corner of the house. He began to run. All she could manage when he caught her up in his arms was the name of her husband.

As he carried the moaning woman upstairs, Brent called out loudly that Savannah was going into labor. Instantly, the others were all about him, turning down the bed, fetching blankets and towels, and pulling the curtains to block out the piercing light.

"I'll take over, Colonel," Caroline said brusquely, sensibilities stunned when he began to loosen her sister-in-law's bodice.

"It's all right, ma'am. I'm a doctor. That is, I'm going to be. I would appreciate your help, though. This one is going to be my first and I want to do it right for my niece or nephew."

Caroline had no other protests, bowing to his authority without hesitation. She was used to hearing the same tone from his brother and knew arguing would only waste time and her breath.

Savannah groaned mightily and squeezed Brent's hand, calling him by another name. Thinking the discomfort had her confused, he bent down and wiped her brow.

"Sky's not here, Savannah, but I'll do my best to deliver a son or daughter for him. I'm going to need your help too."

"Skyler," she moaned as if in desperation, but another sharp contraction cut off her words.

"Savannah, it can wait, but this baby's not going to for much longer. I want you to do what I tell you. I want you to breathe slow and easy. That's it."

"Another Dr. Reade," she panted with a strained smile.

"Looks that way. Don't be a difficult first patient." His broad, familiar grin suddenly made everything easier, and with a grim concentration, she nodded. "Good girl. You'll do me proud."

The labor was short for a first time and Savannah bore it well. Exhausted and soaked with sweat, she delivered Skyler's child. Weeping in weary relief and amazement, she took the wrinkled child to her bosom. Looking shaken but all grins, Brent kissed both mother and child and left them their privacy for the babe's first suckling. He wandered out onto the porch to breathe in the cooler early evening air. He felt good. He felt strong. He felt the humbling power of bringing new life and finally understood his father's and Palmer's devotion. His father would be pleased to hear that. He only wished he could tell Palmer as well. Perhaps, he knew.

He was about to sit down when the flutter of a crumpled paper in the dirt caught his eye. They were the sheets Savannah was clutching when she went into labor. Curiously, he went and picked them up, smoothing out the wrinkles.

After seeing Savannah safely asleep and the child tucked into its cradle—the same one that had served all the Russell children—Caroline suddenly remembered a bottle of apricot brandy she had hidden away to celebrate Darcy's homecoming. This felt like a celebration too. Smiling, she fetched it and two glasses, and went to find the younger Reade, who had proven himself in her eyes just as his brother had before him.

"Colonel? Brent?"

Caroline stepped out onto the veranda in puzzlement. He was sitting on the top stair, hugging his knees, face buried in his arms. To her dismay, she realized he was weeping. The low, mournful sounds were muffled but heavy with loss and pain. It was a sound she had heard too many times before. Not even daring to suppose, she walked to him and sat at his side. After a moment, she took the papers he held in his shaking fist. They were from James Ambrose. There was no message, just two separate lists. She didn't need a heading to tell her what they were a part of. Swallowing with difficulty, she scanned both pages, eyes stopping where a name had been marked on each sheet.

"Oh God. This has to be a mistake," she wailed. "It has to be wrong."

But the words were clear and bold.

Captain Darcy Russell, South Carolina Legion—Dead

Skyler Reade, Major, United States Army of the Potomac—Dead

Slowly, numbed, she put her arm around the sobbing boy and together they sat in the fading embers of a glorious spring and mourned their losses.

The room was darkened, and groggy as she was, Savannah's heart gave a sudden leap when she saw the slumped figure in the door. But it wasn't Skyler. It would never be Skyler again. Feeling the hot scald of her tears rise once more, she held out a hand and Brent came to kneel beside her bed, fair head resting on the coverlet. He was no longer weeping but his voice was raw and aching.

"What are we going to do without him?" he asked in a hushed grief.

"I don't know, Brent. I can't even imagine it. Does Caroline know about Darcy?"

The ashen head nodded. "She's going to tell Hillary."

"I want him brought back. I want Skyler home, here with me. Can you do that, Brent? Can you see they send me his—his body?" Tears trembled on her words as she struggled for control, struggled not to surrender to the depthless pain that said nothing mattered now that he was gone. But something did. She had his child and he would live for her in that tiny figure. And so she must go on.

"I'll do whatever I can, Savannah. I promise you." He strengthened with that vow, straightening and giving her a narrow, pinched smile. "I'll see about your brother too."

"Thank you, Brent. We'd all appreciate that." She looked directly into his brown eyes, for seeing his face was too difficult. "You should get some rest. You look all done in."

He nodded in resignation. "I want to see Hillary first, to see she's all right."

Savannah smiled. "I'm sure she'd like that. Good night."

"Good night, Savannah."

He lingered for a moment, then awkwardly bent to kiss her cheek. She fought the desire to cling to him, to hold him close. He wasn't Skyler. It wouldn't give the same comfort. Instead, she touched his silken hair and let him go to her sister.

Alone in the great emptiness of her bed, Savannah held up her hand so her rings caught in a sliver of light from the hall. They glowed with such warmth, such fire; she couldn't believe all they represented was cold and gone.

No, she wouldn't believe it. There was too much alive in her thoughts, in her heart, in this room. Skyler was in all of them, grin dazzling, eyes alit with a challenging deviltry, chest broad, golden, and warm, profile a strong silhouette against the moonlight that played on his hair. No, there was too much life here, too much love, too much hope. And he had promised and he never broke his word.

No, it had to be a mistake. Such cruel mistakes were made all the time by both sides. That was it. Someone was wrong, just as they'd been wrong about Brent. He was here and alive and so would be Skyler. She would silently cling to that belief for strength.

And if Brent brought back his body, she would accept it and mourn. But for now, Skyler was alive and she would be waiting, never surrendering hope of that reunion. No piece of paper could convince her that vital love was gone from her life. No single word would make her believe it was so. Nothing short of physical evidence would break her stubborn Rebel pride and get her to admit she was wrong.

So like her mother before her, she began to wait. It had to be a mistake.

Chapter Thirty-One

Major Skyler Reade sat on the back of his horse, the glow of the fire reflecting in his somber grey eyes. It was disagreeable work, so much of this mission he was on with Phil Sheridan, and it gave his conscience little rest. Since Sheridan had taken over, Grant had given him two directives: to defeat Jubal Early and to remove the Shenandoah Valley from the war. Early had led a small Confederate army to the edge of the Washington suburbs, and though he had been forced to retreat, the threat he presented to the Northern heartland had caused widespread panic among the diplomats. Skyler could share that worry with Philadelphia being vulnerable along with the rest. His family's safety was uppermost in his mind. The Valley itself had proven strategic to the South. It was a fertile region for meat and grain, feeding Lee's defending army at Richmond. Grant ordered its lush acres despoiled so it would no longer support the Confederates.

The fighting, even with three-to-one odds, was difficult, for Early's group was comprised of hardened sinewy veterans who had proven themselves in combat again and again. Killing those soldiers of the South in confrontations of life and death he could justify, but the cold rape of the land soured him to his duty. It was merciless, systematic destruction, the scorched earth policy Sherman mimicked in his infamous sweep, destroying the Southern economy by leaving them no means of survival. No matter that innocent Union sympathizers as well as women and children would suffer. War showed no sympathy and that ideal caught in Skyler's throat.

The only thing that kept him going was the need to see the strife end. Savannah's letters fueled that concentration, making him long for the time he could go home to her. Her words of encouragement and love fed his starved soul and balanced the scene he witnessed even now. He had helped torch the entire upper Valley. The smoke was so thick it turned day to night and lit the evening sky with an eerie incandescence. Such barbarity made him fear for the safety of those at Rising Sun.

He had seen savage fighting both at Winchester, Virginia and again three days later at Fisher's Hill. The greatest threat was not from the lean army but from the unseen soldiers of the bush, the guerillas who raided outposts, burned supply trains, shot sentries and couriers, and forced Sheridan to employ a large guard detail. Snipers created a fear of panic in even the most seasoned officer. Dying in battle at least gave a man a chance. Guerillas were treated as criminal murderers and were hanged if captured. In retaliation, they hanged their Yankee prisoners. War did bitter things to men. He didn't care much for what it was doing to him.

He was about to turn his horse back toward camp when a sharp brittle crack snapped a branch beside him. As he reached for his carbine, another shot sent his hat flying. The carbine caught in its boot and after a desperate tug, he gave it up, flinging himself to the ground with a low curse. Scrambling madly in the crisp autumn leaves, he rolled and propelled himself for cover. As his hand fell on the butt of his revolver, a cold metal circle pressed to the base of his skull. He lay perfectly still, breathing in the loomy scent of the earth in hurried gulps. His eyes squeezed shut, awaiting death and hoping it would come here instead of at the end of a rope. The image of Savannah's face rose startlingly clear, her voice echoing in fatalistic warning: "Skyler, I can't lose you."

The Reb's caustic tone intruded on her gentle words, jarring him back to the present.

"You forget there was a war on, Yank? Just out here for a Sunday ride in the country?"

The rush of Skyler's breath stirred a rustle of leaves and dirt. Slowly, hands carefully distanced from his sides, he rolled to face the tattered man on horseback whose half smile taunted him.

"Horses are mighty scarce for you to be so careless of yours," Darcy Russell chided, extending the reins. Savannah's brother looked as hard as the packed earth beneath his horse's hooves. His face wore the same gaunt, hungry look of all the South, but his eyes were a brilliant glitter of life. The faded uniform was worse for wear, patched repeatedly but still worn with pride. The rifle he held, of Union issue, was cradled harmlessly across his knees.

Skyler rose warily and dusted himself off before reaching for the leads. He felt loose tremors of relief mingle with an odd sense of chagrin. "You ruined my hat," he grumbled.

"Better than your head. If you had any brains in it, you'd stay closer to your own."

"I plan to in the future" was his curt remark. He swung up onto his gelding so he could meet the other's eyes directly.

"Another word to the wise if you want to see my sister again. Sharpshooters aim for those shiny brass

429

buttons you boys are so fond of. Spend less time polishing them and keep your head down."

"I'm in your debt," Skyler said stiffly. It was hard to warm to the cold-eyed man who stared at him.

Darcy's lips curled sardonically at the vow. "No you ain't, Yank. We're even now. We don't owe each other anything the next time we meet unless its over a bourbon in the parlor."

There would be no pleasantries between them, no well-wishing. The color of the uniforms and the place dictated the current of hostility. A debt owed had been paid. Looking into the glassy blue stare, Skyler had no doubt that this man could kill him without a flinch if the occasion warranted it. He snapped off a formal salute but Darcy only nodded. Skyler wheeled his horse about and nudged it into a canter, wondering as he rode if fate would arrange another meeting between them.

The winter months were long, weather preventing much movement of troops and postponing the inevitable. The Confederacy was dying for the lack of food, ammunitions, clothing, men, and spirit. The weight of numbers alone was staggering, but the weary grey army still hung onto its capitol and its lost cause.

The thaw of spring found Skyler Reade a changed man. Battle had hardened him, toughening his outlook to near callousness. He no longer saw faces above the coats of grey and butternut. He no longer saw men but rather an enemy that was keeping him from home and he hated them for it. That hate and the will to survive sustained him as Savannah's letters once had. He hadn't received one from her for two months and only hoped his warning to flee would reach her in time. He was no longer the lofty dreamer who clung to ideals of

430

humanity. His senses were deadened to all but a keen edge of self-preservation. His uniform was dirty and torn, the brass buttons clipped off and replaced by plain flat black. His face was unshaven, his eyes cold and empty of all but a single purpose. There would be no pangs of conscience after this battle. He hadn't felt them for a long time. He hadn't felt much of anything but a fatigue that lent him a sharp edginess and a lean, dangerous look, the look of a veteran soldier instead of a politician playing at one.

Sheridan's cavalry moved on the Five Forks road junction to break Lee's railroad connection with the South. That would force the evacuation of Petersburg and Richmond and place them between Lee and Johnston. Rains had slowed everything, turning roads into rivers of mud. But on that April 1 afternoon, while the Confederate generals were at lunch together, their troops were swamped by Sheridan's dismounted men. Magazine guns echoed in the pine woods to sound as though several army corps had opened fire, while Warren's infantry converged on the rear of Pickett's troops. By dusk, five thousand of his seven thousand men were taken prisoner. Pickett was a general without a division.

Skyler didn't know until later what happened. He was advancing rapidly through the copse of pines when a sudden force lifted him from his feet, hurling him bodily through the air. He hit the ground hard. While sounds of the battle roared about him, he lay stretched out on his back, stunned and oblivious to his own condition. A sticky warmth on the side of his face brought a vague awareness. He'd been shot. There was no pain, no panic, just a numbing heaviness that kept him from moving even when he saw figures rushing by him in hazy shadows of blue and grey. Then a voice came so close and so familiar he doubted his sanity.

431

"Still can't keep your head down, eh, Yank?"

Darcy Russell's features wavered in his limited scope of vision. The world tipped with a dizzying abruptness as he was lifted up and draped belly down across a saddle. He recognized the dull yellow hide of the horse beneath him.

"I must be crazy but Vannah'd skin me if I didn't bring you back to her. Now you owe me, Yank. Let's get the hell out of here."

As Darcy climbed up behind him, he gave a sudden lurch and a short blurt of surprise. Laying heavily across Skyler's back, he kicked the horse into a jolting gallop. After several minutes of watching the ground somersault in his upside-down position, Skyler closed his eyes and let unconsciousness rescue him. The next thing he was aware of was the blackness of the Virginia sky spread above the soaring pines.

Movement brought a wave of hurt and sickness that cancelled all else. When that crippling tide finally ebbed, he was more cautious. He lay on the cold mossy ground several feet from the grazing yellow mare. Slowly, he turned his head to find another still figure sprawled beside him. Darcy.

The night was still, the sounds of battle only echoes within his head. An acrid scent lingered with the crisp fragrance of the pines—gunpowder, the perfume of war carried on the evening breeze. But from how far away? Where were they? Why had no one found them?

Gritting his teeth with determination, Skyler rolled toward the unmoving form. It was too dark to see well. That darkness made the red staining the back of the grey coat look black and greasy.

"Darcy?"

He winced at the thunder of that single word as it rumbled mercilessly between his temples. Fumbling about, he found the warmth of the other man's neck and a faint rewarding pulse. The wetness on his back was centered between his shoulder blades. That wasn't good.

He sat beside the still figure and looked about. Now that his eyes were accustomed to the darkness he realized why no one had found them. They were at the bottom of a deep gully, well out of sight from above in the shield of boughs overhead. The mare looked up at the sound of his tuneless whistle but soon lost interest. He calculated the distance between them and the horse. It might as well have been miles. Even if he could drag Darcy that far, how could he ever get them both into the saddle? Where would they go in the darkness? He started to run his fingers through his hair in a frustrated gesture but the sticky matting stopped him. He felt tenderly along his forehead until he reached a deep furrow that disappeared into his hairline. The ache there was tremendous. He was still bleeding, rivulets of it streaking down his face and wetting his shirtfront. Painstakingly, he wadded up his handkerchief and bound it to the gaping wound with his belt.

The night was cold or was it him? Shivering fitfully, he looked again at the little mare and at the promising bulk of a blanket behind its saddle. Softly, he called the horse's name. The shell-like ears pricked forward. When he called again, the mare took several tentative steps toward him. Regretting the things he had said about the ungainly creature, he smiled and pulled himself up on his knees.

"Come here, Aurora. Come here, girl."

The horse wickered softly and walked up to him. With a silly laugh, he clung to the reins and tried to gather his strength.

"Whoa, girl. Steady now. Don't run off and make me curse you stubborn South Carolina ladies."

As he spoke, he pulled himself up on the mare's front

433

leg. The horse snorted in uncertainty but didn't bolt. Once on his feet, the world swayed mightily about him. Using his hands as blind guides, he moved along the quivering haunches, skipping over the rifle in favor of the saddlebag. He tugged at it, the effort causing him to lose his precarious balance.

He fell hard but the smack of the bedroll across his shoulders was ample reward for his discomfort. Aurora danced several feet away but then lowered her head to crop more of the stingy grass. It was as though the little horse didn't want to weather the darkness alone any more than he did.

Skyler returned to Darcy's side with a crablike crawl. His head was agony and the chills shook him so hard the rattling of his teeth provoked more of the discomfort in his temple. The bedroll yielded one thin blanket. He lay down close to the unmoving figure and used it to cover them both. It was only slightly warmer but it made him feel better. Someone would come in the morning. Blue or grey, someone would come to help them. If he felt better at daybreak, perhaps he would try to get them both on the mare. They must be near one of the armies. They only had to find them. His only thought was to get help for Darcy. The man had saved his life. At least he had done everything he could. And so would he, Skyler determined. Even if he had to spend the rest of the war in Andersonville, it would be worth it. He no longer dreamed of the train. Savannah was with him, and knowing she was in his future was his strength, a strength that could endure anything as long as he knew she waited for him.

Feeling miserably sick and cold, he closed his eyes. "I'll get you home, Darcy. I'll get us both home."

Dew glistened jewellike on the tattered blanket as

434

three soldiers looked down on the two prone figures it covered. The men were ragged and tired, their uniforms discolored by powder and smelling of battle. The sound of the horse had brought them down to investigate. No one passed up a good horse. It was then that they found the two men.

"Dead?"

"Looks like it. Dead and cold."

"Wonder what he was doing with one of theirs?"

The first man shrugged, prodding one of the scuffed boots with his toe. He needed a pair and they looked his size. This man wouldn't be needing them anymore. It was a shame they should go to waste. He was rewarded by a soft groan.

"This one here's still breathing," he said in amazement, then bent to feel for a pulse. "Don't know how, but it looks like one of 'em made it."

Chapter Thirty-Two

The setting sun was bright, making Caroline squint to see the lone rider coming slowly down the drive. All she could make out was the outline of a man and horse until they were nearly upon her. She rose from her chair, a name catching in her throat in disbelief. The funny-looking yellow horse was Savannah's and the figure slumped in the saddle, Hardee hat shading his face, wore grey.

Tears blinding her, Caroline flew down the steps, catching the dusty arm as the man dismounted. Then the brim of the hat rose and her sobs turned into a sickened wail. With all the fierceness of her crushed hopes, she slapped the bearded face. Not waiting to see the anguish in the tired eyes, she fled back to the house, stumbling blindly and nearly falling on the steps. She clung to the rail, racked with grief and bitter disappointment. She flung off the hands that took her arms, not wanting to look on that cruel joke that mocked her fleeting dream.

"I brought his things, Caroline. I'm so sorry," he said softly. "I wanted to bring him back home to you. I wanted us all to be a family. He saved my life. I wish to God I could have saved his."

With a weary sigh, Skyler let his hands fall impotently to his sides. He had no strength left to turn her hate with helpless words. Words wouldn't change him into the man she wanted to see come up the drive. When she turned, he half expected another attack but not the arms that went tightly about his neck. He held her in a loose circle as her tears made damp splotches in the heavy travel dust that coated the blue of his uniform.

"Will you tell me how it happened some time?" she asked finally. "I should know so I can tell Jeffery when he's older."

The fair head nodded. "You can tell him his father was a brave man."

She brushed a kiss against the whiskered cheek and stepped back. "Welcome home, Skyler."

A soft spoken oath of amazement made him turn and regard the other with equal stupefaction. Then the brothers came together in a wordless embrace, each clinging hard so the contact would assure him of the other's existence. When they stood away, they eyed each other for a long moment, noting the battle scars that marked flesh and spirit so deeply.

"What are you doing here, Brent?" Skyler asked huskily, hand rumpling through his brother's fair hair.

"I gave the ladies an escort from Charleston."

"Charleston?"

Brent laughed at his confusion. "Someone had to look after them," he said with a grin. In spite of the dirt and the wariness and the white ominous line that marred his forehead, his brother had never looked so good to him.

"Is everyone all right?" he asked in concern.

Arm in arm, Brent led him into the house, explaining as they walked the events as he knew them, including the death of Adelaide Russell but omitting one very important one. That should come from his wife. And when he asked for her in a constricted voice, Brent grinned wider.

"See for yourself."

She stood in the terraced garden where she had once seduced him. Only both had changed since that long-ago night. The gardens were overrun with a tangle of weeds, neglected out of necessity. Savannah much thinner than he remembered, tall straight figure dressed in simple calico over a single petticoat. The sad disrepair of both touched his heart. Not knowing what to say, he walked down the gentle slope of lawn until he stood behind her. While he was deciding just how to take her in his arms, she must have felt his presence for she gave a slight shiver before he reached out to brush aside a wisp of her hair. She turned, eyes uplifted, eyes the color of the stormy sea that had brought them together. There was no surprise in that long, savoring stare, as if she had been expecting him.

"Oh, Sky," she whispered as her arms glided about his neck. "I knew it wasn't true. I knew you'd keep your promise to me."

They held to each other for a long moment, each loathe to let go, but there was so much to be said.

Savannah swallowed hard on the knot of her tears. "But Darcy won't be coming home, will he?"

"No."

"I never really believed he would. Oh, Sky, it's so good to hold you."

Skyler crushed her close, feeling the supple contours of her body so inviting without the hard cage of corset or hoops. The feel of her was an unexpected jolt. It flooded him with sensations nearly forgotten during the stress and weariness of war. The bitter horror of those long, terrible months was swept away by the strength of that rekindled longing, by the love he held for this one special woman, his wife.

Savannah looked up into the dirty, bearded face,

eyes soft and glistening. He looked different, harder, aged, worn, but the warmth in his eyes was the same. Her voice was heavy with emotion.

"They said you were dead. A man in your unit told Brent he had seen you fall but I just couldn't accept it. I was beginning to think my hopes were as thin as my mother's. What happened? Where have you been?"

He touched the half-healed furrow in his head as he spoke. The concussion from that wound had kept him unconscious and unidentified for nearly a month. During his lengthy recovery, the news that Darcy hadn't survived filled him with a different quandary of emotion. Darcy had died for him. What if his family didn't see the sacrifice as worth it? What if they hated him for taking yet another one of their loved ones? Weak and delirious, he spent several weeks considering returning to the North without a stop at Rising Sun. But he owed it to Caroline to see her husband's sabre and belongings home, and he couldn't bear to go on without at least seeing Savannah again. He had to be assured that she was all right even if she no longer wanted him. Instead, he had found this warm, welcoming embrace and it shook him mightily.

"Darcy died because of me," he said flatly, scanning her expression for the expected twist of accusation. But it remained serene.

"Darcy died for a cause he believed in. Part of that cause was family. Uncle Jonah was imprisoned because of his greed. You're not to blame for either of their choices," she corrected, to put an end to the subject between them. "You look tired and hungry. Come up to the house and let me see to your comfort."

His eyes glittered. "I need more than food and sleep to see me comfortable."

"Then we'll see to that, too."

Tugging his arm, she led him back inside. She didn't

440

pause at the dining room but continued on to the curving stairs.

Seeing the tall uniformed man with her sister, Hillary gave a delighted cry, but her pursuit of them was halted by an arm about her trim waist. She turned to Brent with a sullen pout. He merely grinned and tapped her under the chin.

"They don't need you right now," he advised quietly. "Wait until your welcome will be more appreciated."

Hillary's brows rose in dawning knowledge, then she giggled coyly. "I guess I would be a rather unwelcomed intrusion."

"Never to me," her fair-haired suitor vowed silkily.

She regarded him through the lowered sweep of her lashes. He was so handsome and so unpredictable. She was never sure he wasn't laughing at her. But he never mocked her. Softly, she murmured, "Why, Brent Reade, whatever are you trying to say to me?"

"Only that now that Skyler's here, I'd like to go home and resume my study of medicine.

Her face fell with stunned disappointment, the pretty blue eyes growing shiny with genuine dismay. "Oh."

"And if it's all right with Savannah," he continued, "I'd like to have you accompany me."

The tears vanished in a surprised blink. "Do you mean that?"

"It would be just for a few weeks, then I'd see you back. I'm sure in that time you can buy out the best stores in Philadelphia. I'm going to be very busy with studies, but I'm sure you could convince Sky to bring you up for holidays. Then, we'll see."

The petal-soft mouth pursed thoughtfully as she ran a finger down the lapel of his coat. "Yes, we shall see."

From the entrance of the library, Caroline watched the two couples in bittersweet reflection. Within her family, the healing of North and South had begun. A

441

tug at her skirt made her look down at the beautiful child's face that peered up at her, questioning her tears. With a tremulous smile, she bent and hugged the boy to her.

At the top of the stairs, Skyler could control his lusting no longer. He spun Savannah about and crushed her lips beneath his in a rough, demanding claim. The vehemence of her protest shocked him into releasing her. She stepped out of his arm's reach to observe his obvious impassioned state with a cool, appraising stare. The rebellion in her eyes sharpened when he caught her up with a now-controlled ease.

"I vowed once I'd take you on these stairs," he growled in warning. "I'm not above doing it now."

Her hands pressed to his dirty shirtfront in denial, permitting him to draw her no closer. Nor would he release her.

"Skyler, we have to talk," she began firmly.

"Talk?" His brows rose in an incredulous sweep. "My dear wife, we have years and years in which to talk at long length about anything you choose, but for right now, I'm at a loss for words."

There was no resisting him as his arms bent and hers collapsed. His mouth moved in an urgent hunger over hers, gentling when her lips parted to grant him entry between them. Her fingers plied restlessly through his hair, then clenched to pull him closer. Swamped by the intoxication of her desire, his hand rose to knead the heavy fullness of her unfettered breast. Its quick, stiffening response ended all restraint.

Savannah gave a startled gasp as Skyler scooped her up in his arms and bore her purposefuly down the hall. Outside her door, her protest returned in a hurried rush.

"Sky, wait. I have to explain. We're not alone. There's someone inside you have to meet first."

442

He set her down so abruptly she nearly fell. Of course, his stunned mind chided. She had thought him dead. How could he have expected her to wait? A woman like Savannah so full of love and life. He should have known.

"I'm sorry," he blurted hastily. "I guess I'm intruding. I never stopped to think you might have found someone else."

Now it was her turn to look blank. Then she saw the hurt and anguish he was struggling to conceal so poorly and began to laugh.

"Oh, Sky, don't be ridiculous. How could there be anyone but you?"

He flinched away in uncertainty when her palm touched his cheek, strickened gaze going to the closed door. Not discouraged, she caught up his unresponsive hand.

"Come, let me introduce you to your rival."

Skyler followed reluctantly, confusion mounting as his eyes swept the empty bed. Then lit on the lacy bassinet. He moved like a sleepwalker to the side of the wicker basket, hand squeezing Savannah's unconsciously. He stared down at the small bundle through round, awed eyes until Savannah's words broke his reverence.

"Mary Elizabeth Reade."

His glistening eyes flickered to her briefly, the pleased glow warming her tenderly. His hand reached down to touch the downy head of wispy blond hair. It was the first time she had ever seen him at a loss over a child.

"Our child," he said vaguely. "My daughter. When? Savannah, why didn't you tell me? I should have been here."

It wasn't the time to argue reasoning, so she told him simply, "Brent delivered this one. You can be here for the next half dozen."

"But Savannah—"

She rose on tiptoes to cover his mouth, ending his questions and challenges. Her lips lingered over the sensuous heat of his, delighting in the taste of him the way she would a rare, precious vintage. She let him go reluctantly as his stunned gaze returned to the basket.

"Go ahead and pick her up. She'll want to meet her daddy."

Skyler hesitated. He looked almost afraid. "I don't want her to see me like this." His hand rose to the scratchy chin. "I'd scare her witless. I just want to look at her for a while. I have to get used to the idea that she's real."

"And I have to get used to the idea that you're really here. I've missed you so."

Her husky tone made him forget the child. His hands fell lightly on her shoulders.

"Skyler, I love you," she whispered and stretched up for his kiss. She gave a delicious shudder as his mouth scorched down her throat amid the tantalizing tease of his beard.

"And I love you. I'll never leave you again," he promised fiercely, holding her to him. "This is my home, our home, our family's home. You see to the land and I'll see to the repairs to the state. There are going to be a lot of changes, more of a bitter struggle now the war is over. Carolina's going to need men to guide her back into the Union and see to her recovery. I'm going to be one of those men because I have an important stake here. I'll have to go to Washington for a time to see to an appointment, then I'd like to go home to my family for a visit. It can wait until the baby's ready to travel because I wouldn't think of going without you."

"One condition," she said firmly.

"Anything."

"No Rhea Sherwood this time. If anyone's going to cling to your arm at those stuffy parties, it's going to be me. I want everyone to see how proud I am of my husband and to know I'm behind whatever he does."

"As a politician, you have to know what's a priority," he began.

She smiled into his dusty coat, hearing the persuasive campaigning in his tone. He would be good for the state and she knew he was good for her. "And what might that be?"

"Locking our door for at least three days." His large hands moved down her back then up again, the power in them making her tremble in excitement.

"There is one thing about Mary Elizabeth," she said softly.

"What's that?"

"She's a very sound sleeper." Her deep blue eyes rose to meet silver, both growing dusky with expectation. Savannah's fingers began to move down the buttons of his jacket. "Didn't you also promise once the war was over this uniform would never come between us again? Well, it is now. Take it off."

"And didn't I promise I'd melt your Rebel heart?" he countered, busy with her buttons as well.

"You have, Yankee. You have."

FREE Preview Each Month and $ave

Zebra has made arrangements for you to preview 4 brand new HEARTFIRE novels each month…FREE for 10 days. You'll get them as soon as they are published. If you are not delighted with any of them, just return them with no questions asked. But if you decide these are everything we said they are, you'll pay just $3.25 each—a total of $13.00 (a $15.00 value). **That's a $2.00 saving each month off the regular price.** Plus there is NO shipping or handling charge. These are delivered right to your door absolutely free! There is no obligation and there is no minimum number of books to buy.

TO GET YOUR FIRST MONTH'S PREVIEW…
Mail the Coupon Below!

THE ECSTASY SERIES
by Janelle Taylor